KT-145-689

"I AM CALAE,
PRINCE OF THE COLONNAE."

The spectre then turned to Del and an even more gentle puff blew by. "Truly I am sorry, Jeffrey DelGiudice, but your friend, Ray Corbin, has passed from this world."

Del's eyes widened. The being had just read his mind and answered his unspoken question.

"You still think we're not dead?" whispered Billy. The breeze came again.

"Take comfort, Billy Shank. By the power of the Colonnae, you have passed through the dark realm and are healed. We could not permit your deaths, for this is a time long awaited, and a great adventure lies before you. Your actions may well determine the destiny of a new world."

"Come," he said, opening his arms as a father to his children. "Sit by me and I will tell you a marvelous tale that shall answer many of your questions and instill in you many more."

Compelled by this superior will, the mortals could only comply. The breeze came again. "Let me begin," it whispered to them, "at what you may perceive to be the end. . . ."

SIGNET (0451)

FLIGHTS OF FANTASY

☐ **THE GOD BOX by Barry B. Longyear.** From the moment Korvas accepted the gift of the god box and the obligation to fulfill its previous owner's final mission, he'd been plunged into more peril than a poor dishonest rug merchant deserved. Now it looks like Korvas will either lead the world to its destruction—or its salvation. . . . (159241—$3.50)

☐ **SORCERER'S SON by Phyllis Eisenstein.** "Outstanding"—Andre Norton. "Fantasy at its best!"—J.E. Pournelle. As Cray Ormoru, son of enchantress Delivev, grows to be a man in magical Castle Spinweb, he yearns to find his father, who disappeared years ago on a heroic mission. Cray sets out on a journey full of danger and sorrow—a baptism of fire for the sorcerer's son! (156838—$3.95)

☐ **THE CRYSTAL PALACE by Phyllis Eisenstein.** From the acclaimed author of *Sorcerer's Son*—a magical tale of a mortal's quest to find and free the soul of his one true love . . . Cray was intrigued by the image of the young girl in the magical mirror, but who she was remained a mystery until he discovered she was Aliza, a prisoner in her own magnificent crystal palace. (156781—$3.95)

☐ **THE MAGIC BOOKS by Andre Norton.** Three magical excursions into spells cast and enchantments broken, by a wizard of science fiction and fantasy: *Steel Magic*, three children's journey to an Avalon whose dark powers they alone can withstand, *Octagon Magic*, a young girl's voyage into times and places long gone, and *Fur Magic*, where a boy must master the magic of the ancient gods to survive. (166388—$4.95)

☐ **GAMEARTH by Kevin J. Anderson.** It was supposed to be just another Sunday night fantasy game—and that's all it was to David, Tyrone, and Scott. But to Melanie, the game had become so real that all their creations now had existences of their own. And when David demanded they destroy their made-up world in one last battle, Melanie tried every trick she knew to keep the fantasy campaign going, to keep the world of Gamearth alive. (156803—$3.95)

Prices slightly higher in Canada

Buy them at your local bookstore or use this convenient coupon for ordering.

NEW AMERICAN LIBRARY
P.O. Box 999, Bergenfield, New Jersey 07621

Please send me the books I have checked above. I am enclosing $________ (please add $1.00 to this order to cover postage and handling). Send check or money order—no cash or C.O.D.'s. Prices and numbers are subject to change without notice.

Name________________________________

Address______________________________

City ____________ State ____________ Zip Code ____________

Allow 4-6 weeks for delivery.
This offer, prices and numbers are subject to change without notice.

Echoes of the Fourth Magic

by R.A. Salvatore

A ROC BOOK

To the memory of Geno Salvatore, my dad,
and to my wife, Diane.
Their inspiration and unconditional support
made all of this possible.

ROC
Published by the Penguin Group
Penguin Books USA Inc., 375 Hudson Street,
New York, New York 10014, U.S.A.
Penguin Books Ltd, 27 Wrights Lane,
London W8 5TZ, England
Penguin Books Australia Ltd, Ringwood, Victoria, Australia
Penguin Books Canada Ltd, 2801 John Street,
Markham, Ontario, Canada L3R 1B4
Penguin Books (N.Z.) Ltd, 182-190 Wairau Road,
Auckland 10, New Zealand

Penguin Books Ltd, Registered Offices: Harmondsworth, Middlesex, England

First published by Roc, an imprint of New American Library, a division of
Penguin Books USA Inc.

First Printing, September, 1990
10 9 8 7 6 5 4 3 2 1

Copyright © R.A. Salvatore, 1990
All rights reserved

Roc is a trademark of Penguin Books USA Inc.

Printed in the United States of America

Without limiting the rights under copyright reserved above, no part of this publication may be reproduced, stored in or introduced into a retrieval system, or transmitted, in any form, or by any means (electronic, mechanical, photocopying, recording, or otherwise), without the prior written permission of both the copyright owner and the above publisher of this book.

BOOKS ARE AVAILABLE AT QUANTITY DISCOUNTS WHEN USED TO PROMOTE PRODUCTS OR SERVICES. FOR INFORMATION PLEASE WRITE TO PREMIUM MARKETING DIVISION, PENGUIN BOOKS USA INC., 375 HUDSON STREET, NEW YORK, NEW YORK 10014.

There are so many people I wish to thank, too many to list here, for their help and support over the course of this project. My special thanks to Dave, Jean, Kent, and Sheila for lending me the benefit of their experience and expertise in those areas in which I needed help the most.

Map courtesy of Kent McKenzie

GREAT CRYSTAL MOUNTAINS
SHELF OF THE MOON
ILLUMA
MTN GATE
BLACK MERE
AVALON
FIELDS OF ELADAIN
SOUTHERN CRYSTALS
JUSTICE STONE
Calva
PLAINS OF CALVA
GREAT FOREST
CORNING
FOUR BRIDGES
LOCH SOLACE
PALLENDARA (CAER TUATHA)

Chapter 1

The Passage of the *Unicorn*

The *Unicorn* ran deep, ran smooth, gliding with the ease of an eagle on wing. But no hunter this; she was a ship of peace, the pride of the National Undersea Exploration Team, NUSET, pelagic counterpart of NASA. Every member of NUSET looked upon her with satisfaction and deep respect, for this submarine was the epitome of technological achievement. More than that, in accordance with the legend of her mythical namesake, the Unicorn had become a symbol of hope for the future of mankind amidst the constant threat of technological annihilation. For NUSET was an organization truly dedicated to the peaceful application of science. And that, more than anything else, was the true victory of the *Unicorn.*

More than five miles of water now separated this new generation of submarine from the sunlit surface. All was dark here and quiet, save the gentle hum of the ship's engines and the ping-poc of the hydraulic system beating back the tremendous ocean pressure. Powerful searchlights cut a swath of illumination through the lightless waters as this lone sphere of civilization prowled the Atlantic's depths.

On the surface she had bobbed nervously about, each swell threatening to spin her over, but in this watery environ, she swam swiftly and effortlessly. Here she was made to be at home, and yet for all of her detailed and near-perfect designs, here she remained a stranger.

Morning sparkled in bright reflections on the glassy surface, but this depth knew only night. So began the *Unicorn*'s thirty-second day out of Miami, her first without a dawn. Down she had gone. Down from the curious Russian trawler; from the beating of the navy helicopter's blades; from the clamor of a mechanical world. Deeper than any hint of the sun could reach, deeper even than the fish dared swim.

Jeff "Del" DelGiudice lay back on a weightlifting bench and clasped the metal bar. "Five miles up and a hundred across," he mumbled, his thoughts inevitably drifting back to Miami. Again, as always, he found he found himself examining his relationship with Debby, trying to find some answers to his unresolved emotions. He cared for her—deeply—but it wasn't the passionate desire that he had fantasized love would be. That special spark, the tingling excitement that brightened even the blackest moods, was simply not there. But Del was as content as he could be, he supposed, for he doubted the existence of his romantic love. That was the substance of a poet's pen, not the reality of the world.

And yet, again he had run away.

But even this escape was a lie, and little protection from the profound sadness within Del. He had never learned the joy of existence; the simple pleasures of perception and experience, and that was his frustration. Instinctively Del perceived an emptiness, a void within himself that craved fulfillment, but his materialistic and fiercely competitive world gave him no comfort.

"Lift, lift," Del repeated over and over. No good. Every time the ping-poc of the hydraulic system sounded, his concentration broke and he remembered Debby and those haunting questions. He slipped his hands from the bar in frustration.

On the forward bridge, navigator Billy Shank studied his instruments. "Any minute now, Captain," he said, his voice edged with excitement.

"Put the signal from the screen to the rest of the monitors on the ship," said Captain Mitchell, a giant, scowling man. His voice and visage held rock steady, but the simmering glow in his eyes belied his calm facade.

The alarm blasted just as Del finally managed to start his lift. The weights crashed back to the rack and Del scrambled across the room, his mind whirling. He charged into the hall, colliding with a crewman. His panic changed to embarrassment when he saw the cooler of beer.

"Carry on," Del said, as though he had known all along.

"Look at those legs!" came a voice from behind. It belonged to Ray Corbin, the *Unicorn*'s second in command.

"Ray," Del replied, watching the easy saunter of his approaching friend, the one man Mitchell had personally requested for the crew.

But Mitchell and Corbin were far from alike. Intensity, Mitchell's trademark, was not a mainstay on Ray Corbin's diet. Still, everyone on the crew understood Mitchell's choice. A quiet, unassuming first officer virtually guaranteed the dominating captain uncontested control.

Or did it? Truly Ray Corbin would not openly oppose Mitchell; dogfighting wasn't a part of his makeup. But Corbin was an officer sympathetic to the needs of the people around him, and he realized the pressures that a tyrant like Mitchell could exert on a crew. He needed a foil for Mitchell's dominance, a release valve for tension, and he found it in a man recommended by an old skipper of his. Corbin's secret weapon was Jeff DelGiudice and he had pulled quite a few strings to get Del into the project.

"You going up front?" asked Corbin.

"You think I'd miss this?" replied Del. "Probably the only excitement we see on this tub for eight months."

"You want excitement?" Corbin remarked. "Wait until Mitchell sees his junior officer in gym shorts on the bridge." Corbin smiled inwardly as he pictured the captain's face burning bright with rage. "But you do have cute legs."

"He won't mind just this once," Del said unconvincingly. "Besides, they're navy issue."

"The legs?" quipped Corbin, heading down the corridor.

Both of them were handed a glass of beer when they entered the control room. Most of the staff and several crewmen were there, all holding glasses and intent on the viewing screen. Mitchell sat straight-backed in his chair, a microphone buried in one of his huge paws and a beer surrounded by the other. "Refrigerator with a head," Del mumbled when he viewed the square-bodied captain. Mitchell gave his two officers a quick glance, but immediately returned his attention to the screen.

Del breathed easier that his outfit had apparently gone unnoticed.

Suddenly the screen brightened as the searchlight reflected back off of the ocean floor. Buried for centuries untold under an inconceivable tonnage of water, the pressed stretch of mud and rock offered little artistic inspiration, but to the men of the *Unicorn* the view was grand indeed.

Mitchell cracked a rare smile as he clicked on the com. "The deepest spot in the Atlantic, gentlemen," he said, lifting his glass of Old Milwaukee in a toast. "The floor of the Milwaukee Deep."

A tiny sip and Mitchell's perpetual scowl returned. "She's all yours, Mr. Corbin," he said as he headed for the door. "And get rid of the beer."

Corbin shrugged impotently to the disappointed crew and motioned for one of the crewmen to collect the drinks.

Del was as thrilled as anyone aboard to finally realize the goal of their months of preparation, but a five-second toast and a sip of beer wasn't exactly his idea of a celebration. "Big deal," he grumbled, errantly believing the captain to be out of earshot.

The room hushed suddenly when Mitchell's head

popped back in the door. He eyed Del for a long minute.

"Mr. DelGiudice," he began, teasingly calm. "You're invited to join me in my quarters in ten minutes." His grin became an ugly grimace. "In uniform!"

Del just sighed helplessly as Corbin strolled over to pat him on the shoulder. "Maybe he didn't like your legs."

Billy Shank bit his lip and tried hard not to laugh.

Two uneventful days passed as the *Unicorn* crawled along the floor of the Atlantic. Forty-eight hours of rocky abutments and flat bottoms, captured in a relentless progression on the ship's monitor, and Del felt like a cartoon character running past the same background scenery again and again. He was on the bridge most of the time, pulling extra duty at the personal request of Captain Mitchell.

Good-behavior reward, he supposed.

Three others, Seamen Jonson, Camarillo, and Billy Shank, worked with him, but they went about their duties with disciplined efficiency and did little to relieve the boredom.

Finally a voice dispelled the solitude.

"Unbelievable," muttered Billy Shank. "Come see this!"

But even as Del rose from his chair, a loud peal blasted out of Camarillo's sonic equipment and spun the others on their heels in surprise.

His visage locked in a contortion of shock and terror, Camarillo could not answer their questioning stares. Unblinking, he toppled to the floor.

The three men ran to him. "Back to your station!" Del told Billy. "Full stop! Get the captain and Doc!"

Del rolled Camarillo's body over, his stare answered by dull unseeing orbs. He removed the headphones and found the speaker cloth torn wide and wet from the blood that still trickled out of Camarillo's ears.

A moment later Ray Corbin and Doc Brady rushed in, followed closely by Mitchell and Martin Reinheiser, the civilian physicist who had earned the distinction of becoming Mitchell's right-hand man. They ran to DelGiudice, now working furiously on the body.

"I've got him," Doc Brady told Del.

"He's dead," Del whispered as he rose. He felt his own pulse pounding as he watched helplessly.

"What happened?" Mitchell demanded.

Billy Shank answered with a shrug. "The indicators on my panel started jumping beyond the range of the gauges. I've never seen anything like it. And then there was a loud noise and Camarillo just fell over."

Mitchell glared at Del, who couldn't meet his accusing gaze, too vulnerable to argue with the captain this time. Del wasn't at fault, but he had been in command.

Secure in his victory as Del's head drooped, Mitchell turned to Reinheiser. "What could it be?"

Reinheiser snorted at the absurd request. "I believe I should examine the tapes before I make any guesses."

Doc Brady shook his head and closed Camarillo's eyes.

A dead crewman. Mitchell fumed at the implications to his record. "Put the ship on alert!" he roared. "And get me a damage report!" He rushed over to the security of his command seat, all the more angry at the lack of focus for his ire.

The alarm whined incessantly and the commotion could not ease Mitchell's impatience.

"The rest of the ship reports no damage or casualties, sir," reported Jonson.

Mitchell glanced at Del.

"Just one speaker," said Del. "It'll still work."

"Minor damage here, too," called Billy Shank.

Martin Reinheiser had torn off some printouts and was referencing them over a gridded chart. "I believe the disturbance came from right about here," he said, pointing to a spot on the grid. "About a quarter mile dead ahead."

"Get us there, but keep it slow," Mitchell snapped at Billy. "I want to know what killed my crewman."

Del eyed the viewing screen, now perceiving the beacon of the searchlight as an unwelcome invader of this secret and suddenly hostile darkness. We're heading right into something that killed Camarillo from a quarter mile away, he thought, and he was not the only one in the room troubled by that fact.

Billy Shank's indicator needles flickered in warning.

"Captain . . ." Billy began, but his voice trailed off when he noticed the astounded expressions on the faces around him. He looked to the screen and brought the sub to a halt.

Blackness. The searchlight knifed down and abruptly disappeared. It didn't reflect back; it simply stopped.

"What is it?" asked Mitchell.

"A cavern?" Reinheiser questioned rhetorically, certainly not expecting any answers from the men around him.

"My instruments are acting strange again," Billy remarked loudly, but they seemed not to notice him.

"We must get a closer look," declared Reinheiser, unconsciously leaning toward the screen.

"Move us in," Mitchell ordered flatly.

"But, sir," replied Billy, "my instruments aren't functional. I'll have to guide us manually."

"Take it nice and slow then," said Mitchell. "DelGiudice, have you got that speaker fixed yet?"

"Yes, sir."

"Get us a replacement for Camarillo."

"I can take it," offered Del, thinking his act of bravery might earn him some grudging respect from Mitchell. It didn't. Gingerly he slid the headphones over his head.

The sub inched downward. Still the light could not penetrate the void before them. The sonic equipment issued its signals, but they, too, were absorbed into the blackness, never to return.

"We must be within twenty feet," said Billy nervously. "I don't know how much closer I can get."

"Stop her, then," said Mitchell. Then to Del, "Have you got anything?"

"Nothing," answered Del. "The equipment seems to be working, but I'm not getting any signals at all."

"Damn!" Mitchell growled under his breath.

"We should back off and study the situation," Ray Corbin suggested. "We don't know what we're up against."

"It would seem prudent," Reinheiser agreed, realizing the futility of a visual examination without supporting information from their instruments.

Mitchell closed his eyes and rubbed his hands over his face. "Take us up a hundred feet."

Del's sigh of relief was audible.

"Mr. Corbin," Mitchell continued, "have everything inspected and bring me a complete status report as soon as possible." He turned to Reinheiser. "I'd like your evaluation the minute you get a chance to study all of the data."

And so the *Unicorn* hovered in the eternal gloom, a mere forty yards above the unexplained void. On the surface, a mighty electrical storm vented its fury in spasms of untempered violence, but the men of the *Unicorn* couldn't know that.

Not yet.

The ship came off alert before an hour had passed. Del found himself in command of the helm again as Mitchell and Corbin held a conference with the scientists. Most of the crew went to their barracks, trading rumors and trying to get what they figured might be their last rest for quite a while.

"These indicators are acting strange again," Billy said to Del a short time later, using the informal tone that marked their friendship. As the only black man on the *Unicorn*, Billy's own hesitance prevented him from having many friends on board. He had heard the quiet references to "NUSET's token black," an insidious thought that often crept into the back of his own mind. Del knew better, though, and he had proven a great comfort to Billy.

"It acts like there's something going on just above

us,'' Billy explained as Del approached. The needles jumped and a blip appeared on the tracking grid for just a second, then was gone. ''See? There it goes again!''

''Can we get a look above?''

''We can try.'' Billy began manipulating some controls. The viewing screen darkened as its camera turned away from the illumination of the forward searchlight.

''That should be about right,'' said Billy. ''Now, if I can get some light up there . . .'' As he reached for the controls, a bright arc cut a blinding line across the screen. Seaman McKinney, working the sonic booth, cried out and flung the crackling headphones to the floor. The screen flashed again.

''Jesus, it looks like a thunderstorm!'' cried Jonson.

''Sounds like one, too,'' added McKinney, rubbing his ear.

''Yeah, but underwater?'' questioned Billy. He looked blankly at Del. ''I think you'd better get the captain.''

But before Del could move, the lights, the screen, even the hum of the reactor shut down. Dread drifted in with the silence and blackness, inundating all aboard in the knowledge that they were utterly helpless, freezing them with the certainty that something terrible was about to happen.

Then the storm hit.

It struck amidship, by the crew's quarters, attacking with a raw power that mocked the sophistication of the *Unicorn.* Steel beams and hydraulics that had held back the pressure of 30,000 feet of water bent like rubber in the face of its strength. Bolt after bolt of lightning blasted into the sub, scorching and searing her sides. Currents wild with might wrenched mercilessly at the hull, tearing apart metal and splitting welded seams with unrelenting fury.

And through the holes, death streamed in, oblivious to the screams and pleas of the doomed crew.

Del was battered, but still conscious, clinging desperately to the bolted chair. His mind spun with the turnings of the sub, whirling around, then over, again and again. His terror heightened as he sensed that they were falling, hurtling uncontrollably toward the ocean floor, into the maw of the perverse blackness that had defied the intrusions of light or sound. Del tightened his hand on the arm of the chair, its tangible material his only grip on reality. Metal groaned in protest of the wrenching impact as the sub pummeled into and then through the black barrier.

And DelGiudice knew no more.

Chapter 2

Riddles Beyond the Blackness

Billy Shank's eyes opened upon a surrealistic scene of destruction. The glow of the emergency light reddened the misty shroud of steam and smoke that wafted through the air and distorted his perceptions of familiar images. He recognized Del, stretched out facedown on the floor, somehow still managing to hook his arm around the support of the captain's chair. Billy watched mesmerized as a dark liquid flowed out from under Del and made its way toward the wall.

"Listing?" he heard himself whisper, and then he looked again at the liquid and wondered if its blackish hue was another trick of the light.

Perhaps it was red—red like blood.

The realization that Del was dying before his eyes shook the grogginess from Billy. But when he tried to sit up, he found that a support pole had bent over to pin his shoulders. He struggled with all his strength, but he had no leverage to push the pole away. "Damn!" he screamed, raising his eyes to an unmerciful god. "You would make me watch him die?" Ignoring the protests of his flesh as the metal cut a deep line across his upper back, he twisted and jerked wildly.

Then a sickly-sweet odor caught Billy's attention. Out of the corner of his eye he saw a charred body lying on top of a shorted-out electrical panel.

McKinney.

"Jonson!" Billy called.

No answer. Billy scanned the room, searching for some hint of the crewman, squinting to penetrate the steam and smoke and the tears that welled in his eyes.

He saw a form resembling a foot sticking out from under a toppled computer bay. Yes, it was a foot. A moan escaped Billy's lips as he imagined Jonson's body squashed under the heavy case.

"This is the end," he said softly. He gave in to the pain and weariness that hammered dully at his senses and put his head down and closed his eyes.

And wondered what death would be like.

In his dazed state Billy could not track the minutes as they passed. Delirium swept over him and he could not react when the door crashed open and four wraith-like forms drifted in. Couriers to escort him to the land of the dead?

Never before had Billy imagined that the sound of Mitchell's shouting could bring him comfort.

"What the hell happened?!" the captain screamed. He stormed across the slanted room to the intercom, taking no notice of his injured crewmen.

Doc Brady didn't hesitate when he saw Del's life-blood streaming out. He tore a makeshift bandage from his shirt and dove down to stem the flow.

"This one's gone," declared Reinheiser as he peered under the cabinet at Jonson's crushed body. "And I don't think there's much hope for that one," he added callously, pointing to McKinney's smoldering corpse.

"Nasty cut," Brady chided with a wink and a calming smile. He pressed the shirt hard against Del's neck and helped Del to sit up. "Might need a tourniquet."

But Del hardly heard the Doc; his eyes focused on Billy.

Ray Corbin answered the concerned look evenly. "He'll be fine," he assured Del, turning the bent support aside. Billy moved to rise but Corbin held him down. "Just relax, Doc'll be with you in a minute."

Mitchell stared blankly at the dead indicator panel. "Something very big hit us," he growled. "And we didn't react. We just took it!" Mitchell realized that what had happened had been unpreventable, but he couldn't accept the loss of his ship. He needed a scapegoat to catch his wrath. "Someone up here, in command of the bridge, did nothing! Not even a goddamn warning!" He spun angrily and charged at Del, but Corbin and Brady saw it coming and cut him off.

"There was nothing I could do," Del snapped back, but he had to repeat himself several times as a litany against the guilt Mitchell had laid upon his shoulders.

"Stop it! Listen!" shouted Reinheiser, and the others quieted, surprised by the physicist's uncharacteristic outburst.

"Listen," Reinheiser instructed them again.

A few seconds passed, the only sound an occasional creak of settling metal.

"I don't hear anything," said Doc Brady.

"Not a thing. Nothing at all," emphasized Reinheiser. "Not even the hydraulic system." Terror seized all of the men with the expectation that they would be instantly crushed, as though they believed that death, in a final stroke of cruelty, had waited patiently for them to fully realize their doom.

Reinheiser was the only one unafraid enough to break the silence.

"Why aren't we dead?" he asked, echoing the thought that reverberated in all their minds.

They remained silent, trying to sort out a rational answer to the question. And if they weren't perplexed enough, the main lights suddenly brightened, indicator needles jumped to life, and the familiar hum of the *Unicorn*'s mighty turbines returned. The men jumped in unison when a shaky voice crackled over the intercom.

"Hello . . . anybody," it pleaded, balancing precariously on the edge of hysteria. "This is Thompson. Can anybody hear . . . oh, God, please don't make me be alone!"

Mitchell ran to the com. "What's going on back there?"

"Captain?" Thompson cried.

"Where are you?"

"Auxiliary power with Sinclair. He's pretty bad off. I don't think he's gonna make it."

"On my way," called Doc Brady, and he headed away.

Thompson heard and screamed back, "No! You can't!" Doc turned back to his companions, all frozen by the sheer desperation of the wail.

The prospect of one of his men, reputably the finest crew ever assembled, losing control enraged Mitchell. "You had better explain yourself!" he barked into the microphone.

"Flood, sir," Thompson answered evenly. "Everything between the gym and auxiliary power is underwater. You crack the hatch to forward barracks and you'll flood the front of the ship, too."

"The crew!" Mitchell cried. "What about my crew?"

Thompson's inevitable response stuck like a dagger in Mitchell's heart. "Dead, sir. Everyone's dead except for me and Sinclair and you guys up front."

Once again the survivors were reminded of the hopelessness of their situation. Eight men, six on the bridge up front, two in back, with fifty feet of flooded rooms between them.

"Seems we're in trouble," said Corbin offhandedly.

But Mitchell didn't view things that way. He put this situation into the perspective of one more challenge, probably the greatest he would ever face. His entire life, from city streets to the merchant marine to his naval commission had been one continuous fight. He had done more than survive, he had become a leader. "Stow it, Corbin!" he growled. "We've got a job to do." He motioned at Billy and Del. "I want those two ready to work tomorrow."

"That's impos—" began Brady.

"Tomorrow!" bellowed Mitchell. "Set up the conference room as an infirmary." He turned to Reinheiser. "See what you can do about cleaning up this air. You and I," he told Corbin, "will get this room back in order. I want those viewing screens working as soon as possible."

Mitchell didn't slow the pace of his growing momentum. "Thompson," he called, "what's your situation?"

"I'm a little banged up, sir. I sprained my wrist pretty bad, but I can work." He sounded a bit steadier.

"Then get that damn engine room back in shape and give me as much power as you can!" ordered Mitchell, using just the right timbre of anger in his voice to convey two messages: that he had faith in Thompson's ability and that he held Thompson solely responsible for getting the job done.

"Aye, aye, sir!" came Thompson's enthusiastic reply.

Del stared at the captain. He hated the man, but he couldn't deny Mitchell's effectiveness as a leader. Under Mitchell's command, nobody dared surrender. They all had jobs to do and, under the captain's demands, had no time to worry about the implications of their situation.

A few hours later, Del tossed uneasily on a makeshift cot, his dreams a lament for the security he had left behind. In that distant world, Debby celebrated her seventieth birthday huddled with her grandchildren in a placebo called a bomb shelter.

"Doc says I can go back to work," Billy announced to Del the next day. "I'm on my way to the bridge now. How about you?"

"R and R for at least another day," Del replied with a sly smile, clasping his hands behind his head.

"I'll come back and see you later," Billy said, and despite his feigned contentment, Del envied him. Sitting around idly allowed too much time to worry.

"I don't know what to tell you, Captain," said Corbin with a shrug. "It seems to be operational."

"How can we be in a hundred feet of water?" Mitchell snapped, though a twinge of hope found its way into his tone.

"That gauge operates by measuring the pressure on

a foot-long wand protruding off the side of the hull,'' explained Reinheiser mechanically, as though he was reading out of a book. ''It's a new design, untested really. Perhaps the wand was snapped off and the equipment has been fooled, taking the total pressure on the remaining piece and calculating it out over the whole length.

''Or perhaps we are in a place sheltered from the pressure of the ocean depths,'' he added, his analytical mind searching out every possibility.

''How deep could we be without the hydraulic system?'' asked Mitchell.

''About seven thousand feet,'' answered Billy from the door. The men turned to him. ''Reporting for duty, sir.''

''Where's DelGiudice?'' Mitchell demanded, a sour look on his face as though merely speaking Del's name left a bad taste in his mouth.

''Doc wants him to rest another day,'' explained Billy.

''I'll deal with that jerk later,'' Mitchell whispered under his breath. ''Get going on that viewing screen, Shank.''

Billy moved to the intercom, knowing that he would need some help from the engine room to test the power levels to his panels. ''Thompson,'' he called.

An empty pause.

''Engine room, come in.''

Still silence. Mitchell grew worried and reacted with typical anger. He grabbed the com away from Billy. ''Thompson!'' he shouted.

''Here, sir,'' came the unsteady voice, much like the tone they had first heard the day before.

''What's the matter?'' Mitchell demanded.

''Sinclair's dead,'' muttered Thompson. The men took the news stoically. Corbin rubbed his face to brush away any intruding emotions and Billy Shank let out a resigned sigh.

Thompson's voice came with sudden determination. ''How deep are we?''

Mitchell rarely felt sorry for anybody, but he pitied

the man on the other end of the intercom, trapped alone in the steamy engine room. "We're not sure," he replied calmly. "The gauge says one hundred; we think it's broken."

"Then mine must be broken, too," said Thompson, again stubbornly. "I'm going out. I'll be up front soon."

"Don't be a fool!" shouted Mitchell. "If that gauge isn't right—"

"I'll be killed," Thompson interrupted with a resigned, almost sedated, laugh. "So what? I'm alone back here with no food or water. I'll be dead soon anyway." He ended any further arguments by shutting off his mike.

"He'll never make it," muttered Reinheiser.

"Unless the gauge is right," snapped Billy, not appreciating the physicist's too-sure pessimism in an already dismal situation.

They went back to work halfheartedly, unable to concentrate on their tasks as each of them, even Reinheiser, waited and prayed that somehow Thompson would make it through, that the gauge would be right. But as minutes passed, the miracle seemed less likely and finally, Reinheiser took it upon himself to defuse the tension.

"Gentlemen," he said with his customary formality. "Since Seaman Thompson hasn't arrived yet, we must assume that he is dead. We must all simply concentrate on our assigned duties and get this ship back together."

Corbin and Billy exchanged helpless glances. They hurt at the loss of yet another companion, but once again they had to push their emotions deep inside and refuse to acknowledge the pain.

"How's that screen coming?" snapped Mitchell, trying to bring everyone back into the tasks at hand.

"Good, sir," replied Billy. "I should have something for you in a few minutes." He concentrated on his work, tried to forget that a friend of his had just died, taking what was probably their last hope with him.

"We aren't going to see much without the outer searchlights," remarked Reinheiser. "Let us hope they are still working."

"Even if they are, all we're going to see is dark water and gray stone," Billy mumbled to himself, too low for anyone else to hear. But he, too, hoped that the screen worked. At least then something would be fixed.

Billy flicked a switch, and the screen crackled sharply and filled with snow. As Billy tightened a patched connection on a broken wire, the picture came clearly into view for just a split second and then returned to snow.

"Did you see that!" cried Corbin.

"I'm not sure what I saw," gasped Mitchell. "Shank, get that damned picture back!"

"Trying, sir," replied Billy, confused as to why they were all so excited. He hadn't seen.

"The hull of an old warship," said Reinheiser.

"But did you see its condition?" cried Corbin. "It looked like it just went down!"

The screen flickered a couple of times, the picture came clear again, and the four men gaped at the eerie sight. Settled on a rocky reef less than twenty yards ahead loomed the spectacle of an old frigate. The name on its side read U.S.S. *Wasp*.

"Explain that," Mitchell challenged Reinheiser.

"We should get Del—I mean Mr. DelGiudice, sir," offered Billy. "He's always reading books about naval history."

"Go," said Mitchell and Billy was off. He returned moments later with Del and Doc Brady.

"Well, mister, what do you make of it?" Mitchell asked.

It took Del a minute to find his voice. "The *Wasp?*" he spoke aloud, trying to jar his memory. "That name sounds familiar."

"Late 1700's by the looks of it," said Reinheiser.

"Early 1800's, I think," corrected Del. "I could tell you more if I could get to my quarters. I've got some books about warships and—"

A bang sounded above them.

"The outer hatch," observed Corbin. "Thompson?"

The men surrounded the ladder leading to the sub's squat conning tower and Mitchell called over the intercom to the air lock. "Thompson, is that you?" he asked into heavy static.

The handle of the inner hatch began to turn.

"It better be Thompson," muttered Billy grimly, casting a wary eye at the old ship and clutching a heavy wrench.

Water gushed in as the inner hatch opened and a pair of black leather boots dangled through the hole.

"I knew it!" cried Billy, and he whacked up at the legs.

"Hey!" came a startled cry from above.

Mitchell recognized the voice and grabbed Billy as the legs were pulled back into the air lock. After some shuffling, Thompson stuck his head through the hatchway.

"Have you all gone crazy or something?" he asked of the startled faces below him. Eyeing Doc Brady, he added, "Have I got something for you! You aren't gonna believe this!" And he disappeared back through the hole.

After more shuffling, the dangling legs came through again. "Give me a hand with this guy, he's waterlogged," said Thompson. Stunned, Mitchell and Brady mechanically helped lower the body, a man in his thirties, dressed in a gray suit, complete with tails and a gold pocket watch.

"All he's missing is the top hat and cane." Corbin laughed, too overwhelmed by the unreality of it all, and too relieved to see Thompson, to be apprehensive.

"Got that, too," said Thompson. He slid down the ladder, a cane in one hand and a gray top hat on his head. "Well? What do you think?"

"It looks like he just died," said Corbin.

"Very little decomposition," agreed Doc Brady, but his attention was on Thompson, and the seaman's frenzied actions.

"Like that hull," remarked Reinheiser.

"They're all like that," Thompson teased.

"What are all like that?" demanded Mitchell, having no patience for Thompson's antics. "And what the hell took you so long?"

"All the ships outside are like that, sir," replied Thompson. "I had to look around.

"I closed my eyes when I left the ship. I really expected to die. But the gauges are right and the pressure wasn't bad at all.

"When I opened my eyes, the first thing I saw was an old schooner lying just off our tail. This guy was all tangled up in a rope on the capstan. I couldn't believe it. I started swimming toward him and noticed that all around were these other ships!"

"How was visibility?" interrupted Reinheiser.

"Not bad. A couple of hundred feet at least," replied Thompson. "And at first I couldn't understand that, either. By my figuring it's nighttime up top. So where's the light coming from? I saw these weird flashes up above us and I headed for the surface. But when I got closer I realized that there's solid rock above us."

"What?" Mitchell and Corbin asked together.

"Solid," reiterated Thompson. "We're in a giant cave. Back a couple hundred yards there's a funnel going up into the ceiling—the light's more intense there. I would have checked it out closer, to see if it opens up to the surface, but I couldn't get near it; I kept getting shocks—static, or something. I picked this guy up on the way back. I had to show you."

"How does the ship look from out there?" asked Mitchell.

"Bad," replied Thompson. "Real bad, sir. There's some holes midship, but that's the least of it. She's listing to port up here, but she's listing to starboard in back."

"Impossible!" Reinheiser argued.

"The middle of the ship got twisted," continued Thompson earnestly, putting his clenched fists one on top of the other and turning them in opposite directions. "I'd figure at least a thirty-degree discrepancy between the two ends."

"It's a miracle we're alive," said Reinheiser.

Mitchell didn't hear him. He just stared blankly ahead, dismayed by the now indisputable fact that his ship was gone beyond hope of repair.

But the brutal damage report didn't daunt the others. Something very strange was going on and they were intrigued, especially Martin Reinheiser. At this point, curiosity outweighed worry.

"I've got to get out there," Reinheiser begged Mitchell, his voice almost a whine.

"I'd like to get back out, too, sir," added Thompson. "I want a closer look at our damage."

"And I want to get at those books in my cabin," said Del, refusing to be left out of the excitement.

"No, you don't," cut in Doc Brady, still examining the corpse. "Thompson will get them for you. You're staying here and getting healthy!" Del would have argued, but Mitchell's outburst stopped him short.

"Do what you want!" the captain roared, his face contorted into an angry scowl. It was Mitchell's turn to feel the hopelessness, to believe that nothing he did in this situation could make any difference. He knew the gloom would pass. The violence within him had been able to push all his hurts away since he was a child, but for now he just had to get away from the others. He turned on his heel and stormed out of the room.

The others blankly watched him go, confused by the solid captain's sudden despair.

"He has lost his ship," observed Reinheiser. He studied the tenseness of the captain's stride, logging this newest revelation of Mitchell's disposition.

"Help me get this body to the conference room," Brady told Del. Del's face drooped in disappointment.

"All right," Brady conceded. "Maybe I'll let you go for a dive later."

Del smiled. "Let me tell Thompson where the books are." He bounded across the room, mesmerized by the potential adventure that awaited him outside the *Unicorn,* able to forget, for just a while, the carnage around him.

And the inevitability of his own impending doom.

Chapter 3

To the Tick of a Different Clock

"What did you bring that for?" grumbled Mitchell.

Reinheiser glared at him from across the table. "From the *Wasp,*" he explained, holding up the untarnished belt buckle for the rest of the men to see. Etched into the upper-left-hand corner were the initials "JB."

Reinheiser pointedly turned away from Mitchell. "The ship's captain, judging from his uniform," he said. "If we can find any records of the *Wasp,* it might prove useful."

"Always thinking, aren't you?" remarked Mitchell.

Reinheiser ignored the comment, unsure whether he had been insulted or complimented. "I also positioned a microphone under the break in the cavern ceiling. The funnel narrows considerably, but remains, I believe, large enough to admit the sub. The black area at its top seems similar to the one we were observing before the storm hit."

"You're assuming that we were forced downward by the storm, through that hole," said Corbin.

"We did go down," insisted Del, unconsciously clenching his fist as though he was still grasping the chair. "And we were pushed right through that hole."

"We must consider all of the possibilities," said Reinheiser. "But whether or not we went through the hole, that funnel is generating some sort of electrical disturbances, pulses, if you will, that I believe deserve some study. With the sonar equipment, we might be able to find some pattern to the pulse intensity."

"And then?" Mitchell asked, his tone still edged with sarcasm.

"Possibilities," was all that Reinheiser bothered to reply. He turned to Thompson, who had accompanied him on the last dive. "Do you know more on the status of the ship?"

"She'll never swim again, that's for sure," replied Thompson. "Our propellers are completely destroyed and we're bent and twisted in the middle. And we've got at least three fair-sized holes in us. There may be other smaller ones, too. The engines are in pretty good shape, though, considering the beating they've taken."

"Could you get her up?" asked Reinheiser.

"Surface?" Thompson balked at the idea. He started to chuckle, as though he believed the question a jest, but the physicist's visage told him otherwise. Embarrassed, he cleared his throat and continued. "Well, I can patch the holes and I think we can muster the power to blow our ballast tanks. But half the sub is full of water and we haven't got pumps to handle that. There's no way we can carry that load!"

"Let me worry about that," said Reinheiser in a condescending tone that conveyed the message to Thompson, and to all of them, that their role was to follow orders and leave the thinking to him. "How long to patch the hull?"

"A few days, and I'll need someone to help me."

Reinheiser nodded and patted his goatee. With a look, he indicated to Mitchell that he had heard enough from Thompson. Billy Shank was the next to speak.

"There's not much more to tell about the bridge," he began despondently, not enjoying his role as a prophet of doom. "The screens work, the com works, and the sonic equipment is okay; here's the latest readout." He handed the papers to Reinheiser. "Apparently, the depth gauge is functional, too, but that's about it. Everything else is dead and I really don't see how we can fix any of it."

"What you're saying is that we can see and hear anything that's in our area," Corbin remarked grimly. "And that's all we can do."

Even Mitchell seemed touched by the apparent finality of Corbin's statement. The sense of personal mortality descended upon the men, its weight bowing their heads low.

But not Reinheiser. He studied the sonic printouts, oblivious to the despair.

"What about supplies, Mr. Corbin?" he asked in his emotionless tone.

"There's enough food in the storage compartments below the galley to last several years," Corbin replied. "Water could be a problem, though. As far as I can tell, we've got about two weeks' worth with strict rationing, and we aren't likely to get any more. Our purification units are both completely destroyed."

Mitchell watched, fuming, as Reinheiser scribbled more notes on his little pad. The physicist was taking control.

"You seem to have this whole thing figured out," the captain snapped at him. "Why don't you let us in on it?"

"In due time, Captain," replied Reinheiser coolly. He turned away from Mitchell with a smirk. "Tell me, Doctor, based on your examination, how long was that cadaver in the water?"

"I don't know." Brady shrugged. "There must be some type of preservative in the water. But assuming that things were normal, I'd say that he was in the water about a day." The other men knew that the body was in good condition, but the confirmation from Brady shocked them nonetheless.

"Could you be more specific?" pressed Reinheiser, his excitement revealing that Brady's estimation figured into the framework of his escape plans.

"Twenty-two to twenty-five hours," replied Brady.

Reinheiser merely petted his goatee again and absently eyed the sonic printout. "Interesting," he muttered.

Del almost chuckled out loud as he imagined switches clicking on and off behind the physicist's eyes. He managed to cough as a cover, but a second later, Reinheiser looked straight at him with his information-devouring eyes and Del felt sure that his mind had been read. "Mr. DelGiudice, do you have anything to tell us?"

Del cleared his throat to compose himself. "If that ship on the screen was really the *Wasp,* she's over 180 years old. She was lost without a trace early in 1814, commanded by Johnston Blakely."

"That matches the JB initials on the belt buckle," observed Billy.

"Could you find anything else about the schooner off our tail, where Thompson found the corpse?" Reinheiser pressed.

Del looked down at the notes Thompson had given him, naming the various wrecks around them. "The *Bella,*" he replied. "Lost in 1854."

"What?" Brady gasped. Putting a specific date on that ship, labeling the corpse over 140 years old, simply wasn't in accordance with the precepts of medicine.

Reinheiser nodded his accord and smiled smugly.

"There's more," Del continued. He held up a book, one of the many written about the mysteries of the Bermuda Triangle. "All of the ships Thompson saw out there are listed in here. Lost at sea twenty, fifty, even 150 years ago." Del paused to let it sink in, knowing that his next revelation would stun the others even more.

"And the planes," he began.

"Planes?" echoed Corbin.

"World War II fighter types," Del explained. "Five of them and a larger rescue craft."

"Flight 19," Doc Brady gasped.

Del nodded. "Flew out of Florida on a training mission and simply disappeared," he said, though the legendary tragedy needed no explanation to the group at the table.

"So we've solved the mystery of the Bermuda Triangle," Corbin said grimly. "Or at least we know where everything went."

"Not to see the surface again," Billy found himself saying. He fell silent and slumped back.

Mitchell slammed his hands down on the edge of

the table and leaped up from his chair, leaning ominously over them to give them a closer look at his scowl. "You keep your minds on your work! Got it?" He turned impatiently on Reinheiser. "Are you ready to talk yet?"

Martin Reinheiser stared intently at the men around the table, trying to determine the best way to present his theories. He fixed his gaze on Doc Brady.

"First of all, let me assure you that conditions here are normal and within the framework of our laws and calculations. There are no preservatives in the water, no special oxygen or chemical balance to keep a cadaver fresh." Brady shook his head insistently and Reinheiser held up his hand to block any interruptions. "I understand your doubts, Doctor, but there is another explanation. I believe the key to this riddle lies in the fourth dimension, time."

"Are you saying that we were thrown back in time?" demanded Doc Brady. Incredulous stares came at Reinheiser from every direction.

Idiots, thought Reinheiser. I knew that this was beyond them. "No," he countered, his voice a knife's edge. "Not pushed back, but pushed into a different frame of reference."

They didn't seem to understand.

"Our concepts view time as relative," he explained. "An hour to a man on a rocket approaching the speed of light would be days, weeks, even years to a man on Earth. This illustrates what I believe has happened to us. We have been pushed into a time frame where 140 years of our history has been condensed into twelve to fifteen hours, judging from the doctor's report on the cadaver."

"I said that the body was in the water for about twenty-four hours," corrected Brady.

"Yes, Doctor, but we were in this frame for approximately ten hours before the body was recovered."

"Wait a minute," demanded Del, looking hard at the physicist. "If what you're saying is true, and we've been down here for about fifteen hours, then . . ."

"Then one hundred and forty years have passed on the surface," Reinheiser finished. "And everyone we ever knew is dead and buried."

With the unreality of all that had already happened to them, they found it hard to dismiss Reinheiser's conclusions. Shaking their heads and muttering denials, they looked around to each other, searching for confirmations to the absurdity of the explanation. This angered Reinheiser even more, not because they didn't believe him—he hadn't expected them to—but because of their outright trepidation, even horror, at his suggestion. Could they be so inane as to disregard the incredible implications?

"Think of it, gentlemen!" the physicist exclaimed. "A new world awaits us. Think of the advancements in science! In medicine, Doctor!" He was almost pleading with them, holding out hope that they weren't as small-minded as they appeared.

"Bullshit!" blurted Mitchell. He towered over the seated physicist, not even trying to conceal his disappointment. "Is this the best you've got for me?"

"I assure you, I intend to prove my theory," Reinheiser replied, knowing full well what Mitchell needed from him.

"And how can you do that while we're still down here?"

"That shouldn't be hard," answered Del. Startled, Reinheiser and Mitchell looked over at him. "Tomorrow morning we send out divers to recover two bodies, one from our ship and another one from the *Bella.* If the theory is right, Doc's autopsy should show our crewman to have been dead in the water for about thirty-four hours and the body from the *Bella* for forty-six to forty-nine hours."

Reinheiser's surprised look turned icy. He was amazed at Del's show of reasoning, but mostly he was angry, preferring to explain his own theories without any help from a layman. "Precisely," he hissed at Del, narrow-eyed.

"Whether or not my theory is correct, I believe that we can escape from here," Reinheiser said. "If we can patch the holes and get the sub up, magnetic influences should force us to the funnel. A storm might push us out, just as one pushed us in."

"It won't work," said Thompson, immediately stifling the hopeful looks of the others. "No way can I make the patches strong enough to handle the kind of pressure that's on the other side of that hole."

"Our hull couldn't sustain that kind of pressure if it were intact," retorted Reinheiser. "The hydraulic system was destroyed."

"Then how?" asked Corbin.

"I'm gambling that we won't have to worry about the pressure."

Mitchell huffed sarcastically, the tone itself refuting Reinheiser's assertions.

"Look around you!" Reinheiser fumed, fed up with being ridiculed by his inferiors. "Do I have to spell it out to the letter? Why wasn't the hull of the *Wasp* crushed under the pressure of 27,000 feet of water? That corpse still had its top hat and cane!" His voice mellowed as he perceived that the puzzled expressions of the others no longer held any hint of protest, only intrigue. "The only possible explanation is that the electromagnetic storms which brought these ships and planes here shielded them from the pressure."

"But we didn't have anything protecting us when we went through," Del pointed out.

"We didn't get caught *in* the storm," Reinheiser explained. "We got hit *by* the storm, outside its bubble, merely in the way of devastation's chosen path."

The men looked around to each other with hopeful shrugs. Perhaps they didn't believe Reinheiser on a rational level, but they had a desperate need for some sliver of hope.

"But we don't have the supplies to just float around and wait for a storm," said Del. His voice wasn't hostile; he was asking, not arguing.

"We shan't wait long," replied Reinheiser. "That portal is the barrier between two very different magnetic fields. The interaction of those fields constantly produces violent electrical storms."

"But how often?" argued Mitchell, disgruntled at the second apparent flaw in Reinheiser's plans. "Every couple of months? Or years apart? We don't have that much time."

"Again you are looking at things from the wrong point of view, Captain. The storms occur every few weeks or so on the other side of the barrier, the other frame of reference. Down here that translates to minutes or even seconds."

The physicist looked around at the others, noting the slight, hesitant, glimmer of hope on their faces. Give them what they need to hear, he reminded himself, and he looked straight into each set of pleading eyes.

"We can escape."

Chapter 4

Eulogy

Wonderment overwhelmed him. Every escapist instinct Del had told him to swim away from the *Unicorn* and lose himself in history. He had thrust himself into the heart of an untainted legacy. More than a museum, this . . . unfabricated, unbiased testimony to worlds and ways with a purity that books, models, even restorations could not begin to approach.

Del's first order of business was a bit more grim, though. He had to remove the bodies of his dead shipmates from the sub and select one for Brady's test of Reinheiser's time theory. He moved to the jagged tear in the *Unicorn*'s hull and peeked inside.

The destruction was total. Splintered bunks, shredded blankets, and blasted footlockers floated about and lay jumbled in uneven heaps.

And scattered all about the mounds, meshed in like just so much more debris, were Del's shipmates.

Del set a determined visage and squeezed in through the hole. Working methodically and with as much detachment as he could muster, he laid his shipmates to rest in their watery graves and brought one back to the air lock.

Now he had to get a body from the *Bella*. This task both scared and intrigued Del, his imagination having launched several promising plots for horror movies. But at the same time, Del could not repress his curiosity about the wonders around him.

When he first went aboard the *Bella*, he moved gingerly, like an archaeologist brushing sand away from an ancient relic or an historian leafing through a delicate medieval manuscript. Before long, though, he realized that this ship was not in any way fragile with age. Her flooring remained unwarped and her masts stood straight and firm. Del was convinced that if she were raised and patched, the *Bella* could sail proudly once again.

He moved without hesitation to the door leading belowdecks and found a suitable cadaver for Brady as soon as he had opened it. But Del pushed his way past the corpse, determined to get a closer look at whatever relics lay below.

It exceeded anything his imagination could have hoped for. Everything that wasn't bolted down had been jumbled and battered, but that included just a small fraction of the room's contents. How well the people of this age were prepared to handle the tossing of heavy seas! Del had always known that danger was a very real fact of a nineteenth-century sailor's existence, but he had never really appreciated just how powerful an influence the unpredictable savagery of the sea had been. In honor to the *Bella*'s gallant crew, and to all the sailors who had braved the seas when the advantage was so lopsidedly on nature's side, he cleaned up the room.

And the treasures he found! Trinkets and artifacts, masterfully created by human hands. He wanted to scoop everything up and take it with him, but of course Mitchell would have had his head if he did. There was one item he couldn't resist, though, a small silver box, sealed and locked, perhaps a jewelry case, and bearing his initials "JD."

That night, after an exhausting stretch of work, the crew headed for their beds in the conference room. More interested in privacy, Del stayed behind on the bridge, assuring Doc Brady that he'd sleep better alone. Brady suspected that something was up, for the agitated look on Del's face made it obvious that he had no intention of sleeping.

Finally, when he was alone, Del broke open the silver box and found a small pistol, a derringer, again engraved with his initials, a solid silver bullet, and a note:

> To my dearest Judith,
>
> My but you are a difficult person to buy a conventional birthday present for! I have, however, proven my resourcefulness once again! In all modesty, I present to you, dear Judith, the prototype of my new pistol. You shall find this firearm is well suited for a lady, as it is small, light, and easy to conceal. Look for it on the market sometime next year; you can always say that you got yours first!
>
> Your loving cousin,
> Henry

"I'm keeping this," breathed Del. He thought for a moment, then shoved the pistol and bullet into the inside pocket of his shirt.

By the sixth day, all of the patches were in place and Reinheiser was ready to make the attempt to blow the water out of the sub. The only chance was to use the Atmospheric Control Unit to force great gushes of air into the flooded sections, displacing water out an open diving hatch. It proved a tedious and dangerous chore, for the physicist couldn't possibly produce enough power to empty the entire ship all at once. Del and Thompson had to remain in the flooded sections and seal off each room as it cleared.

The process had to be repeated several times; twice Del and Thompson weren't quick enough in securing a room and the ocean charged back in as the pressurized air burped out a hatch in a great bubble. But the patches all held, and near the end of the day, Del closed the outside hatch and the interior of the *Unicorn* was dry once again.

After a few hours of final cleanup, jettisoning everything that wasn't nailed down, all was ready for their desperate attempt. No one gave any speeches or assurances; they all knew their odds and faced them individually.

Thompson remained in the engine room at the controls for blowing the ballast tanks while the other six men used belts to strap themselves down on the bridge. Each of them held supplies of some sort—food, water, clothing. Corbin clutched an inflatable life raft, a going-away present from his father on the day the *Unicorn* had sailed out of Miami.

Mitchell carried the largest pack, four rifles strapped together in a plastic bag. Del saw no need for the guns, and the sight of the volatile captain holding them disturbed him. He shook his head incredulously—guns wouldn't save them from drowning. Yet the rifles were indeed a comfort to Mitchell. He could accept that they might all die in the escape attempt; this was Reinheiser's game and he'd let Reinheiser worry about it. Mitchell was more concerned with situations that he could control—that he and his guns could control.

"Let it begin," Reinheiser said when they had all settled.

Mitchell took the com and called back to the engine room. "Thompson?"

No reply.

"Thompson!" Mitchell growled more loudly.

"Here, sir." Brady winced at the uneven timbre.

"Our lives are in his hands?" remarked Del.

Mitchell spoke calmly, but firmly, "Blow the tanks."

But again, no reply.

A few more seconds of silence broke Mitchell's patience. "Blow those goddamn tanks, mister!" he roared. "Now!"

The sub shuddered with the release of water. Mitchell shut down the intercom and congratulated himself for his prowess in handling his crew.

The *Unicorn* began to rise.

Their moment of hope was upon them; almost as one they clutched the belts that held them. They said nothing, too engulfed by the probability of impending death to think of anything else, those feelings being too personal and unresolved to be shared. Involved with their work during the last few days, they hadn't had time to come to terms with this moment and all of them welcomed the silence as conducive to the contemplation they now needed.

It didn't last. Suddenly the door burst open and a terrified Thompson rushed in, tears streaming down his face.

"Oh, no," groaned Doc Brady.

"I've got him," shouted Del. He wiggled free of his restraints and pulled Thompson down to the vacated seat.

"Get the hatch!" screamed Mitchell. Del ran to the door. Dismay stole his breath when he got there.

"The rest of them are open! All the way back!"

The *Unicorn* thudded to a stop and Del was knocked to his knees. He froze and did not try to rise.

"We've hit the top of the cavern," said Reinheiser.

"No time, man!" Brady cried to Del. "Get back."

Del secured the hatch and dove down, trying to slip under the belts with Thompson, just as the *Unicorn* started moving again.

Mitchell looked to Reinheiser. "Currents?"

"Magnetic force," answered the physicist. "Drawing us to the center of the field interaction." Suspecting what was about to happen, he warned, "Hold on."

Just as he finished, it grabbed the sub. Like a great untamed beast, the newborn storm sprang upon the *Unicorn,* seeking an outlet for its uncontrollable power. It raged about in torment, aimless at first, but then suddenly finding a direction. Its power became purposeful anger, guided toward the black portal by vengeance, as though it blamed that area for its agony. The storm raced in, pulling the helpless sub along, and tore through the barrier.

The men's knuckles whitened under a grip of terror. Up and up they went, spinning and swirling. Up to a world that had once been their home.

But not anymore.

Chapter 5

The Wrath of an Angry God

The minutes passed slowly as the *Unicorn* spun and bounced through the five-mile trip to the surface. Up and up she went, and then, as suddenly as it had started, the violent thrashing stopped.

The *Unicorn* righted herself and sat calm, but the seven men did not release their grips on the belts. "We've stopped going up," Del dared to whisper at length.

"The surface," added Corbin. "And we must have broken clear of the storm." Wide smiles curled up from every lip.

But even as the seven men began freeing themselves from the straps, the lights went out. And in the blackness an ominous sound became evident, a sound that every seagoing man dreams of in his worst nightmares. Somewhere toward the back of the *Unicorn*, the ocean had again found its way in.

"We're taking on water!" cried Billy. As if to confirm his statement, the sub tilted to starboard.

"She's going to roll!" shouted Mitchell. "Get out!" Coolheaded Ray Corbin was the hero this time. At the first sign of danger, when the lights went out, he had groped his way to the base of the conning tower. "I'm at the ladder," he said calmly. "Follow my voice."

Mitchell found him first, and with the captain in position to guide the others, Corbin stated loudly enough for all to hear, "I'm going out with the raft."

Little light entered when Corbin opened the outer hatch, the sky being starless and pitch black. Undaunted, he threw out the raft and blindly scrambled onto it as it inflated.

Reinheiser was next up the ladder, then Doc Brady.

"Hurry up!" Mitchell urged as the sub leaned further.

But Del had a problem: Thompson was frozen in terror, refusing to move despite every effort. As time seeped away, Del grew angry. He grabbed Thompson's shirt and hauled him up the incline.

"Help me!" he yelled to Mitchell. The captain latched on to the terrified seaman's shirt and heaved him up the ladder, where Billy Shank was waiting.

But just as they got Thompson safely into the raft, the *Unicorn* suddenly rolled further to starboard. Mitchell was braced by the ladder, but Del lost his footing and plummeted into the darkness.

"DelGiudice!" cried Mitchell.

"I'm okay," replied Del, rubbing a new bruise on his shoulder. Unmercifully, the *Unicorn* assumed an even steeper angle. "I'll make it," he assured Mitchell. "Go ahead up."

Mitchell shook his head, not so certain that Del could get back to the ladder. But the captain had no way to help. He moved out of the sub.

Del heard the men on the raft calling as he groped around on all fours. He could not find the ladder! Then the sub rolled some more and the ocean rushed through the open hatch, hungry to claim its prize.

"She's on her side!" came Billy's distant cry as the raft drifted away. "She's going over! Del!"

Del slumped back against the now vertical floor, resigned to his fate. He didn't notice that the water pouring in was strangely hot.

Suddenly he felt himself rising, and not with the water; it wasn't deep enough. His eyes darted around. What sort of delirium had gripped him? He was floating in the air! And then miraculously, he was on the ladder!

"How?" Del asked aloud, but he didn't wait for any answers. He fought his way out the hatch and swam toward the dim outline of the raft and her six passengers.

They hauled Del aboard silently and gathered to the edge of the raft.

All was quiet save the rustle of wet clothes and the occasional groan of a soft-soled shoe on the rubber raft. Behind them, far off now and racing away, the wild storm raged, but the men took no notice. They stood solemn, peering into the blackness, waiting for a part of their lives to come to an end. And with a gurgle, the vast, unconquerable ocean took the *Unicorn.*

"Well, she's gone," said Corbin, staring vacantly into the void of night.

What more could they say?

They settled in for the night along the perimeter of the twenty-man raft and lay quietly in blackness as the empty hours passed, remembering and wondering. The crisis and great loss of the past few days forced Del into a contemplation of his own mortality. Despite all his efforts, death remained unanswerable and irreversible.

For perhaps the first time in his life, Del was experiencing the emptiness of his rational inability to accept religion.

A few hours later, without warning, dawn exploded over the eastern horizon, shattering the black calm of night and whatever tranquility the men might have had. Startled from their dreams and thoughts, they faced the surprising light.

Even though its lip had just broken the horizon, the raging sun burned their eyes, and as it climbed into full view, the sky turned a bright red and the temperature soared. Waves of heat ripped through the air above the raft. The ocean flashed bloodred as choppy swells caught the sky's fire in brilliant reflections, appearing as sheets of flame flicking against the sides of the raft.

"What the hell is going on?" cried Mitchell as he reflexively dodged the splash of red water. The very sky above them was battered and torn. Only one thing could have caused that devastation.

"They must have done it," realized Corbin, scrambling unsteadily to his feet. "They finally did it!"

"War?" gasped Mitchell. He turned to Reinheiser, who was staring blankly at the merciless sun. "Nuclear war?"

Reinheiser shrugged his shoulders listlessly. "There could be other explanations," he said unconvincingly, overwhelmed by the apparent betrayal of his cherished science. What had they done with the marvelous tools and inventions?

"Whatever happened, we've got to get some protection from this sun before it burns our skin away," said Doc Brady.

"Get the cover out," Mitchell said absently, his voice subdued. This horror transcended anger, leaving nothing but emptiness in its wake.

"We are gathered together on a most solemn occasion," Ray Corbin proclaimed, still standing. The men watched him with unchanging expressions as he deliberately reached down and picked up one of Mitchell's rifles. "We stand alone as witnesses to the ultimate stupidity of mankind. We have come to bury the dead." He raised the rifle above his head in uplifted palms, then tossed his offering into the red water.

The shoulders of the sitting men visibly slumped even lower. Mitchell wanted to choke Corbin, more for destroying what little morale was left than for throwing away the rifle. But he found that he couldn't even shout at the man. Corbin's sarcasm had touched him, made him realize his own frustration at the very real possibility of a barren earth.

Billy Shank took many more shifts than the others outside the tent of the raft's cover, and he stayed out hours at a stretch, until his eyes burned from the dazzling light and he lay near dehydration in a puddle of sweat. It wasn't a form of self-persecution; Billy was simply determined to live the last few days of his life in defiance of the horror.

Black thoughts and empty silence dominated the atmosphere under the tent. The men faced the grim reality in private, more alone than any of them had ever been. For Del, though, a sliver of hope fought back against the despair. Tugging uncomfortably at the rational side of him, which refused to admit blind faith, was the notion that a miracle had saved him on the bridge of the sinking *Unicorn.* And on a deeper, still ungraspable level, the thought of intervention by some angelic overseer hinted at a sense of comfort beyond anything Del had ever experienced.

Day was a brutal trial of endurance in the sweltering 120-degree heat. Even outside the stuffy tent, a good breath of air was hard to come by. Lungs and throats ached with fire in the parching dryness and lips cracked within cracks. Strained eyes, bloodshot from the uncanny brilliance, stung relentlessly even when closed.

Nights were better. When the temperature dropped to more tolerable levels, some of the men ventured out to join Billy, hoping for a nostalgic glimpse of normalcy, a relief from the constant pressure. And yet they were always disappointed, for the night sky was ever the same unblemished black. Not a single star would grace them with its fantasy-spawning light nor did the moon arise with her alluring glow. Del focused on this perversion and to him it became the greatest tragedy of all. He desperately wanted to see a star again before he died.

On the afternoon of the fifth day, their water supply nearly exhausted, Billy lay alone outside the tent. The sea sat calmer this day, a smooth, dull crimson below the thin mist that hugged the surface. Billy lay across the edge of the raft, his hand drawing shapes in the water. He fell asleep in that position, unaware that the raft had entered a strong current and was steadily accelerating. Several hours and many miles later, Billy woke and looked up with a start. Dead ahead, his sweat-filled eyes beheld a beautiful sight.

"A mirage," he gasped, and he closed his eyes tightly and rubbed the sleep from them.

But when he looked again, the vision remained.

Their way was blocked by a wall of golden light stretching from the sea to the sky and for miles in either direction.

Billy's breath came in short puffs. What barrier was this? The gateway to death? To heaven? Or had the heat brought him delirium?

The raft continued toward the golden sheet and Billy's apprehension grew. He needed someone now—Del, or anybody. "Hey!" he shrieked between gasps. "Come see this!"

The men under the tent reacted slowly to the call. Some were asleep, other lost in daydreams or distant memories.

"Hey!" Billy yelled again. Heads finally appeared from the tent, and amid questioning and unbelieving exclamations the six men moved to the front of the raft.

"A giant sunbeam." Del chuckled.

"What could it be?" Mitchell asked Reinheiser, a slight trace of panic in his voice as he was once again faced with something unknown and beyond his control.

Reinheiser just shrugged his shoulders and shook his head. He wasn't talking much these days. He had expected a future world of marvelous machines and great discoveries, but something had gone very wrong. Someone had pushed the wrong button and washed away his technological dream. The bitter reality around him had forced him to question the value of his entire existence.

"Here we go!" Del said as they rushed into the light.

Instantly the temperature dropped to a comfortable level and their vision became a yellow-golden blur, bereft of individualizing shadows and shades of depth. Everything, the orange raft, their blue clothes, Billy's black skin, melded together in the uniform hue of their background.

The raft exited the golden sheet without any warning and the startled men were greeted by a cool breeze and blue skies and the bluest water any of them had ever seen. After a moment of shock, they cried out in delight, even Mitchell and Reinheiser, and Thompson sobbed with joy. Some of the world had escaped the devastation, it seemed.

Again Mitchell turned to Reinheiser and again Reinheiser merely shrugged his shoulders and shook his head.

"Now we've got to pray for some rain or a place to land," Ray Corbin reminded them. "Blue skies won't fill our water bottles."

But the men paid little attention to Corbin's words. Their salvation was at hand and they would hear no more of death. Not now.

The raft continued to drift in an easterly direction for the rest of the afternoon and through a beautiful, crimson sunset. And that night, clear and cool, the stars came out, a billion it seemed, and Del was overjoyed to witness their twinkling for the first time in weeks. Truly a night to lie back and appreciate the gentle sway of the ocean below and the vastness of the heavens above, far beyond mortal comprehension yet intimately pleasing to the soul. So the men lay serenely about the perimeter and unanimously agreed upon a pact that if anyone awakened before dawn, he would rouse the others, that they, too, might enjoy the first wonderfully normal sunrise. One by one, they drifted into the comfort of untroubled dreams.

Del opened his eyes just before dawn, the sky a deep blue as the still-hidden sun worked the inevitable transition from the black of night. He stirred the others and the raft became noisy with shuffling and yawning as they all positioned and prepared themselves for the coming event.

They talked and joked and stretched the night away with complacent groans, but when the watery rim of the eastern horizon glistened suddenly in sparkling reflection and the sky above it steadily pinkened, the men hushed in unison.

It came as the visual music of the cosmos, timeless

perfection; the first ray of the sun peeked at them across the mirror-calm water. She mounted higher, the giver of light, on the unseen, untiring wheels of spherical order. Seven men stood as one and applauded, and in every mind was the fleeting realization that before them was a moment of spiritual awareness, too often taken for granted. For most, the thought would pass as quickly as the dawn, rekindled far too infrequently to make any difference in their character. But for Jeffrey DelGiudice, the experience was lasting. Never again would he look at the beautiful world about him in quite the same way.

When dawn turned to day, though, the men discovered a new problem. The raft sat still on the water, nothing but unmoving blue ocean as far as the eye could see. Corbin's warnings about the water supply loomed suddenly before them. They had dared to believe that the currents that had pulled them from the devastation would be their path to salvation.

This newest dilemma was more than Thompson could take. He leaped to his feet and punched at the sky. "Will you get it over with!" he screamed to the gods above. "Bastards! If you want us dead, then do it now and no more games!" He looked around suddenly, as if a revelation had stricken him, meeting his seated companions' unbelieving expressions with a sincere look of understanding. "That's it! Don't you know?" he howled with hysterical glee. "It's all a game!"

Mitchell turned a menacing glance at Brady and Corbin and warned in all seriousness, "Control that idiot or he's going overboard."

But even as the captain spoke, Thompson dropped to the raft, alternating wild laughter and sobbing. Tears streamed freely down his face and he kept whispering, "Just a goddamn game," desperately begging anyone to agree with him.

Later that morning, they drank the last of the water, and then sat helpless, quiet, betrayed.

Suddenly their contemplations were stolen by a loud splash, and then another.

"Dolphins!" shouted Doc Brady as a large bottle-nosed dolphin broke the surface and arrowed into the air. In seconds, the water around the raft churned as dozens of dolphins danced and soared all about them, silver-flitting needles weaving intricate patterns in the azure fabric of the sea.

"Unbelievable!" Del whispered, seeing the display in an inspiring light. A week ago, he might have viewed the dance as a pleasing diversion, but now his vision went much deeper. In their evolution, the dolphins had become perfectly suited for their world, the embodiment of nature's ability to flow toward perfection. They were the flesh-and-blood music of universal law and divine order. Del wanted to share his revelation and see if the others, too, saw the true beauty of it all, but no words good enough came to him.

The ballet went on for several minutes.

Then a dolphin sat up in the water, half of its blue-gray body effortlessly still in the air a few feet in front of the raft. It stared with intelligent eyes into seven puzzled faces and began clicking and whinnying and waving its long nose frantically.

"He's talking to us!" Billy laughed.

"Don't be stupid!" retorted Mitchell, but Del's perception showed him that Billy was right, and moreover, he somehow felt that he understood. He darted under the tent and tore away some of the cord that edged the canvas, quickly securing one end to the raft. He ran back up front and threw the other end toward the dolphin.

"What are you doing?" demanded Mitchell. But even before Del could respond, there came a great tug and the raft started moving as several dolphins pounced on the rope and took it in tow.

"Incredible," was all that Doc Brady managed to mutter.

"I just had a feeling," said Del, with an embarrassed shrug of his shoulders.

The dolphins pulled due east. On and on for hours and hours, and when those on the rope tired, they were replaced by fresher companions. Once again the men took faith in their salvation and by midafternoon their prayers were answered.

"Land!" cried Billy, and sure enough, edging the eastern horizon, loomed the black silhouette of distant mountains.

"Any idea where we are?" asked Mitchell.

"None," Billy answered. "We've been going the wrong way for Florida. Could be Haiti."

"We'll know soon enough," said Corbin. The dolphins continued their incredible pace, and less than an hour later, the raft was barely several hundred yards from the shoreline.

The dolphins let go of the rope and graced the men with a final dance. Perhaps it was a farewell salute, the dolphins' way of saying good-bye; or perhaps they danced simply for the joy of it, cutting sleekly through the water and leaping in pirouette or somersault. Then, as precisely as any drill team, they formed into a line and headed back out to sea, skimming the surface in majestic flight. Del hung over the edge of the raft, calling out good-bye.

Not even Mitchell berated him.

"The tide will get us in now," observed Corbin.

A few minutes later, the raft beached onto the sand of a new world.

Chapter 6

Ynis Aielle

The beach was dreary and gray as the sky above. Soggy clumps of seaweed, disgorged offal of the ocean, lined the high-tide mark as monuments of neglect. Dead fish and crabs, untended by scavengers and parasites, festered in the sand. Something was terribly wrong here. What should have been a place of revitalizing, cleansing tides offended the senses like a fetid, unmoving swamp. Nature seemingly had abandoned, or had been forced from, this stretch, leaving it in total decay. Yet the men were undaunted, for this land, however discouraging, was their salvation, their deliverance from the very fires of hell.

After a couple of minutes of quiet thanks (none of them had even stepped out of the raft), Mitchell remembered his responsibilities. "We've got to find some water," he said. "And I want to know where we are."

"And when we are," quipped Reinheiser. Brady's test of the cadavers had gone exactly as he had predicted, though Reinheiser and the doctor decided to keep their findings private until the more serious problems had been addressed.

But none of the others missed Reinheiser's remark, and for the first time, Del seriously contemplated the possibilities. The devastation beyond the golden sheet had convinced him that there had been a nuclear war, but occupied with other pressing issues, he hadn't really considered that perhaps the devastation came fifty or even a hundred years after the *Unicorn* had sailed from Miami. The prospect of a new world, of meeting a man from the future, now intrigued Del. A very large part of him hoped that Reinheiser was right.

"We'll split up into three groups," said Mitchell, looking at the three remaining rifles. He surveyed the landscape. North, faintly visible through the light fog, loomed the distant shapes of huge boulders, a rocky prelude to great dark mountains. South, the beach remained redundantly gray for as far as the eye could see. Due east, inland, was a marshy plain, flat and misty, misshapen black puddles of salty backwash blotting a gray-green background.

"Pull the raft up above the tide line," Mitchell told Del and Billy. "Then head north. Mr. Corbin, take Thompson and go south."

"Thanks a bunch," mumbled Corbin.

"The rest of us will head inland," continued Mitchell. "Each group get a rifle. We've got about four hours until sundown and I want you all back here before then."

Del and Billy moved at a swift pace, excited and anxious to discover their whereabouts and, as Del put it, their "whenabouts." Two hours and several miles later, they found themselves stomping along the only twisting trail they could follow through the great boulders and sheer rock faces. It rose and fell, more up than down as they steadily climbed higher and higher. Off a few hundred yards to the left and below them, came the incessant pounding of the waves vainly bashing against the invincible cliffs.

"There's no end to these rocks," muttered Del, his head down, watching his step; he had already stubbed his toes several times on the unyielding stone. The path was only a couple of feet wide at this point, barely a crack in a huge slab of solid stone, and the incline was fairly steep. Approaching the summit of the rise, Del looked up and beheld a magnificent sight.

"A castle!" he gasped, and he darted up the trail. Billy followed Del's lead. The fog thinned out momentarily, and sure enough, he, too, saw the black walls and imposing towers of an immense fortress far in the distance, set upon a cliff face overlooking the sea.

Del stood on the lip of a ledge, his hand shading his eyes as he tried to gain a better view of the castle through the alternately thick and thin patches of fog. He still hadn't looked at the drop beneath him.

Billy did when he got there.

"Get down!" he whispered harshly. He grabbed Del by the shirt collar and pulled him back from the ledge and to the ground.

"What are you . . ." began Del, but he shut up when he saw Billy trembling and readying the M-16.

Ray Corbin carried his rifle casually, barrel down over his right arm. Thompson had first grabbed the weapon back at the raft, but Corbin had witnessed too much to let the unsteady seaman anywhere near it. The two traveled slowly, for though Thompson was excited, Corbin insisted they take things easy.

They had moved inland just off the beach and were traveling over a line of parched bluffs covered by scraggly brown grass. Corbin's easy pace had subdued Thompson a little and both walked silently, deep in thought—Corbin worrying about the fate of his family in New England, and Thompson, who had already convinced himself that he had saved the *Unicorn* single-handedly, fantasizing about the presentation of his medal.

As they approached a high bluff, the sound of voices abruptly ended their daydreams. The two looked at each other and Thompson was about to blurt something out when Corbin slapped his hand over the seaman's mouth. He motioned for Thompson to follow and began crawling up the side of the hillock. As they neared the top, the croaking voices became clearer; guttural, sounding somehow not human, but talking in a broken form of English. Corbin squirmed to the top and looked down on the speakers.

Hideous they were, mutated as though nature herself had rebelled against their very existence. Nine of them stood naked except for scant lizard-skin loincloths tied about their waists and sheathed swords strapped to their sides. They were shorter than a man, but stocky, their sinewy trunks were supported by bow-legged, powerful legs and pallid green skin blotched by uneven clumps of knotted, filthy hair, hung about them in loose flaps. Their faces were worse yet, lipless mouths stretched thin, straining to cover cruelly pointed, yellow-stained teeth, twisted, boil-infected noses, and evil eyes, bulbous and yellow, like barren desert cracked by rivers of blood. Twisted arms hung crookedly at their sides, nearly reaching the ground.

Thompson's face went bloodless at the sight, and much to Ray Corbin's dismay, he let out a blood-curdling scream. Instantly, the creatures wheeled and drew their wicked swords. Corbin put his head in his hands.

"Well, Thompson, I guess it's time we met our new neighbors," he said with as much calm as he could muster.

Furious at the intrusion, the creatures charged the bluff. Corbin reacted quickly. Springing to his feet, he pointed his rifle into the air and fired a thunderous volley, freezing the creatures in surprise. The largest member of the group stepped through the line of its terrified comrades, the steady set of its grimace showing it unshakable. Even the gunshots hadn't unnerved it.

It eyed Corbin with cool contempt. Corbin returned the stare, but felt the sweat on his temples. Thompson stayed huddled in the grass, not daring to move.

"Friends?" Corbin asked weakly. Then in a lower voice so that only Thompson could hear, he added, "I don't think they've seen you. Stay low and get back to the raft to warn the others."

But Thompson didn't move.

"Go!" said Corbin as loudly as he dared, and he kicked Thompson in the ribs. Still quivering, Thompson inched down the hill.

"Gunfire?" Mitchell gawked.

"Probably DelGiudice and that other moron playing games," snapped Reinheiser, rising from the stagnant pool he was examining. "Just the sort of thing that appeals to idiots."

"Del wouldn't do that," Brady came back angrily. "He doesn't fool around with guns. Besides, those shots came from the south."

Mitchell agreed. "Get everything together, we're heading back."

"Miles!" protested Reinheiser. "And still we have found nothing fit to drink." He threw a clump of weeds back into the fetid pool. "We need water, Captain!"

Mitchell's hesitation further showed Brady the growing relationship between the captain and Reinheiser. Lately, Reinheiser's recommendations had taken on the tone of command.

"All right," Mitchell conceded to Reinheiser. "We'll go a little farther. But keep your ears open!"

Brady just smiled away his distaste.

Corbin stood eyeing the leader.

The creature growled a command to its troops and they began slowly approaching, weapons in hand and all too ready.

"Put the swords away!" warned Corbin, and he blasted a second volley into the sand in front of their feet. This put Thompson, now at the bottom of the bluff, into a dead run. Terrified, he sprinted over the dunes, stopping only when he was a safe distance away. Looking back from the top of another knoll, he could see the creatures fanning out, encircling Corbin.

The second volley had again scared the creatures, but their leader remained calm and by its strength kept them from panic. It began an ominous chant, "Men die. Men die. Men die!" and snarling, the others soon joined in.

The trap around Corbin was firmly in place and still they chanted, "Men die! Men die!" their frenzy growing with every repetition.

Corbin recognized the suicidal violence gathering

like the black clouds of a hurricane about him. My God, I have to kill, he told himself. His stomach turned in protest, a scream of disgust rising in the back of his throat.

To murder.

Trembling, his muscles arguing with every move, he raised the rifle to his shoulder. "I don't want to kill you," he pleaded.

The leader recognized the human's weakness. It raised its arm and issued a command and the others halted immediately.

Corbin wondered if his threat had worked.

The leader's wicked grin dispelled his hopes. It had stopped the others, desiring in its bloodlust to make the kill alone. It puffed out its chest and strode defiantly at its foe, confident of Corbin's inability to kill.

Yet the beast had miscalculated. As it approached, its twisted smile widening with every step, Corbin sensed a pervading vile aura; indeed, he was nearly overwhelmed by the absolute evil of the beast. His inner conflicts were suddenly resolved. This was no unfortunate, ignorant creature, he realized. This was a monster, a demon come straight from the torments of hell. He tightened the rifle's butt against his shoulder. "I don't want to kill you," he repeated, and truly he didn't, for it was not his way to pass judgment, even obvious judgment, upon another. The beast never slowed and Corbin growled, the flavor of righteousness on his tongue, "But I will." And he squeezed the trigger with passion.

Click.

The gun had jammed.

The creature jerked in sudden horror when Corbin unexpectedly pulled the trigger. But as it tried to regain its courage, it saw that Corbin had a problem. Unwilling to give the human a chance at another surprise, the monster charged right in and swung mightily with its sword. Corbin blocked the blow with the rifle.

"I don't want to fight!" he pleaded. But the beast, consumed by rage, was beyond hearing.

It wailed away wildly at the man, each blow more

savage than the previous. Corbin became a release for furies and frustrations too base and vile for him to understand.

In hopeless desperation, he parried a few more attacks. But then, regaining its control just long enough for a slight feint, the creature evaded his defense. It howled with delight as the cruel blade gashed through flesh and muscle and shattered Corbin's collarbone just to the left of his head. Corbin realized he was sitting now, dropped straight to the ground by the force of the blow. He felt the searing pain.

And he watched, all too aware, as the evil beast slowly, agonizingly, withdrew the jagged blade, darkly stained with his lifeblood. All the while, the creature eyed him as well, hissing a laugh, reveling in the man's torment.

But then, for some reason, Corbin no longer felt any pain and his fear, too, had flown. All that came to him was a sudden, mystical insight into the id of the evil beast and he pitied the thing, that it could never know the joy of goodness or of mercy. Truly, it was a damned soul. "Why?" he asked calmly as the creature began to raise its sword. Corbin offered no resistance, he just sat there and repeated, "Why?"

The creature's delight turned to confusion. No screams of pain? No hint of fear? It looked to its companions, who, undaunted by Corbin's passive reaction, were yelping with glee and jumping around wildly, throwing sand in the air. Infected by their frenzy, the creature looked back to Corbin.

Corbin sat swaying, nearly overcome by the vicious wound. Darkness edged his vision, but he saw the sword slowly and deliberately rise up above him and he heard the creature hiss, "Men die!" before the fatal blow bashed in his skull. In the distance, Thompson had seen enough—too much. His vision blurred by tears, he ran north along the beach and back to the raft.

Mitchell's group had just started moving again when Corbin's second volley went off.

"Those are definitely gunshots," said Doc Brady.

"That's enough," said Mitchell with a certainty long absent from his tone. "We're heading back." He wheeled around before there could be any arguments, starting toward the beach with Doc Brady right behind. Reinheiser halted and sighed in dismay. Reluctantly, but without alternatives, he followed.

"What did you do that for?" whispered Del, rubbing his bruised elbow.

"Did you look below you?"

"No, I was looking at the—"

"Well, look!" demanded Billy, and he pushed Del toward the ledge. Del peered over into the dense fog.

"I can't see a thing!"

"Give it a minute. It'll thin," whispered Billy, a bit more calm now. "And keep your voice down."

A gust of wind thinned the opaque veil.

"Lizards!" exclaimed Del. And there were indeed lizards. Huge lizards. Dozens of them, trapped in a wide pit and crawling all over each other, their intertwining bodies a grotesque orgy of scales and claws.

"I don't think they can get out," said Del. Just as he spoke, a dark beast, no less than fifteen feet long, scampered to the base of the wall directly below and lunged up at him.

"I certainly hope not," said Billy clutching the M-16. But it soon became apparent that the lizard was trapped. It rose up on its hind legs, its forelegs on the wall and its uplifted head only about ten feet from the two men. Frustrated at its unattainable quarry, the lizard hissed viciously and opened its huge mouth, displaying rows of jagged and all-too-numerous teeth. It held the pose for a moment, letting Billy and Del truly grasp its formidability. Then, lightning quick, it snapped its mighty jaws.

Billy blew a low whistle. "Wouldn't want to get caught in that, would you, Del?" But when Billy turned his head, Del was gone. Panicking, Billy spun around, and sure enough, there was Del walking swiftly down the path.

"Hey!" Billy shouted.

"Yup, Billy boy, I think we've seen enough here," replied Del in a squeaky voice, still retreating as he talked. "It's getting late anyway. About time to get back."

"You coward!" Billy laughed.

The lizard in the pit roared and Billy passed Del before he even realized that he was moving. He never looked back.

When Mitchell, Brady, and Reinheiser arrived back at the beach, they found Thompson frantically dragging the raft back out into the surf. Brady called out to him, but that only made him pull harder to get away.

"That son of a bitch!" growled Mitchell, and he charged into the water and viciously plowed Thompson under.

"Just what in hell are you doing?" the captain roared. He grabbed Thompson's shirt collar and dragged him and the raft to the water's edge. Instinctively, Brady went for Thompson, but Mitchell shoved the raft at him and told him to help Reinheiser pull it up onto the beach. Thompson offered no resistance to the great strength of the captain. In fact, Mitchell had to hold Thompson's limp body upright, and this angered the captain even more.

"Well?" Mitchell barked. Thompson plopped down onto the muddy beach and rolled to a sitting position, cross-legged, with his head down.

"I'm talking to you!" yelled Mitchell. With no reply forthcoming, he grabbed Thompson's sandy-blond hair and jerked his head back. "Where's Corbin? And what were those shots about?" Thompson stared blankly ahead. Mitchell tore his hand away, taking clumps of hair with it, and slapped Thompson across the face.

Doc Brady had seen enough. He stepped between the two men, trying to hold the giant captain back.

"It's no good, Captain," Brady reasoned. "You're just scaring him more."

"I want to know what's going on!"

"Let me try," Brady begged. Mitchell turned with a disgusted wave of his hand and stormed away. Brady half carried Thompson up the beach and sat him down on the edge of the raft.

It took a lot of coaxing and soft talk, but finally Brady had Thompson ready to speak. Mitchell and Reinheiser gathered around while the seaman gave a jumbled and confused account of Ray Corbin's death.

By the time Billy and Del came in sight of the group, Thompson had finished his tale and was in the middle of yet another breakdown. Doc Brady took him by the arm and led him away.

"What's going on?" asked Del.

"Corbin's dead," replied Mitchell.

"What!" exclaimed Del and Billy in unison.

"He was killed by a monster—a goblin." Reinheiser sneered. "That is, if one can believe our less than sane friend over there."

"Lying bastard," grumbled Mitchell.

"Imagining is a better word for it," replied Reinheiser. "I believe our deluded friend shot Mr. Corbin—by accident probably," he quickly added seeing that Del and Billy were about to protest the accusation. "His warped little mind then concocted these creatures so that he wouldn't have to face the reality of what he had done."

"You're wrong," argued Brady, returning to the group. He had left Thompson lying on the sand. "I believe him." Mitchell snorted in amazement as Brady explained, "There was too much detail in his description for him to be imagining the creatures."

"Of course there was detail," retorted Reinheiser. "Those monsters actually exist in his mind. They probably have been there since his childhood days, the essence of countless nightmares."

"No way."

"Oh, Doctor, please." Reinheiser sighed. "Might we try to remain logical and ration—"

"Logical!" Brady laughed. He pointed accusingly

at Reinheiser. "Will you just listen to the time traveler here telling me to be logical!"

"Enough!" roared Mitchell, his voice edging on violence. The muscles in his arm twitched dangerously. Even Reinheiser refrained from any comments under that imposing glare and Mitchell cooled at the immediate respect shown him. "I've got an officer missing, probably dead, and all I've got to go on is some bullshit story from that nut!"

He spoke loudly.

Thompson heard.

Mitchell raved on and the others, watching him, didn't see Thompson rise and charge across the beach. He bowled into the captain, clawing at his throat and screaming hysterically. "You idiot! You'll get us all killed!"

Mitchell regained his balance in a second and easily pulled free of Thompson's grasp. He was about to retaliate viciously, Billy, Del, and Brady poised to intercede, when Thompson suddenly stopped fighting.

"Buy maybe that's it!" Thompson proclaimed excitedly as he spun away from the captain, unconcerned about his defenseless posture. As with his tantrum on the becalmed raft earlier that morning, his abrupt mood swing halted the others in confusion. Mitchell backed off a bit and waited curiously for Thompson's next move.

"Don't you see?" Thompson looked around from man to man. "We don't belong here. I wanted to escape on the raft, but that's no good. Nowhere to go. Don't you see? We don't belong anywhere anymore. This isn't our world." He looked Mitchell straight in the eye. "Corbin found the only way out!" Brady went to calm him, but Mitchell did it his own way, connecting on Thompson's jaw with a wide arcing left hook that lifted the seaman clear over the edge of the raft and dropped his limp body inside. Del began to protest, wanting to mention the castle in hopes that it might lend credibility to Thompson's story, but the resounding *boom boom* of a drum stopped him short.

The startled men turned and, in the fading daylight, saw their impending doom.

Fifty yards away, rank upon rank of creatures lined the beach, most standing, but some riding saddled lizards. Those mounted brandished long spears and the others crude but wicked swords and black shields. In front of the files stood a standard bearer, his unfurled yellow banner emblazoned with the red foot of a bird of prey, blood dripping from its talons.

"What was that word you used, Reinheiser? Goblin?" said Billy with obvious contempt for the physicist. "Good word."

"That Thompson must have a huge mind to keep this army bottled up in it," remarked Del.

"Cool it," said Mitchell in a low steady voice. Unlike the uncontrollable elements of the storm, Mitchell understood the crisis before them and knew that it was within his realm of influence. "We're not dead yet, not with these." He patted his M-16.

"Boom! Boom!" tolled the drums as a huge goblin strutted in front of the standard bearer. It presented Corbin's smashed rifle to the men, then bared its teeth in a growl, threw the weapon down, and spat on it. Mitchell walked out a few steps.

"Do you understand pain?" he threatened, pointing his rifle at the creature. He was amazed that the beast was capable of answering.

"We know pain," it croaked. "Men taught us pain long ago." Suddenly its voice rose in proclamation. "We give pain back to men!" Wild-eyed, it turned to its army and bellowed a command. "Give death to men!"

The drums thundered to life and the ranks began chanting the liturgy of their race, "Men die! Men die!"

Sensing that the attack was imminent, the men moved several yards apart and formed a line, Billy and Mitchell on opposite ends with the two remaining rifles. With all that was happening in front of them, they didn't notice that Thompson had climbed out of the raft and had found a large rock. He crept up behind

Billy Shank and, as a drum resounded, brought the rock down on Billy's head. Without a moan, Billy dropped to the ground.

Thompson had a rifle.

Suddenly the drums went silent, their last note hanging in the air like a death summons. The leader turned slowly back to Mitchell and flashed him an evil smile. It raised its arm and commanded, "Marguluk!"

Two creatures emerged from the throng, pallbearers to Ray Corbin, his "casket" a pole supported horizontally on their shoulders, his shredded, mutilated corpse tied twisted to it, left wrist and right ankle.

Del spun away in horror and fought back the bile in his throat. Likewise, Brady and Reinheiser averted their eyes. But Mitchell reacted differently, more than ready for a fight. "Bastards!" he roared. "Murdering bastards!" and he fired a burst at the bearers. They dropped, as did several creatures behind them, riddled with the leaden extensions of Mitchell's fury.

The beast leader howled in rage.

Mitchell imitated the cocky grin it had flashed earlier and blew it away.

Awed and terrified, the creatures verged on panic. Many of them fled, especially those in the farthest ranks; others ducked quivering behind their shields; some even bowed to Mitchell.

"Look at them!" shouted Mitchell, his anger turning to ecstasy under the aphrodisiac of instant power. "Look at them run and hide!" He fired a volley into the air. The creatures cowered.

"Do you realize what this means?" Mitchell laughed and turned to the men, a sated look in his eyes. "We're gods!" he proclaimed. "We'll own them!"

"Wrong, Captain," came Thompson's voice, steady now, off to the side. Mitchell, surprised, turned to the seaman, and looked down the barrel of an M-16.

"We have no right to kill them," declared Thompson. "This is their world."

"What the hell are you doing?"

"Shut up!" snapped Thompson, and Mitchell froze,

expecting Thompson to fire. Suddenly, though, Thompson seemed calm again. "Don't you see?" he pleaded, begging for some confirmation. "We're the ones who don't belong here. We've got to escape . . . like Corbin." His head drooped in despair, and Mitchell, seeing an opening, inched the barrel of his gun toward him. Thompson was alert, though, and he snapped his glance back on the captain.

Mitchell swung about desperately, clearly recognizing his death in Thompson's feverish eyes.

But Thompson's rifle roared first and Mitchell felt fiery explosions as bullets invaded his body.

Doc Brady lunged at the mad seaman, but stopped abruptly when Thompson wheeled around, the smoking rifle still ready.

Del noticed Billy, his head opened and blood flowing freely. He wanted to go to his injured friend, but fright and confusion held him in place. Reinheiser looked about, searching for an out, calculating his chances and the best possible escape route and counting on Del or Brady to distract Thompson.

"Thompson, please," said Brady, trying to appear calm. In the background, he saw the creatures regrouping, also trying to make sense of Thompson's crazy actions. "For God's sake, man!"

The three were still in a line, Del frozen on one end, Reinheiser in the middle and leaning away, and Brady on the closest end, bending toward Thompson, reaching out with pleading hands for the rifle.

"Why was I picked for this?" mumbled Thompson, tears streaking the sand on his face. He looked at Brady, still several feet away. "Why am I the only one who understands?" With a sigh of helplessness, as though he had no other choice, he clenched the rifle determinedly, and the others, like Mitchell, knew.

Reinheiser broke for the raft, Brady dove for the barrel of the rifle, Del never moved.

But it didn't matter.

Thompson, sobbing openly, but certain of his duty, made one thundering sweep with the death dealer.

And they, all three, felt the fiery explosions.

Chapter 7

In the Halls of the Colonnae

Void.

Time passed . . . irrelevant.

Del opened his eyes. Perhaps they had been open all along and his mind just now caught up with them. Instinctively he clutched at his midsection. Too late, he knew, the bullets had already ripped through his belly.

He lay on his side, shrouded by a thick gray fog. Strangely, he felt no pain. He raised his hands to his face.

No blood. Had it been a dream? Trembling, he looked down, his breath coming in short gasps as he moved the tattered strands of his shirt aside. A jagged line of scars crossed his belly, the round scars of bullets.

He realized that he wasn't on the beach, that the floor beneath him was smooth and cool as marble. Struggling against his disorientation and bordering on panic, he forced himself to his feet, but as his head emerged from the waist-deep fog, his confusion only increased. He was in a vast dark hall, illuminated in reflections of wispy gray from the transient fog. To Del's left was a seemingly infinite row of huge pillars glowing blue white. Del saw no walls or ceiling, just the massive columns, each rooted beneath the low-riding fog and stretching upward as far as the eye could see, into the blackness, and beyond. Unearthly, beautiful, yet hauntingly surreal.

"I must be dead," he muttered.

"Hardly," came a voice behind him. He spun to face Martin Reinheiser.

"Del? What happened?" came another voice. Del recognized it immediately, and then saw Billy rising from the mist at his right. "Last thing I remember was those goblins on the beach and getting whomped on the head."

"Thompson," explained Del.

"Figures," replied Billy, shaking his head. "That guy's got a real problem."

"He took your weapon and opened up on the rest of us," Del went on.

"But you two got away."

"No, I got shot. So did Reinheiser, I think."

"A dozen times at least," confirmed the physicist.

Billy folded his arms across his chest and shot them an angry glare. "What?" he demanded, his voice louder.

Del understood his friend's impatience. Holding Billy's stare with his own firm but compassionate visage, he slowly pulled the tattered shirt away from his abdomen. Even from several feet away, the vicious scars were unmistakable.

Billy's arms fell unfolded and his eyes bulged in disbelief. "Are we dead?" he gasped.

"You two seem preoccupied with that subject," said Reinheiser. "These are not the bodies of spiritual entities; we remain flesh and blood. We are not dead!"

"But you just said you got shot," protested Billy. "Don't tell me that those goblin things know anything about medicine."

"Apparently—" Reinheiser began, but Del cut him off.

"Ssh!" he hissed, and he went tense. Billy and Reinheiser also went alert, straining their eyes and ears in search of the danger Del had sensed.

Suddenly, a low growling noise came from somewhere under the fog nearby.

"What the heck is that? A bear?"whispered Billy breathlessly. He moved next to Del, half expecting some hideous beast to spring at them from out of the fog.

A second later, though, the growling sounded more

like snoring and Billy and Del looked at each other and smiled. "Mitchell!"

"The captain, too," said Reinheiser. He stroked his goatee at this new revelation. He knew he had been shot, but that being the last thing he remembered, he wasn't sure of the extent of his injuries. Immediate aid might have saved him. The captain was a different story, though. Reinheiser had seen Mitchell blasted apart by a hail of bullets, certainly dead even as he fell to the ground. Nobody could possibly have survived that volley.

Following the thunderous snores, the men had little trouble finding the sleeping giant. Waking him was a bit more difficult, though, for Mitchell was deep into his dreams and didn't appreciate being disturbed. He flailed and kicked, punched and bit. Eventually, they managed to rouse him, and though he didn't believe a word of their story, he had no choice but to accept it.

"Let us continue searching," suggested Reinheiser, "perhaps the doctor is here as well."

Almost immediately, Billy stumbled over Doc Brady, peacefully asleep under the gray blanket.

Before they even woke him, Del pressed on. "That makes five," he said. "Let's keep going." And he started away.

"Do we really want to locate that idiot Thompson?" argued Reinheiser.

"We've got to keep looking," Del pleaded. He wasn't looking for Thompson at all, secretly hoping that Ray Corbin was there, somehow recovered.

"Del's right," agreed Billy. "If Thompson's out there and he's got that gun, we've got to get him before he wakes up."

"Then let's get going," growled Mitchell, remembering the pain and shock of the bullets. "I want Thompson found. Then his ass is mine." The captain grinned. It wasn't often that a dead man had a chance to pay back his killer, and the thought of twisting Thompson's neck filled Mitchell with glee.

They searched the immediate area, but the fog remained impenetrable and Thompson didn't seem to be close by. Frustrated by the futility and scared of the possibilities—perhaps Thompson watched from a distance even as they searched, a crazed smile on his face and a ready M-16 at his side—Mitchell needed a showdown and began calling out, "Thompson!" The others, except Reinheiser, joined in.

"Wonderful," muttered Reinheiser, and he crouched low into the safety of the opaque veil. "That lunatic is probably training his rifle on their voices this very minute."

Suddenly a gentle puff of wind blew across them. And it carried words in its wake, words in the purest tone that any of them had ever heard, clear as an unblemished bell and, like the great hall about them, supernatural in beauty. "Your Mr. Thompson is not here."

They turned to the voice.

Halfway between the five men and the columns, limned in ghostly evanescence, stood a tall man in a flowing white robe of fine silk. A golden crown adorned his head, and in his delicate hand he held a many-jeweled, golden scepter. Hair of the starkest white, yet thick and rich with vitality, hung loosely about his shoulders, and though his skin was incredibly pale, almost translucent, his presence was undeniably powerful.

Even from a distance, the being's calm demeanor soothed Del's apprehension. The eyes held a flickering blue flame that radiated unbounded knowledge and serenity.

Mitchell stood firm before the wondrous specter, his anger sufficient proof against any feelings of awe. "Then where is he?" he demanded. "And who are you?"

The being made no motion, yet a breeze emanated from him. He did not move his lips, yet the breeze carried words. More than words, actually. Within that gentle wind were emotions and sensations beyond the spectrum of hearing that the five men felt throughout their bodies and souls. "It is best to say only that Michael Thompson's destiny followed a different path from yours. As to your second question, I am Calae, Prince of the Colonnae." The specter then turned from Mitchell to Del and an even more gentle puff blew by. "Truly I am sorry, Jeffrey DelGiudice, but your friend, Ray Corbin, has passed from this world."

Del's eyes widened. The being had just read his mind and answered his unspoken question.

"You still think we're not dead?" whispered Billy to Reinheiser. The scientist, completely at a loss for an explanation, wasn't so quick to dismiss the possibility this time. But before he could seriously consider that theory, the breeze came again.

"Take comfort, Billy Shank. I assure that you are not dead. By the power of the Colonnae, you have passed through the dark realm and are healed. We could not permit your deaths, for this is a time long-awaited and a great adventure lies before you. Your actions may well determine the destiny of a new world."

Their understandable doubts had been foreseen. Calae raised his scepter and permitted the men a glimpse of their recent past, an image that had been mercifully erased from their memories. Each alone in a form not quite corporeal, yet somewhat substantial and inescapable, they walked among black mounds, barrows of broken shale, under unknown stars, and looked upon the shadows of Death's domain. A lonely journey, an endless trek, for not another being stirred in the never-ending plain and every horizon promised nothing but continued blackness. Even Martin Reinheiser was stricken dumb, this episode being too far beyond any mortal experience to be believable. Sympathetic to their confused distress, Calae released them from recollections they could not comprehend. "Come," he said, opening his arms as a father to his children. "Sit by me and I will tell you a marvelous tale that shall answer many of your questions and instill in you many more."

Compelled by this superior will, the mortals could only comply. They approached and sat before Calae on the cool floor, barely conscious that they were moving.

Calae closed his eyes and contemplated his tale. He didn't want to overwhelm the fragile mortals any more than was necessary. The breeze came again. "Let me begin," it whispered to them, "at what you may perceive to be the end, though it was in fact the beginning. You have been quite perceptive and have already guessed much." Calae's eyes softened in sympathy and sadness. "The war long-feared by your race came, swift and terrible, a mere fifty years after you departed the sunlit world. Mankind's machines of destruction wreaked fiery devastation across this beautiful world. Nothing could stand against the fury, the very stones screamed in agony! Nation after nation loosed their weapons in full knowledge that the poisonous wake would leave naught but a barren, unlivable earth.

"Yet they loosed their weapons!" howled a mighty wind. The men cringed as Calae grew suddenly tall and terrible before them.

But then Calae calmed again, a hint of tears rimming his eyes, and he continued, "For in the end it was the folly of man to put country before conscience, pride before pity, might before mercy. Your race was doomed by its own hands, and that was the tragedy.

"Yet know this, mortals, know it as I am the proof: There are powers in this universe far greater than Man and far beyond Man's creations. And the beings that looked upon the ravaged earth were saddened, for, though evil dwells in man's domain, it is not an inherent trait of the race. Even HE who is supreme was moved to pity. Thus it was decreed that Man be given another chance to survive, to evolve above this fatal flaw of pride. Amidst the devastation, Ynis Aielle, isle of hope, rose from the sea, shielded from the fires by a golden barrier that was HIS blessing. And HE summoned the Colonnae.

"At the time of doom, great ships sailed these waters. Of the hundreds aboard them, only the children and four adults were saved. The others had been touched by the killing fire and, more importantly, had tasted of the mighty magic, technology, that had wrought the fire. This knowledge demanded their deaths if the world was truly to begin anew.

"Thus the Colonnae became the guardians of an orphaned people. We guided the ships to this land and set them upon a southern beach. And the four chosen adults came away with us to learn higher levels of consciousness that they might one day return and help guide the new race of Man down a truer path.

"Under our protection and with our blessings, the children flourished. Soon a large settlement, a city named Pallendara, had grown on Calva, the southern plains of Aielle. She was a beautiful city of art and poetry and true brotherhood, a community untainted by greed and governed by philosophers who followed unerringly the will of the people. Learning was the common goal, knowledge gained only to be shared, and the earth knew its greatest peace since before the Jericho of your history many thousands of years ago.

"The mercy of the ONE is without bounds, yet it is bestowed upon those who prove themselves worthy. Thus, in the seventh generation of Pallendara, a test was unveiled. Mutated children of irradiated heritage, the lingering curse of technology, were born unto the innocents.

"Yes," answered Calae to the question in all of the men's minds, "these were indeed the forefathers of the creatures you encountered on the beach.

"As the first cursed child breathed Aielle's clear air into its tainted lungs, our time as guardians was ended. Thus, the Colonnae departed the shining halls of Pallendara. The trials of the ONE had begun, the time for your race to prove itself capable and worthy." Calae looked into the fog beyond his audience and smiled fondly at the distant memories of the early days. Again the tears came to his eyes. "It was difficult to leave," he explained to the men. "We had grown fond of your race, had come to love them as parents to children. Yet we knew they had grown beyond our care; it was time for them to stand on their own. The four we had instructed returned to their people, but we remained close by to observe.

"The curse lasted ten years. Every woman with child prayed to us for the health of her coming baby, but we could only watch helplessly. Cries of dismay in the night oft told neighbors that a new mutant was among them. One hundred times during that decade of horror a new mother looked upon her child and despaired.

"Yet the Calvans loved and cared for the misshapen babes, for they knew naught but love. In their innocence, they could not perceive that these creatures were the perfect incarnation of all that is evil in your race, an embodied mirror of the darkest errors of Man's past.

"At first, the mutants caused only minor problems, but as the years passed, they grew strong. They found each other and forged a brotherhood of evil, bonded together by a common purpose of destruction. They met in shadows, carefully plotting every attack. They were indeed devious, keeping their crimes within the borders of Calvan mercy. The people, ever trusting and forgiving, fell easy prey.

"The crimes worsened as the mutants gained confidence, soon openly roaming the streets at night, cutting a trail of destruction across the city. With great sorrow and disappointment, the Calvans were forced to admit that love and compassion offer no protection against true evil. Three of our students, the fourth having long since departed from the city and the ways of man, joined the Calvan Lords at council in the Citadel of Justice to decide the fate of the mutants.

"An angry crowd gathered outside, promising violence if the Lords offered no better solution. Inside the chambers was a similar scene of frustration and rage. The gentle Calvans had no response to the evil that had befallen them. After hours of yelling and angry debate, one of our students, Thomas Morgan, who called himself Morgan Thalasi, offered a solution. 'I shall lead these foul beasts away from our fair city,' he said, 'and far over the plains to a place where they will trouble Calva no more. And I, Thalasi, shall watch over them, that their evilness be contained.'

"He lied. It was our greatest fear that one of the four wizards we had trained would fall victim to the lust for power that had been the foulest bane in your history and had eventually led to the destruction of the original race. And it was to our ultimate distress that it was Morgan Thalasi, mightiest of the four, who fell into evil ways. The Calvans believed him. They accepted his offer with great joy and praised him for his sacrifice.

"Thus, Thalasi departed with the cursed hundred. He named them 'talons' after himself, an arrogant act that hinted at some of the events to come. North they marched and then west to the sea where the wizard wrought Talas-dun, bastion of darkness."

Del recalled the castle he had seen in the mountains. Somehow his vision now was clearer than it had been through the fog, as though Calae's empathy had enhanced the image to a point more distinct than reality. He saw now in his mind black battlements iron strong and awesome towers spiraling to the sky, extensions of the very strength of the rock mountain they rooted in. And Del felt, strongest of all, the pervading evil that bound the place together, a force that was still very much alive. A shudder shook the vision from him.

"There Thalasi bred his army and waited," continued Calae. "And time mattered little, for the Colonnae had bestowed upon the Four the gift of long years. He could have spent centuries preparing an army that would have swept everything away before it, but his thirst for power overcame his patience. Two-score years after the forging of Talas-dun, Thalasi, the Black Warlock, led the mutants back to Calva.

"The talons could not hope to defeat the more numerous Calvans in open battle, but Thalasi counted on surprise to carry him through to Pallendara. He knew that if he could get to the city and overthrow the Overlord quickly, the scattered hamlets of the plains would not organize against him. And in his arrogance, Thalasi believed the two remaining wizards to be no match for him. Yet the Calvans were not caught unaware. The second of the Four, kindly Rudy Glendower, had privately questioned Thalasi's motives when the mutants had first been led away. Ever the wary guardian of peace, Glendower, had anticipated the eventual return of Thalasi and had always kept one eye toward Talas-dun. With his warnings, the Calvans had time to assemble a great force. They charged westward across the fields to meet the invaders at the great river Ne'er Ending. Thalasi's army came on only to find the four bridges that spanned the river blocked by the Calvan force. Ever merciful, the Calvans offered peace, ordering the talons to return to their mountain homeland and demanding Thalasi as a prisoner. But Thalasi's years of torment had worked wickedly on his charges and the self-named Black Warlock truly believed himself invincible. Even with the plans for surprise ruined, he attacked. The ferocity of his army was great and at first they drove hard into the Calvan ranks, but Glendower and the third wizard, Perrault, managed to keep Thalasi at bay while the Calvan wave countered, smashing and scattering their ill-bred foes."

A second image blossomed in Del's mind as Calae imparted to him the scenes of that fierce battle. The armies clashed upon four arcing stone bridges spanning a shining silver river, though the water steadily reddened with the blood of fallen combatants.

The sheer savagery of the talons appalled Del. With total disregard for their own lives, they launched themselves at the Calvan spearmen, thrashing wildly with their short swords, biting and gouging. They swept through the first ranks, overwhelming the civilized men with demonic ferocity, and pushed their foes back to the end of the bridges. But as the monsters came on, not just killing, but goring and mutilating the men caught in their savage rush, the Calvans, too, turned ugly. Faces twisted in rage, they surged into the mutant throng, matching the talon brutality blow for blow. The defined lines of the opponents disappeared as the battle became an entwined cluster of slashing swords and thrusting spears, and soon the howls of fury were drowned out by screams of agony. Several times man and mutant, grappling in mortal combat, fell from a bridge to the mighty river below. Even then they continued their frenzied struggle, though it meant that neither could escape watery death in the powerful current.

Attrition gradually thinned the smaller mutant force, and as the outcome became obvious, the vision faded from Del's view. Sweat stung his eyes. He looked to his companions and their stunned expressions told him that they had also witnessed the horror of the struggle.

"Thalasi was thrown down that day and believed killed," Calae continued when the men regained their composure. "But evil does not die so easily, and the spirit of Morgan Thalasi lurks ever in Aielle, with patience bitterly learned, awaiting a second chance.

"The treachery of Thalasi tolled heavily on the Calvans. Many men died at the Battle of the Four Bridges and those that survived carried and passed on to their children scars of suspicion and fear. Thus, the new race of man lost its innocence and its trust. And thus it remains today." Calae paused, his eyes downcast. Thalasi's deceit weighted heavily on him, too.

"This is not the end of my tale," he continued after a few seconds. "The Battle of the Four Bridges was a long, long time ago. Ten years after the battle, there was born in Pallendara a second mutation of Man. Unlike the talons, these children were very beautiful and their joyous smiles curled unblemished by evil. Yet the untrusting Calvans were ever wary and grew fearful as more mutated babes were born. Though these children had committed no wrongs, a time of prejudice and unwarranted anger overtook the city. Once again a council was convened of Pallendara's Lords and the two remaining wizards.

"Enduring are the scars of Thalasi's deceit, and enduring are the tests of the ONE. With the second mutation, the character of Man came to trial again.

"Never has the Citadel of Justice known such a travesty," declared Calae. "The Lord Umpleby, a wretched, gluttonous man who had gained power through deceit, opposed any change, fearful that it might endanger his ill-gotten position. He demanded the deaths of the innocent babes and his twisted beliefs were not without support among the truly frightened people.

"But Ben-rin, Overlord of the City, was a kinder man. 'We kill no children,' he commanded. 'We have risen above the legacy of our heritage and are not murderers. The children will be watched, but no harm shall befall them!' And so set was he in his belief that he welcomed no debate.

"Ben-rin's compassion was admirable and his motives true, but disgusted and enraged by even the suggestion of murder, he had thrown aside due course of Calvan law and had overstepped the bounds of his title. No one man ruled Pallendara, however justified in his actions. There was then a great confusion in the Citadel, for more than the fate of the children had now come to trial. Lord Umpleby was quick to counter, his voice rising above the commotion. 'Our Overlord,' he hissed, 'has declared himself Emperor!' Ben-rin's glare was cold and firm, but he knew at once that he had erred in his anger and he dared not command Umpleby to silence.

"Umpleby continued his assault on justice, his raving antics kindling the memories of anger and fear engraved by Thalasi and the first mutation. He knew that his only chance for victory was to entice the others to a level where rash emotions denied mercy. 'Must I remind you of our past? Might it be that you have forgotten the terror in our own streets?' Angry shouts of agreement gathered about him. 'My Lords,' he pleaded with mock concern, 'can we ever wash the stain of blood from the stones of the Four Bridges? These freaks might be worse! For the sake of all that we deem good, I demand their deaths!'

"Umpleby achieved his level of chaos. The furor split the council, pitting lord against lord in an angry debate that bordered on violence. Though the emotional tide swept against his cause, Ben-rin remained calm and resolute. 'We shall kill no innocent children,' he repeated. But Umpleby had swayed too many, the Overlord's edicts would not be enough.

"Across the room, from a forgotten corner of the council table, came an unexpected response. 'Then I shall kill them.' All sat in silent shock, Ben-rin nearly collapsed, for the speaker was the gentle wizard, Rudy Glendower. The other wizard in attendance, Perrault, understood and nodded his approval.

"Perhaps Umpleby, never trusting, also understood, for he confronted Glendower. 'You?' He laughed. 'Once we put our faith in a wizard and our blood ran freely for it. Yet we are to believe you?'

"Glendower rose tall above the Lord. 'I, too, have felt the stinger of Thalasi,' he breathed with convincing anger, cold death in his eyes that Umpleby dared not question. 'Tomorrow, I go north with the children that there should be no blood in the city, and I shall slay them mercifully.' Umpleby's face chalked beneath the glare of the mighty wizard. 'And you alone shall accompany me!'

"Glendower turned and looked deep into Ben-rin's eyes and the Overlord understood. Ben-rin agreed, hiding his relieved smile and thus the council was ended.

"The solemn caravan left Pallendara and traveled in solitude across the rolling plain, shunned by fearful farmers. At nightfall on the seventh day, they came to the foothills of the Southern Crystal Mountains, the northern edge of the Calvan fields. 'We will sleep first,' said Glendower. 'And in the dark of the night, that none bear witness, our foul deed shall be done.' Umpleby found sleep easily, for this task bothered him not at all. And Glendower came to him in his slumber and worked an enchantment upon him. In his dreams, Umpleby stood witness as the wizard slayed the mutants one by one on a wide flat rock and buried their bodies in an unmarked grave. In truth, that night Glendower stole away with the children and hid them in the mountains, having already provided for their care with a secret friend. Glendower and the deceived Umpleby returned to Pallendara bearing tidings that the deed was done. Many times during the years of the second mutation, Glendower drove a cart of new mutants north, supposedly to the Justice Stone, as Umpleby had named the flat rock, but actually to the secret refuge.

"By day the children stayed hidden for fear of discovery, but under night's black veil of protection, they danced joyously. Glendower named them Illumans, Children of the Moon, and their home, Illuma, Lochsilinilume in the tongue of wizards. And that their number might remain small and easily concealed, he, Perrault, and their secret friend joined their powers together and enchanted the children with the gift of long years.

"Villagers of the northern fields told fireside stories of the night dancers of the Crystal Mountains, and legends of the Illumans spread throughout all of Calva. But Ben-rin and then his heirs, with the help of the wizards, had little trouble dismissing the rumors as fanciful children's tales. In this manner, Aielle remained at peace for many years.

"But," Calae went on, his voice suddenly grim, "one-score and ten years ago, Ungden the Usurper, a descendant of Lord Umpleby, overthrew the line of Ben-rin and proclaimed himself Overlord of Pallendara. He banished Glendower, for he had somehow guessed the deception at the Justice Stone. With the noble heir of the line of Ben-rin and his supporters killed and Glendower exiled, the only hope for peace in Pallendara was Perrault, who had come to be known as Istaahl the White. But Perrault, beyond belief, has supported the new Overlord and war has been averted only through Ungden's inability to find the secret mountain refuge."

"You speak of generations and hundred of years," Reinheiser interrupted. "How long has it been?"

"More than twelve centuries have passed since you went beneath the sea," answered Calae.

Mitchell snorted.

"Believe what you will," Calae replied to him. "But dwell not in the past. Your destiny lies not there, but here in Aielle. A war is soon to be fought. A conflict not of good against evil, as was the Battle of the Four Bridges, but of nation against nation. Aielle is about to have its Jericho, its first unnecessary war, and if that comes to pass, the new race of man may well embark upon the same path that led your race to its ultimate demise. The lessons of the past may yet save this world, and thus, the Colonnae have guided you here.''

''Guided us?'' exclaimed Mitchell.

Calae remained silent, letting the men sort things out for themselves. Doubts and confusion closed in on them; all of this was simply too much to digest. They sat with knotted brows, reflecting on the events that had befallen them, searching desperately for a logical explanation. Not Del, though. He leaned back comfortably on his arms, smiled and winked at Calae. He remembered the miracle at the ladder of the sinking *Unicorn* and had known since that someone was looking out for him.

At length, Calae's breeze came again. ''A people call out to you,'' he said. ''Your path lies east, to Illuma.

''But now, sleep, ancient ones, for the road ahead is hard and long, and sorrow and weariness will find you in the days to come.'' As he spoke the mist returned, bringing with it suggestions of slumber the mortals could not resist. They collapsed into a deep and restful sleep.

Calae looked down upon them, mere shadows under the shroud of gray, and realized again that he had grown fond of this being called Man and cared deeply about this race's struggle to find its true path.

''Go, ancient ones,'' he said softly. ''Go hence to Lochsilinilume. Seek out the Children of the Moon and teach Aielle the lessons of the past.''

Chapter 8

The Desolation of Thalasi

Dusty sunlight woke them sometime later, and they struggled to orient themselves, trying to distinguish reality from dreams. Gone was the cavern, or had that, too, been just the delusions of wounded men? They were outside now, sitting on the parched dirt of a desert that stretched brown and barren as far as they could see in every direction except north, where loomed the great stone mountains, ominous pillars of unrivaled might standing resolute and undiminished by the dulling veil of sea fog. Del shuddered with dread as he viewed that towering range, jagged and foreboding, for the image of its black heart, Talas-dun, remained unnervingly clear.

Dressed still in their blue and white uniforms, each of them now had a hooded gray-brown cloak tied about his shoulders and a sheathed sword strapped to his hip. Waterskins and packs of provisions lay at their feet.

More riddles.

Despite the new situation, the pervading thought that pressed upon them was the image of Calae, and they understood him least of all. The memory of the angelic specter flooded each of them with distinctive, powerful feelings; frustration and even anger to Mitchell, for in the presence of such a being, he was small and unimportant, and against the power of the Colonnae, he had no recourse. Reinheiser was also frustrated, not because he felt belittled, but because the mere existence of the Colonnae disputed the foundation of logic that had guided his entire life.

Billy and Doc Brady accepted the Colonnae Prince as the embodiment of peace and serenity. Del felt that inner comfort as well, but in a more profound way. Calae was the promise of answers, the guide to truth and to a level of existence beyond the human experience.

Finally, Mitchell could contain his rage no longer. "What the hell was that thing?" he snapped.

"Hell?" echoed Billy, contentment stamped indelibly upon his face. "Nothing to do with hell." Doc Brady chuckled in agreement, but Mitchell glared at him and Reinheiser was quick to attack.

"May we leave naive spiritual fantasies out of this?" he huffed. "I know your type. Something happens which you can't readily explain and you yell 'miracle' and fall on your knees to recite hollow prayer verses!"

"You got a better explanation?" retorted Billy.

"All of this and still you doubt?" added Doc Brady.

Reinheiser stroked his goatee. "Have you considered that this entire episode might be part of an elaborate deception?"

"Bull!" they retaliated in unison.

Del tuned out of the heightening argument. He considered discussions of Calae to be pointless. He didn't understand everything that was going on, but that wasn't important, for Del knew that the science and rationale of his time offered no explanations to what had occurred. Logic, as they understood it, did not apply here. So Del broke through the limitations imposed by his inadequate knowledge and experience and released himself to the boundless acceptance of his imagination. He embraced Calae's tale and this new world, not with his mind, but with his heart.

Ignoring the others, he turned his attention to the sword at his side. A sense of wonderment engulfed him as his trembling fingers felt the exquisite detail in the hilt. This came from no assembly-line mold. Its delicate designs were crafted with the patient workmanship and love of caring hands. He marveled at the sword, not as a weapon, but as a symbol. Something about it set his imagination free to wander in lands of soaring dragons and dark dungeons of treasure and danger. And, of course, beautiful maidens waiting to be rescued from loathsome beasts by him, the Hero. Consumed in his fantasy, he drew the sword from its scabbard and swung it about slowly, getting used to the feel of its perfect balance.

The sounds of the argument suddenly stopped and Del realized that all eyes were upon him. He tried to hide his embarrassment behind a screen of comedy.

"Goblins!" he roared, a smile fighting through his serious facade. "Bring on the goblins!" He tightened his muscles into a fighting pose and grimaced away his growing smile.

"Talons!" Billy corrected lightheartedly.

"Bring them, too," clowned Del. "For my vengeance is great and my sword is hungry!" He thrust the weapon to the sky in triumph.

"Hey, jerk!" shouted the captain, in no mood for games. "Put the toy away.

"Swords," Mitchell spat. "I'd trade the whole lot of them for one rifle. Or even a stupid pistol, for that matter."

At the mention of the word "pistol" Del instinctively grabbed at his shirt pocket and felt the familiar bump of the derringer.

"I . . ." began Del reflexively as he fingered the bullet, about to tell the others. Suddenly he realized the implications and changed his mind. He remembered the frightening image of Mitchell on the beach, wild-eyed and bordering on delirium with the power of a rifle. Best that the derringer remained his own little secret.

"What?" snarled Mitchell in open contempt.

"Nothing," answered Del quietly, hoping the issue would be dropped. Mitchell glared at him, searching for some further way to vent his frustration.

"I told you to put that damn sword away!" he raged. "When I give you an order, you jump, mister!" Now satisfied that he had put his junior officer in place, Mitchell's need for power and domination was temporarily satiated. He turned to Reinheiser. But this time Del wasn't going to let him have the last word.

"Not again," he said under his breath. "Time to

get some things straight." And as Mitchell swung back at Del to blast him for mumbling, Del looked him square in the eye and asked firmly, "Why?"

"Why what?" demanded Mitchell incredulously.

"Why do you give the orders?" asked Del as calmly as he could, taking extra care to make sure there wasn't even a trace of sarcasm in his voice.

"You got guts," Billy whispered to Del. He took a cautious step away from his doomed friend as Mitchell approached.

Del held his ground. "If the country blew up 1200 years ago, the navy, and NUSET, went with it." Mitchell listened unblinking, his muscles corded dangerously, on the verge of an explosion. But Del had committed himself and had to finish his point. "We're civilians."

Angry fire coursed through Mitchell. The others stared in disbelief. The captain turned to them and pretended to relax, grinning wickedly as he heard Del's relieved sigh behind him. "Did you hear him?" he asked calmly, the smile broadening. "He wants to know why I'm in charge."

Suddenly, he wheeled back, the masking grin torn away by a snarl of unbridled rage so evil that it turned Del white. "I'll tell you why," Mitchell growled, and *Thwop!* his huge fist smashed into Del's jaw.

Del reeled backward under a wave of dizziness. His knees wobbled but he refused to let them buckle. "I'm not going down," he groaned softly, and by sheer determination he held his balance. Then *Thwop!* came the second blow and Del felt the warmth of the blood running freely from his nose.

"I'm not going down" he grunted angrily, covering his face with his arms just as Mitchell began unloading punches on him. The others quickly jumped in and separated the two.

"Enough!" shouted Mitchell, and he pulled away from Billy and Brady. "It's over!" He pointed ominously at Del. "You're asking for more trouble than you can handle, mister!"

Del kept his eyes averted, but couldn't ignore the threat.

"I don't think it's broken," Doc Brady said, holding Del's head back to stop the flow of blood from his nose.

"I wasn't going down," said Del with grim pride, firmly convinced that he had achieved a victory without throwing a punch.

"Maybe you should have," replied the pragmatic doctor. "He probably wouldn't have hit you again."

"That's not the point!" retorted Del, frustrated that Brady didn't share his dedication to principle. "We're civilians now, we can't let him push us around!"

"Humor him, Del," advised Brady. He looked back over his shoulder as he started away. "Or he's going to kill you."

"Yea, right," muttered Del, too low for anyone to hear. He rejoined the others. Mitchell eyed him threateningly, but again he didn't return the look.

Satisfied with the lesson, the captain broke off the stare and turned his energy to more important issues. "How do you figure all of this?" he asked Reinheiser.

The physicist shrugged. "I have no answers for you."

"Well, then what the hell do you suggest we do?" snapped Mitchell, flustered that even Reinheiser offered no help.

"What can we do?" answered Reinheiser. "We cannot stay here and I've no desire to go back to the beach and meet those creatures again."

"Only one choice left," cut in Brady.

"Play along, Captain," advised Reinheiser. "Go east as the being instructed us. Perhaps our answers are there."

Mitchell closed his eyes in dismay; he had feared that advice. To him, going along with this game meant accepting it as real, and he wasn't prepared to do that. "Okay," he said finally, out of options. "Then let's get going. Shank, take the point, and Doc, you and him"—he motioned at Del—"bring up the rear." The situation may have had Mitchell confused, but he was still shrewd in handling his crew. He knew that he had to keep Del and Billy as far apart as possible if he was to maintain control.

And so the five men picked up their gear and set off eastward across the barren plain in search of answers. They plodded on in silence, each examining possible explanations. Del, though, having fully accepted the situation, was more concerned with the people he had left behind. He determined that this would be his time of mourning and yet he found no tears to shed. Perhaps it was the unreality of the adventure, the subconscious expectation of awakening from a dream at any moment; or maybe, Del hoped, it was his newfound awareness of the universal mysteries. With his heightened insight, he didn't perceive his father or Debby as dead. Rather, they existed in a different time than he. Separated by aeons, yet all very much alive. Immortality within our own little bubbles of time-space?

Del hoped he wasn't dreaming.

For most, the deep reflections soon passed. The relentless sun and the choking dust simply weren't conducive to contemplation. As the distraction of thought passed away, Billy got bored all alone up front, but knew better than to argue with Mitchell, given the captain's mood. He wouldn't have found much company with the other four anyway. Mitchell and Reinheiser had begun a private planning session, discussing courses of action should certain situations arise. Del had lightened his thoughts, but they remained private. Now he was enjoying another fantasy as a warrior engaged in a heroic battle. And this time the loathsome beast was Hollis Mitchell.

Brady, too, was preoccupied, stubbornly trying to sort out a general uneasiness with this whole situation. His concern ran too deep for the discomfort of the desert to distract him. Something just didn't seem to fit.

The sun climbed high above them, its penetrating rays draining their energy with every step and weakening their determination to go on. Finally, lathered in sweat, with dust clinging irritably to their wetness, they took their first break. There was no shade to be found, but at this point they gladly settled for a bit of food and more importantly, something to drink.

Their packs contained dried, bland-looking cakes that the men eyed with grudging acceptance, if not hungrily. But they were in for a pleasant surprise. One nibble turned their lips up into delighted smiles. The cakes were wonderfully delicious and the sweet-smelling liquid in the skins was incredibly refreshing, revitalizing their lost energy with every drop. Their resolve returned with their strength, for they knew that this gift from the Colonnae would sustain them across the wasteland. All too soon, they felt themselves sated, but in packing up, they were stunned to find that they had actually consumed very little.

"It seems that we have more provisions than we thought," said Billy cheerfully.

"Probably just means that we've got farther to go," grumbled Mitchell, equating anger with alertness. He was scared now, not knowing what to expect next, and would not allow himself to be caught unawares.

They traveled on that afternoon, and the land remained brown and foul. Even the air tasted unwholesome and the colorless and empty sky offered no hopeful promises. Jagged cracks gouged the landscape like parched mouths begging the unhearing heavens for water. The men saw no living thing, for they traversed the land of Brogg, the Brown Wastes, a desolation wreaked by Thalasi in the early days before the Battle of the Four Bridges to discourage any curious adventurers who might discover Talas-dun and his secret army. Even centuries later, the scourge of the Black Warlock was complete upon this land.

Night came suddenly, cool and refreshing. But it was all too short, and almost without warning, the morning sun burst over the eastern horizon. Again the day was hot and dry, as the men realized every day would be in this desert. To further their misery, a sharp wind came up, whipping stinging sand into their eyes and mouths. Still they saw no signs of life, and all of them grew more sullen and quiet, particularly Doc Brady. Something deeply troubled the doctor. He seemed uneasy, worried, his eyes constantly darting about as if in search of some impending disaster. But when Del asked him about it, he shrugged it off and would not answer.

Day turned into night, and night back to day. And when the days became a week the land still had not changed.

The first week was brutal. The relentless sun took its toll on their skin and the hike had their feet aching and swelling tight within their boots. On Doc Brady's suggestion, the men tightened their laces and didn't remove their boots even when sleeping, fearing they wouldn't be able to get them back on.

The second week proved worse. Physically, the men improved, their blisters turning to calluses and their skin tanning a deep brown. But boredom pressed in upon them. Each day became nothing more than putting one foot in front of the other in a countless procession that seemed to accomplish nothing in the never-changing landscape. The wasteland remained physically trying, but its demands multiplied when their hearts went out of the journey. Even Del had tired of this adventure. He had run out of fantasies to explore and now there was only tedium. They trudged on, though, having nowhere else to go.

In the third week the tops of dark mountains reappeared far in the north and the men's packs grew noticeably lighter. They prayed that this meant that their travels were nearing an end, but with the eastern horizon before them still an unbroken line of scorched brown, they feared otherwise.

Near the end of that week they passed a few scrawny bushes widely scattered and nearly as scarred as the broken earth. The desperate men welcomed even this small change as a blessing, though their hopes sank quickly as several more miles of nothingness slowly rolled by.

Then, so suddenly that it took their dust-reddened eyes a few moments to adjust, they breached the top of a sandy slope and found themselves on the edge of a green field with rich blue skies overhead. Birds fluttered excitedly about at the approach of the strangers and small coneys lifted their twitching noses high to examine the unfamiliar scent.

Del fell to his knees and muttered a sincere thank-you to the heavens above. More than once Billy wiped tears from his eyes, explaining it as sweat, though the others shared his feelings and knew better. Only Doc Brady remained sullen. For some unknown reason, the change in scenery did little to lift his spirits.

The green carpet spread wide before them, rising and falling gently in a series of rolling hills. The tall northern mountains seemed much closer now, and the men could also discern a low, rocky range off to the south. These majestic peaks were different from the foreboding mountains they had left far behind in the west. Curling streams of mica crisscrossed the mountainsides like icicles on a Christmas tree, sparkling brilliantly in countless reflections of the sun.

The great range stretched eastward for many miles and then swung south, so that ahead of them, still a day's journey or more, the men could see the towering landscape that they somehow knew held the refuge of Illuma. Perhaps Calae had ingrained this image in their minds as a guide. They picked up their pace considerably, for their hearts pounded with excitement at the prospect of finding their goal, and finding some answers.

Hours and miles later, the northern mountains loomed even closer and the narrowing vale sloped gradually down. The spirited men could have gone on for hours more, but soon the light began to wane.

Crimson splayed across the western sky, marking the end of the day, igniting a thousand red fires on the mica rivers of the mighty northern mountains. Even Mitchell gaped in awe at the overwhelming beauty of the Crystal Mountain sunset.

And then, freed from their trance as the sky turned a deep blue and the mountains became dark and cold, the men set up camp under the sheltering branches on the western edge of a small, thick wood.

Chapter 9

Blackemara

Anxious to finish the trek, they broke camp long before the yellow ball of the sun peeked over the lower summits of the Crystal Mountains. But the forest proved rough going. Undergrowth piled upon undergrowth, vines hung all about in tangled clusters, and plants, bent over by the weight of other growth, crisscrossed under their feet at every step. The thin trees were tightly packed; there was simply no room for large trees to grow, as though all the life that had been stripped from the soil of the Brown Wastes had taken root here in a jumble of living chaos, an upraised pillar of defiance against the perversion of the lifeless desert. The men pushed in anyway, seeking the most direct route and hoping to find some sort of path.

The hours passed more quickly than the miles and the tangled mass of life did not relent even a bit. Exhaustion became a factor, for the men constantly had to tear themselves free from shrubs or vines that seemed to grasp at them as they passed. Sheer stubbornness kept them going, and each step brought them deeper in and lessened their desire to admit their mistake and turn back to find a route circumventing the wood. Noon was fast approaching when Billy, who was once again up in front, gave a welcomed call.

"There's a break up ahead," he yelled as he surged forward. The others, too, picked up their pace when they came in sight of the open area, but their hopes were dashed when they caught up to Billy.

A dimming mist rose before him as he leaned with his back to a tree and his head down in frustration.

The others couldn't understand until they were beside him.

Beside him on the ledge of a deep gorge.

The cliff fell almost perfectly straight for hundreds of feet. At its base a river, swollen by the spring thaw, thrashed southward about its rocky course, sending up the fine spray. Barely a hundred yards away, the other side seemed a reflection in a foggy mirror, with a cliff just as sheer and the thick forest continuing undisturbed atop it.

"Damn!" moaned Mitchell.

"We're having one hell of a day." Billy chuckled with lighthearted sarcasm. He looked despondently at the drop and sighed. "No way we're climbing down that."

Del remained undaunted. "Can't find something you don't look for," he muttered to himself, disappearing into the mist northward along the ledge.

"This river obviously flows from the northern mountains," said Reinheiser. Like Del, the physicist was more interested in finding a solution to the problem than in grumbling about it. But while Reinheiser based his hope on logical structure, Del was playing on a hunch, an eerie, overpowering feeling that something was needed to complete this hauntingly familiar scene.

"So?" quipped Mitchell at the unremarkable revelation.

"So," continued Reinheiser, perturbed at the sharp reply, "judging from the line the river takes, it must intersect with the lower mountain range to the south of us." Mitchell's expression remained impassive, almost oblivious to Reinheiser's attempt to right their course. The physicist's eyes narrowed to dart-throwing slits as he went on. "Our eye level is well above the base of those mountains. So"—he emphasized the word with contempt—"the land obviously slopes down to them. A slight grade no doubt, but sufficient to bring us down to the level of the river."

Surprised at such an easy answer, and a bit embarrassed by his pouting, Mitchell considered the logic, when "YEEEAAA!" came Del's shriek.

The four startled men spun toward the sound, expecting some approaching danger. Mitchell began to draw his sword, but Del's subsequent shouts dispelled his fear.

"I knew it!" yelled Del in delight. "It had to be here. Hey!" he called to the others, but they were already on their way to him.

They came upon him suddenly in the mist, his arms folded triumphantly across his chest and a smug look on his face as he leaned on an anchor post for a railing to an old rope bridge. It stretched out, just a silhouette in the heavy spray until it disappeared altogether about halfway across the span. Even in the misty veil, the men could see that several planks were missing, and the remaining wood sounded precarious at best, creaking and groaning like an old man's bones as the bridge swayed and rolled gently on the updrafts and swirling currents of air.

They were thrilled at the discovery, anyway, for the bridge was the first sign of civilization they had encountered since the Halls of the Colonnae. Still Mitchell had no intention of crossing the aged and rickety thing.

"How far to where the land gets low enough to cross the river?" he asked Reinheiser.

"A couple of miles, no more," answered Reinheiser, sharing the captain's apprehensions about the bridge.

"Why?" asked Del incredulously. "What are you talking about?" He was as certain of the bridge's safety as he had been in knowing it would be here in the first place. Somehow it all fit together for him, like pieces of a puzzle to which he had learned the key.

"You think we're going to cross that?" snapped Mitchell. Del shrugged as though he didn't even understand the problem. "Well, be my guest," chided Mitchell. His grin turned sadistic as he motioned to the bridge, inviting Del to lead the way.

Del swung around the post onto the first planks,

meaning to march straight across. He hesitated, though, as his senses gripped him in spinning, vertiginous fear. He snapped his eyes shut and swallowed the terror and, demanding of himself that he trust his new insight, he started out.

Gaining confidence with every step, he soon passed from the others' sight. About two-thirds of the way across, he came to a gap several feet wide where the boards had broken away. Assured that he wasn't meant to die now, he casually hopped onto one of the rope supports and grasped the cord rail in both hands.

But the support was slick with spray, and just as Del moved from the safety of the boards, a blast of air rushed into his face and sent the bridge on a wide swing. He leaned into the wind, using it to secure his balance, moving as though the gust was but a minor inconvenience. Unafraid, he didn't pay complete attention to what he was doing and overcompensated for his lean. When the bridge reached the limit of its sway, it jerked back violently and Del's feet fell free.

He dangled there, stunned and terrified, for several long seconds as the bridge continued to roll about and the cord railing bit mercilessly into his straining fingers. The river seemed to get louder as his senses keened to the fate laid out before him.

Was I wrong? he asked himself as his grip weakened. He grimaced in anger at the thought of missing the adventure, and growled defiantly, "Not going to die now!" Swinging his legs in time to the bridge's sway, he was able to heave one up over the rope support, and he managed to pull himself up to straddle it. He inched his way to the far side and rolled onto the boards. Looking over the edge at the rocks below, he repeated, "Not going to die," less convincingly, and quickly added, "unless I get stupid!" Humbled, he continued on much more carefully, taking shorter steps and gingerly testing each board in front of him before he put his full weight on it. Soon he reached the other side and called back to his companions that it was safe to cross.

Fearing that the scowling captain would order them

to go around the chasm despite Del's crossing, Billy immediately sprang onto the bridge and rushed to join his friend. Mitchell shook his head and huffed angrily as Billy disappeared from sight, but with two of his crewmen going over, the captain had to relent.

"I'll go last," he volunteered to Reinheiser and Brady. "I'm the heaviest."

Doc Brady was of a different opinion.

"Let me go last," he insisted. And he finished his thought silently, Today I die anyway, and if it's to be here, then let the rest of you all be across before the bridge falls.

Disgusted at being upstaged by Del, Mitchell didn't care enough to argue with Brady. The doctor was relieved that he wouldn't be endangering the others, and at the temporary stay of his expected fate, but all too soon Reinheiser and the captain were across the gorge calling for him. For many minutes, he stood frozen in fear, unable to take that first step.

"Hurry up!" came Mitchell's snarl. "Or we'll go on without you!' "

On the planks now, his breathing coming in short puffs and beads of sweat cold on his forehead, Brady forced himself ahead. It didn't get any easier, his terror heightening with every step to the point that he almost wanted to just throw himself off and get it over with. And yet, before he knew it, he was on the solid ground of the other side, surprised, but nearly faint with relief.

With the gorge behind them, they continued on in even greater anticipation. Shortly after noon, they emerged from the wood to a disheartening sight.

They had come to a meadow of tall swaying grass. The land before them sloped down a long grade as it continued to narrow, and at the bottom was a second wood, this one dark and gloomy. North and east the great mountains towered over the low ground, and to the south a high ridge of gray stone, as though the land had split apart, blocked their way. The ridge ran eastward, curved north for a short distance, and then turned back toward them again along the base of the northern mountains forming a horseshoe-like ring around the dark wood.

"A box canyon," groaned Mitchell over a chorus of sighs.

"Just a minor delay, Captain," said Reinheiser. "All we need do is double to the southwest and find where the ridge starts. It can't be far. We should be up on that plateau in a few hours." But Mitchell had once again grown angry and frustrated at this whole business and his stubbornness overruled reason. His retort startled Reinheiser.

"We're not doubling back," the captain fumed. "Not yet. There might be a way through that wall ahead, a tunnel or something. Or maybe it's climbable. I want to know for sure before we waste the rest of the day going backward!"

"But, Captain—" began Reinheiser.

"No arguments!" yelled Mitchell. "You don't even know if we can get back across the damn river without using that rope bridge again. You want to do that? That thing in the hall said go east. We go east!"

"I don't know," said Del. "I don't like the look of that forest." But Del's disagreement only strengthened Mitchell's resolve and he started off down the slope, ripping aside the tall grass as he went. Del wanted to argue further, somehow the mere sight of the wood below them offended his senses and promised danger, but the thought of facing Mitchell again made his jaw and nose throb with the acute memory of pain. He shrugged his shoulders, sighed, and followed with Brady and Billy.

Reinheiser hesitated, though. He stood for a few moments petting his goatee and considering the captain's tirade, amazed that Mitchell had turned on him with such anger. "You should not have spoken to me like that," he muttered under his breath. And with a wicked chuckle that warned of retaliation, he started after the others.

The sun all but went away when they entered the dark forest. Huge black trees bent nearly in two by thick strands of gray-green moss formed an unbroken roof above them. Though it was springtime in Aielle, no vibrant colors of fresh-blossomed petals decorated this landscape. Perhaps it was due to the dim light, but Del sensed that even in full sunshine this wood would remain dreary with decay. It was as though the life about them had gained dominance in a past age and refused to relinquish it to new growth. There was no rebirth here, no seasonal cleansing. Even the scent of the few flowers had long ago gone stale.

Though there was little undergrowth, no tall grass, the path remained difficult. Knotted roots crossed every course, twisted from the ground as the ancient trees leaned wearily. Too large to step across, the men had to climb over or crawl under them.

Eventually the group came to a wide expanse of towering ferns, as tall as a man and taller, with stems nearly an inch thick. Still not daring to argue with the determined captain, they reluctantly drew their swords and hacked their way through.

Out of the corner of his eye Del saw a squirrel the size of a small dog leaping across high branches. It didn't seem out of place, not here in this grandfather of woods, so Del brushed it off with a shrug and made no mention of it. He understood now the nightmarish fears of the romantic poets so far removed from the bricks and highways of his world, for all about him the trees and plants, and all the life of the wood, seemed to close in, scowling with passive, yet stifling, hostility. This was a place where a man could be completely overwhelmed by the vast dimensions and sheer power of nature; a place where a man could realize his own insignificance.

Mitchell had no time for such reflections. The dismal surroundings and the fern barrier only made him grit his teeth and push on harder. He hacked mightily with his sword, leveling fern after fern, driving the men ever deeper into the black shadows of the decrepit wood.

Then the insects came. Mosquitoes mostly, biting them and buzzing in their eyes and ears and flying up their noses, making this leg of the journey even more miserable.

The ground was getting softer under their feet. Reinheiser and Billy understood the signs and they both fully expected what lay ahead when, finally, Mitchell cut through the last line of ferns and found himself on the muddy bank of a swamp. It meandered lazily about the trees ahead, great pools of black water sweating wispy vapors into the already rank air. Stillness surrounded the men, but it was an uneasy, anticipating silence, like a predator's hushed crouch before its spring.

Following Mitchell, they labored on as best they could, but every path ended at one of the stagnant pools and the obstructing roots had become slick with slime and nearly impassable. The ground oozed mud now, threatening to swallow them up with every step.

Every time Del wiped the sweat from his forehead, he left behind a streak of mud and slime. Thoroughly wretched, he was fed up. "This is crazy," he cried. "We should've turned back hours ago."

"I didn't ask for your opinion!" retorted Mitchell, though he, too, realized the folly of continuing through the swamp. He certainly wasn't going to let Del point out his error. He puffed out his chest and glared, daring Del to defy him.

Shaken by the threat, but determined that he was right, Del continued cautiously. "I'm just trying to point out that this place . . . if we get lost in here we're dead." A mosquito buzzed in his eye. "And these bugs!" he added angrily, slapping futilely at the pest.

"Listen to him, Captain," pleaded Billy. "We had a swamp back home where I grew up, and I'm telling you, it's a bad place to be wandering."

Mitchell snapped his menacing gaze on Billy. "What's the matter, little boys?" he whined sarcastically. "Are the bad buggies biting you?" Then he squared his shoulders, eyes squinting in an ominous threat. "We go on!" he growled.

Del wouldn't challenge him this time, nor would

Billy, but Mitchell's renewed fury only prompted Reinheiser. The physicist truly desired to leave the swamp and the dark wood altogether, but more than that, he wanted to test the extent of Mitchell's defiance of his advice. "Perhaps you should listen to them, Captain," he stated flatly. Mitchell wheeled around as though he had been struck.

"You too?" he blurted in disbelief. "Again you back these two jerks. Who's side are you on, anyway?"

"This is not a contest," began Reinheiser, but before he could elaborate a loud splash ended the debate.

The fen before them churned and bubbled, its gray ooze rolling in sickening contrast to the pale whiteness of the frothing. Then as suddenly and unexpectedly as it had started, it stopped, the rancid water quickly settling to flatness under the weight of its muck. In a second, only a widening ring of dissipating ripples hinted at a disturbance under the mirror smoothness of the pool. The men sensed a presence—close, under the surface—and knew they were being stalked. In frozen terror, they awaited the wild rush of water as the predator charged.

It didn't happen like that. The creature came slowly, deliberately, confident of the inability of its prey to escape. Without causing even a ripple, almost as if it were an extension of the mere itself, a head appeared out of the dark water, a great lizard head with a forked tongue flicking between long, pointed teeth and bulbous black eyes with evil yellow slits.

Oh those eyes! though Del, and he mustered up all of his willpower and broke free of their binding gaze. He was nearly limp with terror, but he managed to grasp the hilt of his sword.

The lizard monster rose from the fen and reared up on its hind legs, lean and sinewy and very tall—even twenty feet away it towered over the men. It almost seemed to grin as it looked down at them, sizing up its dinner and swaying slowly, hypnotically, back and forth. And all the while, its wicked little forelegs twitched in anticipation of the juicy morsel they would soon hold steady for its great maw to feed upon.

Most frightening of all were the creature's "whips." Two tentacles, twin serpents they seemed, protruded sideways from its shoulders, hanging down the creature's side until they disappeared into the dark water. Del couldn't tell how long they were, for most of their length was hidden beneath the mere, but he did get a look at the end of one, a nasty barbed hook, as it broke out of the water for an instant in a menacing twitch.

"Good God," muttered Del, and he drew his sword, preparing to meet his doom.

"Do we try to run, or fight?" he asked softly, trying not to spur the monster to action.

The others could not hear him.

"Well?" he said louder, panic in his voice. He glanced over to his right. There stood Billy, Mitchell, and Reinheiser staring blankly ahead, transfixed by the gaze of the loathsome beast. Over at Del's left, Doc Brady, too, was held immobile by the bulbous eyes.

"Hey! Hey!" Del yelled, shoving Billy Shank, who was the closest to him. But the lizard's eyes held Billy so firmly that he didn't even blink.

A voice inside Del's head, his instinct for self-preservation, told him to run. He resisted, unable to leave his friends in this predicament. He was obviously no match for the monster, but figured that if he could hurt it, the lizard might just settle for him and leave the others alone.

Del sucked in his breath and prepared to attack. Truly, he wanted to charge, but again that basic instinct refused to let him rush to his death.

Now it was the creature's move and Del watched anxiously as one of the tentacles began inching out of the water, arcing up behind the shoulder slowly, teasingly, until the barbed claw just cleared the water. Then crack came the snap of the whip and the tentacle rocketed off past Del's left and thudded into Doc Brady's chest. The claw tore through flesh and bone and exploded out of the Doc's back, its barbs catching fast on a piece of vertebra in the splintered backbone. So quick and clean was the blow that Doc Brady never moved. Nor did he change the expression on his face. He just plopped facedown in the muck, and the beast began reeling in its skewered quarry.

"Doc!" screamed Del.

Its meal secured, the beast released the other men from its paralyzing gaze.

"Get out of here!" Mitchell ordered to his remaining crewmen.

"Come on, Del" cried Billy, grabbing Del's shoulder.

"I'm not leaving him!" rasped Del. He shook himself free of Billy's grasp and rushed to the body of his fallen friend, now nearly halfway to the beast.

The creature was ready for Del, though, and just before he reached Doc, the other tentacle snapped. At that moment, Del stumbled on a rock and hunched over, trying to regain his balance. That slip saved his life, for the claw razed his back, severing his cloak, but it could not dig in. Del felt the burning flash of pain and then the warmth of his blood. He dove forward into the mud and scrambled on his belly to Doc Brady.

"Doc!" he cried. "Oh, Doc!"

"Del!" screamed Billy, and he took a step forward.

"That's far enough, mister!" roared Mitchell. Billy turned to the captain, who was already backing away. "Let's go!" Mitchell ordered.

Billy saw Reinheiser moving to the safety of a nearby root. From behind, he heard Del moaning over Brady. Faced with the same choice that Del just had, Billy, too, could not leave. He met the captain's eyes firmly and stated, "No."

Mitchell lunged for Billy, meaning to pull him forcibly away, but he stopped short as an arrow suddenly whistled by, just inches from his nose. His face went bloodless with shock and fear.

The arrow wasn't aimed at the captain. Even as the lizard readied a death strike on Del, the missile found its mark, thudding into the beast's chest and knocking it off balance. Its tentacle fired wildly as it staggered under the blow.

"Oi, Avalon!" came a cry. Mitchell and Billy turned just in time to see a warrior charging at them through the muck, brandishing a huge sword. Billy braced himself and Mitchell, unsure if this man was friend or foe, grabbed at his sword hilt. He never got the weapon out, though, as the warrior crashed through, sending both the captain and Billy sprawling in the mud, and bore down on the beast.

The lizard began wriggling the tentacle impaling the doctor, frantically trying to free itself in order to better fight this new foe. But Del saw the lizard's intent. "You're not getting away!" he cried, and with a great fury he brought his sword down on the tentacle.

The monster tried its other tentacle again, but the warrior had rushed too close and just pushed it harmlessly aside before it could snap. On he charged and the beast responded with a snarl. It remained unafraid, believing itself more than a match for any man.

But this warrior was no ordinary man. He moved right in, deftly dodging the maw's initial attack, and snapped his sword against the lizard's side, just under its foreleg. His agility and speed surprised the beast, though it remained unhurt as its scaly armor easily repulsed the blow. The warrior stayed calm as the two squared off, taking good measure of each other. He had fought this type of monster before and knew how to defeat it.

He let the lizard be the aggressor, using his energy defensively, dodging its deadly jaws and parrying the lightning thrusts of its razor-clawed forelegs. He bided his time, patiently waiting for openings, and when they came, he brought his sword to bear, always on the same spot on the beast's side. Frustrated, the lizard stepped up its attack, but this merely gave the agile warrior more opportunities to strike. Again and again his sword crashed in and now with every blow the beast grimaced in pain.

Billy and Mitchell watched the battle in horrified awe. Reinheiser backed away a bit, further securing his escape should the monster be victorious, or perhaps even if the unknown warrior won. Del was blind to everything except the focus of his rage. He hacked away at the still-twitching tentacle that impaled Doc Brady.

The lizard wasn't standing straight anymore. It hunched to the side in pain as the concentrated blows began to take their toll. Desperately the beast lunged at its foe, but tiring from its frenzied attacks and off balance from its crooked posture, it stumbled and the warrior easily dodged aside. As the beast struggled to regain its footing, the warrior had his best chance yet. He grasped his sword hilt tightly in both hands and hammered it into the battered scales, jolting the monster several inches off the ground. Scales splintered and flaked away, leaving the lizard's blue, bruised hide exposed. It shrieked in agony as the warrior wound up for a deathblow.

But the monster wasn't defeated yet. With desperate ferocity, it transformed all of its rage and pain into one last, vicious lunge at the man. The warrior had figured the battle won; the sudden attack caught him off guard. He somehow managed to get his weapon up in front of him, blocking the beast's jaws from his face, but the force of the blow snapped off the blade of his sword and dropped him on his back in the mud.

Billy gasped and started to charge but the lizard was in control again. It waved its free tentacle menacingly and held Billy at bay.

The warrior scrambled to his feet and faced his doom. He knew he couldn't flee; even if he managed to get ahead of the beast, its tentacle would easily find his back. He concentrated his thoughts on a final plan of attack.

The lizard looked down on the man and exhaled a long hiss. It hesitated, savoring the moment of its victory.

A fatal mistake.

The warrior flung his broken sword hilt at the monster's head and pulled a hand-ax from his belt. As the beast raised its forelegs to block the projectile, the warrior dove. He crashed in heavily, his free arm hugging tightly, pinning the lizard's forelegs against its chest, while his other arm chopped away with the ax at the unprotected hide, peeling away the tough flesh with mighty strokes. The monster tried to bite him, but he was in too close and the beast couldn't manipulate its head that way. The lizard struggled wildly to break free, but so strong was the warrior, so ironlike was his grasp, that he held tight with one arm.

Dark blood gushed from the monster's wound, staining the persistent ax and reddening the water at the combatants' feet. The lizard managed to free one claw, digging it deep into the warrior's shoulder and sending a stream of blood down his back. He grunted and grasped tighter and, incredibly, the flexing of his cordlike muscles pushed the claw out.

And all the while, the ax dove in relentlessly, tearing and splattering the beast's entrails.

Then, with a final scream of agony, the lizard burst free of the hero. He backed away a few steps, his ax held ready, but as he watched the reeling monster, its breath coming in short, labored gasps, he knew that the battle was over.

With one last shudder, the beast rolled back into the mere and was swallowed by the filth that had spawned it.

Chapter 10

Belexus

Del managed to sever the tentacle just before the beast disappeared beneath the mere. He rolled Brady gently over onto his back. Blood trickled out of the doctor's mouth, a macabre red-black blend with the mud and slime on his face.

"Oh, Doc," Del moaned.

"Don't worry about me," gasped Brady, opening his hollowed eyes.

"You're alive!" Del cried, amazed.

"Not for long," said Brady calmly. He grasped Del's arm gently to comfort his frantic friend. "It doesn't hurt, Del. Calae told me it wouldn't."

"Calae?" asked Del. "What are you talking about?"

"This adventure . . . not for me," replied Brady, now laboring for every breath. "A mistake that I was here. Same with Corbin. Calae came to me that first night . . . on the road. Explained. Apologized to me . . . promised it wouldn't hurt." He coughed up some more blood.

"They're coming now, Del," he said, and he turned his eyes up to the heavens. His face brightened with joy as the greatest mystery of the human experience unfolded before him. "They're coming for me!" he asserted as loudly as he could, trying to convince himself of the reality of the moment of his death.

"Don't worry about me," he continued soothingly, and there was true excitement in his voice. "I'm okay now. I'm not afraid. Everything's okay now." And he kept repeating those words until his voice trailed off and his eyes rolled to white.

"Doc," groaned Del. He lifted Brady's head and hugged him close.

"Be strong, buddy," said Billy, who had come over. He helped Del to his feet just as Mitchell walked up.

"Is he dead?" asked Mitchell hoarsely. Del nodded.

"Come. And be quick now," called the warrior as he finished wiping the blood from his ax. "We huv got no a minute to tarry."

Covered with mud from being knocked to the ground, Mitchell was confused, embarrassed, and angry. The beast had scared him and the arrow had unnerved him. Doc Brady lay dead before him, and it was his own bad judgment that had caused it. And Mitchell wasn't sure that he appreciated being rescued; in his fantasies, he was the only hero. "And if we refuse?" he snapped, belligerence his only defense.

As the warrior approached, Mitchell put his hand on the hilt of his sheathed sword.

"Are you nuts?" Billy whispered to Mitchell. "That guy just saved our butts."

The warrior slid the ax into his belt and strode right up to the captain. Del eyed the man with sincere respect. He wasn't as tall as Mitchell, but sturdier, with huge, knotted muscles. His tousled hair glistened raven black and his eyes shone clear, untainted blue. He wore high boots and a short, brown tunic, belted by a wide leather girdle. Studded bracers adorned his wrists and he had a thin, red band tied around his right arm at his massive biceps with a matching headband crossing his forehead, weaving in and out of his unkempt locks.

"I do'no understand," he said calmly.

"To follow you," explained Mitchell. "If we refuse?"

"Then yer bones are for vultures," replied the warrior matter-of-factly. "For no doubt ye will die."

Mitchell, not quite sure of the stranger's intentions, clutched his sword hilt.

"Behold Blackemara—Black Mere," continued the warrior, sweeping his arm in a wide arc. "And her name comes from the color o her heart, not her water. Ye must not know where yer going, for ye cannot go much further into the swamp. She's too soft for the way ye fill yer boots. And if a bog do'no swallow ye, suren one o her fiends will!

"Blackemara," he repeated, rolling the name off his tongue like the ominous rumble of an approaching storm cloud. "Good thinkin for ye to berth her wide in comin days. Few enter here, not a one but the Rangers o Avalon e'er leave."

Mitchell relaxed his grip on the sword, but still eyed the stranger with icy suspicion.

"What's your name?" said Del, trying to end the tension.

"I am Belexus," replied the stranger.

"Jeff DelGiudice." He extended his hand and Belexus clasped his wrist firmly. "Call me Del."

"Del," echoed Belexus, smiling. "Tis noble to chance yer life for a friend. I bow in respect o yer braveness." The compliment from such a man thrilled Del, but Mitchell moved quickly to diffuse Del's pride.

"He was stupid," the captain snorted.

"And who ye be?" asked Belexus, eyeing Mitchell angrily, affronted by an insult to the man he had just honored.

"Mitchell, Captain Mitchell," the captain proclaimed, emphasizing the "captain." The pride in his voice only antagonized the warrior more. Not usually a judgmental man, Belexus saw no reason for Mitchell to show such arrogance, especially since he hadn't even tried to do something to help against the monster.

"Ye show a strange mind for a captain, Mitchell," Belexus said. "A man followin his heart to a danger his mind would'no face is not stupid. Nay, he's a man I wish to raise sword beside when battle is joined. A true leader knows the worth o loyalty." Having nothing more to say to Mitchell and wanting to hear nothing more from him, Belexus turned to Billy.

"Billy Shank," said Del.

"Health o yer kin," said Belexus, warmly clasping Billy's wrist. Not knowing quite what to say in his amazement of this magnificent man, Billy just nodded blankly. But Billy didn't have to say anything, he had already earned the warrior's respect. His attempt to help when the monster had gained the upper hand had not gone unnoticed.

"By yer unheared names and ne'ersseen clothes." Belexus sighed. "And ye come no from the land, for suren ye do'no know her ways. Troth be in seein, ye are standin proof to the Witchin Prophetics."

"What do you mean?" asked Reinheiser, who had come from hiding when things appeared safe. He brushed off Belexus's offer of a handshake with a quick pump. "What are these Witching Prophetics?"

"A gift o the Lady," replied Belexus, undisturbed by the callous efficiency of Reinheiser's greeting. Something had struck a chord in his heart, a faraway memory or a pleasant image, and a sparkle like the twinkling of a distant star edged his eye. "Old tales and long in the tellin."

"I thought you said we didn't have much time," cut in Mitchell's openly hostile voice.

"That I did," replied Belexus, taking no care of the captain's tone. Insults directed against him didn't bother Belexus unless they came from someone he respected. He turned to Reinheiser. "By the words o the prophecies, a time o great trial is come upon us. A time for valor and courage. And honor. And the tales tell o the comin o strange men—ancient men to deliver us. Or mighten be they come to damn us. 'And they shall be the shapers of Aielle, the changers of all that is to pass,' " he recited. "But the prophecies do'no tell for good or for evil. Me sire, Bellerian, Ranger Lord o Avalon, sent me in quest o the ancient ones. I found yer tracks in the vale above and the rest ye huv seen."

"And we must be the ancient ones," said Reinheiser.

"May that ye be," replied Belexus. "And bein so, I must beg yer trust o me and bring ye to meet me sire."

"I have to bury my friend first," said Del. "It is our custom."

"As tis ourne," explained Belexus. "But we huv no the time. I huv no likin to see this foul swamp at shadowtime, and even now, the sun rides low. Blackemara takes care o her victims.''

Del looked at the fallen doctor. ''Then, if you'll excuse me for a moment,'' he said softly, ''I'll say my good-byes.'' With Billy at his side, he walked to where Brady lay fallen and knelt over the body. Belexus bowed his head in respect.

In deference to Del's injured back, Belexus led them at a steady, but easy pace. Del wasn't too uncomfortable, though, the cut being superficial.

Walking behind Belexus, Del was stunned by the grace of the Ranger's movements. Belexus seemed unhindered by his bulky muscles as he easily glided over or around any obstructions they came upon. And Del was even more amazed when he noticed that Belexus, though heavier than any of them except Mitchell, left only a slight depression, barely visible in the muddy ground, while Del and the others sank in nearly to their ankles with every step. Del smiled as the meaning of Belexus's earlier words, ''too soft for the way ye fill yer boots,'' came clear to him.

They emerged from the swamp as the day began to wane and backtracked up the grassy slope with the sun, riding low in the western sky, in their eyes. When Belexus felt assured that Blackemara was safely behind, he veered sharply off toward the southern range. They made the cliff wall just before sunset and moved westward along its base. The great river, red-speckled in the last rays of the daylight, rolled on methodically a ways ahead of them, and as they approached, they saw that it flowed into a wide tunnel in the cliff wall. Belexus led them in, walking along a narrow rock ledge beside the flowing water. A short distance in, he stopped.

''Pray turn yer eyes aside,'' he requested.

''Why? Don't you trust us?'' protested Mitchell, but Reinheiser hushed him quickly.

''You embarrass me, Captain,'' he scolded. ''Turn away and let us get on with this adventure.'' Still grumbling and stung by Reinheiser's comment, Mitchell realized that he had no support in his hostility toward the ranger. He spun around and the others followed suit. Belexus put his hand in a small crack in the wall and pushed a hidden lever. A large slab of rock silently slid away, revealing a narrow, carved stair spiraling upward into blackness.

Del's jaw dropped open when he turned back.

''Wizard's workin in a fore age,'' explained Belexus. ''A free path from the vale in times o need. Come.'' And they entered the stair. Just inside the opening Belexus pulled a torch and tinderbox out of a cubbyhole. A few steps up, he stopped again to work a second lever and the rock moved quietly and securely into place behind them.

Ever upward wound the stair, always arching at the same angle to the right. The walls were cracked and chipped, though not nearly as broken as the exaggerating torchlight shadows made them appear. This passage didn't appear to have been cut; Del got the impression that an incredible force had literally torn the rock from between the walls.

Up they went, and up some more. A thousand stairs passed, then two thousand. Only Belexus kept the spring in his stride; the others struggled for every breath and their legs ached. Reinheiser lagged behind, but Belexus didn't relent the pace. In near blackness, the physicist stumbled on, scrambling to keep within the area of torchlight. Finally, just when the men thought they could go no further, they came to a short, level landing ending in a large stone door. There they waited for a minute to find their breath and to let Reinheiser catch up. Then with a great heave, Belexus opened the door.

A cool refreshing breeze rushed in on them and the cries of a nightbird and the chirping of crickets mercifully washed away the monotonous echoes of weary boots scraping on stone. But it was the clear night sky that held Del's thoughts. A canopy of black velvet it seemed, a million twinkling little lights strung upon it.

''Beauty in the spring, Aiellian Sky,'' recited Belexus, sensing Del's delight. "Soothin freedom for wall-wearied, wintered eyes."

The men stepped out into the night and Belexus closed the door behind them. From the outside it seemed to be part of an immense boulder and not a crack was visible to indicate that this was an entrance.

"Incredible workmanship!" exclaimed Reinheiser. Belexus smiled and nodded, but before he could elaborate any details to Reinheiser about the door, the group was accosted by a voice from the darkness.

"Stand where ye are!"

The men halted obediently at the threat, but Belexus knew the voice. "Andovar?" he called.

Immediately several torches blazed up and a dozen powerful-looking, well-armed men surrounded the party. Del knew right away that these men were of the same clan as Belexus, for they, too, exuded health. There was a rightness about their physiques, a natural beauty and strength, hardened by the labors of winter, yet softened under the warmth of springtime sunshine. Their visages reflected that strange combination, with jaws set strong and grim on a face not unaccustomed to smiles. They put their weapons away quickly when they saw that it was indeed Belexus.

"Wait quiet," Belexus instructed the men, and he walked over to one of the warriors.

"Bringin people here," said the man. "Suren that be folly!"

"Ayuh, Andovar, in troth t'would" agreed Belexus, "were they not the ancient ones."

The man, Andovar, blew a low whistle. "Ye be certain?"

"By their clothes," said Belexus. "And the skin o that one." He pointed at Billy Shank.

"Five by the tales," argued Andovar, "but only four before me."

"Five they were," said Belexus grimly. "Even as I came upon them, a whip-dragon showed one to the other world." He held up his broken sword.

"Blackemara?" exclaimed Andovar, his eyes wide with disbelief. "It is an evil place for meetins." He shook his head and sighed. "Still ye should no huv bringed them. Calva's spies feel the belly o every rock."

"No choice was to me," answered Belexus. "They do'no know the land. One more night on their own would huv seen to their deaths."

He turned to another man. "Fetch me sire and be quick." The man nodded and sprinted off into the darkness.

"Bellerian is just beyond the firelight," said Andovar, and even as he spoke, the man returned with the ranger Lord. He bore the same strong and steady features as Belexus, diminished not at all by his silver hair or by the fact that his back was bent nearly double and he used a cane to walk, crippled from a wound that had occurred in a battle with a whip-dragon.

"Sire," began Belexus, "I huv brought the—"

"Ayuh, me son, I huv heard," said Bellerian in a voice steady and cool with the confidence of experience. "Ye did right in bringin them here. Knowin their path may help us find ourne."

"And what of our guest?" asked Andovar with deep concern.

"It is a risk," agreed Bellerian. "But tis a risk we need take. Too much has happened for us to heed not the Prophetics, Andovar. Might that these be the ancient ones. I wish now to question them."

Belexus pointed at Del. "Speak to that one. I huv seen his heart bared and twas true. Unless me eyes be seein lies, a good man he is."

"Call him, then," said Bellerian.

"Jeff DelGiudice," called Belexus, "please if ye would come and speak with us."

Surprised, Del glanced at his companions and shrugged. Though he turned right away, he hadn't missed the look of jealous rage on Mitchell's face and he fully expected the captain to say something as he started toward Belexus.

"Watch what you say," came the growled order behind him. Del smiled at the predictable captain, but otherwise ignored him, tired of bullying threats and commands Mitchell issued solely for the purpose of making himself seem important. Del knew that he was a better judge than Mitchell of what he could and could not say to these men.

"This is Andovar, me friend, and me sire, Bellerian," said Belexus when Del reached the small group. Del nodded his greeting and clasped their wrists firmly.

"Just call me Del," he said with a friendly smile.

"Me father wishes to ask o ye some questions," explained Belexus. Again Del nodded.

Bellerian stared searchingly at the man before him, reading every detail about Del. As the seconds passed silently, Del grew uncomfortable, feeling naked under the scrutiny of the ranger Lord's gray eyes, orbs clear and sharp with crystalline awareness. Seeking a defense, Del began his own visual study. Immediately he recognized the pride and honor that was in Bellerian. And he saw incredible strength in the older man's gaze, might of mind that belied the bend in his back. Their eyes met and locked in stares probing for the truth of each other's character.

A good test, Del thought, and he gathered up all of his willpower and tried to stare Bellerian down. He had recognized strength in Bellerian, but he had no idea how deep and true that vein ran. The two remained held in mental combat for several long minutes. Determined as he was, Del proved no match for the ranger Lord. Visibly shaken, sweat on his face and neck, he backed off. Bellerian never flinched.

"What business might ye huv had in Blackemara?" Bellerian asked pointedly but politely. No trace of arrogance edged his voice, as if he had already put the contest behind him. His gracious attitude heightened Del's considerable respect for the rangers. Would Mitchell, he wondered with a chuckle, have let him off the hook so easily after such a defeat?

"We were looking for a pass through the cliff," he answered, anxious to please. "We were told to go east." Bellerian's eyes lit up and Del wondered if he'd said too much.

"And who might huv told ye?"

Del hesitated for a moment. He remembered Mitchell's warning, but his judgment told him that these men could be trusted. He glanced at his companions. Mitchell stood with his arms crossed and his head defiantly back, looking as stubbornly proud and belligerent as ever. That was all Del had to see. "Calae sent us."

The three rangers gasped in unison at the mention of the Colonnae Prince. "By the Lairds o the Endless Hall!" cried Andovar. "Tis in troth an omen o good!"

"Where ye be goin? Or lookin to go?" pressed Bellerian excitedly. Again Del hesitated.

"Do'no be feared," Belexus assured him. "In his own breast, a Ranger o Avalon would catch an arrow aimin for ye, if a friend o the Colonnae ye be!"

"We are going to . . . to Illuma."

"Lochsilinilume," said Bellerian, and his face lit with a smile of pleasant recognition. "The Silver Realm. Ayuh, that was me guess." He eyed Del directly and soberly and Del knew there was no falsehood in his words. "If yer business is with the Colonnae, me friend, then yer business is yer own, and I ask no more o ye. Be at peace, ye huv made the right choice in trustin us. Now go back to yer friends. Rangers will be taken ye to Illuma after ye huv rested."

Del relaxed, certain beyond any doubt of the friendship of the rangers. He bowed, it seemed appropriate, and went back to the others.

"They stay in the Emerald Room till once around the morn," said Bellerian. "Then ye two guide them to Mountaingate."

"But Benador is at yer house!" argued Andovar.

"He goes to the wood for hidin till they leave," replied Bellerian. "There's much the danger in these men. And much the hope. I want to be keepin them under me eye. Know ye me will: not a one speaks to them and they do'no leave me home till ye depart. Now no more o yer arguin. Take them to the room. A hard road behind them and mighten be harder a road to come. They be needin rest."

Chapter 11

The Emerald Room

Belexus and Andovar led the four men eastward along the cliff face overlooking the vale and Black Mere. The stony ground beneath them was cracked and uneven, occasionally studded by a cairn of piled rocks that served as markers to the house of Bellerian.

Andovar still did not like the idea of outlanders in the ranger camp, but he honored absolutely the requests of venerable Bellerian. For the last thirty years Bellerian had been his teacher and guardian. Indeed, he was to Andovar as a father, as he was to all the Rangers of Avalon, for when they were but children, sons of the nobles of the court of Ben-galen, Overlord of Pallendara, the infamous Ungden seized the throne and killed their fathers. Ungden had planned to do slaughter to them as well, to extinguish the lines of noble blood completely, but Bellerian, with the help of Glendower, shuffled them away in the darkness of that bloody night to the outskirts of Avalon. There, under the watchful eyes of Bellerian and one other secret friend, the new rangers grew strong and true. Now as adults, they had achieved a whispered reputation among the farmers of Calva's northern fields as mighty fighters. This was a wild land, open to bands of marauding talons or to monsters that slithered out of Blackemara. Yet such intruders, no matter how many or how mighty, were always cut down before they could cause much mischief, and when the farmers found the slaughtered remains left along the roadsides for the vultures, they knew that the fierce rangers were watching over them.

The party came to a small cliff, a great block of stone rising up before them.

"Behold ye, we are to the door," said Belexus, pointing to a dark crack at the base of the slab.

"That's it?" asked Billy. "You want us to go in there?"

"This is your father's house?" added Del incredulously. "I thought he was a Lord."

"Indeed, and that he is," answered Belexus. "But a Lord o Rangers."

"A ranger is a soldier o the spirit," explained Andovar. "We are but a simple folk and huv no need or want for palaces to name as home. The meat o our table is not fineries, but honor and sense o purpose. We huv a duty, and the given o self to it is comfort enough."

"And just what might that duty be?" asked Reinheiser, curious to know more about this people, to understand completely their ways and motivations. For Reinheiser, knowledge was the greatest advantage over enemies or friends alike.

Andovar didn't answer, wondering if he had said too much to the strangers already. Belexus interceded.

"Come, let us enter," he said. "Ye may find that we are not as poor as ye believe." With that Belexus crawled into the crack and disappeared from sight. The others followed, Billy somewhat reluctantly, with Andovar taking up the rear. Belexus soon had some torches burning and the men found themselves in a wide chamber. Furs were scattered about the floor and a firepot sat under a natural chimney in one corner. A rack of weapons lined one wall, brimming with well-crafted spears and swords and fine chain-link armor. On pegs along the opposite wall hung cloaks and saddles.

"Looks pretty crude to me." Mitchell snickered.

Belexus pulled a torch out of a holder. "Follow," he said coldly, his eyes on the captain. Mitchell smiled inwardly with the knowledge that he was bothering the ranger.

Belexus pushed on a rock and a section of the wall

slid away to reveal a short tunnel sloping down into blackness. He entered first with the torch, its light revealing an iron-banded wooden door at the tunnel's other end. Belexus took out a key and opened the door and the men caught a shadowy glimpse of a room beyond. But then, with a look of contentment aimed at Mitchell, and much to the surprise of the men, Belexus put out his torch.

"What the hell are you doing?" shouted the captain above a chorus of wondering murmurs.

"Silence!" commanded Belexus abruptly. Surprised by his sudden outburst, the men quieted. Reinheiser and especially Mitchell grew nervous. They were in a precarious situation, surrounded by two grim warriors, one of whom was angry at Mitchell, and they were helpless in the complete darkness. Only Del held calm in his trust of the rangers.

"Take hold o the hand o the man in front o ye and follow me lead," instructed Belexus. He grabbed Del's hand and, after Andovar called from the back that the chain was complete, led them into the room beyond. Andovar shut the door and they heard the dancing music of a swift-running stream. They stood silent in anticipation for several seconds, but neither Belexus nor Andovar made any move or offered any explanation.

"Well?" snapped Mitchell, strung out with anxiety.

"Behold ye the home o Bellerian," answered Belexus flatly.

"It's awfully dark," said Del.

"Ye be wantin light?" Belexus chuckled. "Then ask for it." Over by the door, Andovar began to laugh.

"Would you please light your torch?" asked Del, not quite understanding what Belexus was hinting at.

"Do no ask me," replied Belexus, straining to hold back his own laughter. "Tis the room ye should be askin."

"What?"

"The room," repeated Belexus calmly and in all apparent seriousness.

"But be askin politely," added Andovar. "Take care ye do'no offend it!"

"Okay, I'll play your game," said Del, his confusion turning to curiosity. Billy and Reinheiser, too, were no longer afraid, sensing that the rangers had something amazing in store for them, something of which Belexus was obviously very proud. Mitchell, though, was fuming. He had no patience for surprises or for jokes made at his expense, and he perceived these mysterious actions by the rangers as an attempt to pay him back for his earlier insults.

Del thought for a moment about what to say. If he was going to play along, he was going to do it in grand style. "Oh, great room!" he began, but he was interrupted by the laughter of Andovar.

"Quiet!" shouted Del, a smile crossing his face.

"Oh, great room!" he began again. "We humbly beseech you to shed your magnificent light upon us!" Instantly, the room lit up with blinding white light, its intensity stinging the eyes of the four ancients. (Belexus and Andovar had known enough to close their eyes when Del said "magnificent.")

Mitchell yelled in anger, snapping his eyes shut. "Damn it!"

"Light!" commanded Belexus, and the brightness of the room immediately mellowed. Andovar opened his eyes and jumped in front of the men.

"Behold ye," he cried, "the magical chamber of Bellerian, Ranger Lord o Avalon!" As their eyes adjusted, the men were treated to a sight they would never forget, a vision so wondrous that even Mitchell lost his anger.

They were in a domed chamber, its floor smooth white marble streaked with red-brown veins. A gully several feet across, and running from wall to wall parallel to the door, divided the room, the water singing its melody from within. A marble bridge arched delicately over the midpoint of the gully and, therefore, over the exact center of the floor. Incredibly, the posts and handrails of the bridge, though also made of marble, were shaped into intricate twists and turns. Del knew at once that only magic could have worked stone in that manner.

On the wall opposite the door, the men saw beautifully crafted furniture; a desk, chair, and bookcase, all adorned with bas reliefs of dragons and wizards and arcane runes, and overfilled with scrolls and parchments. Off to the side was a small cabinet and Bellerian's bed, many-pillowed and covered with purple satiny sheets.

Most magnificent of all, though, were the curving walls and ceiling of the room, for they were the source of the light. They were of translucent, many-faceted crystal, a magical glow flashing through them in brilliant reflections of spectral color. Rainbow rows of gemstones, all polished to a sparkling glitter, ran up the walls like many-hued ladders of starlight and converged at the center of the ceiling in a kaleidoscopic burst. Just below this, suspended in midair, hung a clear crystal ball rotating slowly on an unseen axis. Set in its center was a huge, six-sided emerald, perfectly cut, almost as if it, like the shapings of the bridge's rails, had been formed naturally to that design.

Mitchell stood dumbfounded at the magnificence before him, having no witticisms sufficient to retaliate against this place of beauty.

"We are but a simple folk!" Andovar chuckled proudly.

"Soldiers o the spirit," added Belexus.

"This is unbelievable!" cried Del when his breath came back.

"Incredible," agreed Reinheiser. "How could you possibly have made this?"

"Twas made by no hands o ourne," answered Andovar.

"Then who?" pressed Reinheiser, eager, almost frantic, to know what power in Aielle was capable of creating something like this.

Andovar seemed unsure of how to answer the physicist. He and Belexus exchanged questioning glances, wondering how much they should say to the strangers. The men noted the caution in Belexus's reply.

"We do'no know," he said. "Bellerian says only that it was made by a friend."

"Sit, then," said Andovar, quickly changing the subject, "and know yerself blessed in seein the power o the Emerald Room!"

Anxious for more of this wondrous place, the men readily complied. As they made themselves comfortable on some plush furs that Belexus had brought along, Andovar walked to the middle of the bridge. When everyone was settled, he looked up at the crystal ball and spoke to it.

"Blue!" he commanded, and instantly the room was bathed in blue light, gleaming through the crystal walls.

"Red!" said Andovar, and the room obeyed.

He looked at the strangers and their amazed expressions urged him on with his demonstration. "The water!" he ordered with proud conviction. The room went black. Then the walls of the gully lit up, the light dancing enchantingly through the water of the stream in flickering designs about the room. Every now and then came a silver flash as a cave fish flitted by.

"Dark!" cried Andovar, and the room went black.

"Witness to the night, Andovar," came Belexus's request.

"By yer wish," Andovar replied. A quiet hush held for a moment. Finally, when Andovar felt himself prepared, he raised his eyes in the blackness toward the crystal ball and called clearly, "The night!"

The room remained dark for a second. Then a crimson ball, a perfect representation of the setting sun, appeared low on the wall opposite the door and the room lit up accordingly. The ball sank quickly behind an illusionary landscape turning the western sky of the dome fiery red in a beautiful sunset highlighted by the black silhouette of a lone cloud.

Soon the red dissipated into the deep blue of dreamy twilight and dots of light, stars, made their first twinkling appearance all about the sky. Blue deepened to black and a million stars shone clearly. The men stared in blank amazement as a huge, silvery moon rose on the wall directly behind them and made its way overhead. Soon it, too, disappeared behind the room's horizon and gradually the room began to lighten until the first rays of dawn peeped from the wall behind the men. With this first hint of sunlight, Andovar's request was completed and the room faded to darkness.

"Light," commanded Andovar to bring back the normal illumination.

"My God, Belexus," whispered Del.

"Magnificent!" exclaimed Reinheiser. "I must know more about this room!"

"Me sire suren be glad ye're pleased," said Belexus, but he halted Reinheiser's coming stream of questions with a wave of his hand. "Ye must be restin now," he explained. "The night hus been windin long as we tarry and me and Andovar huv duties before dawnslight."

"When will you return?" asked Del.

"On the two-morn, the day behind the morrow's night," answered Belexus. "We will come for ye when the time's for goin. Until then, ye stay here and rest. Ye'll find yer food in a sack under the table o'er the bridge."

"Steps go into the brook where it flows out o the room by the wall," added Andovar, pointing to the wall on the right. "There's for washin. Back against the pull, she's drinkin clean."

"Ask o the room as pleases ye," said Belexus. "But be wary, for tis the strength o yer own mind that truly brings the changes." His voice went low with seriousness. "And bein a friend, I warn ye, hopin ye will heed me words; the tomes and scrolls across the way are alone for the eyes o Bellerian. They'll no abide the gaze o any other."

With that, the rangers bowed low in farewell and left. The men heard Belexus lock the door behind him.

Del was obviously enchanted with the room. "Better than any planetarium I've ever seen," he declared.

"I don't get it," said Mitchell, confused but certainly not enchanted. And with the captain, confusion usually led to anger. "They walk around with swords and they've got the technology to do this!"

"This room has nothing to do with technology, Captain," offered Reinheiser.

"Oh, really," snapped Mitchell, suspecting Reinheiser's thoughts. "Then how does it work?"

"The man Andovar named it," answered Reinheiser, hesitating as though he was making a reluctant concession. "Magic."

"You're as sick as the rest of them," declared the disgusted captain.

"Perhaps," retaliated Reinheiser. "But I know what lies plain before me! Think of all that has happened to us!" he continued in open anger. "You yourself carry the scars of bullet wounds that should have killed you instantly, and yet you stand here talking to me! How, Captain? How is that possible?"

"I don't know!" shouted Mitchell. "Maybe they're advanced medically—or maybe these scars aren't real!"

"An illusion?" retorted Reinheiser. "Yes, of course, this whole experience could be an illusion! Or maybe a dream."

"Yes!" cried Mitchell, seeing the revelation.

"No!" shouted Reinheiser right back at him. "Don't you see the trap, Captain? Why is this an illusion? Perhaps the illusion was our lives before the *Unicorn.*"

"That's crap!"

"Of course it is," agreed Reinheiser. "And it is also ridiculous to think that this land, Aielle, is imaginary. An image that persists for days, weeks, is not an illusion, it is reality! And as insane as this all seems, it is truly happening!"

"I wouldn't expect this of you," Del said to Reinheiser. "I mean, you being a scientist, devoted to laws and precise calculations. I didn't think there was room in your world for something as illogical as all this."

"Laws, measurements," snorted Reinheiser. "They are only tools. They have their uses, but they are limited. No, there is something else here. I can feel it, I can taste it. There is a power, a magic in the air, that the laws of science as we understand them cannot explain."

"Bah!" blurted Mitchell. He threw up his hands and stormed away. Reinheiser shook his head and smiled as though he pitied the captain's inability to comprehend.

Despite the tense atmosphere, they all slept better that night than they had since the Halls of the Colonnae.

The next day was difficult for Mitchell. As anxious as he was to get this whole business over with, certain that its end would somehow bring about a reasonable explanation and a return to normalcy, the frustration of sitting and waiting quickly became more than he could bear.

But that day was anything but boring for Reinheiser. He set to work with enthusiasm, testing the limitations of the room's power. That would have been absorbing enough to satisfy him if the parchments and scrolls on the desk had not been a constant torment to his insatiable curiosity. He stayed away from them, though, for he believed in this magic he had witnessed and, not yet understanding it, respected it enough to heed Belexus's warning.

Del and Billy spent the day recuperating from the trials of their weeks on the road. They were both excited and charmed by this strange world in spite of its dangers, especially Del. But being forced to accept one impossibility after another had created intense pressures and both of them needed to unwind. They talked with nostalgic fondness about old times and wondered what was yet to come, all the while enjoying the show provided by Reinheiser's experiments.

"Maybe I was wrong about him," said Del, noting the physicist's enthusiasm as he worked the lights and illusions.

"No, you weren't," answered Billy with flat certainty.

"But look at him." Del smiled. "He's thrilled about this whole thing."

"His old rules are defective. They don't explain what's going on, so he's trying to find new ones that can. That's all there is to it."

"I don't know," argued Del. "He threw out that Mr. Computer act of his and got emotional last night, even defended this completely impossible place against Mitchell. That's not the Reinheiser I know."

"Emotional?" replied Billy. "No, you've got it wrong. He got excited, but he never lost control of his emotions. He found a new toy to play with, a new frontier to explore. It was the same way on the *Unicorn* when he figured out the time distortion and thought we were going to find an advanced society. There's nothing wrong with being curious or wanting to learn, but Reinheiser's got this self-destructive need to know absolutely everything."

"Yeah, you're probably right," Del sighed. "I just thought there might be hope for him."

"Believe me, buddy," said Billy, "that snake is as cold-blooded as ever."

No one visited the men that day. But that night as they slept, Bellerian came and woke Del. He motioned Del to keep quiet and led him out into the torchlit tunnel.

"By the words o me son, I can put me trust in ye," said Bellerian after he had silently closed the door.

"You can," said Del, intrigued. He hoped that Bellerian would ask something of him. Though he knew little of the rangers and their ways and understood not at all their dedication to the unknown duty that Andovar had hinted at, Del realized that these men were unquestionably honorable. Seeing in them the qualities of the proud and principled heroes that his calculating and mystery-less world so desperately needed, he was anxious to prove himself worthy of their company and respect. "I owe the rangers my life. I won't betray you."

"Good in hearin," said Bellerian. "Then I beg a small favor o ye."

"Name it."

"Take this." He handed Del a bone cylinder, both its ends capped with cork. "When ye be in the realm o Illuma, seek ye the Silver Mage and give him this. Tell him I gave it to ye and that it is from our friend o the wood."

"Mage?" asked Del. "You mean wizard?"

"Ayuh, a very great wizard indeed is Rudy Glendower."

"Wow," whistled Del, thrilled at the prospect of meeting such a man. This world was growing more and more fantastic to him every minute. What would a wizard be like? he wondered. What kind of power could this Rudy Glendower command, if any at all? Suddenly, Del remembered the incredible magic of the Emerald Room and he looked at the venerable and iron-willed man before him with a surprised and questioning expression.

Bellerian read the look on Del's face and smiled. "No, me friend, I am no enchanter. But only a mortal man belike yerself. No but four wizards be chantin spells in Aielle."

"Of course, the Four trained by the Colonnae," said Del, remembering Calae's tale. Bellerian's nod confirmed Del's guess and he pressed on, even more excited.

"Tell me how to find this man."

"Ye should'no huv a difficult time o it," replied Bellerian, "he bein the only one in all Illuma whose blood runs pure to human. And lestin the ways o the dancin children huv changed, Ardaz, as they name him, is ever about.

"Show that to no one," continued Bellerian soberly, indicating the bone case. "And bechance someone sees it, tell him ye found it by the roadside. Keep it our secret."

Del assured the ranger Lord that he would carry out the task. As Bellerian turned to leave, Del called him back. "You've trusted me and I thank you for that." He studied Bellerian's every reaction as he spoke, hoping to word his request just right. "Could you trust me some more? Could you do me a favor?"

Bellerian nodded cautiously.

''I want to know about the room,'' asked Del. ''Is it the magic of one of the Four? Did the Silver Mage create it?''

Bellerian hesitated for a moment. Having asked of Del in friendship and trust, he had no choice but to return the courtesy. ''Suren the mark o Ardaz is upon it,'' he said. ''But in troth twas more the dweomerin o another. No more can I tell ye.''

''I understand,'' said Del, satisfied. ''And thank you for saying as much as you did.''

''Go now and rest,'' said Bellerian. ''Tomorrow finds ye on the road.''

Del rejoined his companions and quickly fell into a sleep filled with heroic dreams of magics and swordplay and rescues from the fiery maws of evil dragons. But then one image held him, dominating his train of thoughts with disturbing incessancy.

An eye was watching him.

A green eye, studying his every move and penetrating deeper to scrutinize his thoughts and the very feelings within his heart.

Finally the eye released him from its probing and Del dreamed that he was floating in the air. Up he went, past the trees and clouds and beyond to a million stars. Stars that spoke to him with their flashing lights, showed him fleeting glimpses of wondrous secrets and powers. They limned the edges of his consciousness, teasing him with unimagined knowledge, but he could not grasp them in to decipher their flickering code.

Suddenly he was back in the Emerald Room, weightless still and hovering beside the crystal ball that hung above the bridge. And the eye was in the ball!

He awoke in darkness, the others breathing deeply around him and all as it should be. He looked above the bridge and thought that he saw a flicker of green before all went black.

Del did not sleep the rest of the night. He wasn't afraid, just curious. Something was calling to him and he longed to know what it was.

Chapter 12

The Witch of the Wood

Reinheiser prepared a little surprise for his companions the following morning. He had learned much about manipulating the powers of the Emerald Room, even to the extent of coinciding its magic with events in the outside world. Confusion greeted Del, Billy, and Mitchell when they were awakened by the illusionary light of a sunrise within the room at the same moment that the real dawn was breaking outside. They barely had time to stretch the restful sleep out of their muscles and reorient themselves to their surroundings when Andovar opened the door.

"Come," he said, "suren a merry day and Avalon awaits."

And when the men emerged from Bellerian's house, they saw that Andovar was not exaggerating: it was indeed a beautiful day, comfortably cool with a winsome spring breeze carrying the fragrances of budding life. Puffy white balls of clouds floated across the rich blue sky and the sun beamed as if rejoicing that the last traces of winter had at last been left behind.

"Get yerself a mornin meal," said Andovar. "We huv the time. Belexus is gone scoutin the road ahead and sha'no return for a while. And I huv a notch in me sword needin to be fixed."

Del drew his own sword. "Do you really think we'll need them?"

"No for guessin," replied Andovar. "Evil ones do'no stalk the grounds o Avalon, but sunpeak shall pass above us afore we see her blessed boughs. The road is e'er filled with dangers in the wild northland." Del and Billy exchanged disheartened looks. "Do'no worry, me friends,'' Andovar added to console them, ''for this day ye ride beside the mightiest blade o this age.''

''My, aren't we humble,'' grumbled Mitchell, his sarcasm undiminished by a good night's sleep.

''I speak not o meself,'' retorted Andovar coldly. A proud man, proven in battle, he didn't take lightly being insulted by an outlander. He stared unblinking at the captain and continued in a low, grim voice, ''Me blade is worthy, alike all o the rangers, but Belexus is the one makin the deeds for the singers o songs.'' Mitchell ignored the words and the glare, acting as though Andovar didn't even exist.

''Killin the whip-dragon to save yer lives marks Belexus at fifteen,'' Andovar told Billy and Del. ''And he is no but a young man. The great Bellerian killed but twelve in his fightin days, and the beasts were more about back then. And Belexus once showed a true dragon to the other world. Not a big one, but even a small dragon is a foe beyond the strength o mortal men.

''But not beyond Belexus,'' Andovar explained, his smile one of admiration untainted by envy. ''By what me own eyes huv seen, even the largest o the dragonkind would be hard put to it by the ringin sword o Belexus Backavar, son o Bellerian and Prince to the Rangers o Avalon.''

''Backavar?'' asked Del.

'' 'Iron-arm' in yer tongue,'' explained Andovar. ''Tis a name he hus earned since his first fightin days. I am no wrong in sayin, me eyes as witness, that he is a mightier warrior than Arien Silverleaf himself!''

Their looks told Andovar that they did not recognize the name.

''Arien Silverleaf,'' the ranger repeated. ''Ye'll be meetin him soon enough, for he is the Eldar o Illuma and very great and wise. But no more o yer questions. Things are needin doin and time is not enough!''

Belexus soon returned and once again the four outlanders were left speechless. They were in a grassy meadow, sheltered by a ring of huge boulders that seemed purposely placed to maintain secrecy. Andovar and another ranger were with them selecting horses for the journey, and the men were indeed relieved that they wouldn't be walking this time. Suddenly the horses began whinnying and stomping their hooves.

Del jumped back from the horse he was brushing.

"Lord Calamus draws near," Andovar answered to his questioning look.

"Who?"

The ranger pointed towards the eastern sky. "Calamus," he repeated solemnly, "winged Lord o Horses." The men looked to the sky, shielding their eyes from the early-morning glare. They stood with their mouths agape, for coming in low, under the fiery ball of the rising sun, was the unmistakable and unbelievable silhouette of a winged horse bearing a rider.

"Pegasus," muttered Reinheiser.

"It can't be," gasped Mitchell. He stood perplexed. Everything that had come before, the talons, the Colonnae, the Emerald Room, even the whip-dragon, Mitchell could rationalize away as a deception of makeup or technology. But now this. Pegasus! There was no explanation. The beast approaching was not mechanical or a trick of makeup. His breathing coming hard, he had to concentrate to keep his balance, forced now to accept that this whole adventure wasn't merely a game. Even amidst the craziness and the death, he had held on to the hope that it was all some elaborate scheme.

Reality was persistent, though. The building proof had pushed Mitchell's belief further and further back in his mind, and now this flying horse shoved it out completely, taking with it all his hopes of returning to a more controlled, more organized, and more familiar environment.

Seconds later, the magnificent steed landed in the little knoll and Belexus hopped off its back. It was pure white with a thick silvery mane that shimmered in the sunlight and coal-black saucer eyes sparkling with pride and spirit, and hinting at an intelligence that transcended its equine frame.

"Where did you get him?" asked Del, actually trembling with excitement.

"Belexus won him," answered Andovar. "Spoil o the dragon's lair."

"Won him?" said Belexus. "No, Calamus can'no be won." He patted the mighty steed's muscular neck and met the saucer eyes with his own, as though he was directing his words to the horse. "Calamus can'no be won," he repeated, "for he can'no be owned. His own master and woe to any who might try a rope on him!" The horse lord snorted its accord.

Belexus spun back to the men, a boyish smile of exuberance stretched from ear to ear. "But now's for goin," he proclaimed. "A clear road and a climbin sun. To Avalon!"

Del marveled at the ranger's enthusiasm and envied that smile. It was untainted, pure joy unleashed for no reason other than the glory of the world about, an exuberance spawned by the simple thrill of existence. Del wondered if he would ever smile like that.

"Avalon!" echoed Andovar with the same innocent grin, and thus began the final leg of the eastern trek.

They moved southeast at first, gaining even more distance from the great cliff, as further "guardin from watchin eyes lurkin in the northern mountains," explained Belexus.

Soon they swung around directly eastward. The ground sloped up slightly as they climbed toward the Crystal Mountains. Their trail was rocky and bare except for an occasional sprig or bush, but off to the south, the ground fell away more steeply and in the distance was a wide expanse of grassy fields. Hillocks rolled relentlessly southward like green ocean swells on and on as far as the men could see and winding through them, a silver-blue snake, the great River Ne'er Ending.

Presently the trail leveled and the clip-clop of hooves on stone changed to softer thudding as the path became earthen. Many rocks were still about them, but every stride took them deeper into more hospitable terrain. Grasses and scattered trees grew more general, and then, almost without warning, they came upon the mighty forest. Great oaks, tall and proud, stood thickly packed before them, running in a long line all the way down to meet the green plain. Belexus quickened their pace at the sight, and shortly after midday the travelers dismounted and ate their lunch in the shadow of Avalon.

Del directed most of his conversation toward Belexus, reiterating his sincere thanks for the rescue in the mere.

Belexus was a humble man. He said little and seemed uncomfortable with the subject.

"Killing that monster was a feat of great strength," mentioned Del. Mitchell chomped hard on his biscuit.

"A whip-dragon is indeed a mighty foe," agreed Belexus. "But more o test o courage than strength, for ye must charge the beast and no waitin. If ye let it use the whips, then tears to yer kin. But if ye get too close for the snap, the beast is for beatin."

"Of course, it's a whole lot easier if the damned thing is already busy with five other people," snapped the captain.

"In troth," Belexus replied with a condescending grin, "tis easier when the beast is at peace, and not ready for a fight."

Del knew that Mitchell was looking for trouble and would push this issue, so he shouted, "Time to go!" and jumped to his feet.

"Ayuh," agreed Belexus, still smiling down at the captain. "Past the time, by me thinkin."

As they began making ready to leave, Belexus pulled Del aside. "Me friend," he said, "if e'er ye're faced with battle, keep to me words: The greatest advantage of a true warrior is neither strength nor quickness, but courage. Courage keeps yer head clear so ye might remember yer strengths and pull the mask off yer opponent's weaknesses."

"That's advice I'll hold on to," said Del as he mounted his horse. And remember it he did, much to his benefit in the days to come.

* * *

They set a leisurely pace in Avalon—no need or want to rush in this truly glorious wood. The trees were tall and straight and the leafy ceiling thick, but unlike Blackemara, the wood of Avalon was not a gloomy place. There were clear, flat paths to follow and the sunlight seemed to sneak in everywhere, flowing around leafy branches and warming the earth with its penetrating rays. And, oh, the colors! Wildflowers of white, red, violet, gold, and every hue imaginable clustered at every turn and the air was rich with their scents.

And the grass was the deepest, truest green, primeval in its purity, as though it was the original conception of the color. All the greens of Del's world seemed but cheap imitations of it.

This was a place for poets and lovers, an unblemished dreamscape of colors and aromas that stirred the senses to new levels of awareness. And it was a clean place; no ghouls lurked behind the trees of Avalon. Being here, Del felt that he better understood the rangers. Nurtured on the fruits of this perfection, a man could only grow strong and true. Del was overwhelmed by the wood; Billy, too, but Reinheiser had other things on his mind and hardly noticed it and Mitchell held on stubbornly to his anger and his envy.

Wildlife abounded. Rabbits, squirrels, even an occasional deer or wild pig turned a curious eye as the party passed, and countless birds squawked and chattered in the branches like gossiping old ladies, spreading the word that strangers were about in the wood. One animal in particular caught Del's eye, a large squirrel hopping along the branches, apparently following the party. Del had the strange feeling that this was the same squirrel he had seen in Blackemara and he was more than a little curious about it.

He trotted his horse up beside Belexus. "That squirrel is following us."

Mitchell closed in on Belexus and Del, hoping to catch their private conversation.

"Hush about it," whispered Belexus. "Pay it no heed."

"But I saw that same squirrel in the swamp," continued Del, copying the ranger's respectful whisper.

"And I've seen too much of it!" Mitchell announced loudly. Recognizing the ranger's reverence for Avalon and her inhabitants, the captain saw an opportunity to vent his seething frustration and truly outrage both Belexus and Andovar. He slid from his horse and picked up a stone. "Where are you?" he yelled to the trees. As if in answer, the squirrel hopped to an open branch and cocked its head in study of the raging man.

Mitchell smiled wickedly. "Your ass is mine!" he growled, and he raised his arm to throw.

"No!" screamed Del, every instinct within him revolted by such an act. He leaped from his mount and crashed in just as Mitchell brought his arm forward, and the stone skipped harmlessly wide of its mark. The infuriated captain regained his balance quickly, intent on pummeling Del, but Belexus and Andovar were already between them.

"By the Colonnae!" roared Belexus. "In troth ye be a fool to huv done such a thing! Avalon opens her arms wide to friends . . ." He stopped as Mitchell met his shock with a stare of open challenge. How the ranger wanted to accept that challenge! Realizing he was bound otherwise, Belexus settled for a warning that came out unmistakably as a threat. "She welcomes friends, Mitchell, but keep me words, she destroys enemies!"

Together they turned to the squirrel. It sat motionless on the branch for a moment, taking in the scene, before it disappeared into the shadows of the trees.

"At least the bastard's gone." Mitchell laughed.

"Swallow yer words!" shouted Andovar, his ire dashing all reason. Quicker than the ancient ones could follow, his sword was out of its scabbard and the tip in at Mitchell's throat. "Or defend yer crooked mouth with yer life!"

"Hold, Andovar," ordered Belexus calmly. "By the Prophetics and our quest, ye huv no the right to do this.'' Andovar paused a moment, weighing the consequences. He sheathed his sword grudgingly without releasing the captain from his penetrating glare.

''Ye huv chased away one animal,'' said Belexus. ''But the eyes o the wood are not few and sure to be watchin even more closely, now.''

Mitchell tried to hide his horror at how easily Andovar could have killed him. He ignored the ominous stare of Belexus and turned to Del, a more easily intimidated adversary.

''I'll remember this, DelGiudice,'' he growled threateningly.

''Oh, so will I,'' retorted Del in the same tone. ''I'll remember all of it.''

Surprised that Del would stand up to him, Mitchell gave an angry snort and went back to his horse. But the steed would not let him near, and the other mounts shied away from him as well.

''Beasts o Avalon,'' Andovar explained with a chuckle of deep satisfaction. ''Ye be walkin.''

Mitchell did just that. He walked with his head held high in proud defiance of the wood and he did not speak another word that day.

They all went on in silence throughout the afternoon. Soon the sheer beauty and wholesomeness of the wood had Del feeling happy again.

Such was the power of Avalon to heighten the awareness of friendly observers that they might recognize a harmony here that transcended the normal and took on almost magical proportions. It was a twofold beauty, both simple and profound: simple in the dances of the animals on the ground and in the trees above, in the constant flow of songs from countless birds, in the unified craning of a group of wildflowers seeking out the patches of sunlight that sifted in through the branches of towering oaks. And yet it was the deeper sense of order, the profound beauty of Avalon, that overwhelmed Del. The realization that every single being that lived and grew here belonged to a system that was delicate yet ever enduring and so complete and balanced that it reflected the orderly perfection of the universal scheme.

They made camp in a small glen as the sunset pinkened the sky behind them. The tops of several of the closer mountains were visible to them and once again they were treated to the sparkling spectacle of the mica-river fires on the Crystal Mountains.

The stars came bright and clear when the cold dark closed in, but were soon dimmed as the full moon peeked his silvery face through the valleys between the mountains in the east. The air grew chill, but not uncomfortably, for a gentle wind came up from the south.

Something about this budding evening flickered recognition in Del's heightened senses. "Am I wrong," he asked with a puzzled look, "or is this the same night that we saw in Bellerian's room?"

"It does look the same," agreed Reinheiser, and he, too, was puzzled.

"It feels the same," said Del.

"Might that it be, " said Andovar. "Tis in the power o the magic o the Emerald Room to huv foreseen this night."

"Suren be beautiful, then," said Belexus. "But we can'no keep our eyes open to it, for the road is yet long before ye and moren so if yer weary. Now is the time to sleep."

Lulled by the rustling leaves and the wind's mournful song, they complied almost immediately, except for Andovar, keeping watch, and Del. Though Del was certainly comfortable in this enchanted wood, sleep would not come to him. As he settled down for the night, the bone case that Bellerian had given him caught his attention and pulled incessantly at his curiosity. He realized that he should be stronger than the temptation, but with all the wonders going on about him, he couldn't resist.

Finally he gave up trying to sleep and walked over to where Andovar sat patiently. Del couldn't help but chuckle as he approached, for as he suspected, the ranger's eyes weren't turned outward against any threat from the wood, they were fixed on Captain Mitchell.

"I'm not tired," Del explained when he got to the small fire. "I'll take the watch if you'd like."

"Nay, the watch is mine," replied Andovar. "The soft nights o Avalon are me deepest love and I do'no weary from ridin. But I would welcome yer company." He motioned a friendly invitation for Del to sit.

"I'd enjoy your company, too," said Del, returning the ranger's warm look. "But first, if it's all right, I'd like to take a walk. The woods don't scare me; they seem to call to me. And the moon is bright."

"Ye huv the makins o a good ranger." Andovar laughed. He studied Del's face. "Me friend, there be a sparkle in yer eye as I huv seen before. So ye've seen it, huv ye? The magic o the wood." Andovar's ability to see right through him embarrassed Del. "Ayuh," continued the ranger, " she's shown ye the beauty and health o the place—the strength o the trees and the richness o the earth below. Know yerself a lucky man.

"Go take yer walk then and enjoy the wood. But do'no stray too far. A man might get lost even in a friendly wood!" As Del started off, Andovar called after him, "Keep the fire in yer eyes!"

Del soon found a break in the trees that let in enough moonlight to read by. He pulled the bone case from under his cloak, his eyes wide and his hands sweating with excitement.

I shouldn't do this, argued his conscience.

But his conscience was no match for his curiosity.

"Bellerian didn't say I couldn't look at it," he rationalized, and before his conscience could argue back, he popped off the cap and pulled out a scroll, trembling as he slowly unrolled the parchment.

The first thing Del noticed were sketchings of a man going through various motions. "It must be some kind of a magic spell," he whispered happily, for that was what he had hoped.

His excitement turned to frustration when he saw the runes. They were wizards' writings, of course, and try as he might, Del could not make any sense of them. He studied them for a few moments longer, hoping that some magic within the runes would reward his perseverance. Nothing happened, and so, with a sigh, he put the scroll away and started back to the camp.

But then he heard the music.

It floated on the wind through the trees, clear as the clearest bell that ever rang, the sweetest music ever heard. Del's heart was drawn to it, pulled uncontrollably within the sphere of its notes. It led him away from the camp, out of sight of the fire, but he didn't care—following the course of that harmony became his only concern.

He came to a row of pine trees on a small banking. The source of the song was close now, perhaps just over the rise. Belly-climbing to the top, Del cautiously peeked out around one of the trees. He was on the edge of a wide field blanketed with plush grass and lined on all sides by the thick pines. Scattered patches of wildflowers added a preternatural touch to the scene, surrealistic wisps of dull color in the silvery moonlight.

But Del hardly noticed the field. His eyes were fixed upon the heart of Avalon's song, a hauntingly beautiful woman dancing carelessly in the moonlight, leaping high into the air and floating down gently, a leaf in autumn, caught by currents of unseen breezes. She wore a black, flowing gown with many layers of gossamer that displayed, with every twirl and rushing leap, her graceful form in ghostly silhouette; and as she descended from her entrechat, a silken cape floated behind, a shadowy extension accentuating her mysterious essence. Her skin was creamy and porcelain smooth and her thick hair floated about her shoulders, a golden mane so rich in color that even the quiet light of the moon could not diminish its luster. And her green eyes sparkled a light that could penetrate even the blackest night.

Lithe as any ballerina, her moves as distinct and meaningful, yet she was less rigid and precise, more in tune with the natural flow of her spirit. Del could sense the joy of that spirit. He could feel the cool, moist evening grass under her bare feet. And he felt the free rush of air as she rose in yet another great leap, ascending on a moonbeam and floating gently, delicately, back to the earthen realm of mere mortals.

Del watched entranced as the minutes passed and the woman tirelessly continued her dance. Suddenly she stopped and stood staring in Del's direction, her eyes wide with surprise.

No way she can see me in this light at this distance, reasoned Del. Yet, all logic aside, he knew that she had sensed his presence and could indeed see him.

Cautiously, the woman walked across the field toward Del, stopping a mere dozen yards away. Leaning over to get a better view of him, she brushed her thick hair back from her face and Del saw a sparkle of green in the middle of her forehead, though he could not discern its source.

He wondered whether he should run away or simply stand up and introduce himself. But any choice he might have made was irrelevant, for a combination of awe, even to the point of fear, of this mysterious woman before him, and a deeper passion, one that was wonderfully new to him, rooted him to the ground and rendered his tongue useless.

The woman studied the area around Del for a few seconds. When she was satisfied that he was alone, her gaze probed deeper. Del felt naked before her green eyes, certain that she could read him to the very core of his soul. And yet, when he grew uncomfortable, she seemed to read that, too, and immediately broke off her examination and looked at him apologetically.

Del longed to know this woman who was so perceptive and responsive to his feelings. He felt kindred to her spirit, and prayed that she shared those feelings. As if in response to his silent hopes, the woman lowered her eyes and turned a blushing smile, and with a sudden burst of energy like a child breaking free of its embarrassment, she began spinning around, her form blurred by the floating layers of her gown. Around and around she twirled, faster and faster. And then she leaped from the spin onto a moonbeam and simply vanished into the evening air.

Del jumped to his feet, the emotional bonds that had held him torn apart by his shock. His mind reeled, blurred by an image of a woman he would keep until the end of his days.

When his thoughts cleared, with sudden panic, Del realized that he didn't know where he was. He had a notion of the general direction of the camp, so he started back, keeping an eye out for landmarks that would jog his memory and lead him true. But whenever he felt that he was making progress, expecting the firelight to come into view with every step, the vision of the woman ebbed back in, muddling his thoughts. Soon he was wandering aimlessly in the darkness.

Minutes became hours as Del meandered. Luckily, his random path led him in circles, not far away in one direction, and in the deep blue of predawn, Belexus and Andovar were upon him.

"DelGiudice!" cried Andovar. "Did ye no hear our calls?" Del looked around reflexively at the sound, but his barely opened eyes did not register the forms of the two men that stood near. As he resumed his confused journey, Belexus sprang in front of him and blocked his path, holding him by the shoulders at arm's length. Nearly asleep on his feet, and indifferent to what was going on, Del offered no resistance.

"What might be wrong with the man?" asked Andovar.

"I fear an enchantment is upon him," replied Belexus. He grabbed Del's chin and tilted his head back so that he could look into Del's eyes. He waved his hand in front of Del's face, but the entranced man did not respond. "His eyes are lookin somewhere other.

"DelGiudice," Belexus called softly, and he shook Del slightly.

"It's all right," slurred Del, "she won't hurt me."

The startled rangers looked at each other wide-eyed.

"The Lady!" whispered Andovar, barely finding his breath. "Might it be?"

Belexus shrugged uncomfortably and turned back to Del. ''DelGiudice!'' he shouted as he studied the glazed eyes with new concern. He shook Del fiercely. The first finger of dawn traced through the trees then, and Del's eyes popped open, freed of their trance by the reality of morning.

''Belexus,'' he started to say in surprise when he saw the concerned face inches from his own. ''Time to go already?''

Andovar rushed to say something, but Belexus stayed him with a wave of his hand.

''Had ye a good sleep?'' asked Belexus.

''Wonderful!'' replied Del. ''Who wouldn't sleep well in this place?'' But then his face crinkled as though he were trying to remember something. ''I had a strange dream . . . I think.'' Fleeting visions of the dancer flashed about in the recesses of his mind, just out of the straining grasp of his consciousness.

Try as he might, he couldn't catch them.

''I can't remember,'' he said with a frustrated shrug of his shoulders. Again the two rangers glanced at each other.

''Where are the others?'' asked Del, even more confused as he looked around at the unfamiliar surroundings. ''And the horses?''

Belexus pointed in the direction of the camp.

Del decided to look for answers some other time; it wasn't important. Right now a more pressing need was upon him. ''Then let's go,'' he said, walking away, ''I'm starving!''

''By the Colonnae, Belexus, he hus seen her,'' said Andovar in a low voice.

''Then suren a blessin light shines on that one,'' replied Belexus. ''He is indeed a fortunate man.''

The others were awake when the three returned to the camp, Billy and Reinheiser setting up for breakfast while Mitchell sulked against a tree in the distance. Again Del wondered why he hadn't woken up in the camp. But he didn't worry much about it, not while his empty stomach called.

They ate a hearty breakfast and were soon back on the trails. Images of the night before skipped in and out of Del's thoughts, teasingly close but unattainable.

They rode easily across the smooth ground, allowing Mitchell, whose horse still refused to let him ride, to keep up with them. It was pleasant and quiet and they enjoyed the sounds and colors of the wood and the mild breeze of another perfect spring day. Scents of newly bloomed flowers mingled their sweet perfume in a rich collage of natural fragrance in the clean air.

The path wound on and soon the party came to a wide grassy field bordered by thick pines. Instantly Del's visions returned and the events of the night before began to fall into place. He quick-stepped his mount up between the two rangers.

"This field," he stammered. "It was in my dream! I came here." He pointed to the small bluff on the side of the field where he had lain the night before. "Over there. And this beautiful wom . . . " He paused helplessly, mouth hanging open, eyes wide. It was clear to him now, all of it. "It wasn't a dream," he declared, and he looked at the rangers, searching for some explanation.

"The Lady," said Andovar with a gleam in his eyes. "Tell me o the Lady."

"Beautiful," answered Del. "Golden hair and green eyes." He closed his eyes to focus on the image. "And she had something here." He put his hand to his forehead. "It shone green in the moonlight."

"An emerald," explained Belexus. "Her gem mark, for she is the Emerald Witch."

"Then it's true?" gasped Del. "There really is such a person?"

"Tis spoken she can be to every man what most he desires in a woman," said Andovar. "Ye are o the very few to huv seen her."

"Have you?"

"Not I."

"Nor I," added Belexus, "but me father knows her as well as any."

"Yestereve, I named ye lucky and suren ye are," said Andovar. "Tis in me heart n hopes that I might gaze upon the beauty of the Witch o the Wood before me time for leavin this world."

Del floated in a happy trance the rest of the morning, seeing the wood as many times more beautiful now that the memory of the witch rang clear in his mind. More than once, he imagined he saw her slipping behind a tree or dancing in distant shadows. This was her realm, a reflection of her beauty, and her magical presence pervaded its very essence.

But as the morning waned, Del sadly realized that they were nearing the end of Avalon. Rocky spurs of the towering Crystals rose up out of the trees just to the south and the east.

Then the mountains were lost from view as the party came upon a thickly packed grove of oaks with a canopy that let in little light. The dimness wasn't a problem, though, for here the straight road rolled wide and distinct, sloping upward and cutting through impassable walls of oak and elm that formed a green and brown tunnel around it.

A speck of light showed the far end of the tunnel, ever growing as they approached. Even sooner than Del had expected, they had come to the abrupt end of Avalon. Beyond the trees, lay a grassy field and, in the distance, a mountain wall of gray stone.

When they were a few yards from the exit, still under the protective shadow of the trees, Belexus wheeled his horse around. "No further do we rangers go," he said. "Yer horses, too, huv reached the end o their road."

"But Bellerian said you would take us to Illuma," said Billy.

"And so we huv," replied Belexus, "for beyond the wood, at the northern end o the field called Mountaingate, lies the entrance to the Silver Realm. There, by the tellins o Prince Calae, ye shall find yer destiny."

Del didn't want to leave. Since the Halls of the Colonnae he had followed the road gladly, letting it take him where it would, and looking for adventure around every bend. But now, whatever might lay ahead, the road was taking him from the place he most wanted to be. Billy dismounted quickly and moved to support his friend. Truly he felt for Del, realizing that he, too, would have surrendered to the enchantment of the wholesome wood under a different set of circumstances.

He led Del out slowly, letting him savor every last second. As they passed the rangers, Del stopped and looked to Belexus.

"How can I leave?" he asked, honestly torn between his desires and his responsibility.

Belexus understood the torment in Del's eyes.

"Ye huv me pity, me friend," he replied. "Many are the sorrows on the road o life, yet oft the grief o partin is the most unlooked for and the most hurtin. Yet ye must be goin. By the words o Calae himself, Lochsilinilume is the land o yer purpose and yer destiny."

No reason for leaving seemed good enough to Del at that moment, but he continued on sadly, vowing in his heart that he would one day soon return to Avalon and seek out the mysterious witch.

Mitchell and Reinheiser walked up next, their stride considerably different from the lingering steps of Del and Billy. These two were anxious, Reinheiser to see what would come next, and Mitchell to get away from the rangers so that he would once again be the one in control. Andovar stepped his horse out, blocking their path. "Keep me warnin, Mitchell," he promised grimly. "Should ye bring any hurt to DelGiudice, the sword o Andovar will part yer head from yer neck!"

"And all o the rangers will hunt ye down," added Belexus. "And to yer terror, I know o greater powers more horrible in their wrath than anything ye huv ever dreamed, that will be wantin a piece of yer stubborn hide!"

Mitchell just sidestepped Andovar's horse and kept on walking, pretending to ignore the rangers altogether. He heard their words, though, and he marked them well.

"Martin," he said to the physicist when they were clear of the rangers and not yet up to Del and Billy, "someday, with you at my side, I'm going to own this world. Then I'll pay back those rangers and especially that damned DelGiudice."

"If you plan to dominate this world, Captain, you are going about it all wrong," Reinheiser replied. "You reveal your enmity to some very powerful foes when gaining their confidence would better suit your purposes."

Mitchell considered Reinheiser's words and, except for a thoughtful grunt, remained silent.

The four men emerged from Avalon into a bright noon sun. They were on the edge of a flat, green field stretching about a quarter mile south to a grouping of mountains, and twice that distance north, where the main range of the great Crystals lay dormant like resting giants, comfortable in their confidence that they were truly unconquerable. The field was barely two hundred yards wide, bordered on the west by the cliff ledge overlooking Blackemara, running from the feet of the northern mountains to the expanse of Avalon. A towering stone spur lined the eastern side of the field, ending abruptly just south of where the men stood, allowing the field to spill out around the southern mountains into a wider rolling plain in the southeast.

The men walked slowly northward, approaching a rising wall of trees and stone. In the middle of this imposing barrier stood two trees, similar to elms, but with silver-hued bark and leaves colored white as a puffy cloud. They bent to meet each other, their intertwining branches making them seem almost as one, forming an arched entrance to the lone trail up the mountain.

Chapter 13

City on the Mountain

"I'm in for it now," Del whispered to Billy when he saw that Mitchell and Reinheiser were nearly caught up to them. But the captain was still considering Reinheiser's advice, and he knew that Belexus and Andovar were probably watching from the shadows of Avalon. He wasn't about to invoke the rage of the rangers; not yet.

"I'm in charge again," Mitchell declared as he walked past Del and Billy. "And from now on, if we meet someone, I'll do the talking." Too relieved to worry about the implications of Mitchell's command, Del let the point pass without an argument.

As they approached the silvery archway, it became obvious to the men that there was something special about these trees. They emanated a magical aura, a fairy-tale flavor of the happy dreams of a child's bedtime. Visibly the tension eased out of the men's strides and taut muscles unwound with every step toward the wondrous boughs, and as they came under the shadows of the white leaves, a nonsensical, yet innocently joyous singing filled their ears. It seemed so appropriate that they hardly noticed it and a long moment passed before they realized that they weren't alone. They peered up the sloping path with renewed caution, but the contrasting patches of shadow and sunlight blurred everything beyond a few yards.

"Do you think they know we're here?" asked Billy.

The singing stopped.

"They know," answered Reinheiser.

Mitchell slipped aside, hoping to blend into the surrounding woods to gain a better vantage point. He had barely started moving, though, when an arrow cracked into a tree inches from his head.

"On your lives, halt and be recognized!" came a command. A young woman's voice, or perhaps even that of a boy child, and certainly not ominous. But the arrow was several inches deep into the tree. The men froze.

"Cast your weapons to the ground before you," ordered the voice. Billy and Del looked at each other. They were perfectly willing to surrender their swords, not really knowing how to use them anyway, but they expected a confrontation. Mitchell, after all, certainly wouldn't give up easily to a voice so removed from violence.

The captain was indeed itching for a fight. When the command to throw down their weapons came, his first reaction was to clutch his sword hilt. But then Reinheiser's advice came to him once again. He looked to the physicist, who nodded toward the ground in front of them. To the absolute surprise of Billy and Del, Mitchell drew his sword and threw it down.

"Do it!" he growled at the gawking men, though they needed no encouragement; their swords were already in the air.

A slender figure clad in a short brown tunic stepped out from behind a tree and skipped down the path to the swords. Sparkling blond hair, short-cropped and straight, bounced above his pointed ears with every springing step. He seemed in his early teens, shorter than a man and not nearly as heavy. His face was angular, yet very fair; nose straight and thin, but not sharp, and eyes accentuated by slanted brows. It was by these marvelous eyes, big and round and blue, so rich in hue they appeared almost black, that Del could tell that this was no child. Although on the surface they reflected that unblemished joy of youth, these eyes were far from shallow, and within their depths they revealed to Del's sensitive scrutiny a sorrow gathered in the experiences of many, many years.

The boy's skin glowed with a hint of a golden tan, but Del clearly recognized that his being had not seen much of the sun in his day. A "night dancer," he surmised with a secretive grin, and he realized that it was the twinkle of the stars, not the shine of the sun, that highlighted the lad's hair.

"Who . . . what the hell is this?" Mitchell balked as the Illumans gathered up their swords in long, graceful fingers and started back up the path.

"It's an elf," explained Del, but his smirk disappeared when the shocked Illuman stopped short and wheeled around to face the men. Surprised whispers issued from every imaginable hiding place near the trail.

"What name have you branded upon me?" demanded the Illuman in a near shreik. He stalked toward Del, hand firm on the pommel of his sheathed sword.

"I think you blew it," Billy whispered to Del.

Del cleared his throat and responded meekly to the suddenly imposing Illuman.

"An . . . elf." Again the mountain hissed with whispers.

"By what right do you dare utter that word?" demanded the Illuman, his voice ringing both anger and confusion.

Martin Reinheiser quickly cut in. "It is what we would call you in our land," he explained. "Certainly no offense was intended; the word was not meant as an insult."

"And what land is your land?" asked the Illuman a bit less sharply. "Talons you are not, luckily, for if you showed but a trace of that cursed breed, an arrow would have cut you down where you stand. Yet you do not appear as Calvans. What manner of being are you?"

"We are men," replied Reinheiser. "Men from across the boundaries of time." He put great weight on the word "time," studying the Illuman for a reaction, gambling that these people were familiar with the same folklore that had guided the rangers' actions toward his party. From the amazed expression staring back at him, Reinheiser knew that his guess had been correct. He decided to put things bluntly to measure the Illuman's excitement.

"Yes," he continued in a breathless rasp of importance, "we are men from another world, an older world. The ancient ones have returned!"

"Bey-ane cairnliss Colonnae!" cried the Illuman in the enchantish tongue of wizards. His trembling hands could not hold the swords as he ran stumbling to shelter up the path. This time the tumult of whispers sounded more like gasps and Del imagined dozens of arrows being notched to bows trained on the four of them.

But the noises died away and soon the Illuman reappeared, accompanied by a beautiful elfin maiden. She had the same stature and skin tone as the other and was likewise clad, but her hair was as dark as his was light. Not empty as the darkness of a void was the black of her lengthy locks; rather a shimmering hue, as if every other color had blended there in overabundance. And from beneath the raven's coat of her hair, her bright blue eyes peeped in startling contrast.

The two approached the men cautiously, obviously as unnerved as their counterparts.

"I am Erinel," said the first, "and this is—"

"I am Sylvia," interrupted the other, "daughter to Arien Silverleaf, Eldar of Lochsilinilume."

"Then this is a fortunate meeting," proclaimed Mitchell with overfriendly abandon. Sylvia raised an eyebrow at him.

"It is your father we came to see," Reinheiser quickly explained.

Sylvia backed a step and studied them, thinking the same thoughts Belexus had when he first viewed these otherworldly men. She, too, knew the tales, but she was tentative, for the consequences of her decision were much more severe. Illuma was a secret refuge hidden from powerful enemies, and Ungden the Usurper would bestow a king's reward on any man who discovered the whereabouts of the Silver City. In the end, it was Billy Shank's black skin that convinced Sylvia that these men were not of her world and she decided to grasp at the faint glimmer of hope that had entered her oppressed heart.

"If you are truly the men spoken of in our legends, my father shall indeed grant you an audience."

"Then lead on," said Mitchell, and he took a step up the path.

"Halt!" commanded Erinel. "I will respect your judgment in this affair, Sylvia. Yet we must also honor the laws of our land. You know as well as I that it is forbidden for any man to gaze upon the paths to the city."

"Yes," she conceded to Erinel, and then to the men, "You must be blindfolded."

"No problem," agreed Mitchell quickly. Again Del and Billy were both stunned and pleased by the captain's uncharacteristic behavior.

As soon as the blindfolds were in place, the men heard the sound of many light footsteps and chattering whispers gather around them. Sylvia gave some instructions and the troupe started off.

The path was crossed by many roots and stones, causing the unseeing men to stumble constantly despite the earnest efforts of their captors to guide them carefully and keep them steady. The only one not having much difficulty was Reinheiser, for all of his steps were evenly spaced and very deliberate and he exaggerated all of his turns, making them as close to right angles as possible. The Illumans thought the man crazy, but there was indeed a method to his madness.

An hour later, they stopped climbing and began moving horizontally across the face of the mountain. Suddenly the blindness became blacker and the cool mountain breeze ceased.

"We're in a cave," observed Reinheiser as soon as they entered.

"A tunnel," corrected Erinel. "You will find the ground smoother in here."

"Please!" Reinheiser cried in sudden terror. "No caves!" Del cocked his ear in surprise, suspecting that the physicist was up to something. A man of Reinheiser's disposition would not allow himself such an irrational fear, and the exaggerated tone of the physicist's despair gave Del the impression that he was lying.

"Could I travel near a wall?" begged Reinheiser. "Something to hold on to." Del cringed at the blatant deception but, not understanding the motives behind it, remained silent.

"I do not understand," said Erinel. "Why—"

"Please!" shrieked Reinheiser, noting the overlying tone of guilt in the voice of his pitifully sympathetic captor. He smiled inwardly. He knew that he could play on these softhearts as easily as if they were his puppets. "I am afraid of caves!"

"Yes, yes," agreed Erinel, trying to comfort the frantic man. He took Reinheiser by the hand and led him the few steps to the tunnel wall. "I will stay beside you," he assured Reinheiser, "but be wary of side passages."

That is precisely the point, thought the physicist, burying a chuckle. To be wary of side passages! Now he was thankful of the hood that hid his devious grin. Bless these kindly, simple folk, he mused inwardly. Rustic fools!

A good while later, they exited the twisting maze of tunnels and were greeted by a chilly, late-afternoon breeze. Sylvia stopped the party and told the men they could remove their blindfolds. The did so anxiously, and gazed down upon yet another wonder of this strange new world.

They were on the western edge of a valley, and below them, rolled out like a carpet of magical dreams, lay the hidden refuge of Illuma. Del looked on the city of the Silver Realm with sparkle-eyed wonder, for this place was woven of wizards' spells as surely as was the Emerald Room—on an even grander scale. Certainly this was no ordinary vale; the slopes leading down to it were barren gray stone and shale, in direct contrast to the color-filled floor, overflowing with life. Blue-green grass waved like a rippling pond in the mountain breeze and "telvensil" elms, as Sylvia named the silvery trees, swayed gently with every gust, accepting the wind without a creak or groan of protest. These were larger than the two that formed the archway at Mountaingate, their mighty limbs raised proudly high, and within the shelter of their white leaves were many houses. The constructions weren't intruding upon the sovereignty of the telvensils; rather, they seemed to be natural extensions of the tree, as if somehow the tree had helped in their creation.

The homes scattered about on the ground were of stone, worked and shaped with care into elaborate designs that followed no set patterns, yet displayed a congruity of spirit. Glittered with streaks and swirls of flashing silver and bursts of gemstones, and thick with windows, these joyous abodes were more a creation of love than a product of work.

And such was the valley around them. It was hemmed by three towering mountain mica walls, and the fourth side, directly across from the travelers, spilled into a wide gorge that ran deeper into the range, offering an endless view of mountain majesty. Some of the distant peaks lay cold in the long shadows of late afternoon, while others raised their heads above the gathering darkness to catch the last warming rays of the sun. Cloud collars and rising mists floated in mystical serenity, adding a preternatural, almost holy, touch and kindling profound ponderings of the unanswerable secrets of the heavens. How removed from the noisy existence of men were the unconquerable and silent Crystals.

There was singing coming from the valley, the same innocent melody the men had heard when they first came under the archway at Mountaingate. Here, too, it fit, the sweetest icing on a sugarcoated land. With this strange and wonderful view before him, Del felt the name Illuma inappropriate. He preferred the name Bellerian had used, Lochsilinilume, with its eldritch ring and rhythms conjuring images of faerie lands and legends.

Sylvia led them down into the city, past the curious gazes and giggling whispers of the surprised elves.

Seldom had visitors ever come to Illuma and none at all since Ungden the Usurper had claimed the throne of Calva. And Billy, with his dark skin, was a completely new experience for them.

They passed through the city and approached the lip of the gorge, where sat the grandest house of all, immense in size and incredible in design, its roofs slanted every which way, dotted with lazily puffing chimneys. Spires and towers darted up everywhere for no better reason than to catch the low-riding clouds. Windows dominated each wall, large and small, and swung wide to bring in the sun, the breathtaking view, and the scents of the million flowers that blossomed on the grounds. Balconies and terraces with ivy-covered railings crossed and crisscrossed again and again.

The huge front doors were ridged with ornate carvings and edged by gold leaf, their bulk alone promising tons of weight. But so perfect was their balance and workmanship that they swung in easily at Sylvia's effortless push.

Easily and noiselessly, in silence befitting the hallowed halls within. Even Del, who had perceived this vale as a place of happiness, was a bit taken aback at entering the palace of the Eldar. A hush fell over them all as they stepped through the doorway, belittled by the grand and ornate arches. Yet once inside, they realized that this was a comfortable house, a place not unaccustomed to dancing and merriment. It was a house of art, not akin to a museum holding artworks, but a masterpiece in itself, each individual work a contributing element in the overall design.

Every room had its own large fireplace promising warmth against even the coldest winter nights on the mountain, each as different as the elves that had created them, offering its own perspective with unique twists and turns in the iron grillework and stone composition. Intricate mosaics covered the floors and finely woven tapestries lined the walls, all depicting scenes of feasts and festivals by the light of the full moon. The maidens shown were dressed in beautiful gowns, the men in flowing robes, yet like this house, the regal dressings were offset by a comfortable informality, a pervading sense of individualism and acceptance.

The group crossed through several rooms and a long corridor that opened into a narrow hall, different from any of the other rooms they had seen. Formal and serious, this appeared as a place of grave debates, a council hall for important decisions.

Across from them, on a throne carven of silver telvensil, sat a very tall Illuman, as tall as a man, wearing a light green robe with silver trim. A crown of white leaves ringed his head, making his black hair seem even more vital than Sylvia's. His face was firm, yet fair, and he held his head high, despite his comfortable posture. He was flanked by a more ordinary-looking elf with whom he had apparently been arguing when the great door had swung open.

"Sildarren aht theol baisraquin!" screamed the Illuman standing by the throne, enraged by the interruption. But his second volley of protest caught in his throat and his face went bloodless in horror as he realized that there were humans in the party. The elf on the throne started forward in surprise, but quickly regained his composure and glanced questioningly toward Sylvia.

"Father, I bring four distant travelers who seek audience with you," explained Sylvia.

"To bring men to the Silver City in these times!" cried the standing Illuman. He pointed menacingly at Sylvia, his finger trembling with outrage. "You have betrayed us!"

"They surrendered their swords willingly," retorted Sylvia. Her face flushed with anger and the looks the two exchanged made it obvious to all present that their dislike of each other ran deep.

"You do not, then, remember the laws, my lady Sylvia?" he hissed sarcastically.

"Enough, Ryell," the seated Illuman casually requested, all too accustomed to the bickerings of these two.

"The laws?" jabbed Ryell, heedless of the other.

"And do you not remember the tales?" the elf on the throne scolded in response, clenching suddenly, taut and ready as a bent bow. He hadn't shouted, but his clear voice resonated with power, and the sheer strength of its insistence broke the lock of anger between Sylvia and Ryell and turned them both toward the speaker. Immediately he relaxed back in his throne. "These men are special, I believe," he said to console Ryell.

"They are men," spat Ryell, venom dripping from his words. "That alone makes them enemies to Illuma! You look too much to old tales, Arien, for the answers to problems we face."

He swung back at Sylvia. "You searched them, of course," he stated matter-of-factly, though he fully expected that Sylvia had not searched the men.

"They surrendered willingly," stuttered Sylvia. "I—"

"Search them!" roared Ryell, and apparently he held some importance, for several elves moved to the men.

Panic hit Del when he remembered the scroll in his cloak. He locked into Arien's gaze, begging for a stay of the search. The elf-king caught the desperate plea in Del's eyes.

"No!" Arien commanded, immediately halting the search. "They have trusted us and we will not return their trust with suspicion!"

"Do not be a fool, Arien!" screamed Ryell. "They are men! By the law penned in your own hand, they should be imprisoned!" Arien remained unblinking and resolute.

"You will bring us all to ruin with your trust of humans!" yelled Ryell. Suddenly the expression on his face eased as though a revelation had come over him. "But then," he continued too calmly, "your parents were the children of humans, were they not? Back in Caer Tuatha when the land was young."

"I should choose my words more carefully were I you, Ryell," advised Arien evenly, a sudden and calculating coldness in his control promising that his warning was more than just an idle threat.

Unnerved, Ryell shrank back from the Eldar. He knew that he had pushed too far, elevating the debate to a level where he was no match for Arien. Fearful of continuing the confrontation, he threw up his hands in frustration and marched for the safety of the door. "Come, Erinel," he said as he stormed by.

"But, Uncle . . ." protested Erinel.

Ryell wasn't listening to any arguments. "Come!" he commanded, and Erinel had no choice but to follow.

"Oh Father, why do you keep him at your side?" Sylvia asked when Ryell had gone. "He is so disagreeable, and so stubborn!"

"Ryell holds old grudges, but he is not evil," replied Arien, the tension eased from his face and his lips turned up in a disarming grin. "And it is good for an adviser to be disagreeable; he shows me a different point of view for many important problems. His eyes see what mine do not. Ardaz has been too busy to sit by me since midwinter. I am grateful for Ryell."

Del perked his ears up at the mention of the wizard.

"Ryell forces Ardaz away," said Sylvia. "He is always calling him an 'old buffoon' and other—"

Arien raised his hand to stay her. "We shall discuss this another time, dear child. I have guests with a tale to tell—one that I am very anxious to hear."

He motioned for the men to approach and sit before him. Mitchell walked out in front and introduced his companions and, with a low bow, himself as their leader. Then at Arien's bidding, he told their tale from the rescue by the dolphins to their encounter with Sylvia and Erinel at the silver archway on Mountaingate. He was careful to omit the episodes that showed him in a bad light, nor did he tell of the rangers, for he wasn't certain of the relationship between the Illumans and the warriors of Avalon.

He continued for over an hour, and though he wasn't much of a storyteller, the strangeness and importance of his tale had Arien leaning forward on his throne, absorbing every word. After the captain finished, Arien sat with his chin resting in his palm, studying the travelers for several long moments, playing their story over and over in his head to test it against his own perceptions.

"It is a good tale," he said finally, "You shall not be imprisoned, nor shall you be harmed in any way, but I insist that you be my guests for a short while."

"May I ask what that means?" asked Mitchell.

"You are free to roam the valley, as though you were of my own people," answered Arien. "But you may not leave the city. You would not find your way out of the mountains anyway."

"Your judgment is more than fair," said Mitchell, and again he bowed low.

Billy and Del looked at each other with disbelief.

"What's with him?" whispered Billy.

"Beats the hell out of me," answered Del. "But I still don't trust him."

"Less than ever," agreed Billy.

"Would it be possible for me to acquire pen and paper?" asked Reinheiser. "I wish to log our adventure now that I have the chance."

"Sylvia will see to all of your needs," replied Arien. "At this time I have other matters to attend." They understood his meaning and bowed and turned for the door.

"DelGiudice is to stay," commanded Arien. "I have yet words to speak with him." Del stopped in midturn, stunned at the request and more than a bit apprehensive. Mitchell stopped for a moment, too, a scream of jealous rage sticking in his throat. With no other choice, though, he left quietly, as did the rest.

Only Del remained in the somber hall to face the Eldar of Lochsilinilume.

Chapter 14

Ardaz

"Perhaps you will show me now what it is you are hiding," said Arien in a friendly tone. He sat relaxed and calm, secure that Del posed no threat.

"I don't know what you mean," stammered Del quickly.

"I have lived for many years," said Arien. "I have seen the dawn of several centuries and witnessed their twilight. Two dozen and ten Kings in Caer Tuatha—Pallendara—have come and gone, yet I remain." He sat up tall and straight and his face grew stern. "Deceive me not with your words, my friend," he warned, "for I read your eyes and they reveal the truth!"

Del dropped his head down, realizing that he was trapped. Arien knew beyond any doubt that he was hiding something, but Bellerian had trusted him to keep the scroll secret. A desperate idea popped into his head and he met the gaze of the elf-king.

"I didn't want them to find this," he explained, an unintentional look of relief crossing his face as he reached into his shirt pocket and produced the derringer.

"What is that?" asked an amazed Arien as he rose from his throne. He guessed that Del was diverting him from some other secret, but the small object intrigued him.

"It's a pistol," Del answered, convinced that his ploy had worked. "A weapon from my world."

Arien recoiled, remembering all too well the tales of the terrible weapons of the ancient age of technology.

"Oh, don't worry," Del comforted, surprised by

Arien's unease. "It's not loaded." He broke open the breech, displaying the empty chamber. "See? It has no . . . no . . ." He paused in search of a word that the elf-king would understand. "No arrows."

"Why then do you keep it?" Arien asked.

"I don't know," answered Del honestly. "It sort of keeps me, I guess. You can have it, if you want." He presented the pistol before him.

Arien thrust his arms out in protest. "No," he snapped, and Del jumped back. Arien realized at once that Del was sincerely confused. "No, my friend, it is for you to keep," he explained with as much calm as he could muster. "It is a burden that has fallen upon you. Keep it safe and well hidden, for the horrors of your age have no place in Ynis Aielle."

Del still didn't quite understand the depth of Arien's horror, but he packed the pistol back into his shirt. The Eldar relaxed as soon as it was safely away.

"I commend your judgment," said Arien. "You did well to keep that hidden."

"I didn't think it would be wise to let everyone see it," said Del.

"Tell me, then," asked Arien, "is it as important a secret as the other you hide?"

"Huh?" Del balked. "I don't know what you mean."

"You do indeed know what I mean," insisted Arien softly. "My friend, play no more games with me. I am sure that you have sound reasons for secrecy, and for myself, I would trust you and let the matter drop.

"But understand my position," he declared, and he stood up straight. "I am Eldar of my people and for them I am responsible. I shall make no gambles on their safety!"

Del turned away to wrestle with his indecision. He wanted to honor his promise to Bellerian, yet realized that his entire relationship with the Eldar of Illuma might well hinge on this moment. Arien had seen right through the deception, and from the tone of the Eldar's voice, Del knew that he meant to get the scroll one way or another. Quickly, so he wouldn't change his mind, Del pulled out the scroll case and tossed it to Arien.

"Ah," sighed Arien, examining the case without opening it. He had guessed that Mitchell left some things out of the story from the way the captain had struggled with certain parts. And Arien knew that these strangers could never have survived Blackemara without the help of others—probably the rangers. "Bellerian gave you this," he stated rhetorically. "So you have met the rangers of Avalon."

"Yes," Del admitted sullenly, disappointed in himself for breaking his word to the ranger Lord.

"Again I commend your judgment," said Arien. "You were wise in trusting me and honoring my request." He handed back the unopened case. "I shall not interfere in your business with the Lord of the Rangers of Avalon. I have had the honor to meet the venerable Bellerian on several occasions in the past three decades and I know him as a man worthy of respect. It is to my sorrow that Ungden's eyes have since turned northward and prevented our friendship from growing, for now no Illuman would be safe wandering from the mountains. Someday perhaps." A solemn look came to the Eldar's eyes, as if he was lost in a silent prayer. He revealed to Del in that moment a deep and profound sadness. But he quickly smiled it away. "Might I ask who the scroll is for?"

"The Silver Mage," replied Del easily, no longer afraid of the intentions of the noble Eldar.

"Of course." Arien laughed. "For his condition."

"Could you tell me where to find him?" asked Del. Arien walked over to a window on the northern wall and pointed to a crack high up on the cliff face.

"Beyond that break in the mountain wall lies Brisenballas, the tower of the Silver Mage," he said. "You will find him there, I expect."

"How do I get way up there?" asked Del.

"There is a stair." Arien chuckled. "But you must search it out carefully, for it is invisible to the eyes of all but Ardaz." Del cocked his head in disbelief.

"I do not jest with you," insisted Arien. "The stair

is truly there. And fear it not, for it runs solid and straight and without a break. You must hurry, though, the shadows grow long and you mustn't miss Luminas ey-n'abraieken."

"What's that?"

"You shall see tonight." Arien smiled. "Go now, and quickly."

"I'll see you soon . . . friend," said Del, and he bowed low and headed for the door. He stopped when he reached it and turned back to Arien, who was still at the window. "One more thing," he announced.

Arien turned to acknowledge and Del was rendered speechless for a moment. Half of the elf-king's face was shining in the last rays of the day, streaming through the window, the other half lay darkened in shadow. A fitting image of the paradox of the elves, Del thought. The same unresolvable conflict he saw within the eyes of Sylvia, a mixture of the light sparkle of joyous innocence and the dark shadows of profound sadness.

"Why did Erinel get so upset when I called him elf?" asked Del. From within the depths of the twilight shadows, Arien's eyes glowered and Del quickly qualified the term. "It's not an insult."

Arien seemed satisfied that Del meant no harm. "Elf." He sighed, his voice mellow, almost subdued. "It is an old word; a name branded upon the firstborn of my race by the Calvans of Pallendara who sought our destruction." The Eldar's jaw clenched with the undeniable pain of the legacy of his people.

Del, too, felt the sincere sorrow of his new friend. He mumbled an apology silently and opened the door to leave.

"Wait!" called Arien. Del turned back to find that the anger and sadness had cleared from Arien's face. "Elf," Arien said again, in a louder, more affirmative voice. "From your not unkind lips, it is not such a bad word. You, DelGiudice, may call me elf, and my people elves," he declared with a broad smile. "So say I, and so shall it be done!"

"I am honored, Lord Arien Silverleaf, Eldar of

Lochsilinilume!'' returned Del with due respect. He bowed low and skipped from the room and set out to find the hidden tower of the Silver Mage.

Del weaved his way through the curious glances of many elves to the base of the northern wall, noting with relief that almost all of the looks he received were friendly. Ryell's angry comments had made Del unsure of the elves' feelings toward the strange men, but any worries were dispelled by the time he neared the wall. Half doubting, but filled with anticipation, he worked along the stone in search of the invisible path. Suddenly his shin cracked into something hard.

''No kidding,'' he gasped as he eagerly felt along the unseen object. Indeed, it was a stair.

He started up, cautiously testing each subsequent step before trusting his full weight to it, and hugging the visible mountain wall. He had to climb less than seventy feet, but it took him a long time to ascend the stair. Normally Del wasn't afraid of heights, but he couldn't escape the logic that overruled his heartfelt desire to believe in the magic. His eyes told him that he was standing in midair and should be falling.

He was relieved when he reached the entrance to Ardaz's home. It had seemed no more then a split in the stone from below, but now Del saw that the left wall was actually a few feet back from the ledge, and overlapped behind the right to form a corridor. The passage went just a short distance and turned a sharp corner and Del found himself in a small, circular glade carpeted with the same thick grass as the valley floor. High stone walls surrounded it, keeping it ever in shadowy dimness though it was open to the sky. In the west end stood a small telvensil, and carved into the north wall, like a gigantic bas relief, was a singular mica-strewn tower with two thin windows flickering from the firelight within like the watching eyes of a dragon.

The tower's great wooden door was banded by silver and decorated with the carvings of many arcane runes. Even as Del admired its craftsmanship, it banged open and out hopped a wiry old man in a dark blue robe and a broad silver belt. A great and pointed wizard's cap—much too large for him—kept flopping forward over his hairless face, leaving only his long nose and his mouth, which was constantly in motion, uncovered. He kept thrusting his hands into the countless pockets of his garment, and he grew ever more flustered as his searches brought forth roots and herbs, frogs and snakes, even an occasional bat, all of which he tossed aside with a frustrated stamp of his booted foot. He seemed to be addressing the silver tree with his unbroken stream of words and his volume increased with his excitement.

"Desdemona, Desdemona, where is it? Oh, where? Oh, where? I know I had it—I did, I know I did, but where has it got to? Did you take it? I bet you did, you silly puss. Love to tease me, don't you?"

"Rrow, meow," came a reply from the tree. Following the sound, Del discovered a smiling black cat relaxing on a branch, licking its paws.

"Oh, don't tell me that!" rambled the old man. "You beastly tease! I know you did it. I should, you know I might, turn your tail into a mouse, ha-ha, and watch you chase it in circles forever and ever and ever. Wouldn't like that a bit, would you, Desdemona? No, no, not a bit, I dare say! Ha-ha!"

"That's Shakespeare," interrupted Del.

The old man froze in his tracks and grasped the brim of his hat in both hands. Slowly he slid it back over his pale blue eyes and gaped at Del. "What?" he asked.

"Shakespeare," repeated Del. The old man's face remained twisted in astonishment. "The name, I mean. Desdemona was a character in Shakespeare."

"Shakespeare?" mumbled the old man, scratching his chin and rolling his eyes as though he was trying to recall something. Del remembered then that Shakespeare was a writer of a different age, a long-forgotten time. He tried to think of a way he could explain it to the old man without totally confusing him, but it was the old man's turn to surprise Del.

"Shakespeare!" he exclaimed. "Oh, yes, the Bard, the Bard! A jolly old chap, don't you agree? Why yes, yes, Othello actually and a strange bird—"

"Grrr!" growled the cat.

"Sorry, Des," said the old man. "And a strange cat she was, you know. Don't you agree?"

Del stood dumbfounded.

"Well, don't you? A strange cat, eh?"

"Who?" asked Del.

"Why, Desdemona . . . yes, yes, we were talking about her, weren't we? She was a strange cat, she was, she was, but then, ha-ha, they all are, I daresay, I do daresay!

"Oh, well, it doesn't matter, no, no. But where, oh where did I put it? You don't have it, do you? No, of course you don't! I don't even know you, how could you—" He stopped short and bounded over to Del, again dropping his hat down to the tip of his nose. He didn't bother to lift it; he just tilted his head back and peeked at the stranger from under the brim. "Who are you?"

"Jeff DelGiudice." Del laughed. "Call me Del. You're Ardaz, the Silver Mage?"

"Yes, yes, of course I am. You have a strange name, my son; yes, very strange indeed! Del-joo-dis. Why, it is a name I might have used from the other . . ." Suddenly the old man began trembling and his breath came in short gasps. "You knew Shakespeare," he squeaked, and he pulled up his hat above his hairless brow so he could study Del more closely. The cut of Del's uniform and its synthetic material were familiar to Ardaz, vague memories of clothes he had worn many, many years before, before the dawn of Aielle. This man in front of him was of the older world!

"The ancient ones walk the land!" shrieked Ardaz with a leap, and he threw his hands high in the air. Then, realizing that it should not have been proclaimed so loudly, he slapped his hands over Del's mouth and went, "Sssh! Sssh!" It took him a few seconds to remember that he was the one who had yelled, and he let go of Del.

"Well, well, Ardaz at your service, Del, and very pleased to meet you I am! Ha-ha! I do daresay! A walking tale in my own yard! How very grand!"

Del tried to change the subject, hoping it might calm the frenzied wizard. "What are you looking for?"

"Looking for?" echoed Ardaz, again scratching his chin. "Who?"

"You," said Del.

"Looking for me?" cried Ardaz, more confused than ever.

"No!" groaned Del. "When I first got here, you were looking for something."

"I was?"

"Yes!"

"Oh, yes, looking for! Why, a feather, of course. An eagle feather."

"What on earth for?"

"Earth?" repeated Ardaz. "I know that word. Earth." He scratched his chin. "Hmmm . . . oh, well, it will come to me. To move that infernal rock, of course." He pointed to a large stone resting on the eastern end of the glade. "Why else would I need a feather?"

"How can you move a rock with a feather?" exclaimed Del, growing ever more ready to pull his hair out.

"You can't, of course."

Del moaned and slapped his hand across his forehead.

"Excitable chap, aren't you?" said the wizard, bringing a second moan from Del. "I need the feather for a spell. What else? What else? To levitate the rock out of my yard, of course."

Del's eyes lit up. "Magic?" He grinned. "That I'd like to see. Maybe you could find the feather if you took off that hat. It's way too big for you."

"Too big for me?" Ardaz gawked. "Too big for me! Why, it's my hat, how can it be too big for me? Of course it wasn't, no, no, not when I had some hair, it wasn't. But then the fire went *'poof'* and *poof,* no more hair and you say my hat is too big for me. What nerve!''

''I didn't know,'' apologized Del. ''I'm sorry.''

''Yes, yes, you are at that, ha-ha! But then, of course you didn't. How could you, after all?''

''I'd really like to see some magic. Is there another way?''

''Everyone knows that you can't levitate without a feather,'' huffed Ardaz. ''But wait! Hmmm . . . perhaps there is another way. I do so very dearly want to get rid of that rock. Could go *'kaboom'* I think. What do you think, Des?'' he asked the cat. Instantly, the cat let out a horrified shriek and darted into a crack in the tree.

''Beastly loyal, you know,'' muttered the mage.

''Oh, well, I'll do it! I will, I will! I do daresay. But oh, bother, where is my staff? I shouldn't try it without my staff, no, no. Dear me, don't tell me I lost that, too.

''I really shouldn't try it without my staff,'' he explained again to Del, but the disappointment on Del's face touched him. ''Oh well''—he chuckled—''who needs a staff anyway? Here we go, here we go!''

Ardaz scratched his chin and mumbled as he pieced together the rhymes of the spell. ''Oh, yes,'' he said finally. ''That'll do! That'll do, I daresay!''

He cleared his throat and straightened his hat and began chanting in an arcane tongue and waving his arms in circular movements. He stopped when he noticed that Del was gawking at him. ''Don't look at me, you silly boy! Watch the rock!''

Del turned quickly and Ardaz resumed his casting and a few seconds later, *kaboom!* A bolt of lightning blasted from his hands and sundered the boulder into a million pieces.

Del nearly jumped out of his pants. ''Holy shit!'' he cried. ''How? What the . . .'' He spun around and there was Ardaz, hopping around on one foot and flapping his hands wildly like some demented pigeon, wisps of smoke trailing from his fingers.

''Ow, ow, ow, ow, ow!'' shouted the mage, but his

voice was muffled, for his great hat had breached his nose and fallen completely over his head. "Ow, ow, ow, ow!"

"Are you all right?" yelled Del, rushing over to him.

"Yes, yes," came the smothered reply. "Should've used my staff, I do daresay!"

Del lifted the hat from the wizard's absolutely hairless head and was taken aback, for embedded in the middle of Ardaz's forehead was a gem, a silvery moonstone.

"Was a good shot, though, wasn't it?" Ardaz chuckled, shooting Del a friendly wink.

"Perfect," agreed Del absently, his unblinking eyes riveted on the gemstone.

"What's the matter, my boy?"

"That stone in your forehead . . ." began Del.

"My mark?" asked Ardaz.

"I've seen one like it."

"It is the mark of magic. Not many of these lying around, you know. Oh, no no. Four and no more in all the land. And not on display for anyone to see, ha. But where could you have seen . . . oh yes, you've been to Pallendara then, and seen the white pearl of Istaahl."

"No, I've never been to Pallendara," replied Del. "Did Thalasi have such a stone?"

"Eeeyiaaa!" shrieked Ardaz. He jumped around wildly, eyes darting to and fro as though he expected demons to surround them at any moment. "Sssh! Sssh!" he cried, and slapped his hand over Del's mouth. "Don't speak that name! No, no!" He tightened his hand over Del's mouth as he again glanced all about for signs of impending doom. The wizard had an incredibly strong grip, and try as he may, Del could not break free. Intent on his scan, Ardaz took no heed of Del's struggling and didn't let go until he finally noticed that Del was turning a delicate shade of blue.

"Sorry about that," Ardaz apologized. "But we mustn't speak the name of the Black Warlock! An evil summons if ever there was one, I do daresay! He did have a stone, a sapphire, most powerful stone of all! Deep, oh the richest blue. At first, mind you; but it turned black when his heart turned black, yes, yes, the blackest sapphire. You haven't seen him, I pray!"

"The stone I saw was green. An emerald, in Avalon."

"Clas Braiyelle," whispered Ardaz, his voice even and much calmer, as though the mention of the beautiful witch had shot a sedative through his veins. "You've seen Brielle. You are blessed, my boy, blessed indeed. Please, you must tell me all about it."

"Sure," replied Del, "but first I have to give you something." He pulled out the scroll and handed it to the wizard. "Bellerian gave it to me. He said that you'll know what it's about."

Ardaz snatched the case from Del, popped off the cap, and drew out the parchment. "It is!" he exclaimed. "It is, it is! Oh good! Stupendously marvelous!

"The spell," he shouted in explanation to Del's blank stare. "The spell to grow back my hair!

"But wait! What's this?" he cried when he noticed something on the edge of the scroll. "Oh, no! Oil. Oil from curious fingers. You've touched it! Oh, no!"

"I didn't know," explained Del.

"Oh, bother it all!" groaned the wizard. "That's how it all happened in the first place. Someone touching a scroll. Supposed to make a fire burn brighter, sure, sure, but *poof* right in my face! And now you've handled this one! Oh bother, I'll probably grow hair out of my ears!"

"I'm truly sorry," said Del, biting his lip in an unsuccessful attempt to stifle a laugh.

"You think that's funny?" snapped Ardaz. But his visage mellowed as he thought about it. "I suppose it would be, wouldn't it! Ha-ha! Hair out of my ears! Oh how jolly, how very jolly!"

When they had finished their laugh, Del recounted his adventures to Ardaz. Unlike Mitchell at the court of Arien, Del told of everything that had befallen his party honestly and completely. The wizard listened with sincere interest, but was especially attentive when Del recounted his dream of being watched by a green eye. And he made Del repeat the parts about Avalon three times.

A starry evening was in full bloom by the time Del had finished.

"Ah, Avalon," said Ardaz. "Clas Braiyelle it is called by the Illumans, you know. A fitting nickname." His voice had lost all hints of its frantic edge, as though he had suddenly realized how important the return of the ancient ones could be to his world. "I envy you that you have seen her, but I would not tell anyone else of it, if I were you."

"Why not?" asked Del. "I told the rangers, Andovar and Belexus, and they weren't upset."

"The rangers are wise, very wise," replied Ardaz. "Under the eyes of Bellerian, they remember the past and they understand the power and goodness of Brielle. Most men and even many Illumans fear the witch and would shun you if they knew you had seen her. The Children of the Moon have forgotten what she did for their race back in the distant past. Hah, many have even forgotten what I, Ardaz, did for them at the beginning of their age. It is a sad time that we live in."

"I have to go back," muttered Del. "To Avalon, to her."

"If all that you tell me is true, I think she would like that, too." The wizard smiled. "But let me think about it.

"Now go, my boy, back to the city and quickly. The moon will be rising soon. Wouldn't want to miss the festival, would you?"

"Will you be there?" asked Dell.

"I might," replied Ardaz. "But for now, you've given me much to think about. Yes, very much to think about."

Chapter 15

Luminas Ey-n'Abraieken

Del moved out from the glade and gingerly started down the invisible stair. He was leery at first, remembering the trouble he had coming up here in the daylight, but soon he found that the darkness was his ally. The mountain wall was still easy enough to discern towering right next to him, and his inability to see the invisible steps in the dim light didn't blatantly contradict his logic.

When he got about halfway down, he heard singing coming from the northwestern corner of the valley. Hundreds of elves, the whole city it seemed, were joined in a singular chorus of celebration. Del couldn't make out the words, for they sang in the strange enchantish tongue, but the tune and tempo made the emotions of the song clear to him. They sang a joyful melody, yet mysterious, almost supernatural, as though their song was for the stars and the heavens alone to understand.

When he had finally reached the valley floor—and it seemed a long while indeed—he raced to the gathering of the elves, their haunting song still rising in the evening air. He found Billy with Sylvia and Erinel. Mitchell and Reinheiser were there, too, a little way off, talking by themselves.

"Where've you been?" Billy asked when Del approached. "We've been looking all over for you."

"A little business, that's all," said Del. "Nothing important."

Billy didn't press the issue. The thought of Del going off on some mysterious enterprise seemed perfectly normal to him. Billy was quite sure now that something unique was happening to his friend. Del alone among the remaining crewmen accepted this world with all his heart and soul, and Aielle and its peoples seemed to be returning the welcome. Everyone they met placed Del in high regard.

Sylvia looked at Del with an apologetic expression. "I pray that my father was not too harsh with you," she said, and Del knew that she was truly concerned. "You must understand that this is a dangerous time—"

"Sylvia," interrupted Del with an uncontainable grin, "your father is a perfectly wonderful elf!"

"Again you speak that word," protested Sylvia.

Del quickly hushed her. "Arien doesn't disapprove," he said. "In fact, he, the Eldar of your people, has personally given me his permission to use it. Honest."

"It's really not an insult," added Billy.

Sylvia couldn't resist their friendly smiles. "I shan't argue the point." She sighed. "I suppose that it is the way that a word is spoken that determines its intent."

"What's all this singing about?" Del asked.

"Luminas ey-n'abraieken," replied Sylvia. Del just shrugged his shoulders.

"Abraieken means celebration, a dance," explained Sylvia. "And the place we are going to we name Shaithdun-o-Illume." She sang softly.

Luminas ey-n'abraieken
Mountain shelf of moonlight
Dance your dance of freedom
Children of the restless night

Sparklings of the mirror-rock
Tivriasis's endless song
Lift your arms to the silvery orb
May her passage be bright and long

Luminas ey-n'abraieken,
Shaithdun-o-Illume!
Your light is mine alone!

Sylvia could see that her song had pleased Billy and Del, and that, in turn, brought a smile to her. "We celebrate this festival each month during the three nights of the fullest moon," she explained. "When the shelf is bright in silver light and feet dance to the song of Tivriasis! You will see, and I promise, you will enjoy."

Suddenly the crowd around them went quiet.

"Be silent now," Erinel said to the three of them. "They are about to begin! My uncle has brought the Staff of Light."

The whole gathering remained hushed and all of the torches were extinguished. In front of them, on a rock pedestal, stood Arien Silverleaf, barely more than a silhouette in the starlight. He held a crooked staff before him in one hand and rubbed its knobbed top with the other. "Illu lumin-bel," he commanded the staff. Gradually, the top began to glow, increasing in intensity until Arien was bathed in soft light. Then he clasped the staff tightly in both hands and presented it to the crowd, which responded in unison with, "Illu lumin-bel!" At once the staff obeyed their joined will, its top bursting into bright light.

Arien handed the staff to Ryell. Behind them, on the mountain wall, loomed the blackness of a tunnel entrance.

The Eldar waited for the commotion to die down, then addressed the gathering. "Four guests shall join in our dance tonight," he declared. "Men who have come to us from a far-distant place." Whispers arose throughout the gathering.

"Silence!" Arien commanded them. "The moon will be rising soon; we do not have much time. Shaithdun-o-Illume awaits. Let us find our places!"

With laughter and songs the elves bustled about into the ritual line that signaled the beginning of the celebration.

"Take my hand, DelGiudice," said Sylvia, "and stand behind me. And you, Billy Shank, take my other hand and go before me." And so it went all up and down the group, the elves forming one long chain with joined hands. Arien led the way with the Staff of Light, Ryell directly behind him. There was one break in the chain this time, though, for Mitchell stood behind Del and would not accept Del's hand.

They went into the tunnel with only the staff to guide them. Just a few places back from Arien it was difficult to see, and for those a hundred steps back, or two hundred, the winding tunnel was pitch black. This was a time of joining for the elves, a time of communication and trust in each other. Finding the way around rocks or up unevenly carved stairs depended solely on the person, the link to the light, directly ahead. Just a few feet into the blackness, Mitchell realized the futility of his stubborn anger and grabbed Del's hand.

The tunnel went only several hundred yards into the mountain, but the slow pace and the winding way made the journey seem much longer. Especially for Del, continually assaulted by Mitchell's unending stream of grumbles and complaints.

Finally Arien saw a lighter spot up ahead. "Shaithdun-o-Illume!" he called, and the elves renewed their songs and cheers.

Suddenly the outline of a man appeared at the tunnel exit and Arien stopped short in surprise.

"Who could it be?" asked a frightened Ryell. Many strange things had happened recently, not the least of which the arrival of the ancient ones, and Ryell was certain that Illuma was heading for a crisis that threatened the very existence of his people. "No one entered the tunnel before us and there is no other way to the shaithdun." Their fears were dispelled a moment later.

"Well, I daresay it's about time you got here!" came a familiar voice. "A bit past time, I should say!"

"Pray no," groaned Ryell. "The jester awaits."

Arien approached the exit. "If you wished to join the celebration, you should have come in with the line, Ardaz. The customs should not be ignored."

"Join the celebration?" echoed the mage, confused. "Oh, no no, not for that, not for that! I mean, there isn't going to be any celebration, so why would I come to join it, after all?"

"What do you mean?" asked Arien. He was at the exit, but the wizard stepped in front of him to prevent him from leaving the tunnel.

"Get out of our way, old fool!" snapped Ryell indignantly.

"The Staff of Light must stay in the tunnel!" retorted Ardaz in a suddenly sober and deadly serious tone. "And there shall be no celebration this night!" Ryell spouted in protest, but Arien, reading the danger in the wizard's eyes, silenced him at once.

The Eldar knew well the moods of Ardaz and turned back to him with genuine concern. "Is there trouble afoot?"

Back down the line, the elves and the men wondered what the delay was all about. Mitchell was especially impatient; if he had been given a choice, he wouldn't even have been here.

"Ungden's spies are in Mountaingate," replied Ardaz grimly. "I am sorry, but a party on the shelf would certainly be visible down there."

"How do you know they are there?" snapped Ryell, ever doubting the wizard. "If this is one of your games . . ."

"I know!" retorted Ardaz, and Ryell was knocked back by the bared power in the wizard's voice.

"Never before have they come this far," muttered Arien.

"Never before has Ungden been this determined," Ardaz replied grimly. The wizard feared that something far worse and more dangerous than Ungden the Usurper was behind this latest attempt to discover the whereabouts of Illuma.

Arien was distressed at canceling the celebration, but he heeded the words of the wizard. He handed the Staff of Light back to Ryell. "Have this passed back to the other end of the line," he instructed. "Now is the time for our people to make preparations; the celebration will have to wait.''

''Arien,'' moaned Ryell, ''surely you're not going to ruin this night on the words of that one.''

''Instruct the people to go back to the city,'' Arien continued. Ryell swung around angrily on his heel and started down the line, but Arien wasn't through with him yet.

''Summon the nine second-born and accompany them to the shaithdun. It is time for a council, I believe.''

''Do you wish anything else, my Lord?'' grumbled Ryell with pouting sarcasm.

''I do,'' retorted Arien sternly. ''Have my daughter and Erinel bring our visitors. This trouble may concern them as well.''

Arien waited at the exit to the tunnel to greet the others as they arrived. ''Our council may be grim,'' he said to Del and Billy, ''but at the least you have come at the right time to see Loch-sh'Illume, the Moon Pool, at its height of beauty.''

They stepped onto the shelf and saw that the Eldar had not exaggerated. They stood on a flat ledge of a bowl-shaped gorge surrounded by high mountain walls of mica rock that opened out to the evening sky as they rose. The walls below the ledge were vertical, though, dropping straight down for hundreds of feet to a deep, cool mountain pool. A few yards to the left of the tunnel, a stream rushed out from a hole in the rock face and dove headlong down. This was Tivriasis, ever singing her haunting notes that conjured images of heroic adventures and mystical lands as she danced across the rock walls on her journey to the darkness of the water below.

The only break in the mountain wall was on the southern side of the gorge, starting as a crack down by the pool, but widening as it rose so that all of the southlands were open to the viewer. In daylight, Mountaingate and Avalon were clearly visible, but in the night, only the shadowy forms of the southern mountain range and an occasional light on the wide Calvan plain beyond could be seen.

No torches were necessary on the shelf except on the darkest of nights, for even by the stars, the abundant mica reflected enough light to see by. On a night such as this, with a clear moon rising, the ledge was bright with ghostly silver.

As Del stood mesmerized by the beauty before him, an old man came up behind him and tapped him on the shoulder. At first Del didn't recognize the man, for though he wore a hat and robe similar to those of the wizard Ardaz, he had a long white beard, bushy eyebrows, and flowing white hair that trailed well below his neck. A large raven perched comfortably on his shoulder. It was Ardaz, of course, as Del realized when the wizard pointed to his beard and winked.

Astounded, Del gave the beard a slight tug. The wizard cackled with amusement and twirled away to greet the others coming onto the shelf. Del gave a laugh of his own and followed, glad that Ardaz had come and wondering what manner of magic the wizard had used to gain the ledge before them.

When the last of the council group had exited the tunnel, Arien sat down with his back against the mountain wall and bid them all to sit in a semicircle about him. The Eldar hardly noticed as the others sorted themselves out, his eyes transfixed on the southern gap in the mountains and his mind drifting back across the centuries. He had been the firstborn of the second generation of Illumans, the first elf born of elven parents, and the first child born in Illuma. He remembered the time when he had stepped out onto the shaithdun and first viewed Loch-sh'Illume. Through this same gap in the mountain wall, young Arien Silverleaf had also seen the wide southlands that day and had realized that there was much more to the world than Illuma Vale and the Crystal Mountains surrounding it. His father came to him then and told him of mighty Pallendara, the city the elves call Caer Tuatha, and of wondrous Avalon and of all the wide lands in between.

Shaithdun-o-Illume became a special place to Arien. So much so that when Tivriasis, his wife and the mother of Sylvia, passed from this world, he found solace here. The song of the stream caught Arien's soul that night, its joyful melody so akin to the notes that had guided the life of the elven maid who had been his mate. Thus Arien named the stream in her memory, and on that same night he began the tradition of Luminas ey-n'abraieken.

Arien smiled as he thought of the times long ago when he, Tivriasis, and Ryell had stolen out of Illuma and journeyed to the wood of Avalon or to the northern fringes of the Calvan plains. But those were safer times, the days of Ben-rin and his heirs. Now, with Ungden the Usurper on the southern throne, no Illuman dared leave the mountain refuge.

The smile left Arien's face. Calvans, Ungden's scouts, were right on their doorstep. Even beautiful Illuma, Lochsilinilume, sanctuary of the elves of Aielle, was threatened. Sanctuary, Arien pondered, or prison? He turned to Ardaz, who had sat down beside him.

"How long shall I live, my friend?" he asked softly. "Shall it be long enough to enjoy the day that I might visit Pallendara? Or swim, perhaps, in the sea?"

It brought a tear to the wizard's eye. He understood Arien's frustration, but couldn't respond. The question was rhetorical and unanswerable, for Arien was the eldest of the elves, the first of his kind that the wizards had blessed with the gift of longevity. At this moment, propped as he was against the mountain wall, Arien seemed very old indeed to Ardaz. Since Ungden had assumed power, Arien had been under a terrible strain, and like a caged animal, he was losing his spirit, slipping slowly into a state of lethargy that Ardaz knew would bring about his passing. Even Luminas ey-n'abraieken brought only temporary relief. Other elves showed these symptoms of mortality as well; Ryell, ever walking a line of rage and frustration, perhaps foremost among them. Oftentimes Ardaz would sit at the entrance to his tower home of Brisen-ballas, looking down upon the secret vale, crying for the Children of the Moon. They deserved a better fate, this kindly race that offered nothing less than true friendship. They could bring so much to the men of Aielle, enrich their lives so. If only . . .

"If only they would give you a chance," he mumbled to Arien. The Eldar, preparing to address the council, didn't hear him.

Although it was Arien's place to open the council, an angry Ryell spoke first. Impatient and hoping to preserve at least part of the celebration, he wasn't waiting for anyone.

"How do you know of the spies, old man?" he snapped at Ardaz. "Or is this another joke of yours?" Ryell needed to feel the freedom of Luminas ey-n'abraieken. Dancing on the shelf in the moonlight was his greatest joy, a release from the constant pressures of the enemy to the south, and he didn't like having it taken away.

"No joke," answered Ardaz solemnly. "Though truly I wish it was, I wish it was. No, no." He pointed at Del. "Just after you left, I began to summon a whirlwind to clean up the mess. Of course you know that Desdemona here, trusting me implicitly as always, flew right off." He gave the raven a sarcastic snarl and Del sat confused, for he had met Desdemona as a cat. "She zipped away and I called up the whirlwind. No problem." He snapped his fingers indignantly at the raven; then under his voice so that only Desdemona could hear, he added, "The leaves will grow back.

"Now where was I? Oh, yes. As I was putting my clothes back on, Des came flapping back in a frightful tizzy and told me that there were Calvans coming through the southeast pass into Mountaingate."

"A bird!" cried Ryell. "Our celebration has been stopped by the cackle of a bird!" He jumped to his feet and looked south to the blackness of Mountaingate. "I see nothing down there, old man. Where is the fire of their camp? Do they enjoy the darkness?" But even as he spat his sarcasm, the light of a campfire sprang up on the dark field. Ryell nearly tumbled from the ledge when he saw it, and the others jumped up, gasping with astonishment. Only Arien, never doubting the word of the wizard, was not surprised.

"It seems you owe the bird an apology, Ryell," he said coolly.

"They have never come this far before," said Ryell, subdued now. "What does it mean?"

The Eldar, determined to maintain a calm demeanor, answered grimly, "It means that Ungden has a clue to our whereabouts, for he certainly believes that Illuma is more than a legend. Or it means nothing at all. We cannot be sure."

"Oh, yes we can be sure, Arien," said Ardaz, "Des here listened to them. They search for us and they know we are nearby."

Del studied the wizard carefully. Something about him had changed. He had seen the wizard's serious side once before, when they had spoken of Brielle earlier in the day, but this was something more profound. Before, Ardaz had been energetic, almost frantic, yet despite all of his jumping around, he seemed a fragile old man. Del had even worried that he would hurt himself. Now that fear was gone; the wizard emanated strength, an aura of supernatural power about him. Before, Ardaz had seemed foolish, but now there was no mistaking the knowledge in his eyes. Deep knowledge, understanding beyond what a mortal man could know. Suddenly, the truth about Ardaz, and the implications of Calae's fanciful tale, dropped their full weight upon Del. This man before him was a wizard, one of the Four trained by the Colonnae in the first days of Ynis Aielle. This man had been alive more than twelve centuries! In the shock of his revelation, he nearly blurted it out loud. It wouldn't have mattered if he had; from the awestruck look on Del's face, the wizard had guessed his thoughts anyway. He gave Del a wink and a grin.

"Then we are lost," moaned one of the others above the grumblings.

"Nay," retorted Arien sternly, and the group was

silenced by the firmness of his tone. "We are not lost. Even should the Calvans discover the tunnel entrance, they will never find the passage through the underground maze."

"But if they do find it," said Ryell in a grim voice, "we have barely three hundred spears, Caer Tuatha alone can raise thousands."

The thought of a war intrigued Mitchell. Given time and the proper opportunities, he would rise to power over these primitive folk. His knowledge of weapons alone could determine the victor in this sword-wielding world. With characteristic impatience, he entered the debate.

"Must there be a war?" he asked, hoping that the answer would be yes.

"A war or a slaughter," muttered Ryell.

"If Ungden finds us," said Arien, "he will destroy us. His anger is rooted deep in his past. In his eyes, because we are different, we must die."

"Sounds familiar," whispered Billy. Del clasped Billy's brown hand.

Mitchell rose and strutted to the center of the council circle, acting as though he was a savior sent to deliver these people. "You are not lost!" he proclaimed loudly, savoring the intrigued and hopeful looks that he saw were upon him. "In my world, we had ways and weapons with which a few could defeat many!" He paused, awaiting their enthusiastic cries for him to continue.

He didn't get what he expected. While most of the second-born sat stunned, Ardaz's face went white with horror and Arien leaped up in a burst of rage.

"Silence!" commanded the Eldar. Mitchell was twice Arien's size, but in his anger the Eldar towered over the captain. "There is no place for your weapons or your ways in Aielle!"

"Let him speak!" demanded Ryell. Arien spun on him, his face twisted with disbelief and renewed fury. But Ryell didn't back down. "Perhaps there is some value in what he has to say."

Arien remained unblinking.

"We face extermination!" roared Ryell as if that alone was justification for his position. "A tyrant is Ungden! We are more worthy than he and his miserable humans to walk this land! What of our birthright?" While Ryell realized that he couldn't sway Arien, he knew that some of the second-born were as fed up as he with hiding in fear. The will of the council could force concessions from the Eldar.

Several conversations began all at once and it quickly became apparent that the council was hopelessly divided by Mitchell's hinted proposal. Arien looked to Ardaz for advice and the wizard's return stare was resolute and uncompromising, confirming Arien's instinctive feelings and fears.

"No!" Arien declared flatly. "And I'll hear no more of this! I shall not start a war. Nor shall I bring back the ways of man before e-Belvin Fehte! Have you forgotten the tales of horror? We are morally bound by the simple fact of our existence, by all that Aielle is supposed to be, never to repeat those errors!"

"If we are found," offered one of the second-born.

"Then we will do what we must!" snapped Arien.

"Then it will be too late," muttered Ryell.

Mitchell backed away from Arien's anger and rejoined his companions. Del, trembling with rage of his own, was waiting for him.

"Captain," he gnashed through gritted teeth, "I don't think we were sent here to start a war!"

"No," interjected Reinheiser, "but have you considered that perhaps we were sent to ensure that the right side emerges victorious. This conflict seems unavoidable."

Del was concerned that Reinheiser might be correct in his observations, but he was even more worried about which side Mitchell would consider "the right side." He felt sure that the captain was more interested in personal gain than in the welfare of Ynis Aielle.

And, despite his reservations, Del remained convinced that there was a better way. He detested war and all the evil and pain it wrought. If he couldn't stick by his principles and ideals in a time of crisis, then they were nothing more than useless rhetoric. He believed, he had to believe, that reason, not violence, was the first and most useful step toward resolving a conflict.

"There must be another way," Del said to the council. "An envoy to show Ungden that we pose no threat to him and are willing to live in peace with Calva."

"Not a chance, my boy," replied Ardaz. "No, no, that would never work. I knew Ungden's ancestor and he was just as unbending as this stubborn fool. The Usurper's mind cannot be changed. I was in Caer . . . uh, Pallendara the night Ungden stole the throne. I bear witness to the blood of his methods and the evil in his heart. Believe me, there is no chance for peace as long as Ungden rules in the city."

"Indeed, Ungden has proven himself a serpent with every act," agreed Arien.

"And there is an even greater evil behind his throne, I fear," Ardaz mumbled under his breath.

The uncomfortable silence that followed remained unbroken for a long while. Arien weighed his thoughts carefully, for he knew that all of Illuma would depend on him for guidance.

"Sylvia and Erinel," he said finally, "lead our guests back to the city. Quarter them in my house, and there," he instructed the men, "you shall remain. The debate before us is for the ears of the council alone. We may not return before dawn."

The six stood up to leave. They all had questions or suggestions on their minds, but Arien had made it clear from the tone of his voice that it was not their place to speak. They all bowed, except Mitchell, and turned toward the tunnel.

"There's a torch for you within the tunnel," said Ardaz. Sylvia nodded.

Perplexed, Reinheiser stopped and studied the wizard. The physicist knew his own prowess in observation and he knew there had been no torch in the tunnel other than the Staff of Light. The staff had gone back to the city with the line of elves and no one had been near the entrance since they all arrived on the shelf.

Yet when they entered the tunnel, a torch was indeed lying on the ground in front of them. And when Erinel picked it up, its tip magically burst into flame.

Del wasn't surprised.

The private council began as soon as the group departed. There was much talking and bickering, for there were two very different viewpoints on what course of action to take. Ryell and his supporters wanted to listen to Mitchell's plans and waylay Calva's forces quickly, defeating Ungden before he could truly organize against Illuma. The other view, championed by Arien, was to avoid war for as long as possible at any cost, hoping for relief from within Calva; perhaps an uprising against Ungden. There was much debate, but in the end, very little was resolved. Finally, as the sky brightened with the approaching dawn, Arien called an end to the discussions.

"It seems we are divided," he said. "Hopelessly divided, for the present, at least. Therefore, as the Eldar, it is my decision that we shall stay hidden and wait until we know more of the situation before us." This brought grumbles from Ryell's group. "And none," continued Arien above the murmur, "save those sent out on missions for this council, shall leave the city."

"And what of our guests?" snapped Ryell. "They are men, after all, and I do not trust them." Ardaz shifted uneasily and stroked Desdemona, who had transformed into a black cat again.

"Yet you would trust the one called Mitchell to lead us against Calva," replied Arien sharply.

"I wanted only his plans to defeat Calva," retorted Ryell, "that we could study and learn from them. I would not entrust him with leadership."

Arien closed his eyes and sought the feelings within his heart. He felt that he must bide his time and react to things as they happened, for he simply did not know enough yet to act boldly, and a rash decision could destroy them.

''Of our guests,'' he commanded, ''they shall be given all the comforts we can provide.'' The grumblings began again. ''But,'' added Arien to quiet the complaints, ''they shall not be allowed to leave their rooms, and guards shall be set outside their doors.'' He looked around the council, his eyes alone showing him to be set in his decision, and at the same time begging approval, relief from the tremendous pressures of leadership.

''Agreed,'' answered the others.

''It is a wise decision,'' added Ryell. Ardaz thought so, too, except that he knew a voice from a wood called out to the one named Del. The wizard feared the voice, for he did not understand why it beckoned so, and he knew, too, that its call would not go unheeded.

''Then, as we are agreed, let us end this council and return to the city,'' said Arien. ''And let us hope,'' he added grimly, ''that the Usurper's eyes remain blind to our home.''

Chapter 16

Patience

Del wasn't terribly upset when he awakened at mid-morning and found that he would not be permitted to leave the room. His sleep had been filled with dreams of Avalon and now a fantasy of dancing with the fair Brielle in a moonlit field haunted his thoughts. His surroundings, inasmuch as they were not Avalon, had become irrelevant and one room would do as well as the whole city.

Billy, though, was truly miserable. From the outset of this adventure, he had adopted a stoic attitude. Even when they had first emerged from the depths of the sea and found their world destroyed, Billy had shrugged it off with grim resolve. Grudging acceptance was his only protection, though he realized that the fine edge of discipline necessary to maintain stability cut both ways. He could defend against depression, but to do so in a situation as unpredictable and uncontrollable as this he had to also avoid the emotional highs, false plateaus ringed by sheer drops. Up to now he had kept that edge, even in the face of Avalon's magical allure.

But Billy's discipline had reached its limits. In the afternoon he had spent among the elves, he had come to love Illuma and its inhabitants, with their joyous songs and dances and their carefree way of life. He sat now in dismay, fallen from his unintended plateau, staring out the room's small window at the frolicking below. For though the shadow of Ungden was upon the elves, it could not put an end to their eternal merrymaking.

* * *

In the room across the hall, Reinheiser was trying to calm down the furious captain.

"How dare they?" shouted Mitchell, the veins in his neck standing out in protest. "Locking me up! And after I offered to help them!"

"A hollow offer," snorted Reinheiser. He knew Mitchell well, his desires and ambitions, and knew that the captain wouldn't help anybody unless doing so would bring him closer to his own goals. These elves, so childish and carefree, had no place in Mitchell's final plans. He might use them, or enslave them, but he certainly had no intention of helping them.

"What do you mean by that?" the captain asked warily.

"Come now, Captain. Surely you do not expect to raise an army from these helpless little creatures."

"No," replied Mitchell with a nasty laugh. "But they don't know that."

"Of course not." Reinheiser agreed. "And do not worry, I believe that you have convinced a few of them at least that you are a friend."

"And this is how they repay me!" He slammed his fist into the locked door. "I've got to get out of here!"

"To Calva, I suppose."

"Of course to Calva. And the court of Ungden."

"Where you will take over?" mused the physicist. "I do not think that Ungden is one who will give up his ill-won throne so willingly."

"Of course he won't. But maybe he'll reward a great leader from another world–a man who delivers to him his greatest enemy–with a place of honor in his court, or perhaps even a little kingdom of my own."

"Either of which would be a solid base for you to raise an army," reasoned Reinheiser.

"Yes, Martin, an army with guns!" The captain glowered, savoring his fantasy of power with obscene delight. "Then I'll rule this world!" The light left his face. "Oh, what's the use?" he groaned. "It's all just a dream. Even if we could get out of this room, which we can't, we'd never find our way out of this stupid valley."

"Yes we would." Reinheiser cackled, and he was the one beaming now. He pulled a rolled parchment out of his cloak and presented it to Mitchell. On it was a map showing the way back to Mountaingate.

The captain's enthusiasm returned at once. "Where'd you get this?"

"I made it."

"But how?"

"Child's play," answered Reinheiser. "When the elves escorted us to this valley, I counted my steps and noted the turns and passages we passed in the tunnel."

"So that's why you pulled that damned stunt about being afraid of caves," said Mitchell. "To get next to the wall."

Reinheiser nodded casually, feigning boredom as if it was all but a minor feat for one such as he. "The map is not perfect, but I am sure it will be sufficient to get us out of here."

"You've got some mind," said Mitchell, his face barely wide enough to hold his grin. "When do we leave?"

"Patience, my friend, patience," answered Reinheiser. "The elves will relax their guard when the immediate danger has passed, and then—"

"And then," interrupted the captain, spreading his arms wide as though he was addressing a crowd. "All hail Mitchell, Lord of Aielle!" He began to laugh loudly, a wicked laugh.

Reinheiser joined him, though less heartily. The physicist knew that there were other powers to contend with that Mitchell hadn't considered.

Late that afternoon, Ardaz and Ryell sat on the dais in the throne room as Arien paced uneasily back and forth before them.

"Arien, let him go," pleaded Ardaz. "We can trust that one."

"Trust him!" exclaimed Ryell. "He is a man, how can we believe there is any good in him? Men have shown nothing but hatred for Illumans. If they could find us, they would kill all of us in an instant! And you ask us to entrust our lives to one!''

''Being a man, I certainly resent that opinion,'' said Ardaz, though he understood Ryell's bitterness toward his kind. It was a common tale in Illuma that Erinel's parents, Ryell's brother, and his wife, were slaughtered on a mountain pass by men when Erinel was just a child. Arien doubted the story, suspecting instead that the unfortunate couple had been waylaid by rogue talons, and though Ardaz didn't believe a word of it, he had no proof to dispute Ryell.

''You are different,'' replied Ryell. ''You are a wizard, and harmless enough.''

''What business could he possibly have in the witch's wood?'' asked Arien, keeping the conversation in line. Arguments between Ryell and Ardaz escalated easily and Arien knew from experience that these two could ramble on for hours if allowed to be sidetracked.

''What business, indeed!'' replied Ardaz. ''Why, what business could he possibly have here? This one's path, I think, is guided by forces beyond us, you know, far, far beyond us. I wouldn't think it wise for us to detain him. Might get them mad, you see, and we wouldn't want that. No, if he wishes to return to Avalon, then we should let him.''

''Should we give them all the free run of Illuma as well?'' Ryell sneered. ''And let these unseen forces you speak of lead us to our destruction?''

''No, Ryell, certainly not!'' replied the wizard. ''I speak only of the one called DelGiudice, and he, I daresay, has earned our trust.''

''That he has,'' agreed Arien. ''Still, I do not understand what she could possibly want with him.''

''She probably wants to turn him into a squirrel''—Ryell snickered—''that he can dance among her trees.''

''Now you've gone too far!'' cried Ardaz, and he leaped up, his eyes flashing with fury. Ryell sat composed, impervious to the threat. Wizards were bumbling old fools, he thought, and witches merely the workings of a child's imagination.

"Enough, Ardaz!" commanded Arien, but the wizard did not back away. Arien stepped between him and Ryell and matched the wizard's fire with his own unyielding glare.

"When you returned to us thirty years ago, you agreed to honor my word and abide by our rules," Arien said sternly, offering no room for compromise. Ardaz grudgingly sat down.

"Ryell's years are not numbered as long as ours," offered Arien to appease the wizard. "He does not remember the Emerald Witch, or the old days when magic filled the air. Those times are only tales by the fireplace to him."

"He's going to learn better, then, he is at that!" grumbled Ardaz, but his anger yielded quickly to the memories of that past age that came upon him.

"Arien," he said calmly, "recall if you will, the days way back, the days of Ben-rin and Umpleby and the Justice Stone. I did much for your parents and kin back then, and I asked for nothing in return except your friendship and your trust. Trust me now, I beg. Let DelGiudice go."

"What do you think she wants with him?" asked Arien.

"I do not know that she wants him at all," replied Ardaz. "I only know that he must choose his own path, and now he chooses Avalon. Let him go, Arien. I will have friends watching him, I promise."

Arien knew in his heart that Del had earned and deserved the trust of the Illumans. He knew the consequences as well; Ryell and many others would be furious with him if he let Del go. And this was not a good time for his people to be divided.

But he decided finally to follow his heart, reasoning that the sacrifice of conscience was a far greater evil than anything Ungden could bring upon them. Arien would not accept that loss for the sake of precaution. With grim determination, yet softened with empathy, he looked Ryell straight in the eye. "DelGiudice may go."

Ryell turned away.

"Splendid!" shouted Ardaz.

"But only after," continued the Eldar, "the Calvans are clear of the lower hills around Mountaingate."

"Desdemona is watching them now. She will let me know when they are gone."

"Also on that day, the other three may again walk freely in the valley," said Arien. "We must learn if they, too, are worthy of our trust." Infuriated, barely holding a thin line of control, Ryell turned back and shot Arien a look of utter contempt.

"Be calm, my friend," said Arien. "You I appoint to oversee the watch of the other three, and you yourself shall escort DelGiudice down to the archway at Mountaingate. From there you can see that he enters Clas Braiyelle, and if that wood of peace and order allows him entry, then know he is no friend of Ungden the Usurper."

Though he honestly believed that allowing the man to leave was a grave mistake, Ryell accepted Arien's concessions as a reaffirmation of their friendship and with the knowledge that Arien truly wished to placate him. "And the other three must return to, and remain in, their rooms at night," he suggested.

"As you wish," replied Arien.

"Then I am satisfied."

Del's heart was lifted when Ardaz came to him with the news that he would be allowed to return to Avalon. Billy, too, was thrilled when he learned that he would soon be able to again walk freely among the elves. The wizard thought that he had done them a favor by informing them of Arien's decision, but in truth, the two men grew even more miserable as the days dragged by and still Desdemona did not return with the news that the Calvan scouts were gone.

During this time, Sylvia and Erinel visited the room often and were a tremendous comfort to the two men. Soon the four had become great friends, exchanging fine tales. Del was a bit disappointed, though, that neither Sylvia nor Erinel shared his enthusiasm about his return to Avalon. Whenever he spoke of Brielle, they looked at each other with concern and pity, as though they knew something about the witch that he did not, and they changed the subject at the first chance. Del began to understand Ardaz's advice to him about keeping his meeting with the witch secret. The wizard had apparently been right; even the good people of Illuma didn't fully accept the witch of the wood.

Ardaz spent most of the time in the other room, talking more with Reinheiser than Mitchell. They were a perfect match, for the physicist was an attentive audience and the wizard loved to talk. Reinheiser pressed Ardaz for stories of Istaahl, the White Mage, and the city of Pallendara, which the elves called Caer Tuatha. Try as he may, though, he could not get the wizard to elaborate about the Black Warlock, Morgan Thalasi, other than the common recounting of the Battle of the Four Bridges and of the days before the first mutation.

Finally, shortly after breakfast on the morning of the sixth day, Desdemona returned to Ardaz with the news that Mountaingate was clear.

"They stayed a long time," said Arien when the wizard reported to him. "Do you think they found anything?"

"Oh, no, no," replied Ardaz. "They were just stubborn, that's all."

"Let us hope," Arien replied. "Go then and inform DelGiudice. He will want to be off right away. And tell the others that they may now leave their rooms."

"Oh, simply splendid!" cried Ardaz, and he bolted out of the room.

"Take Erinel along with you and DelGiudice," Arien said to Ryell.

"Yes, Eldar," answered Ryell, "and woe to him if the wood refuses him."

"It shall not."

* * *

A short time later, Arien and Ardaz were seeing the three off at the tunnel entrance on the western edge of the valley.

"Well, let's get moving," said Del impatiently. "Do you have a blindfold for me?"

"No, friend," said Arien. He gave Ryell a sidelong glance. "This time you may travel without one."

"I'm flattered," replied Del. "I really am, but I'd prefer to be blindfolded. If something goes wrong and I'm caught by Calvans, it'd be better for all of us if I honestly couldn't lead them here."

Ardaz burst out in laughter. "There, Ryell, he has passed your silly little test."

Arien, too, smiled broadly. "We hoped that you would see this wisdom." Again he eyed Ryell. "We hoped that you would care enough not to jeopardize our safety." He tossed Del a hood. "Farewell, my friend, I look forward to your return."

"I'll be back," Del assured them. "Good-bye for now. And take care of Billy for me!" He shouldered the pack they had prepared for him, donned his hood, and entered the tunnel with Ryell and Erinel.

"There he goes," muttered Mitchell, standing with Reinheiser a short distance away.

"It is better that he leaves," replied Reinheiser. "DelGiudice would fight you if he knew your plans, Captain."

"He's an insect!" growled Mitchell. "And I'm going to come back and step on him!"

The journey to Mountaingate didn't seem long at all to Del. He skipped through the tunnel and down the trail full of anticipation, his feet barely touching the ground. He could hardly stand still when the time came for Erinel to remove his blindfold.

"We are at the field, and there lies your destination," grumbled Ryell, pointing to the distant line of trees and glad that this whole thing was almost over.

"Ardaz will know when I return?" asked Del. "I don't want to be stranded down here."

"He will know," Erinel reassured him. "And do not worry, someone will be here to meet you. Now, off you go!"

"Good-bye, then," said Del, and he raced off to Avalon and his dream, his heart pounding.

But when he got to the forest, Del found no entrance. The road was gone! Confused, he began searching up and down the line of trees, yet no trail was to be found. In fact, the trees always seemed thickest wherever he searched, as though they were huddling together before him to block his path. He couldn't even find any opening large enough for him to enter the wood. "That's strange," he whispered.

Under the archway, Ryell fitted an arrow to his bow.

"Uncle, no!" cried Erinel.

"Yes!" retorted Ryell. "It is the will of Arien and all have agreed. Look for yourself, Erinel, Clas Braiyelle will not have him! He is a spy of Ungden, certainly, and we have been deceived!" He drew back on his bowstring and began creeping across the field, Erinel following nervously.

At the wood, Del stood scratching his head. "How strange," he muttered, mimicking the voice of his new friend, the wizard. "How very strange."

Chapter 17

Clas Braiyelle

Ryell raised his bow and took deadly aim.

"Please, Uncle," begged Erinel, "there must be another way!" He grasped the arrow. "Surely he will surrender."

Del didn't notice them, though they were only a short distance away. He stood perplexed, staring at the living barrier before him. He had been here just a week ago, traveled to this very spot down a path through these same woods. Yet now there was no path. The elves called this place Clas Braiyelle, "home of Brielle," and such a name carried implications that went much deeper. As Talas-dun was an extension of the blackness of Morgan Thalasi, so Clas Braiyelle reflected the spirit of its namesake. When Del had crossed through here, he had sensed the magical essence that stamped the name of Brielle upon every aspect of Avalon, but only the very eldest of the Illumans, Ardaz, and the rangers could truly appreciate the relationship between the witch and her wood. She could alter the paths and close the borders as surely as she could clench her fist, could see through the eyes of the birds as easily as through her own. They were one, this woman and the land she had nurtured, soulmates and spirit mates journeying the paths of time in perfect harmony.

"Take your hand away," commanded Ryell. He jerked the arrow from Erinel and refitted it to his bow. "Too much have I heard of this one's lies and I shall accept no pleas for surrender. This human will get all that he and his kind deserve!" He turned back to aim, but Del was gone—gone down a path entering Avalon.

"Clas Braiyelle accepted him!" cried Erinel. "He has not deceived us, yet you would have slain him!"

Ryell said nothing, caught somewhere between relief and his unrelenting anger.

Del trotted down the path, whistling and humming as he went. The sun seemed warmer in here and more friendly, and the breeze that sifted through the trees carried the scents and sounds of springtime and irresistible contentment. Del was truly alone for the first time in this strange new world, yet he remained unafraid, even unconcerned. He felt at home in these woods and welcome, oblivious to the fact that Avalon had allowed him entry only when his life was at stake.

He saw the mark of Brielle everywhere that morning, in the flowered embankments bustling with the frenzy of newly awakened insects, in the evergreen groves, dark and proud survivors of winter's coldest blast, and he heard the rush of her spirit in the song of the streams swollen from the thaw on the mountains. Still, the witch remained ever elusive. Del hadn't given any thought as to how he would find her, he just assumed that she would be there to greet him when he entered her domain. But Avalon was a large wood, stretching many miles westward and many more to the south. In the elation of his fantasy, Del hadn't even considered the scope of the task before him.

He did not see her that morning and was a bit disappointed when he broke for lunch. His mood quickly took a pleasant turn, though, for as he sat in a small clearing munching on a biscuit that the elves had packed for him, several rabbits poked their heads from the surrounding brush to inspect him. Apprehensive for just a moment, they hopped right up to join him.

"So they think I belong here, too." Del laughed, and he happily shared some of his food.

After lunch, Del said good-bye to his little friends and resumed his quest with renewed optimism. But he searched in vain the rest of that day and far into the night. He sat down with his back propped against a tree, meaning only to take a short break, when weariness finally overcame him. Too exhausted to be concerned with comfort, he fell fast asleep in that position. Again he dreamed of starlit fields and dancing with Brielle to the music of the night, and he was at peace.

The dream was all too short, as wonderful dreams always are, and it seemed like only minutes later that the morning sun dispelled the enchantment. The night had been chilly, summer was still nearly a month away, and the hard tree merciless on his back. Groaning with every twist, Del dragged himself to his feet and tried to stretch out the stiffness. Although he was certain he'd wear a grimace the rest of that morning, he refused to be daunted. ''Today will be the day,'' he assured himself.

But it wasn't. The animals danced in the trees, the sun burned warm in the blue sky above, and the magic of Avalon lay deep all about him. Still Del saw no woman that day, and he heard no singing.

Nor did he find her that night; nor the next day; nor the next night. As dawn broke the fourth morning, he was utterly frustrated, his determination ebbing away.

He trudged on, fearing that if he stopped, his eyes would ever after turn to Avalon with an unanswered longing. He shut out the beauty of the wood as much as he could that day, narrowing his vision to a single goal and following every trail he came upon with a rushed and determined stride. One path led him to a tangled cluster of white birch trees. The ground around them was soft, even muddy in some spots from the overflow of a nearby brook, and fallen branches were littered thickly about. Del should have had more sense than to go in, but his frustration had bred a reckless stubbornness. He paid for his foolishness when he lost his footing and, in trying to catch himself, gashed his arm on the sharp point of a broken branch. The wound wasn't too serious, yet it proved more than Del's battered emotions could take.

''Damn it!'' he screamed aloud. ''Where are you, Brielle? Why can't I find you?''

''So, tis for meself ye be seekin,'' came a melodic whisper behind him.

Del stood as if turned to stone. A huge lump welled in his throat, his stomach knotted, and such a great fit of panic swept over him that he had to fight for his breath. It was she, he knew, and he had to face her. He had longed for this and feared it all at once. A million unanswered questions stood behind him, the realization of his fantasy or the greatest disappointment in his life. With all his willpower, he fought off the tension that gripped him and, still trembling, turned to meet his dream.

Del thought he had prepared for this moment, but when he saw her now, wearing a white gossamer gown, her blond hair hanging loosely about her shoulders and her green eyes ablaze with the light of the morning sun, he was overwhelmed.

"And ye huv been lookin for me long?" she asked.

Forever, thought Del, only managing to stammer out, "Four days."

"All ye need do was tell it to the wind," she said.

"The wind?"

"Ayuh," answered Brielle. "If ye speak out yer thoughts in me wood, I shall hear."

Del realized then that in the days he had spent in the wood, he had not mentioned Brielle's name at all. Despite his nervousness, or perhaps because of it, he began to laugh. Brielle responded with a polite smile, though she didn't quite understand what he found so humorous. Then she saw the blood on Del's sleeve. She took hold of his arm and turned it so she could better inspect the wound.

"Ye huv hurt yerself."

"It's nothing," replied Del, and he pulled away from her, embarrassed by the injury and by his stupidity for letting it happen in the first place. "Just a scratch."

"A wee bit more than a scratch, me eyes say to me," Brielle scolded sarcastically, making it clear to Del that he was behaving like a child and she would treat him accordingly. Del recognized the insult and admitted that she was right; the cut should at least be cleaned and dressed. He nearly laughed again at her suddenly motherly tone.

"Come," she said, extending her hand, more of a demand than a request. "I will tend to it."

"Yes, Mommy." Del chuckled under his breath.

Brielle eyed him sharply. "Must I tell ye again that in me woods yer words reach me ears?" But her wrath was feigned and Del recognized the smile behind her scowl. This time, he did laugh out loud, and Brielle joined him.

She led him to a small hillside of soft grass and scattered flowers, topped by a thick row of lilac bushes. She bid him to wait and skipped away under the shadows of the trees.

Del lay back on the slope, letting the sun warm him as he tried to sort out the jumble of emotions playing through him. In truth, he didn't know what he was feeling, recognizing only that when he looked at Brielle he was both calmed and excited. It amazed him how comfortable he felt with her, at how quickly the first-meeting jitters had faded away—for both of them, it seemed. And yet when he looked at her, he consciously had to remember to breathe and his voice threatened to crack with every syllable. Above the confusion, Del understood one thing for certain: He was happy. Just looking at the mistress of Avalon thrilled him like never before.

Brielle soon returned to the hillock bearing a small wooden bowl filled with a muddy paste, pungently sweet, like the essences of all the aromas of springtime blended together. She explained to Del that it would cleanse his wound and help it to heal, and his arm felt better as soon as she put it on.

The two sat in silence on the grass, letting the sounds and workings of the awakening wood drift by them like the lazy clouds overhead. The witch was content and at ease, the serenity and natural order of this land was her strength and her magic. After a few minutes, though, Del began to grow edgy, his eyes drawn more and more toward Brielle. He became self-conscious of the silence, wondering if Brielle expected him to start a conversation. Though he wanted to say something, everything he could think of, like mentioning the beautiful weather, seemed a ridiculous cliché.

Brielle looked at him then, and caught his gaze with her own. Still she sat smiling, relaxed and at peace, while all thoughts of comfort had flown from Del. He could hear his heart racing and was certain against reason that Brielle could as well; though she could have guessed it easily anyway by the flush in his face. To further Del's horror, he felt the sweat beading on his forehead.

Finally, he had to turn away. He glanced all around nervously, feeling more like a fool with every passing second and praying for some distraction to bail him out of this awkward fit. "How about some lunch?" he blurted on a sudden impulse when he noticed that the sun was directly overhead. He lunged for his pack, managed to fumble out one of the biscuits, and offered it to Brielle. She accepted it with curiosity, if not enthusiasm, and after one small bite, handed it back to Del.

"Tis food for the hungry," she said. "Pray ye wait for me here and I'll bring to ye food for the happy!" She tossed her mane and laughed and disappeared into the trees. Del had barely realized her abrupt departure when she returned bearing a large tray laden with the offerings of Avalon: berries plump with sweetness and piles of fruits oozing juice. Del took one look at the approaching feast and dropped his biscuits to the ground.

"Rabbit food."

Then Del tasted of the magic of Avalon, wholesome and delicious beyond comparison; he could feel the health and rejuvenation surging through him even as he ate. When he had finished, Brielle brought a flask filled with water like he had never tasted before—crystalline clear and icy cold from the mountain melt, it tingled all the way down.

He felt totally refreshed after the meal, as if all of the aches and soreness had been cleansed from his body. The paste on his arm had dried to a dust, and on a hunch, contrary to reason, he brushed it away. Sure enough, the wound had completely healed, the only sign of it a thin white line of scar.

"Unbelievable," muttered Del. He looked up at Brielle. "This whole damned thing is unbelievable." She stared back at him with no answers other than her smile.

My God, Del thought, she's beautiful. If my image of beauty were personified, it would be she. Even as he contemplated his good fortune, he remembered Andovar's words about the witch's enchantment over men. Fear swept the smile from his face.

He began cautiously, afraid to ask, yet realizing that he had to know the truth. "Someone once told me that you can be to every man what he most desires in a woman." The witch started in surprise, caught completely off guard.

"Is it true?" pressed Del.

Brielle put her head down defensively and admitted, "There is such a spell."

It was the worst pain Del had ever experienced, an emptiness beyond anything he could imagine. He hoped to believe that he had found that elusive love of his fantasies, the romance he had doubted even existed when he had accepted his engagement to Debby in that world so far away. Now he realized the trap he had fallen into. Lured by the magic of Ynis Aielle, and of this wood in particular, he had allowed his defenses to drop and had dared to dream.

"Then all this," he stammered, barely able to speak, "all this is an illusion, a game you play! How could you deceive me? Why—"

"No!" Brielle insisted, and the flash in her eyes stopped Del short. Again she lowered her eyes, she, too, feeling the pangs of loneliness. The ranger had spoken truly; often men had viewed her from afar only to see their most heartfelt desires. But that was merely a consequence of the honesty and purity of the wood. Perhaps an illusion, but more a glimpse of their own innate longing to live under such an innocent and naturally ordered existence. In her symbiosis with Avalon, Brielle was an extension of the wood as it was an extension of her. And that was her trap, an unforeseen pitfall of being such an image to the world outside her domain. For now she had met a man she might truly care for, and she wanted to be more to him than a fleeting vision in the starlight. How could he trust her? How could he believe in the substance behind the image?

"I huv no deceived ye," she said softly, her voice shaky and nervous. She felt that a lot was at stake for her in this moment and could not dare hope to convince him. "Ye huv me word, I am as I appear."

Far above any doubts he could have, Del knew that there was no lie in the mist in her eyes, for he had truly hurt her with his accusation. His smile returned tenfold.

In her insecurity, the witch couldn't interpret his visage. "Can ye no understand?" she pleaded. "Ye alone see me as truly I be. Even were I to spin the spell ye speak o this very moment, I would appear no different to ye. Ye are under no enchantment!"

But Brielle was wrong. Del was indeed under her spell, and it grew with every word she spoke and every smile she showed him. It deepened each time she tossed her golden mane carelessly about her shoulders, or lifted her face to catch the warmth of the sun, or twirled about in the free air of the unblemished wood. Del was held by the only magic that had remained in his world before Aielle, the only magic that had survived under the smothering blanket of exact sciences and precise technology. Del was in love, and the ten days he spent in Avalon with Brielle were the best he would ever know.

During the hours of daylight, Brielle showed Del a new way of looking at the world. She awakened his senses and heightened the interaction between them, intensifying those mysterious emotions he had been experiencing since that morning on the raft of his first Aiellian sunrise. Brielle helped Del to refine those feelings and understand them, to bring his awareness to new heights of enjoyment. Now, a mere fragrance on the wind could direct Del's eyes to a solitary wildflower, hidden amidst a nest of mossy gray stones. His trained vision translated the flower's texture to his sense of touch, showing him every groove and bend, the softness of the petals and the thorny stem. And what wonderful music the wind played across such an intricate surface! Inaudible to the human ear, but the flower, and Del in his melding, felt every vibration. And thus it went, so that what once would have been just a pleasant forest smell had become to Del a complete experience.

Together they observed the animals and Brielle taught Del to emulate their fluid and balanced motions. His muscles worked in true conjunction, expanding the limitations of his mortal form to levels far beyond his imagination. He felt free, with a sense of rightness and health.

By night, they danced under the stars and Brielle sang to Del songs of beauty and mystery, often in the same strange tongue he had heard among the elves. Ancient and melodic, known to the Four and taught to the elves by Ardaz, it was the song of the angels, the rhythms of the galaxies. Del joined in when he could, and though he had never before been able to carry a tune, in Avalon his voice rang clear and strong.

Thoughts of leaving the wood never entered Del's mind. This was his home now and this was the woman he would spend eternity with. But events of the world don't often allow for such plans, as Del would soon realize.

It was early in the day, the first fingers of the sun stretching out through the thinning mist and the trees. Del, just awakened, was sitting in a patch of bedewed clover in the same pine-bordered field on which he had first viewed the dancing Brielle three weeks previous. He was waiting for her now, to come to him as she did every morning. Sure enough, flashing the familiar smile that rivaled any dawn, the witch of Avalon soon skipped across the grass.

"Good morning," Del called out to her.

"Oh, but it is!" Brielle laughed, and she twirled and danced up to Del and floated down into the clover beside him.

She stared deeply at Del. He was in her thoughts all the time now, as long-forgotten feelings began to stir within her. Del sensed her vulnerability; all his feelings of insecurity had been left far behind in the joy of the previous days and he knew now that she shared his love. He moved closer to her. The time had come for them to share their first kiss.

Suddenly Brielle pulled away from him and sprang to her feet, her expression changing to shock and then anger.

Del fell back, stunned and wondering what he had done wrong, for he, unlike the witch, did not hear a tree cry out in pain.

She stood motionless with her eyes closed, focusing on the breach that threatened her domain.

How? she wondered as the picture came clear. She knew the answer; she had gotten careless.

A distraction had come into her life.

"Ye must be leavin," Brielle stammered, realizing and accepting her responsibility. She continued quickly, before Del could argue, knowing that a protest from him could break her resolve. "Go, I say. Get ye back to Lochsilinilume and do'no return!"

"What are you talking about?" cried Del.

"Go!" commanded Brielle in a tone that drove the words from Del's lips. Del reasoned that she was using some spell to silence him and wanted to resist, but the fire in her eyes was genuine and he knew better than to argue. He squinted to hold back the tears as he watched her crossing the field.

She turned back to him when she got to the pines and whispered, "Sorry, I am."

Del heard her, though he was far away, for a sudden breeze came up and carried the words to his ears.

Then she was gone and Del had no recourse except to follow her wishes. Throwing up an emotional shield of anger, he marched from the field and through the trees, trampling as direct a route to Mountaingate as he could figure. He couldn't sustain the defense and gradually his line began to waver. He was reeling emotionally, hurt and above all confused. Brielle had stung him to the core of his heart, dropped him in a breath from his highest peak to his lowest valley, and still he could not deny his true feelings for her or for this wonderful forest. He loved her and no pretense of anger could change that. His pace slowed and his course meandered, a condemned man clinging to the last minutes of his life and praying for a reprieve.

The fragrance of lilacs led him to the small hill where he and Brielle had shared their first lunch. Del started up and, lost in the memory of that pleasant morn, had nearly reached the top before he heard gruff voices coming from the other side. Startled to caution, he ducked down and crept to the bushes for a look.

Below him on the wide path was a small wagon. His first thought was that some of the rangers were about, but when he noticed the horse hitched to the wagon, he quickly dismissed that theory. Beaten and half-starved, it could hardly lift its head for lack of spirit and strength, and Del knew that no ranger would treat any animal that way. He realized then that something was wrong, though he couldn't have imagined how very wrong until, from a group of trees, pushing and grumbling with every step, appeared a band of talons!

Five of them, each with an armload of freshly cut wood, moved toward the wagon, the largest wielding a great ax and shoving the others. Unclean and loathsome, they stained the beautiful forest with their mere presence and Del barely caught himself from crying out in dismay.

"Do something," he whispered to the wind. "Someone get them out of here!" As if in answer to his plea, a large raccoon crept out of the brush on the far side of the road. It hopped up on the horse's back and began gnawing on the reins. The talons, busy with their arguing, took no notice of it. Although the horse was freed within seconds, it remained in place as though it were following instructions. When the raccoon was safely back in the brush, it bolted.

The talons let out a howl of fury and gave chase, but the horse ran with the taste of freedom blowing in its face and had no intentions of being caught by its wicked masters. Del watched with satisfaction as the miserable creatures returned, pushing and arguing tenfold, each blaming another and threatening some horrible punishment.

Then something else caught Del's eye—Brielle on a distant hill across the road. She danced about, beautiful and terrible all at once, gathering power with every move and reaching for the sky. Del followed the line of her arms upward and saw the thunderclouds. He looked back to the witch, beckoning to the rising storm, menacing and distinct in her white gown against the darkening sky.

The talons hushed when the sun disappeared, their arguing drowned away by the angry rumble of witching magic. Del nearly pitied them, they were so terrified, for they knew their fate was at hand. In a pathetic attempt to escape, they jostled about and tried to break free from each other and away from the wagon.

They had no chance. Even as they started, a bolt of lightning sizzled down from the clouds. Del covered his head and lay as flat and still as he could. Blast after blast exploded and crackled and the thunder rolled on and on, shaking the very earth beneath him.

When all was quiet, Del looked with horror upon the splintered remains of the wagon and the charred, smoking bodies of the intruders.

Then a small twister whistled in just above the trees, not too far from Del. Unafraid, he understood now that this fury was aimed. The whirlwind swept down upon the road and sucked up every trace of the infection that had invaded Avalon, carrying it far, far away from the fair wood and back to the desolated land of Brogg.

Panting for breath and fighting against a wave of nausea, Del looked back at the witch. She stood calm now, unbothered as though she could not see the blood that was on her hands. And as the clouds began to break away, their mission complete, a ray of sunlight descended upon her, lining her form in silvery approval.

The emerald in her forehead sparkled.

"My god," whispered Del. In his own abhorrence of violence, he painted the same face on Brielle now that he had seen on Mitchell that day on the beach. But Mitchell's rifle seemed a toy compared to the incredible power the witch had conjured. In Avalon, Del had viewed the creations of Brielle's magic and he had loved her even more for them. He had never imagined that she could turn that same wonderful ability into such a force of destruction.

Though her brightened form was blurred to him through the tears that had welled in his eyes, Del could see that Brielle was at peace and grimly satisfied. Weakened by confusion and despair, he stumbled down to the road toward Mountaingate.

Soon he had broken into a dead run.

Chapter 18

Caer Tuatha

"It is finished," declared Reinheiser triumphantly. He held up a small splinter of wood notched into an angular design on one end.

"Wonderful." Mitchell scowled, pacing back and forth, his eyes darting anxiously about like some cornered animal searching for an escape. And if the captain's mood wasn't wretched enough at being forced to remain locked in his room at night, earlier that day he had seen DelGiudice escorted from the mountains to freedom. He humored the physicist just to relieve the boredom. "Well, what is it?"

"A key to our door, of course," answered Reinheiser, teasing the frenzied captain with his nonchalance.

At first, the answer didn't register with the distracted man. Then suddenly, Mitchell's face blanched and he spun toward Reinheiser. "Where the hell did you get that?"

Reinheiser laughed casually. "Did you really think that a locked door could defeat me? Come now, Captain, you must show me more respect."

"But how?"

"I formed a mental image of the guard's key and merely copied it," he answered, matter-of-factly. (Though in truth, even Reinheiser wondered how that picture of the key had come so clear in his mind.)

"It won't do us any good anyway," grumbled Mitchell, clutching his negative attitude as protection from false hope. "There are guards outside the door. We'd never make it out of the valley."

"Do not worry, Captain. There are plans to take care of them, I believe."

"Damn it! Will you quit talking in riddles and explain yourself!"

"Not yet." Reinheiser laughed. "Consider it just a call in the night . . ." He trailed his voice away mysteriously. "Patience, my friend, patience. We cannot leave yet. There are arrangements to be made and you have much to learn."

"What are you talking about?" demanded Mitchell.

"About the arrangements, I am not, as yet, sure. But I can tell you with certainty that you must do as I say when we are before the court of Ungden if you wish to attain the lofty goals you desire."

Mitchell scowled, but Reinheiser was adamant. He had learned a great deal about Ungden from his talks with Ardaz and he knew that one wrong word from the captain would cost them both their lives.

Mitchell had no choice but to agree to Reinheiser's demands. Above the fact that Reinheiser had the key and that only he could read his map to get through the secret passes out of Illuma, the physicist apparently had some plan brewing to take care of the guards.

Reinheiser insisted they get right to work, so they spent the rest of that day and much of the night rehearsing scenarios and questions they might encounter at the court in Pallendara.

The wait became even more trying for Mitchell. Now that he had found some direction and purpose to this adventure, he desperately wanted to get on with his hunt for domination. And Reinheiser had asked not to be disturbed and spent entire days in calm meditation. Mitchell reasoned that the physicist was finalizing their plans for escape and knew he should leave him alone, but Mitchell's patience was worn away and he constantly peppered Reinheiser with the redundant "When?"

On a dark and windy night two long days later, the captain's question was answered.

A few stars peeked through breaks in the black

clouds that rushed overhead. Arien's ancient house creaked and moaned against the swirling gusts and the single candle in the room flickered in the drafts. Reinheiser sat motionless, trying to block out the snores of his sleeping companion and attain the relaxed state of his meditative trance. It was a difficult task, even for Reinheiser's disciplined mind, for he was agitated, as close to the edge of his control as he had ever been.

Then a soundless call beckoned to him. In both fear and excitement, he rose and crossed the room to the captain, his shadow dancing in the unsteady light like some monster in the blurred background of a nightmare. "Come, Captain," he whispered, "tonight we are called to leave."

Groggy and not quite comprehending, Mitchell climbed to his feet and began pulling on his clothes while Reinheiser gathered together a torch and two small packs he had stashed under his bed. A trace of mist seeped in from under the door and hung about the floor. Indeed, a ground fog shrouded the entire valley, a very strange mist that had floated in suddenly, a few minutes before.

"Hurry, Captain," Reinheiser encouraged. He slid his key in the lock—it fit perfectly as he knew it would—and opened the door a crack to view the hallway. Satisfied that his suspicions were correct, he swung the door wide and pushed the still-lethargic captain out into the hall. Mitchell perked up immediately, shattered from his sleepiness by the staring face of an elven guard. He raised his arms to defend against an expected assault, but the guard made no motion toward him. In fact, the elf made no movement at all, not to blink or even to breathe! A few feet away, another guard stood rigid in the same comatose state.

"What the hell?" gawked the astounded captain.

Knowing that the situation wouldn't hold for long, Reinheiser cut Mitchell's questions off before they could really begin. "Do not ask about things that are beyond your comprehension," he replied with a pretense of authority, as though he was an intricate part of these strange events. But in truth, the physicist was equally at a loss.

Mitchell was satisfied with the deflective answer. Unlike his companion, he didn't have a need to understand everything about the situation. All he cared about was working toward his goal. "I'll just take this one's sword." He grinned.

"No!" scolded Reinheiser. One more time, he wondered if the benefits of keeping Mitchell around outweighed the aggravations of the captain's endless stupidity. He accepted with a resigned sigh that once again he would have to lead the captain by the hand to get them through. "Take nothing, disturb nothing. If we are fortunate, they won't know that we are gone until the morning. Now, quickly, let us be on our way. We have only a few minutes to get out of the valley."

They hurried down the hallways and out of Arien's house, passing several elves as they darted across the misty city, a couple out for a midnight walk and three dancing in a small clearing. But these, too, were held in time, frozen in midstep and midpirouette.

Soon the two men were deep inside the maze of tunnels, straining their eyes in the torchlight to read Reinheiser's map and counting their steps and the side passages. The eerie mist flew from the valley then, as silently and swiftly as it had come, and the unwitting elves resumed their guarding and walking and dancing as though nothing had happened.

The physicist's calculations proved accurate and the two had little trouble finding their way through the tunnel. When the lower exit came into view, Reinheiser put out the torch so as not to attract any unwanted attention in the open night, leaving himself and Mitchell stumbling blindly down the side of the mountain. They finally made it to the silver archway, their adrenaline pumping with the exhilaration of success, and raced across the field of Mountaingate as quickly as they could. Turning into the southwestern pass, they felt a rush of freedom as the rolling plain spread wide before them.

Mitchell jumped up high and punched his fist into

the air. "We did it!" he squealed with delight. "Think of it, Martin, the next time we see that damned city I'll have an army at my command!"

Reinheiser ignored Mitchell's babbling. "That must be the Calvan scouting party," he said, pointing to the south where the light of a distant campfire broke the even blackness of the horizon. "I believe we can get there under the cover of the night."

The distance was a bit father than Reinheiser had figured and the sky in the east had taken on the lighter shade of predawn when the two came upon a grassy mound, the encampment on its flattened top. The fire in the center of the camp had died down to glowing embers and around it lay the blanketed forms of sleeping men, their horses standing quietly a short distance away on the south side of the hillock.

"These are soldiers?" Mitchell snickered. "They don't even know how to set a guard." But even as he spoke, he and Reinheiser felt the sharp tips of spears against their backs and the supposedly sleeping men within the camp sprang to their feet, short swords drawn and ready. They stood tall and straight in coats of silvery mail and black cloaks, their small black bucklers bearing silver inlays of sharks.

"Right again," whispered Reinheiser sarcastically.

"Silence!" commanded one of the Calvans. "Thieves speak only when they are told to speak!"

"We're not thieves," said Mitchell.

"Silence!" ordered the Calvan, and the man behind Mitchell poked him with his spear.

"We're not even armed," protested Mitchell in a low growl, which drew him a second jab. With the efficiency of trained professionals, two of the swordsmen sheathed their weapons and ran up beside the intruders.

"I am Bracken," continued the Calvan leader, a weathered man with salt-and-pepper hair and a steeled, angular face, "Commander of the First Scouts of Pallendara. As the representative of Overlord Ungden in the northern plains, it is within my power to try and execute you where you stand.''

''For what?'' cried Mitchell. Reinheiser could see that the captain was on the verge of losing control.

Bracken remained cool. ''To approach an official military patrol without proper request and permission is a primary crime against the Edicts of Ungden,'' he recited.

In his stubborn pride, Mitchell was again about to protest when Reinheiser silenced him with a determined nudge. The physicist had recognized a ring that Bracken wore, a black pearl set in gold, and knew better than to argue with this man. Ardaz had warned him of this same symbol during their many discussions. A man who wore such a ring belonged to the Warders of the White Walls, an order of knights that had come into being long before the days of Ungden the Usurper. The sole inspiration behind this band's existence was to act as efficient and unemotional instruments for the will of whomever sat on Pallendara's throne, and their dedication to their creed was absolute. They were few in number now, and older, for none had joined the order in the thirty years of Ungden, but the fanaticism of those that remained had not ebbed, even under the tyrannical new Overlord. Bracken was a dangerous man who had to be handled delicately and Reinheiser knew that meant keeping Mitchell's mouth shut.

The guards were soon satisfied that the two intruders carried no weapons. However, the man searching Reinheiser did find the parchment and quickly presented it to his commander. Bracken inspected it carefully, recognizing it as some sort of map, but the physicist's symbols and notations remained unitelligible to him.

''What is this?'' he demanded.

Reinheiser scratched his chin. It was time for him to gamble a little and he knew he would have to word it just right. He looked around at the other Calvans. Young and naive, ambitious pawns to a perverted king, they would be of no use to him. Only Bracken with his insight founded on years of experience could comprehend the weight of his forthcoming statement. Reinheiser eyed the Calvan leader purposefully. "I beg you forgive our ignorance of your foreign laws," he began. Bracken cocked an eyebrow; a good sign, Reinheiser noted. "We came to you only to present you with that map. A gift for Ungden, rightful Overlord of the city of men, from the survivors of yesteryear!"

The Calvan leader didn't flinch. Eyes boring into the physicist, he slid the parchment into an inside pocket of his cloak and nodded knowingly. Reinheiser smiled in the arrogant assumption that his ploy had saved them, but in truth, this patrol had been sent north not to find Illuma, but in search of the ancient ones. Ungden, or someone in his court, was already aware that the days of the foretold prophecies were at hand.

Assured that these were indeed the men Ungden had sent him to find, Bracken now pondered the implications of delivering them to Pallendara. A crises approached, and these men would help Ungden through it. Bracken's devotion to his oath was on trial, and not for the first time since Ungden had stolen Ben-galen's throne. But the Warder's oath was his strength, and the order his purpose for living. This decision, like all of his choices had been made forty years before, when he had sworn in to the Warders of the White Walls.

"Prepare the five swiftest steeds," he commanded. "We shall escort these intruders to Pallendara, where Overlord Ungden may decide their fate."

Soon they were off, galloping swiftly across the endless sea of green fields. Mitchell and Reinheiser were not treated badly, for the Calvans were not evil men, but Bracken left no doubt of their status as prisoners, and whenever the party stopped for a rest, their hands were tightly bound.

Pallendara was fully a nine-day ride from Mountaingate. Too long for Bracken, who, sensing the urgency of this journey, drove his charges and the prisoners to their limits. They rode their mounts hard long after the sun had set each night and were off again before the next dawn. They passed many farmers out in the fields for the springtime planting, never even slowing down to answer the questioning glances, and they made their evening camps as far from any dwellings as possible.

Impatient to come before Ungden, Mitchell and Reinheiser accepted the exhausting treatment stoically. They were indeed relieved when, on the afternoon of the fifth day, the salty smell of sea water saturated the air.

As they topped a final rise, the last expanse of the Calvan plains opened before them. Far in the distance, beyond the southern shore of Aielle, the blue spray of the Atlantic blurred the line of the horizon. Just below the men, at the end of a long, narrow bay, several groupings of houses lay spread out around an immense white fortress. This was Pallendara, that the elves called Caer Tuatha, the City of Men. Bracken halted the party for a moment at this fine vantage point, for even at this distance the magnificence of the great city stirred him.

Five tall towers dominated the structure, two beside the massive gatehouse in the front, two at the corners of the back, facing the bay, and one in the center of the city. She had been built as a tribute to the artistry of man, a bastion of security dedicated to preserving at all costs the inspired works, and even more, the spirit of creativity and appreciation, that distinguished mankind as a race worthy of the blessings of the Colonnae. A conglomeration of beauty and comfort, the epitome of the best that man had to offer, Pallendara had stood as such for over a thousand years. But three decades of an unlawful king's paranoia had exacted a heavy toll. In the bright days before Ungden, the heavy iron gates were thrown wide day and night, an open invitation to all who would come to partake in the celebration that was this city. Only once in the history of the city, at the time of the coming of Thalasi and his mutant army, had the gates been barred. Now, under the Usurper's wary eye, they remained closed to all and grim-faced soldiers stalked the parapets.

Reinheiser noted this impressive defense as the party trotted the last approach to the walls. He laughed inwardly, realizing that this overblown exhibition didn't put forth the show of strength that Ungden no doubt envisioned. Quite the opposite, it revealed the insecurity, and thus the weakness, of the throne. The physicist also noted Bracken's sigh when the banner of Ungden, a gray shark on a black background, came into view, waving high above the city. Like many of his peers, Bracken preferred the old shield of Calva, four white bridges and four pearls on a sea-blue field. But it was not within the privileges of the Warders of the White Walls to question the decrees of their Overlord.

Bracken gave a call of recognition to a soldier on the roof of the gatehouse and one of the great gates was cracked open enough to admit the horsed men in single file. A short tunnel, its walls lined with arrow slits and its ceiling interlaced with murder holes, led to the open courtyard of the fortress, and Mitchell and Reinheiser uneasily suffered the curious and dangerous stares of many concealed guards as they paced their mounts through. A final portcullis cranked open when they neared, and the captain sighed audibly as they left the passage of horrors and came again into the sunlight.

Reinheiser could only imagine the glory Pallendara had once attained as he looked around him now. A pall hung over the city, a gray fog of lethargy, where men kept at work out of duty and fear, not love. The people they passed stayed huddled and closed with their eyes down in front of them to watch their own measured steps. Everywhere, engines of war dominated the view: a massive catapult belittling a three-tiered fountain and ballistae mounted on the bases where proud statues once stood. Even the unemotional physicist felt a pang at the lost wonders this city must have known. Bracken sensed the disappointment and, as if embarrassed by this, his home, tried to hurry them through the streets.

Nonetheless, a redundant stream of images dogged the trip as they wove around battlement after battlement, one line of defense after another. Every corner carried the same grim visage and they seemed to be going in circles.

Finally they dismounted, and a climb of a hundred marble steps brought them to the golden doors of Pallendara's Throne Hall. Apparently the party was expected, for the guards immediately swung the doors open and escorted them inside. A red carpet led them through the halls and into a long chamber cluttered with statues and sculptures, its walls overlaid with tapestries and paintings; the finest works in all Calva thrown together into a muddled hoard of greed.

The court of Ungden the Usurper.

At the far end of the hall, on an oversized throne of gold and jewels, sat the Overlord. To his left, hunched over and leaning on a cane, stood a man in a white robe, its hood pulled low to conceal his face. Behind the throne, a line of soldiers in the silver and black uniform of the city waited at the call of their Overlord. Everything before him matched the court that Reinheiser had envisioned, everything except for the Overlord himself.

Reinheiser had anticipated an older version of Captain Mitchell, a brutish warrior who had bullied his way to power. But Ungden hardly fit that description. He was slender and delicate, dressed in brightly colored silks with a ruffled collar and puffed sleeves, and overdecked in jewelry, a ring on every finger, two on some, and three on one, and several bracelets that clanked noisily with his every move. From a distance, he seemed younger than the years that the simple arithmetic from the day of his ascent to power would indicate, but when Reinheiser drew near, he recognized this as an obvious illusion of vanity. Powder lessened the wrinkles on Ungden's face and a black wig hid his graying hairs.

The physicist was truly confused; this man who had wrested the throne of a proud and mighty people was, by all measure of his reckoning, a fop.

When the party had settled before him, Ungden threw a leg over one arm of the throne and incessantly strummed the other with meticulously manicured fingers like a bored and impatient child.

"My Lord," said Bracken, bowing low, "I found these men on the foothills of the Crystal Mountains. I brought them here that you might judge if they indeed be the ancient ones the scouts were quested to find." He presented Reinheiser's map to Ungden and moved off to the side.

Ungden scanned the parchment quickly and without much interest, then turned it over to the robed man beside him, who tucked it away in a deep pocket without even looking at it. After the two conferred in whispers for a moment, Ungden focused his gaze upon Mitchell.

"Your name," he demanded.

"Mitchell, Hollis T. Mitchell."

"Well, Hollis T. Mitchell, tell me about this map."

"My friend, Martin Reinheiser, could probably tell you more, Lord Ungden. He penned it himself."

"Ah, yes, I am quite sure that he could," replied Ungden calmly, "but I asked you." He offered no further explanation, as though his simple request contained an indisputable logic to end any further debate. And in this, his Throne Hall, surrounded by his armed and dangerous guard, it certainly did. The Overlord was no fool and his counsel well informed. Just by the way the two men presented themselves, it was obvious that Mitchell was easier prey on a verbal level than Reinheiser, and if these strangers were withholding secrets, Mitchell was the more likely of the two to slip up.

The captain was sharper than he looked, though, and with Reinheiser's coaching behind him, he knew what to say.

"That map, Overlord, will guide you to your greatest foes, the elves of the second mutation."

Ungden's eyes flashed and he started forward in his chair. He caught himself almost immediately and reclined back with feigned calm. The robed man beside him didn't react at all, as though Mitchell's declaration had come as no surprise.

"And why do you freely give me such a map?" asked

Ungden suspiciously. "Surely you must realize the worth of such information. Why do you offer it for nothing?"

"Two reasons," explained Mitchell. "First, it is right that you should know where to find and deal with these mutants." He paused for a moment, trying to remember the way Reinheiser had phrased this rehearsed speech. "The elves are impure, a stain upon the race of man. Like you, I seek to purify the race. I believe that was fate's purpose in bringing us, the ancient ones, to Aielle." Hidden under the cowl of his robe, the wizard beside the throne grinned in amusement. "Second," continued the captain, "I do ask for something in return."

"Then you are a fool"—Ungden laughed—"for I already have your information. You have nothing to bargain with!"

"But I do," argued Mitchell. "I have myself."

Ungden gave Mitchell a sidelong glance and Reinheiser knew that he had coached the captain well.

"Explain, then, your worth to me," demanded Ungden.

"What I ask in return is a position in your army," replied Mitchell. "A position of high rank, that I may aid in the purification of the race of man. That is my destiny."

Ungden lifted his eyebrows at this suggestion. "And what am I to tell my officers when I appoint an unproven stranger among them?"

"Tell them that a Lord is come from another place and another time. A great warrior who knows much of combat and will help lead Calva to victory over its hated foes!"

The wizard leaned over and whispered something to Ungden, who nodded in agreement. "What is the name of this place that you are from, this nation that called you a Lord?" he asked.

"The United States of America," replied Mitchell proudly. "The mightiest nation that this world has ever known."

"Indeed," said Ungden, unimpressed by what he, the Overlord of the grandest nation in Aielle, perceived as a preposterous claim. "And there you were king?"

"No, not king, but I commanded the army for the king, and by his will, so that he would be free to attend to other matters of state. Millions were at my disposal!"

"Millions," mocked Ungden sarcastically, imitating the captain's excited tone. His robed adviser whispered to him again and his taunting smile disappeared. He sat quietly for a moment and tried to compose himself in light of the confirmation from his aide that such an empire had indeed existed.

"My forces are under the able command of Persomy, First Warder of the White Wall," Ungden said. "He is bound to me by an oath of loyalty that cannot be doubted and he carries out my orders without question. And he does so very well, I must say. So you understand that I really do not need another commander."

Mitchell's face twisted at Ungden's unanticipated refusal.

"However," Ungden continued, "my good friend Istaahl has advised me that perhaps you will indeed prove a valuable asset to my army. Therefore, Hollis T. Mitchell, I commission you temporary Undercommander of the forces of Pallendara and the nation of Calva, reporting only to Persomy and to myself. The permanency of your position depends on how we fare against the night dancers, for you and Persomy shall meet today and draw up our plan of attack."

"Thank you, Overlord Ungden," Mitchell stammered through a broad grin. "You won't be disappointed."

Ungden didn't approve of cockiness in an inferior, believing that it constituted a threat to his absolute control. He could neither ignore nor tolerate this, so he promptly reminded Mitchell that gifts from the Overlord of Pallendara did not come cheaply. He leaned forward in his throne and eyed the captain wickedly. "Be assured, Undercommander"—he sneered with deadly certainty—"that I shall hold you solely responsible if we fail."

No longer smiling, Mitchell needed no explanation of the implications of Ungden's promise.

Chapter 19

Shadows of the Throne

The Usurper turned his untrusting eye on Reinheiser. "And what do you ask?" he snarled, his words heavy with the cynicism that dominated every aspect of his life.

"Ask?" echoed Reinheiser with feigned amazement.

"Do not be evasive," warned the Overlord, and he smiled knowingly. The physicist held fast to his naive facade. "What do you ask," demanded Ungden, "in return for your part in delivering the map?"

"Why nothing, my Lord," replied Reinheiser. "I only did what I believed was right." Ungden nodded approvingly, but his doubts remained. Tainted by his own perverted outlook, the Usurper recognized personal gain as the primary motivation for any man's actions and suspected treachery in anyone who claimed otherwise. He knew that Reinheiser was lying. The wizard beside the throne again smiled under his hood. He knew it, too, and furthermore, he understood what it was that Martin Reinheiser sought.

"Although," continued Reinheiser, as if a small favor had occurred to him as an afterthought, "I would truly appreciate a tour of this magnificent palace, and perhaps of the city, too."

"It shall be done," said Ungden. "And more than that, for you certainly deserve it, you shall remain in the palace, comfortable and respected as my royal guest!"

"Thank you, gracious Lord," said Reinheiser, and he bowed low as if honored, though he realized that the invitation was just Ungden's way of keeping an eye on him.

The Usurper accepted the bow with an unenthusiastic wave of his hand, indicating that he was through with the two strangers and the meeting was at an end.

Reinheiser saw many splendors that day, artworks as wondrous as any from his own world. Unfortunately, the manner in which they were thrown together and cluttered about in every room assaulted his senses with an overload of images and insulted the artists who had devoted months, even years, of their lives to create them. Like the dragons of mythology, Ungden hoarded his treasures without any idea of appreciation for them. To the Usurper, owning was an end unto itself and his greed far outweighed any love he had for the art.

Yet Reinheiser, too, had little care for art. His desire to see the palace had nothing to do with observing masterpieces and it took quite an effort for him to hold his facade and convince the guard that he was interested in the tour. It wasn't until the afternoon that he found what he was truly looking for. As his guide led him to his room, they passed a darkened, unadorned hallway. Right away Reinheiser suspected there was something important about this corridor, for it was the only area he had viewed in the entire palace bare of Ungden's pillaged collection.

"Take me down there," he demanded.

"Nay, I cannot," replied the guard.

"You wear the ring of a Warder of the White Walls," Reinheiser snapped at him. "Your Overlord granted me this tour and you are bound to carry out his will. Now, take me down there."

The guard returned Reinheiser's threatening glare with a dangerous look of his own. "I cannot," he stated again. "That passage leads to the tower of Istaahl and he alone determines his guests."

"Even above Ungden?" Reinheiser stated the question rhetorically, meaning to unnerve the guard and remind him of his loyalties. The Warder remained resolute in his refusal.

"Overlord Ungden has granted Istaahl full rights of privacy and sovereignty over his tower. We may approach only by the word of the mage."

Reinheiser had run out of arguments, though it wasn't of much consequence. He had discovered what he set out to find and was confident that he would meet with the wizard soon enough; that had been predetermined. He would have to be patient for a while.

Just for a short while. Conveniently, Reinheiser's room was close by. He entered and shut the door behind him, stopping to listen for steps as the guard departed. But no footsteps moved away; as Reinheiser had fully expected, his room was to be watched. Frustrated, he reclined on his bed, rehearsing the speech he had planned for the wizard and trying to formulate a plan to slip past the sentry. Wearied from the long ride, he was soon fast asleep.

He woke with a sudden start, and thought at first that someone had shaken him, as the last rays of daylight eeked in through the small window of his room. He crept to the door and listened again. Still the hall was silent. "Time to go," he told himself, though he had no strategy completed, deciding in his arrogance and impatience that he was mentally quick enough to ad-lib his way through. When he opened the door, though, he found that wouldn't be necessary, for the guard lay curled up in a sound slumber against the wall across the corridor.

From the impressive tales Ardaz had told him of the Warders of the White Walls, Reinheiser understood this neglect of duty to be more than uncharacteristic. Not about to stop and question his good fortune, he slipped quietly away and headed down the corridor to the tower of the mage, pausing in the shadows beside the iron-bound tower door for a few seconds to be certain that he wasn't being followed. Then, satisfied that he was alone, he knocked lightly on the hard wood.

No response. He rapped as loudly as he dared, but still there came no answer. Reinheiser found himself faced with a difficult and dangerous decision. He knew that he was playing with trouble, perhaps even risking his very life. On the other hand, he realized that he had been fortunate even to get this far and that it was unlikely that this opportunity would come again soon. He boldly creaked open the heavy door and entered the room of the mage.

It was a circular chamber with a stone stairway arching up along the wall on the left to an opening in the second level. There was only one small window, barely more than an arrow slit, meager resistance against the shades of gloom that hung about every nook of the room like splotches of midnight horrors. Reinheiser stood motionless, gripped by an illogical apprehension that disturbing the deathly silence would cue some hidden, poised demon to murderous action.

He gingerly shuffled his way to a chair against the wall behind the open door and softly pushed the door closed. He had to admit to himself that he was intimidated by the mysterious magic of this world. Even so, overruling any fears was the hunger for knowledge, Reinheiser's desire to learn and master this art that hinted at tremendous personal power.

As he scanned the room for clues about its resident, his eyes were drawn to a large oaken desk against the wall across from where he sat, its top cluttered with quills and inkwells and various arcane artifacts: a jeweled knife, a skull, and the eyes of some unfortunate creature. But whether these were actual components in spell casting or macabre scarecrows against inquisitive trespassers, Reinheiser could only guess. Two tall, many-fingered candelabras with twisting and intertwining stems balanced the rear corners of the desk and between them was an upright case sectioned into dozens of compartments, each containing a rolled parchment.

What dark secrets must be penned upon them! Reinheiser thought. Despite the presence of so great a lure, he dared not approach and risk the spells the wizard might have cast to protect his works.

Sunset came soon after and the room blackened quickly. Reinheiser sat very still and noiseless, feeling small and vulnerable to the hiding demons his imagination told him were all about. He fought off panic with every passing second and wondered if these overwhelming fits weren't some trickery of the wizard, a subtle suggestion of promised horror.

After what seemed an eternity, the door creaked open and the white-robed mage entered, bearing a candle. Without taking notice of the physicist sitting in the shadows, he limped across the room, leaning heavily on his small staff, and mumbling a quick spell to close the door and then another to light the candles on the desk. Reinheiser sat amazed and amused at these small feats of wizardry and watched with continued interest, squinting to discern every movement in the weak and flickering light, as the mage's bony hands began slowly pulling back on the cowled hood.

"It should be black, I suppose," Reinheiser said finally, smiling with satisfaction at having caught so wise a man by surprise. The hands kept moving without a hitch, undisturbed by what should have been an unexpected voice, and it was the physicist's composure that was shaken.

"Your mark, I mean," he continued in a less certain, almost defensive tone. "It should be black, since black is the mark of Morgan Thalasi, and that, unless I miss my guess, is who are are."

The wizard turned slowly to Reinheiser and gave a hiss of soft laughter. "You play dangerous games, Dr. Martin Reinheiser," he said calmly, pulling his hood back to let the intruder see what he was dealing with.

Reinheiser shuddered at the sight, for the man before him was indeed the Black Warlock, Morgan Thalasi. He was completely bald, with pallid, sickly skin that seemed stretched beyond its limits just to cover his bony frame. His black eyes showed as no more than holes in deep, sunken sockets, and his cheeks were hollowed and taut, as if he had wasted away, like a starved man who should have died long ago. Centuries of wickedness had exacted a heavy toll on Thalasi, eating at his physical being, but not at his evil will, for that was all-enduring. The many-faceted black sapphire that was his wizard's mark glistened from its setting on his forehead as if newly cut and polished.

"I knew it was you," said Reinheiser, and he laughed meekly, trying to seem at ease. Despite his effort, the tremor in his voice betrayed his true feelings of terror. "I reasoned that only the mighty Thalasi was capable of the feats that the mage, Ardaz, credits to Istaahl."

"So you were right," mocked the Black Warlock, his voice remaining unnervingly calm and sure. "Small comfort in light of the terrible death that is about to befall you."

Reinheiser stroked his goatee and tried to hold fast to the control and reason he needed now to get him through this. Something was going very wrong. He had never figured his meeting with Thalasi to be like this, not even in the worst of his scenarios, and his imagined pictures of the Black Warlock fell far short of the true horrors of the being before him. This man, appearing so physically fragile, exuded an aura of overwhelming evil and limitless power. He was Satan incarnate, a black hole of morality that Reinheiser knew could sweep him away on a whim to an eternity of hellfire.

"Kill me?" he asked incredulously, trying to put the idea into a preposterous light. "Why would you want to kill me?"

"For knowing my identity and intruding on my privacy, or for talking to that slime, Glendower, that you call Ardaz," replied Thalasi. "That is surely reason enough. Or I might dismember you merely for the pleasure of dealing pain." He hissed his wicked laugh again, as though the last idea had appealed to him.

Reinheiser knew without doubt that Thalasi was more than capable of such random murder. "But you summoned me!" he cried. "The mist that allowed us to escape; you had to have sent it! That's how I finally knew your true identity. Istaahl's magic is limited to the seacoast and he couldn't have reached that far inland!"

"I did conjure the mist."

"And the sleeping Warder?"

"A simple task."

"Then you brought me here for a purpose," reasoned Reinheiser.

"For the map, that is all," said Thalasi. "I reached to possess your mind and you, thinking that some knowledge was unfolding before you, let me in. I had not the time to take control, but I saw through your eyes and perceived that you were among the night dancers. Yet I could not discern exactly where that was. So I brought you here for the map, and that is all."

"But Mitchell—" began Reinheiser, desperately grabbing at anything that might save him.

"Mitchell is a fool!" interrupted Thalasi. "I commanded an army of millions, he said. Ha! I, too, lived in the United States before the holocaust, and I remember no General Hollis Mitchell. And I assure you, my memory is excellent.

"I remember you, though," continued Thalasi. "Your work, at least."

Reinheiser immediately saw a chance and boldly forced himself under control. "Then you know that I, too, mastered an art," he stated as proudly as he dared. "I was a master of physics and technology. I thought that was why you sent for me, for if we could combine our knowledge—"

Thalasi cut him off with a loud burst of laughter, mocking the physicist's pitiful attempt to save his life.

"You laugh?" cried Reinheiser, leaping from his seat in anger. He realized that Thalasi would probably kill him then and there for daring to argue, but so frustrated was he by his miscalculations, and so confused by the Black Warlock's responses and attitude, that at the moment he hardly cared. "You doubt the power of science?"

"Power?" roared Thalasi, and Reinheiser huddled back into his chair at the bared strength of his adversary's voice. "It is destructive, yes. That has been proven, but not powerful. You confuse the two. A bomb reduces a city to a pit of bubbling tar, and you term that power. What is gained? Annihilation is not power!'' He clenched a fist and raised his eyes to the ceiling. Reinheiser shuddered at the sheer evil in those smoldering orbs.

''Control!'' hissed Thalasi. ''Bending another's will to do your bidding! Dominating his every move! That, you fool, is power!''

The physicist was still terrified, but also intrigued. Here was the master who held the key to the secrets he desired, and his cravings demanded attention even above the threat to his life. ''And what of knowledge?'' he asked with urgency. ''Does knowledge play a part?''

''Yes, yes, of course!'' replied Thalasi, suddenly sounding more excited than angry. It wasn't often that he found a man who could converse with him on such a level and they were talking about his favorite subject. ''Knowledge of the secrets of the universe and of the absolute powers that exist within it is the first necessity!

''The second part''—the Black Warlock sneered, his fists taut and his eyes squinted evilly to accentuate his point—''is desire. Desire to possess, to own . . . everything. The courage to dare to be a God!'' he shouted. ''And the unceasing determination to see it through!''

''Do we speak of power, or of evil?'' asked Reinheiser.

''They are one!'' retorted Thalasi. ''Oh, the powers of the universe are absolute, and they are there for those who are good and for those who are neither good nor evil, but their strength becomes limited by the restrictions of the conscience of the first, and the lack of purpose of the second. Only the power of evil runs unleashed and unabated!''

''Surely powers are neutral,'' argued Reinheiser. ''Evil and good cannot be considerations.''

''Bah! That is where you make your mistake,'' explained Thalasi. ''There are four schools of magic, all working from the same absolute and universal truths. These truths, these powers, run purest in Brielle, mistress of the first magic. But she is limited in calling upon her power because she lacks purpose. Tied to her wood and to her covenant of preserving the natural order, she becomes merely a watchdog, alerting nature to the intrusions of perversion. Outside of this domain, her magic is inaccessible and thus she is nothing better than a servant.

"You yourself have spoken with Ardaz. His is the second school, the one that the Colonnae intended for me as well."

'To adapt the truths of the universe to fit into the development of the race of Man," offered Reinheiser. "For the good of Man as defined by the codes of morality put forth by the Colonnae."

"Excellent!" replied Thalasi, enthused by the surprising understanding of the physicist. "Then you recognize the trap? The restrictions?"

"Of course. Though more accessible than the first school, the second is more limited in scope and effect, held in check by a strict code of imposed ethics."

"Exactly," hissed the warlock. "But there is a third school, a practice the Colonnae held in reserve for themselves and for those they serve. They kept it from us because they feared us, feared we would rise above them and no longer serve them. I, Thalasi, have found this secret and each day my power grows."

"Control?" asked Reinheiser.

"Control," echoed Thalasi. "I hold no covenants and serve no codes. The powers cannot resist me. I call upon them at will and force them to do my every bidding. It is the most difficult of the magics, a discipline of unceasing concentration. Every thought and every move, I battle the constants of universal order." His eyes glowed with lust and pride. "Do you understand the implications of what I say?" he asked Reinheiser, who sat staring in disbelief, stunned by the magnitude of the potential power the warlock was hinting at. "They are relentless foes, yet so am I. And when I win . . . at those times that I am the stronger . . . with a word, I can pervert the very order of nature and tear a corpse from the arms of death to hold it undead under my control! Or I can steal a spell from the mouth of a wizard to turn it back against him, as I did with Istaahl thirty years ago."

"Then you were the strength behind Ungden's rise." Reinheiser smiled, growing more at ease; this was the way he had imagined his meeting with Thalasi. "You held the Warders at bay until the coup was completed, knowing that their oath would then bind them to Ungden and secure his position."

Thalasi nodded his affirmation of Reinheiser's statement and also in approval of the physicist's continued show of reasoning ability.

"But why Ungden?" asked Reinheiser. "He hardly seems a fitting leader."

"He is not the leader," Thalasi explained. "He is the leader's pawn. A man easy to please, thus easy to control, and no threat to me. And his feud with the line of Ben-rin is rooted deep in the past. Few in all Calva would have turned against the beloved Overlords of that line, yet miserable Ungden was quite eager to drive a dagger into the heart of Ben-galen.

"Ungden is the smoke covering my fire. The Warders would not serve a wizard, and if I claimed the throne, my true identity would soon be revealed. I am not yet prepared for that day, though the time grows near. That is why I need your map. The slaughter of the helpless mutants will break the honor of the truest Calvans and weaken their resistance to me."

"But what of my knowledge of technology? Surely that can aid you."

"Speak not that word!" commanded Thalasi with sudden and renewed anger. "This is the fourth school of magic, a curse upon the wise and a bane to all. What is technology but a harness, making the universal powers available to any, with total disregard to their inner strength? It is an unacceptable danger, lacking all controls and promising nothing except eventual and total devastation at the hands of the foolish!" He didn't have to point out the truth in his premise; Reinheiser had seen the world beyond the bubble of Ynis Aielle.

"The deeper strength," Thalasi continued, his voice

an even whisper, "is the strength of the mind in conjunction with the powers of the universe, and driving those powers by sheer desires and convictions. Given the secrets of the universal truths, you would remain a simple Faustus, playing with firecrackers! But I . . ." He rose up tall and terrible in his wrath and Reinheiser looked away in fear.

"Look at me!" roared Thalasi. "Behold Morgan Thalasi and know you are doomed!"

Reinheiser trembled uncontrollably. He hid his face in his arms and curled up, desperately seeking a hiding place where there was none. He had never really been frightened before; even death he had accepted as an inescapable part of life.

But Reinheiser was scared now. He felt a blackness in his heart, a sense of hopelessness and despair that touched his innermost being. He waited, he prayed, for the deathblow to come quickly.

It didn't fall, and gradually some hope returned to him, though he feared that this was just Thalasi's way of toying with him. Finally, he gathered up enough courage to peek out.

The warlock was sitting again, apparently deep in thought. Slowly, Reinheiser straightened himself in the chair and waited for whatever was to come.

"Perhaps there is hope for you," said Thalasi after several minutes had passed. "You have certainly proven your intelligence, and perhaps, under my guidance, you will become an asset to me."

Reinheiser smiled hopefully, drawing disapproval from Thalasi, who returned a glare that slumped the physicist back in dismay. Thalasi pointed a finger threateningly and growled, "But never oppose me," and Reinheiser felt cold, bony fingers close about his throat, an invisible collar that was Thalasi's will.

The Black Warlock no longer viewed the physicist as a threat to him, for he had faith that his edict of power had once again proven true. With no destruction, no death, he now owned Martin Reinheiser.

Chapter 20

Treachery Unmasked

Sylvia went to rouse the men early on the morning after Mitchell and Reinheiser had made their escape. The early haze had burned away soon after sunrise, leaving the air warm and clean, and Sylvia wanted the three guests to enjoy as much of the day outside of their rooms as possible. Unconcerned and seeking only to make the men's stay more pleasant, the elven maiden could never have imagined at that moment that Mitchell and Reinheiser had just begun their wild ride across the plains as prisoners of the Calvan scouting party.

She sensed trouble as soon as she fitted the key into the door to their room and found it unlocked. This was more than an oversight, she knew, for she had locked the door herself the night before. Yet the two guards beside her, as perplexed as she, assured her that they had been faithful to their watch throughout the night and that she had been the last one in or out of the room.

But the room was empty. Still not quite comprehending the magnitude of the escape, Sylvia crossed the hall to get Billy. The mere fact that he was there to answer her knock brought her a measure of comfort and made her believe that there was a simple explanation for the absence of the other two.

But Sylvia's relief was short-lived, for her question about his companions' disappearance jolted the sleepiness from Billy's eyes as completely as if she had splashed him with icy water.

Every image Billy had of Mitchell since they came to this world led him inescapably to one frightening conclusion. He looked grimly at Sylvia, her innocent and hopeful smile heightening his suspicions, and his anger. "Go find Arien, and quickly," he instructed. Sylvia hesitated, waiting for more details, but Billy couldn't bring himself to tell her that Mitchell and Reinheiser, his companions, were on their way to betray her people.

Sylvia had a good idea where her father would be on such a fair morning. She bid Billy go with her and he agreed, though he dreaded confronting the elf-king with such grim news. They came upon Arien a short time later on a back balcony of the house overlooking the great gorge. He and Ryell sat quietly, enjoying the serenity of the ever-wondrous spectacle of dawnslight on the Crystals.

Arien knew immediately that something was terribly wrong when he saw his daughter, her face flushed and pained. He grasped Sylvia's hands to steady her. "What is it?"

"They are gone!" cried Sylvia. "Captain Mitchell and Martin Reinheiser are not in their room!"

"Treachery!" yelled Ryell. "I knew that no good would come of these men!" He started threateningly toward Billy, but Arien intercepted him with an outstretched arm.

"Find Erinel," Arien said to Sylvia calmly. "Gather your friends together at once and search the tunnels to Mountaingate. Until we know more, those two are to be considered guests and not enemies. But I want them found and brought to me."

"They might yet be in the city," offered Sylvia.

"Doubtful," replied Arien, "but leave a group behind. Instruct them to search the whole of the valley and even Shaithdun-o-Illume. Now go and hurry. We will await your findings here."

Sylvia nodded and was gone. The two guards remained at Billy's side, unsure now of his status among their people and a bit nervous about him being so close to their Eldar. Arien, though, waved them away, steadfastly refusing to let the actions of Mitchell and Reinheiser detract from his trust of this man who had done them no wrong. Ryell, suspicious as ever, and considering all men to be dangerous enemies of his vulnerable people, had a different notion.

"Where have they gone?" he snapped, certain that Billy was in on some conspiracy. Billy shrugged his shoulders and looked away, wisely withholding his theory until more information could be gathered and calmer heads prevailed.

Ryell didn't wait for an answer anyway. Seeking outlets to vent his fury, he turned on the guards.

"And what of you two?" he scolded. "You were supposed to be guarding them!"

"We remained at their door throughout the night," replied one of the unfortunate guards with strained conviction, knowing that he was helpless in the face of such overwhelming evidence.

"Ha!" scoffed Ryell. "If I discover that you fell asleep, I shall—"

"Oh, hush, hush! Hush up I say!" came a voice from behind the guards and the wizard, Ardaz, stepped out onto the terrace, Desdemona wrapped in peaceful slumber like a boneless stole about his neck. "I, too, had eyes posted to watch the ancient ones. Desdemona here." He lifted the limp cat off his shoulder and held her close to his face. "And she wouldn't let me down, would she? No, she wouldn't!

"She kept watch on your house from just outside and saw no one leave, no one at all, not a one," he assured Arien with complete confidence. "Never sleeps either. Not at night anyway. Sleep all day, bother everyone at night; rule of cats, you know." He snorted a chuckle and turned his attention back to the cat, petting her affectionately to make up for his last comment.

"But they are gone," insisted Ryell, reiterating the simple fact to challenge the wizard for an explanation.

"I know that, of course I know that!" replied Ardaz. "Sylvia told me just a moment ago out in the hall."

Ryell shook with frustration. "If they are not here," he asked with deliberate sarcasm, "and that cat assures you that they did not leave, then where are they? Might it be that they simply disappeared?"

"Oh yes, I see your point," replied Ardaz, enlightened and confounded all at once. "And a very good point it is!" He again pulled the cat from his shoulder and shook her awake. "Des, did you fall asleep, you nasty little kitty!" He gave her another shake and eyed her suspiciously. Then, as if talking to her in her own tongue, he uttered a series of varying "Meows," and Desdemona replied with an emphatic "Mrow!" The wizard flopped her back over his shoulder and seemed appeased.

"Says that she didn't fall asleep," he explained to the astounded onlookers. "Doubt that she did, too."

His gaze drifted absently out across the gorge. "Couldn't have disappeared, no, no," he continued, talking more to himself than the others. "There are ways, of course, but they were just ordinary men. Certainly not wizards, after all!" He paused to scratch his bearded chin. "Unless . . ." Arien and Ryell waited for him to let them in on his apparent revelation, but as the moments slipped by and an expression of dark worry crossed the wizard's face, Arien's patience ran thin.

"What is it?" he demanded.

"I am not sure," replied Ardaz, his voice suddenly sobered. He looked back at the Eldar, shaken from his contemplative trance. "Not sure. But I shall find out!" he asserted, and he headed for the door.

"Wait!" called Arien. "You cannot leave now!" But Ardaz kept moving.

"Things to do," he called. "Things to do!" And he scurried away.

"Why do you allow him to stay in Illuma?" groaned Ryell. "He is of no use to us at all."

Arien knew better than that. He knew the side of Ardaz that was the wise and kind Glendower, savior to the elves at the dawn of their race, when Ben-rin ruled Pallendara and Umpleby would have had them killed. Arien was confident that the compassion and power of the wizard were there still, hidden beneath a bumbling facade, but ready to come forth as a shining light of hope in their darkest moments.

"Blame not Ardaz for our troubles," he warned Ryell.

"But what are we to do?" asked Ryell softly, the cutting edge of his anger diminishing with the growing realization of their helpless position.

"We wait," replied Arien grimly. "And hope."

The Eldar sent the guards away to join in the search and he, Ryell, and Billy remained on the balcony, staring out at the towering mountains, seeking refuge from their worldly concerns in the profound contemplations so glorious a landscape oft inspired. They spoke little, each of them finding solace in his private meditation, and a semblance of hope budded among them as the initial shock of the escape faded. Though they did not track the time, it seemed like hours later when Sylvia and Erinel finally returned.

Then their hopes were dashed.

"They are not in the city," said Sylvia.

"Nor in the tunnels," added Erinel. "I traveled as far down as the lower trails above Mountaingate." He looked over at Billy and gave a sympathetic shrug, for he knew that what he was about to say would reflect badly on his new friend. "I found two sets of footprints in several places—less than a day old."

"And were these tracks known to you?" snarled Ryell, intent on tearing from reluctant Erinel confirmation that his own mistrust of the humans had been justified.

"They matched the strange boots of our visitors," replied Erinel.

Ryell eyed Arien smugly, confident that the Eldar could no longer reprimand him. Then he turned his fury on Billy. "What have you to say of this?" he snapped.

Billy was indeed ashamed at the treachery of his companions, but he would not accept responsibility for their actions and he was not intimidated. He looked past Ryell to address Arien. "They've gone to Calva," he declared.

Ryell intervened before Arien could react. "How do you know this?" he shouted accusingly. "And why did you keep it from us?"

"I didn't keep anything from you!" retorted Billy. "I just now figured it out from Erinel's findings." He pointedly turned back to the Eldar. "I admit that I feared this—feared Mitchell. He's hungry for power and will do anything to get it. That night of council on the mountain shelf, he tried to persuade you to grant him an army. You refused, so he seeks it elsewhere. My guess is the court of Ungden."

Again Ryell was quick to voice his opinion. "Bah!" he said. "It seems more to the truth that you were a part of the whole deception!"

"You're wrong," Billy said.

"I am right!" insisted Ryell. "And what of DelGiudice? An emissary sent ahead to prepare the way for his captain? And you were left behind to cover their escape, to keep us from suspecting the worst until it was too late for us to prevent it!"

"No," said Billy, but he saw his conviction slipping away. How could he hold credibility with Arien and the others in light of Mitchell's terrible deception? His pity of Ryell and the elves' desperate situation put him on the defensive, for he knew that Ryell's rage was founded on the very plausible fears that all of Illuma was in mortal danger. "Del and I had no part of this."

"You lie!" screamed Ryell.

"Enough of this!" demanded Arien, and Ryell turned away, biting back curses and accusations through gritted teeth. Then Billy was truly wounded, for the look Arien gave him revealed doubts and suspicion. "Pray tell us all that you know," he asked. "It is important."

"There isn't much I can add," Billy answered. "Mitchell will stop at nothing to get what he wants and you're right to be concerned. But I'll do anything I can to help you and I guarantee that Del had nothing to do with this. He hates Mitchell even more than I do. Those two have been at each other's throats since the first day they met."

"And what of the other one, Martin Reinheiser?" asked Arien.

"Billy shrugged and shook his head. "I don't really know. He and the captain stick together, but I can't figure out why. They're nothing alike. Maybe it's just because they have nobody else to get close to, or maybe each of them needs the other to make up for what he lacks himself. Either way, I wouldn't trust Reinheiser any more than Mitchell. He might not be as openly dangerous as the captain, but he's sneaky, and smart enough to manipulate things the way he wants them."

"I am satisfied," Arien assured him, but the declaration of renewed trust in Billy did not relieve the pained look from the Eldar's face. His people were in grave danger and he could see no way to avoid it.

Again despair smoothed the edge of Ryell's anger. "Then we are lost," he stated with hopeless resignation.

"Not yet," declared Arien, but despite his determination, his voice was strained, and a vein of deep worry stood out clearly on his temple. "Caer Tuatha is many miles to the south and the two have no horses. We do not know if they will ever reach the city, or how Ungden will receive them if they should."

"But if they do get there," said Ryell grimly. "The humans can muster 10,000 spears."

"That would take weeks, even months," replied Arien.

Erinel cut in. "We must know for certain," he said. "Eldar, allow me to go down to the Calvan fields. Among the farmers, I may be able to discern the destination or even the intentions of the two men. Surely it is folly for us to sit back blindly and wait for whatever is to befall us."

Arien looked questioningly at Ryell, granting his friend, as Erinel's guardian, the final authority to permit or reject his nephew's proposal. Both of them knew well the risk that Erinel would be taking if he walked among the Calvans, for both of them had done the same thing many, many years before. But that was when the heirs of Ben-rin sat on the southern throne and the Calvans, though not openly acknowledging the existence of the elves, tolerated them with winks of promised secrecy and spoke to them only in exaggerated tavern tales. With wicked Ungden in power and all of Calva on alert for the mutants hiding in the mountains, Erinel's journey would be much more dangerous.

Ryell sighed helplessly. "We have no choice."

Arien put a comforting hand on his friend's shoulder. "Be ever cautious," he said to Erinel. "Remember that the shadows of the night have always been a friend to your people. I expect and await your safe return." And Erinel nodded his assurance and left the terrace with Sylvia.

"I wish to post a watch at the trees above Mountaingate," said Ryell, and Arien agreed.

In his tower home of Brisen-ballas high above Illuma Vale, Ardaz sat talking to Desdemona.

"You watch over this place while I'm away," he told the cat. "Not that I really want to go, you know. Who would, after all?" An involuntary shudder ran up his back as he thought of what awaited him; Talasdun, the fortress wrought of Morgan Thalasi's black heart. Castel Angfagdt it was called in the enchantish tongue, the castle of utter darkness. A title, Ardaz knew, of well-earned terror.

The wizard rose and shook off his fit of quailing, setting himself with firm resolution to do what he must. "Still, we have to know for certain!" he explained to Des. "I'll be back as soon as I can be back!" He grimaced away a second shudder and, chanting in trancelike monotone and rhythmically dancing through a few twists and turns, he became an eagle and was off.

He soared out of the tower, riding the updrafts of the sun-warmed air rising up the cliff facings, and was soon gliding high along the southern ridge of the Crystals. Ardaz truly enjoyed the effortless freedom of this wind riding. But time was pressing, he knew, so he tilted out away from the cliffs, beyond the reach of the lifting currents, and plummeted into a swoop down toward Blackemara, leveling off just above the swamp and riding the tremendous rush of gathered momentum far out into the desolate land of Brogg.

Unfaltering, the wizard sped on toward the distant shadows of the Kored-dul range and the waiting blackness of Talas-dun, where he hoped to find some answers.

The passing days were agony to the elves and Billy as they awaited Erinel's return. The wait became even worse for Arien when he found that Ardaz, too, was gone.

Chapter 21

The Lines Are Drawn

The trees closed behind Del when he emerged from Avalon as though Brielle were slamming her door at his back. And though Del told himself that it didn't bother him, that right now all he cared about was putting as much distance between himself and Avalon as possible, his heart sank even lower at the sound of the wood shutting him out. He tried in vain to blank the thoughts and images of the witch from his mind, for he had witnessed a terrible and unexpected side of her that had wrenched away his fantasy and broken his heart. Head down, he walked with slow and sullen steps across Mountaingate.

He took no notice of his surroundings as he approached and passed the silver telvensils at the end of the field. His thoughts remained inward in recollections of stately groves of swaying pines and starlit fields and the woman that gave them meaning, and with a resigned sigh he was forced to accept that he would not be so easily rid of his memories of the Emerald Witch.

But even had he been wary, Del would not have seen the three elves, silent as death, slipping down from the concealing branches of the arched trees behind him.

Del continued on a few yards up the mountain path, then realized that he could go no further until an escort arrived. "Damn!" he spat. Even if Ardaz had seen him on the road in Avalon, it would be hours before any elves arrived to guide him back to Illuma. He punched at the air in frustration and turned back to the archway, seeking a shady place to sit and wait.

His relief at seeing the elves was short-lived, lasting only the second it took him to understand that the two bowmen holding their weapons taut and level were aiming at him. And the third elf, standing grim-faced between them, held his slender sword ready in hand, although his recognition of Del was unmistakable.

"What's going on?" Del asked with caution, though he still didn't quite believe that the elves meant to harm him.

"Silence!" commanded the swordsman. "Throw your weapon to the ground in front of you."

"Didn't we already play out this scenario, just a couple of weeks ago?" Del offered with a strained smile, inviting the elves to end their game and admit the joke.

On a nod from the leader, one of the bowmen loosed his arrow. Del whitened in shock at the twang of the bowstring, and jerked involuntarily, expecting to be struck, as the arrow drove itself deep into the ground between his feet.

"I ask you again to throw down your weapon," said the swordsman in a calm, steady tone, and Del had no doubt that the next arrow would find his heart.

There was anger in Del, but against the dizzying swirl of his emotional turmoil, it could not gain a focus or a purpose. Confusion dictated to Del and he was in no frame of mind for an argument, much less a fight. He pulled his sword and dropped it to the ground, dropping his gaze as well, for he had no desire to view the elves in their deadly mood. Were these the Children of the Moon, the same joyful people whose very existence was based in dance and song, in community and friendship? Or had he, perhaps, in his longings for utopia, misperceived this land and its peoples. His whole image of Aielle suddenly seemed to be closing in around him, suffocating him in the same grim visages of reality he thought he had left far behind on the shores of a distant world.

He offered no resistance as an elf came up to bind his hands.

* * *

Erinel trotted across Mountaingate, hugging the eastern cliff face for the little cover it offered. He didn't like moving openly in broad daylight, but the urgency of his news demanded the risk. He crouched low and slowed, though, when he neared the telvensils and heard the voices beyond.

"Blindfold him," said one of the bowmen.

"It is not necessary," replied the elf with Del. "It would only slow us and Ryell is anxious to speak with this one. You remain here to keep the watch," he instructed one of the bowmen. "We shall escort the prisoner back to the city."

"By the Colonnae!" cried Erinel as he stepped through the archway. "Release him at once!"

"Erinel!" exclaimed the elves in unison. The swordsman strode over and warmly clasped Erinel's arm.

"It is good that you have returned, my friend," he said sincerely. "The days of our watch for you have been long indeed in passing, and all of the city is stilled in anticipation of your findings."

"Untie him!" Erinel demanded angrily, and stormed up the path toward Del.

"But it is by the order of your uncle that he is bound," pleaded the swordsman, torn between his loyalties. Fearful of a confrontation, yet obedient to the commands of the Eldars, he rushed ahead to intercept Erinel.

"Then my uncle is a fool!" snapped Erinel, brushing the swordsman aside and continuing on to Del without missing a step.

The three elves looked at each other with uncertainty, then began closing on Erinel and Del. Before they were forced to make a decision on their course of action, Del intervened.

"It's all right, Erinel," he said, trying to soothe his friend's ire and avoid the agitation of another conflict. "I really don't mind. Let's just get back to the city."

Erinel hesitated for a moment. He hated seeing his friend bound, despite Del's assurances, but he realized that he had no time for arguments. "Very well, then," he told the elves. "Let us be off at once. Arien must know of the stirrings in the south!"

Leaving the two bowmen behind to keep watch, Erinel led Del and the swordsman at a swift pace up the mountain. Still struggling with the torment of Brielle's darker side, Del asked no questions and paid no attention to the secret paths. Eventually, though, when they had entered the tunnels and left Avalon far behind and hidden from sight, he was able to focus on the events at hand and he realized that something terribly important and grave must be going on. All of the signs moved him in the direction of one horrible suspicion: that one of his companions must have done something awful to rile the elves so. And Del had a good idea who it was.

Seated at a table of council in the Throne Room of Arien's house, Del noted the grim faces of the elves, trying to mask an undercurrent of desperation, and the quiet, almost cowed visage of Billy Shank. He also noticed, with great concern and renewed suspicion, that Mitchell and Reinheiser weren't present.

"It is as we feared," said Erinel darkly. "They have reached Caer Tuatha."

"Mitchell!" Del blurted, easily guessing now the deceit and motives of the hated captain and angry at himself for not recognizing this possibility sooner, when it could have been prevented.

Arien ignored Del's outburst, working to keep the discussion on track and free of emotional digressions. "And how were they received?" he asked evenly.

"Even as we hold council, the Usurper marches north with an army of a thousand spears," replied Erinel. Above the gasps and frightened whispers that flooded from every end of the table, he added, "And their numbers swell every day as more humans rush to the side of their glorious Overlord to join in his day of triumph over the wicked mutants."

"Barbarism!" shouted Ryell, punctuating his cry

with a slam of his fist on the table. ''Again we bear witness to the treachery of Man!''

''Silence, Ryell!'' commanded Arien, fighting to the last to maintain a rational atmosphere. Yet he, too, wanted to scream out in anger and frustration. He could not, for he was the Eldar, the leader of his people, and was bound to set the proper example of strength. All Illuma looked to him for guidance. He mustered up his composure and stated his question calmly. ''How much time do we have?''

''A few days, no more.''

This time there were no gasps or whispered responses as a silent veil of dread wafted through the room, graying the faces of the elves and dimming the light in their eyes.

Ryell hardened his resolve when he saw his people sinking in the throes of despair. He sought the protection of his anger, clung to an all-consuming rage that allowed no such weakness. ''Pray tell us, Eldar,'' he hissed, making it clear to all present that he held Arien personally responsible for their predicament, ''whatever are we to do now? Would you have us play the role of frightened rabbits as they run and hide before the teeth of the wolf? Perhaps we could find another hole deeper in the mountains that would serve as our prison for the next few centuries!''

The mention of rabbits sent Del's thoughts reeling back to Avalon and the peaceful lunch he had shared on the first day of his return to the wood. Ryell's twisted grimace destroyed that fantasy quickly, reminded Del with painful clarity that his utopian image of Aielle was a distortion founded entirely on his own ignorance.

You're right, Ryell, he thought. Rabbits would run away. They don't confuse pride with stupidity.

Ryell's sarcasm wounded Arien deeply, for he had trusted the humans despite the risks, and now had to bear the responsibility for not taking stronger precautions. Arien remained solid in his convictions about trust and friendship, but the army coming to slaughter his people, to snuff out his entire world, weighed as a heavy consequence on his tired shoulders. He felt the judging eyes of the others upon him, awaiting his response to the accusations of Ryell.

The Eldar steeled his gaze on his accuser. "No, Ryell," he said firmly, "I shall not leave."

The suicidal declaration jolted Del with surprise. Certainly, he hadn't expected such a decision from Arien. "You can't win!" he argued desperately.

"That may be," replied Arien, "but if the entire city departs, the pursuit will be swift and unrelenting. My people must survive, and thus a large group of maidens and the younger of our race, and any else who wish, shall flee into the mountains.

"We must leave more than a token group behind to face down the murderous threat of Ungden, and I count myself among that number. This has been my home for many, many years and I shall not willingly relinquish it to an unlawful king. Perhaps there is parlaying yet to be done. Who but myself should speak for Illuma?"

"He'll kill you all," Del declared flatly.

"Then let him fulfill his rage and be done with it," Arien declared. "We are not a warring people, yet our skill with sword and bow is great. The Calvans will pay a heavy price for their raid. Our fallen will satisfy their thirst for blood, and it may well be that the numbers of their own dead will dim any further desires they have for war. I perceive this to be the only way any of our people shall live in peace again."

Arien jumped to his feet, sending his chair skidding behind him, and stood tall and proud above the gathering, set in a grim resolve that could not be questioned. There was no weakness in the Eldar now, no burden weighing on his shoulders, and all around the table looked on him with respect that bordered on awe.

All except for Del.

He looked away and muttered, "Et tu, Arien," once more feeling the pain of disappointment as keen as a dagger in his breast.

Arien paid him no attention. "These are my words of council," he declared. "Yet in this matter I feel that each of us must make his own choice—to flee to the mountains or to stay and face the wrath of Ungden."

With teeth gritted, Erinel cried out his support. "None shall willingly leave!"

"No," agreed Sylvia with the same fervor. "The people stand behind you, Father!"

"Then let us not stand idle!" commanded Ryell. "There is much to be done!"

Overcome by a dizzying wave of nausea, fighting back the distaste of bile rising in his throat, Del stumbled out to the corridor.

Del returned to the Throne Room several hours later. The place had become a beehive of activity, with elves coming and going and congregating in small groups to discuss plans. Ryell, just a few feet away with his back to Del, was the center of it all. Excited, almost frantic, he called out commands, delegating duties to the younger elves.

"You seem thrilled by all of this, Ryell," Del stated incriminatingly at the back as he entered. "Are you that hungry for blood?"

Ryell wheeled on him angrily. "For freedom!" he growled. "I am hungry for freedom! Too long have I hid in fear from men!"

He looked across the room, leading Del's gaze with his own. Billy and several others were gathered before a large map hung on the wall.

Ryell turned back to Del, eyeing him slyly. "Your friend has offered his aid unconditionally," he said loudly, purposely attracting the attention of some of the nearby elves. "What of you?"

Del knew that Ryell had set him up, put him on the spot before witnesses to wring the desired responses from him. He recognized the expectant looks turning quickly to impatience. He lowered his head so as not to face their disappointment and remained silent.

Del could not give his assistance or his approval for the battle the elves chose to fight. He had hoped for more in this new land than the commonplace wars, the nonsolutions of violence, that were the tainted legacy of his world. And after witnessing that same dark wrath in the woman he had viewed, and loved, as the epitome of peace and beauty, his abhorrence of violence was absolute.

"I need time," he stalled. "I want to talk to Ardaz."

"That fool is gone," snapped Ryell. "He fled at the first signs of trouble."

"Then I'd like to go back to my room," said Del softly.

"Guard!" called Ryell. And Del was grateful to be able to leave so easily with the elf who appeared at the door.

The war councils stretched long into the night, for though the elves had in the past fought many a skirmish with bands of rogue talons, they were totally unfamiliar with larger-scale battles or defensive preparations. Arien and Ryell listened intently as their people presented various plans of action, and together they tried to devise one of their own. Soon they both realized that their only hope rested with the otherworldly knowledge of Billy and Del. Ryell abhorred the idea of trusting the humans again, but the elves were mere novices against the trained Calvan army.

Billy felt awkward in a position of leadership, but was more than willing to help. He quickly dismissed what the elves perceived as their most feasible option: retreating to Shaithdun-o-Illume with its one, very defensible entrance. Even Arien, who had never witnessed war, had failed to recognize the gruesome consequences of a siege.

While the setting moon sent its last silvery rays into the Throne Room through a western window, the council agreed upon its final decision that the elves would make their stand on the field of Mountaingate. Billy had offered them two alternatives, a one-time confrontation on the field or a war of hit-and-run raids, whittling away at Ungden's troops while ever seeking higher, more defensible ground deeper in the mountains. Billy had strongly opted for the latter, believing that the elves had little hope in a pitched battle with so large a force. But the elves, especially Arien, were thinking along different lines.

They perceived their fate as sealed, the outcome of the battle as preordained, and considered it, rather, as a test of their honor. Arien gave little consideration to the short-term victory or defeat, viewing the fate of those who would stand with him against Ungden as inconsequential. His eyes were focused on the aftereffects of the clash, the safety of the Illumans who would flee into the Crystals. The purpose of opposing the Calvans was to gain the respect of the common soldiery, belie Ungden's depictions of the elves as dangerous, murderous mutants. A guerrilla war, Arien feared, would reinforce the negative misperceptions against the elves. And it would be time-consuming. New recruits swarmed to join Ungden's army with every passing day. In the end, Arien's forces would lay dead or hopelessly scattered, and the army celebrating victory on the southern slopes of the Crystals would be ten times the size of the force now approaching. Still believing in its righteousness, the Calvan force would willingly continue its hunt for renegade mutants.

And so, on the next morn, Billy and a group of elves led by Arien and Ryell traveled down to Mountaingate to better organize their battle plans. In studying the area, searching for the most advantageous positions, Billy noticed a long ledge cutting across the sheer face of the cliff that bordered the field on the east, about twenty feet above the grass, and nearly invisible from below, due to the coloration and shading of the rocks. Certainly an army charging into battle would pay it no heed until the trap had been sprung.

"Is there any way to get people up there?" Billy, pointing to the ledge, asked Ryell.

Ryell nodded. "There was at one time a low tunnel behind that cliff wall," he confirmed. "A split in the stone allowed entry to the ledge. It cannot be seen from this angle. But I have not traveled that path for many years; perhaps it no longer exists."

"Ah, but it does," Sylvia interrupted. "Oftentimes Erinel and I have tred that trail to sit upon the ledge and watch the waning sun over Clas Braiyelle."

"Excellent," said Billy. "A few dozen archers up there would thin the Calvan ranks!"

"You forget our number," said Ryell. "We have not the warriors to spare."

"And it would be not quite as great a surprise as you believe, I am afraid," said Arien. "I considered the same plan as we journeyed down here, but it is flawed. Captain Mitchell knows more than the way to Illuma Vale, he knows the number of our people. All of the warriors except the few I have chosen as escort for the departing host will stay for the battle, but if many of them were missing from our ranks, such an ambush might be expected. The Calvans could stay to the far edge of the field for their charge and use their shields to render the archers ineffective. And the number of our people remaining to face the onslaught would be greatly depleted."

"I still think we should put a few archers up there," Billy argued. "We've got to weaken them before they get to us. And you've already told me that your people excelled with bows."

"You doubt our prowess?" Sylvia laughed. "The first you ever saw of Illuma was the arrow I put into a tree by Mitchell's head. Would that I had aimed to kill!"

"You made that shot?" Billy smiled, a plan quickly formulating in his mind.

Sylvia looked at him as though she didn't understand his surprise.

Billy pressed on. "Tell me, then, do all Illuman maidens shoot as well as you?"

Ryell guessed Billy's thoughts immediately and did not approve. "A field of battle is no place for women!" he snapped.

"Normally I would agree," Billy shot back. He

turned to Arien. "Are all of your women to flee into the mountains?"

Arien's face went grim. "They cannot," he admitted darkly. "Our stand would then be recognized as a ploy."

"And if we are beaten, do you really believe that Ungden will show mercy to the women back in your city?" Billy had to ask. "No way. Their only chance is for us to win, so they might as well help where they're needed. You even said that Mitchell knows the number of our warriors. How many is that?"

"Three hundred, perhaps 350."

"Against thousands," Billy reasoned. "We need all the help we can get, Arien. Give some of your women bows and put them on that damned ledge. If the battle is lost, they can retreat back to the city."

"We'll have lost nothing and gained perhaps, a chance," agreed Ryell.

At length, Arien agreed as well, much to the satisfaction of Sylvia, who had steadfastly refused to flee into the mountains, but loathed the thought of sitting helplessly by as her brethren were slaughtered.

Some of the weight was lifted from Arien's heavy heart as they returned to the city, for Billy's strategy offered at least some hope for attaining the goals of their futile stand. Though he saw no alternatives, the decision to fight still troubled the Eldar deeply. For all of their preparations and determination, he was convinced that he was leading most of his people to their deaths in an unwinnable battle.

Del rarely left his room during the next few days. He hung a blanket over its one window, darkening it as his sanctuary against the familiar images of brutality that had suddenly sprung up all about him. He had no visitors, save Sylvia bringing him his meals, and she, incapable of understanding his torment and perceiving his behavior as a betrayal to her people, could not bring herself to speak to him.

Del accepted her coldness stoically, though it wounded him to his soul. The elves had not witnessed the world before the holocaust, and thus could not see among the implications of the coming battle the renewal of a cycle that had only one possible conclusion. They were the children of dance and song and play, and in their innocence lay the hope of the world. But Del could not expect them to shoulder burdens they could not begin to recognize.

Yet he had indeed expected more of Billy. If Mitchell and Reinheiser were to be the demons that would damn Aielle, then Billy Shank was their unwitting agent, bolstering the resolve of the elves to accept the rekindled flames of war by feeding them the false hopes of futile plans.

And the sight of these doomed people rehearsing the scenes of their imminent slaughter with sharpened blades and a common, merciless grimace revolted Del, sent him reeling to his room, the last bastion of his fleeting hopes. Even this walled womb was not impervious to the assaults of the wicked reality, for it couldn't block out the sounds. Every so often, the hollow clang of sword against sword echoed through the air and slashed into Del's heart.

On the afternoon of the third day since his return to Illuma, Del lay quietly on his bed fantasizing that he was dancing with Brielle in the promised splendor of Luminas ey-n'abraieken. A soft knock on the door chased away his daydream.

"What?" he called defiantly at the intrusion.

Billy entered the room, disregarding the challenge in Del's tone. "How're you doing?" he asked through a strained smile.

"I'm all right," Del replied coolly, averting his eyes from Billy's to make a point of his true feelings.

Billy had already suspected that Del was angry with him, but he believed that he was right in his actions and that it was Del who was looking at this situation from the wrong viewpoint. He walked over boldly and sat down on the bed next to his friend. Determinedly, he held his stare upon Del's face until Del returned the look. Then he asked bluntly in a sobered yet softened tone, "What are you going to do?"

"How the hell do I know?" Del replied sharply, and again he looked away.

"Will you look at me!" Bill scolded. "Listen, pal, you had better make up your mind soon. The Calvans are setting up camp less than a mile from Mountaingate and this whole damned thing is going to explode tomorrow morning." Del sat up on the opposite side of the bed, still looking away, and bit his lip at the grim news.

"Most of the elves are already down on the field," continued Billy less harshly, truly sympathetic. "The rest of us are leaving in a little while."

"It's stupid," muttered Del.

"Of course it's stupid," Billy agreed with a chuckle. "Ever know a war that wasn't?"

Del spun on him. "Then why?" he shouted. "Can you just answer me that? You're going down there to die, Billy. To die! All of these wonderful people are going to throw their lives away. And for what?"

Billy shook his head and sighed at Del's ignorance. "For principles, damn it!" he said, rising from the bed. "You live by principles and you do what's right. And if you die by those principles, and for those principles, then your death isn't stupid!"

The two men glared at each other, truly at odds for the first time in their friendship.

"Never mind the Illumans," argued Del. "Think about the Calvans. Your sword is going to be killing men, real men, with wives and children. Not evil monsters, just ordinary, misinformed men who are doing what they're told. How do you feel about that?"

"I feel terrible about it," replied Billy. "Of course I do. But I've got no choice."

"Oh, is that so?" Del taunted.

"Yes, that's so!" Billy mimicked, his voice growing stronger as his anger spilled out. "You know, Del, since we got here, you've been living in some kind of wide-eyed fantasy world. I hate to be the one to tell you, but that's not the way it is!"

"But that's the way it should be!" snapped Del. The two exchanged cold grimaces for a long minute, but neither could maintain his ill feelings for the other. As though they had screamed out all of their rage, had cleared their differences from the air in one quick fit of passion, they soon found their familiar smiles of friendship.

"What's wrong with us?" Del offered calmly. "What is it within our character that makes men fight one stupid war after another?"

"I don't know," Billy said with a shrug. "I don't want this war any more than you do, but it's about to begin and we've got to fight it. What else can we do?"

"We can run, Billy," replied Del. "I'm amazed that Arien didn't do that in the first place. There must be millions of places to hide in these mountains. This battle, this tragedy, doesn't have to be fought tomorrow."

Billy paused for a moment, searching for a weakness in Del's blind resolve that would allow him to communicate his justifications for the battle. "Up on the shelf a couple of weeks ago, Reinheiser said that maybe we were brought here, not to prevent this fight, but to make sure that the right side won. Think about it, it makes a lot of sense. You're right, this whole mess can be delayed. But not avoided. Ungden knows for sure that the elves are here now, and he won't rest until he's got them. Arien realizes that. Why else do you think he'd stick around?"

Del bit down on his lip again and crossed his arms in front of him, his expression a mixture of disdain and disappointment. Billy refused to yield, convinced now of his duty as a friend to open Del's eyes to the truth of the situation before them.

"You've got to face reality," he pressed. "Forget about the elves and the Calvans and just think about this: We don't have the luxury of time to run away. If Mitchell and Reinheiser aren't stopped here and now, they're going to introduce all the wonderful weapons from our world to Aielle. Don't doubt that for a minute. Where will your fantasy world be then?"

Del slumped back, stunned. He hadn't given much

thought to what future damage Mitchell and Reinheiser could wreak.

Satisfied that he had done all he could for Del, Billy walked to the door. He looked back one final time over his shoulder. "You think about it, Del. We leave in half an hour."

Del sank deeper into the security of his soft bedcovers as the door slammed shut behind Billy. Del felt the ghosts of pain and misery, images from the wars and poverty of his world, crowding around him, mocking his hopeless dreams of true brotherhood. He had no arguments to dispute Billy's warning about Mitchell and Reinheiser; he was trapped in this conflict, locked as surely as his ancestors into the unyielding cycle of suffering.

It flooded him with revulsion, paralyzed him for many minutes on his bed in subconscious hopes that the last party for Mountaingate would leave without him, absolving him of his unwanted responsibilities.

Then a vivid memory jolted him. He saw Captain Mitchell standing on a beach with an automatic rifle, holding hundreds of cowed talons at bay and proclaiming himself to be a god.

Del had run out of arguments.

Had that last party already left? he wondered. He leaped from the bed and charged out the door.

Del had a plan of his own.

Chapter 22

Under A Starry Sky

Del caught up to the last party just as they entered the tunnel on the far side of Illuma Vale. Billy had mixed emotions at the arrival of his friend. He was grimly satisfied that Del had apparently recognized and accepted his responsibility, yet he felt somehow a sense of loss for Del's innocent, if unrealistic, way of embracing this new world. Billy had hoped that Del could prove him wrong, could convince him and all of the others that utopia was within their grasp if they only reached for it.

Del walked up to Billy and clasped his hand firmly. The two men stared hard and long at each other, exchanging silent but unmistakable feelings of mutual respect and true friendship, sealing an unbreakable bond that would live on even if they were both slain on the battlefield the following morning.

"You will join with us, then, in our time of desperation?" Arien asked hopefully. All along, Del's reluctance to accept the coming battle as the proper course of action had shaken Arien's confidence in the decision, had made him worry that this man with wisdom bitterly gained in another age might be seeing the situation from a better perspective than he.

"I'm with you," Del assured him. "But first I have something to do. Will you let me go back to Avalon?"

"What trickery is this?" Ryell snapped immediately. "He will not fight beside us! He will run and hide and not return until the vultures pick at our slaughtered bones!"

"I will be at the battle by your side," said Del. "I have to be at the battle." He looked to Billy, his stoic visage dispelling any doubts Billy might have had about his true resolve to carry out his newly perceived duties. "I know that now."

"He's telling the truth," Billy told Arien without hesitation.

"But first I must go to Avalon," Del said with a wide grin. "I have a plan."

Arien did not return the smile, though he had trusted Del even before Billy had spoken for him. "Our problem does not concern Avalon," he said with even certainty, guessing easily enough what Del had in mind. Arien knew that the powers of Brielle could not help them in their struggle with Calva, but he realized that his words had not the conviction to truly dissuade Del. It was Del's right to discover the true character of the witch for himself, Arien knew, but he, as Eldar, would bear the cost of Del's lesson. Already, Arien felt the anger in Ryell's eyes boring into him. You give me more credit than I deserve, Ryell, he said in silent bitterness, yet it was from Ryell's expectations of his courage that he drew the strength to stand by his principles. He nearly laughed aloud at the irony of it all as he told Del with unyielding finality, "You may go."

"Eldar!" protested Ryell, but Arien cut him off.

"DelGiudice has given us no reason to doubt his word."

"There are many who would disagree with you," argued Ryell.

"Then they are misguided," replied Arien in a deliberately calm and controlled tone that reaffirmed his confidence in his authority. "I will hear no more of this, Ryell. We have not the time for a gathering of council, and in the absence of such, my word as Eldar stands."

Ryell trembled with rage, feeling as if his friend had betrayed him once again. "Your hold over the people of Illuma may not be as strong as you believe, Arien Silverleaf. There are many who question your decisions regarding the ancient ones." He could barely hiss out his declaration through his clenched jaw. "They question your intentions as well."

Arien ignored Ryell's treasonous rantings—the elves could ill afford a showdown between their Eldar and his closest adviser at this critical time—and addressed his daughter.

"Go with DelGiudice," he instructed. "See that he is allowed passage to Clas Braiyelle."

Del was surprised that the trees did not hinder his entrance into Avalon. Though his stubborn grudge refused to let him consciously admit it, he was comforted that Brielle had not shut him out. He whistled as he trotted along the path, his senses bathed in the countless stimulations of the fully blossomed forest, and he was able to forget for a while the gathering clouds of misery at Mountaingate and his grim purpose in seeking out the fair witch.

Soon, though, as the sun disappeared over the western horizon and the colors of the wood dulled into the grayed blur of twilight, Del realized that he was running short on time.

"Brielle!" he called, but his only reply was the mournful cry of a loon heralding the onset of the secret world that was the forest night.

Stubbornly, Del scrambled on, calling out again for the witch.

Again the loon answered, and this time its wail beckoned to Del like a lost spirit, akin to his misery. Faithful to its cry, Del turned from the path, stumbling blindly through the darkening brush and thickets to follow the last lingering notes. And when they died away, he called out again and was answered.

Then Del came upon a grove of thick pines, a veritable wall of interlocking, unyielding branches. Undaunted, he fell flat to his belly and crawled beneath their lowest boughs, and when he had finally gotten through, he lifted his head and his breath was stolen from him.

Below him, down a short slide of thick grass, was a small glade thick and soft in swaying petals of white clover. And beyond the lea, a secluded pond, its smooth surface broken only by occasional reeds or cattails, lay quiet and still, as if in meditation under dark reflections of the prestarlit sky. But Del hardly noticed his mystical surroundings, for atop a knoll rising above the green sea of the glade, reclined the gentle Brielle, shadowed in the mysteries of the deepening gloom.

It pained Del to look upon her beauty, though it was she he had sought. He wanted now only to flee this place and this wood and be away from all thoughts of the Emerald Witch. He knew that to be impossible; Avalon would announce his arrival to its queen.

The never-seen loon gave one final cry.

Immediately, Del rose to his feet and started down the slide. Brielle knew he was there, no doubt, and he wouldn't give her the satisfaction of catching him hiding from her in the grass. He conjured memories of the carnage left on the road in the wake of Brielle's wrath and reminded himself over and over of his sole purpose in coming to Avalon, determinedly entrenching his emotions within a fortress of outrage to protect himself from the hinted passions that threatened to sweep him away. His stride stiffened in tense anger as he approached.

But then he was upon her and the ice melted away.

"Hello," he said softly.

Her reply was a smile.

Consciously, Del rebuilt the frosty facade. "I didn't come here to bother you," he said with rough sarcasm. A dark cloud passed across Brielle's countenance. She realized already what Del was leading up to, and feared that she must disappoint him once again.

"I need your help," Del continued, holding tight to his gruff tone. "A battle is about to begin."

Brielle looked away. "It is known to me," she said sadly. "And me heart truly weeps at the misery o the morrow's morn." She paused, struggling, as was Del, with a personal conflict of emotions and principles. The rules of her station were clear and unbending; she had lived by them and for them for hundreds of years. When she turned back to Del, her face was resigned and impassive, and she announced with cool finality, "'Tis none o me affair."

"How can you say that?" Del scolded. "Hundreds of innocent people are going to die! You don't think that concerns you?"

"It wounds me, even as it wounds yerself," replied Brielle, almost apologetically. "But I huv no power for a war o man."

His frustration bordering on rage, Del wanted to scream and cry all at once. "Bullshit!" he yelled. "I saw you, Brielle. I saw what you did to those talons!"

Brielle understood more clearly now that the source of Del's anger went far deeper than her rejection of him. "That I wish ye hud no seen," she said softly, lowering her eyes to hide the welling tears from Del. "It is a side o me life I do'no enjoy." She took a deep breath and reminded herself that she had done only what she had to do.

"But Avalon is me domain and me duty and I am the eyes that protect her," she asserted. "I do'no create the storms, I only show them the harm that is upon the land. Purely evil are the talons, livin only to destroy. They grant no mercy and deserve none. Would ye huv me, then, let them bring ruin to me wood?"

Del had no rebuttal against her logic.

"But the morrow's battle," Brielle continued, softly again, "is a concern o men and I huv no duties, and bein so, no powers for such a war."

Del slumped down meekly to the clover and sighed. With her innocent confession of necessities, Brielle had taught him a lesson in humility. A lot of things fell into perspective for Del at that moment. He remembered the lecture Billy had given him earlier in the day.

Duty.

Utopia had to be earned.

When he recovered from his embarrassment, Del laughed aloud at his arrogant self-righteousness. Then he looked upon the witch and was silent, fearing that she would think he mocked her.

Brielle sat quiet, hugging her knees and staring off across the melancholy pond.

Who am I to judge you? Del asked himself. He owed her an apology, an explanation. So many things he wanted to say to her, and the most pressing one kept repeating over and over in his mind. He crawled across the path of her absent gaze, catching and locking her eyes with his own, and took a chance he had never before in his life been able to take. "I love you."

Brielle blushed, but did not turn her eyes away. "Me heart speaks the same to me."

"But you have your woods and your duty, and I have my battle and mine. My Brielle," Del groaned, and gently stroked her face, "are we never to have any time together?" As he started to turn away, Brielle clasped his shoulders and settled him back in the soft carpet.

She stood up before him, apprehensive, scared even, of this decision she had made. But her heart held little doubt of her love for Del. "The field o Mountaingate is but an hour's walkin and yer battle will no begin ere the light o dawn," she heard herself saying. "We huv tonight."

Del said nothing. He stared deeply at Brielle, stunned that something this perfect could be happening between them. Then he looked past her to the skies, where the first stars brightened as each passing moment deepened the blackness of the evening canopy.

"Beautiful, they are," Brielle agreed with Del's entranced look. "Behold the first stars o summer, for this day marked the solstice. Another spring is ended. Tis a special night."

"It is," Del whispered.

Nervously, Brielle undid the laces in the front of her gown. With a slight shrug of her shoulders the gossamer fell from her and she stood naked before Del. The starlight seemed to emanate from her, enhancing her supple curves, as though she was its source. As if on cue, a slight wave rippled across the pond, carried to the shore by a cool summer breeze.

Brielle trembled, but she knew her heart truly and did not hesitate. She bent to Del and kissed him, and passions she had long ago locked away stirred again within her.

And there, amidst a waving green sea of soft clover, beneath the approving sparkle of countless stars, they consummated their love.

Brielle cried that night. She cried for remembered emotions that had slept for centuries, and she cried at the knowledge that with the morrow's sobering dawn those emotions must once again be put to sleep. Del held her tenderly, cradling her head against his chest. And though the witch could not see it, he, too, was crying.

Chapter 23

The Wizard Unveiled

Shortly before the dawn, Del left Brielle sleeping in the soft clover to begin his long and disheartened trek back to Mountaingate. A gentle rain had come up during the night and it fell still, tapping rhythmically on the leafy canopy and hissing through the mist that rode in off of the pond. When Del had gained the top of the slide, before he crossed through the pine grove, he looked back to the knoll and the fair witch and was dismayed despite his joy in loving her. For though he would carry memories of Brielle into the battle with him this day and forever after, Del's heart told him that he would never look upon her again. Yet then he left her of his own accord, compelled by a responsibility he did not want but could not escape.

Soon after, Brielle awoke from a vivid nightmare. A cold sweat beaded on her forehead as she recalled with frightening clarity an image of Del dying on a charred and bloody field, the head of a cruel spear buried deep in his chest. "This cannot be!" she cried out desperately and helplessly to the heavens. As if in answer, a vision appeared unto her: a small black staff, iron-shod on both ends, twirling about in the air. The sheer wrongness of the thing assaulted Brielle's every sense, a perversion against nature itself. It terrified her and pained her, but she composed herself in angry determination and knew she had found a link to the day's events.

Dawn came as a dulled blur of pink behind the unbroken cover of dreary gray clouds. Fitting weather,

Del noted, for such a day as this. The rain had stopped, but the air hung oppressively thick with moisture.

Del found the elven camp astir in the north, though no signs of the Calvan force were yet apparent in the south. Slowly, head down, he walked across the field, indulging himself as he went with one final fantasy of the way he wished things could be.

The clear note of the watchman's horn announcing his arrival brought the weight of reality back upon his shoulders.

Two horsemen trotted out toward him from the chaos of the bustling camp. Billy Shank rode in the lead, outfitted in chain-link mail and a shining shield and sword, but it was the other rider that Del looked upon in amazement. It was Arien Silverleaf, unmistakably, at that moment, the elf-king of all Illuma, wearing a forest-green cloak pulled back from his shoulders and a light green tunic woven of some fine material. Under the sleeveless edges of the shirt, Del saw closely meshed links of shining mail, much finer than the heavy rings of Billy's armor. Arien wore no helm, but a silver gem-studded crown with a golden inset of a quarter moon, the symbol of Lochsilinilume. Strapped to his left arm was a polished shield bearing the same emblem, and sheathed on his hip in a gem-encrusted scabbard was a broadsword unequaled in workmanship by even the crafted weapon the Colonnae had given to Del. Its hilt gleamed all of silver and its pommel was intricately carved to resemble the head of a dragon, inlaid in gold all down the neck to the crosspiece of the weapon.

"I didn't realize that your people kept such weapons," remarked Del.

"Gifts from Ardaz, mostly," explained Arien, tightening his heels to calm his spirited steed, a great muscled stallion, its coal-black coat glistening from the wetness of the morning and from the sweat of its own tense anticipation. "And some of our own making." He smiled at Del's unyielding sarcasm. "The mountains are wild and dangerous even now, friend DelGiudice. Would that we could hang these devices above a mantel and use them only to enhance fanciful tales!''

The Eldar's face turned serious again as he grasped the hilt of his sword. ''This is Fahwayn,'' he told Del. ''The Silver Death.'' He drew the sword from its scabbard slowly, reverently, and raised it high above him. It gleamed brightly and sharply, in spite of the dim light. ''It was forged with great care many years ago when Aielle was young,'' he said. He lowered the sword and ran his hand along its polished blade, absorbing the sensations of unrivaled craftsmanship and magic that they might invoke images of the past and allow him to wander back to the security of his memories of the early days of Illuma.

With sudden and frightening speed, Arien thrust the sword above him. It shimmered with power, an extension, the focal point of the strength that was Arien Silverleaf. The great stallion, caught up in the ire of the elf-king, reared, and Arien cried aloud, ''Bayr imine eyberg ai'l anais i Sylv Fate-aval!'' He looked at the startled men and cried again with equal fervor, ''By their own evil do they bring the Silver Death upon them!''

His burst of energy satisfied by the proclamation, Arien flashed a calming smile to the astonished gawks of Billy and Del and dropped Fahwayn to his side, swinging the blade in a slow arc. ''At times when talons were abroad, her cut was smooth and sure,'' he said absently. ''But now she sits awkwardly in my hand. I have no thirst for the blood Fahwayn spills this morn.'' He sheathed the sword with a sigh and turned his steed back to the encampment.

''I'm glad you're back,'' Billy said to Del. ''I only wish that Ardaz were here, too. With his tricks, I think we'd have a chance.''

''Ardaz hasn't returned!'' moaned Del.

''No,'' replied Billy. ''But Arien is sure that he'll be here when we need him.''

Arien wheeled his horse around and faced them. ''Even if the wizard does not come,'' the Eldar growled, his face stern and uncompromising, ''we will teach the humans respect for our people. The might of justice flows through our veins!"

"A comforting thought," said Del a bit sadly. "But I'd rather be dancing on the shelf."

Helpless against the relentless assault of Del's chiding, the Eldar could not deter the smile that softened his grim features. "Come," he said. "We must find a horse for you."

Arien led them to the base of the cliff on the western edge of the field, where Erinel stood, hands on hips, defiantly eyeing a white mare. He turned when they approached and smiled broadly when he recognized Del.

"DelGiudice!" he called happily. "Your return brightens this cursed morn!"

"Do you have a horse for our friend?" asked Arien.

Erinel's smile disappeared. "I am truly sorry, but I forgot to keep one for him. We sent the remaining horses running into the foothills after the last of our people were outfitted. Perhaps we have time to find another."

"What about that one?" Del asked blankly, his attention held by the beauty of the small mare.

"That one?" Erinel laughed. "She will take no rider. Several others had the same idea, but she quickly dissuaded them." He displayed a bruise on his arm and laughed again. "She rewarded my efforts to bridle her!"

"Then whose is she?" Del asked.

"I do not know," replied Erinel. "I have never seen her before this morning. She must have strayed from the Calvan camp, though, for she is too well groomed to be wild."

"She'll let me ride her," declared Del as he started toward the mare.

"Be wary!" Erinel called after him. But even as he spoke, the mare nuzzled her nose in Del's neck. He stroked the pure white coat with equal affection.

"How did he do that?" asked an astonished Erinel. Several other elves were now watching in disbelief.

"She will take no saddle," Erinel called to Del.

"Doesn't need one," Del replied, and hopped up on the mare's back. "You won't let me fall, will you, girl?" he asked the mare softly as he patted her neck.

Some of the elves began to chuckle and Erinel blushed in embarrassment. "Or a bridle!" he insisted stubbornly.

In response, Del grasped the mare's snowy mane.

"Will you allow this?" Erinel asked Arien. "He is an inexperienced rider and she is unpredictable."

Arien studied the mare's reactions to Del's petting. "She is his to ride," he replied. "It is not our place to interfere with their love." With a knowing laugh, the Eldar spun his great mount and sprang away to check on other matters.

The watchman's horn sang out and the elves turned their eyes to the south.

Like an endless swarm of insects, the Calvan army spilled onto the field, stretching across the breadth of Mountaingate. They formed into ranks several deep, as still more soldiers appeared through the mountain pass.

"We're going to die," Del stated through his gasps.

"Easy, buddy," Billy said to comfort him, but Billy, too, was dismayed. The force facing them, uniformed in black and silver, was precise and disciplined, fully mounted, and already ten times the size of the elven army.

Finally, mercifully, the procession ended and the Calvans held their positions in silence, thousands of spear tips motionless in the air, patiently awaiting further commands.

Ryell walked his horse over to Arien. "Five thousand?" he whispered.

"Perhaps," answered the Eldar. He looked around at his disheartened troops. They had known from the beginning that they were doomed, but had held out hope for some sort of miracle. The sight of this huge force arrayed against them brought home the full impact of their hopelessness. Yet they had a mission to accomplish, a duty to their kin who had fled into the mountains that would give meaning to their deaths. Boldly, Arien took command. "Form a line!" he shouted.

Barely three hundred strong, the elves heeded the order of their Eldar. And when they had completed their formation, Arien drew Fahwayn from its scabbard and walked his horse the length of their rank to address each of them individually, reminding them of their purpose and rallying them around the basic precept of justice that had dictated their stand on this field. Del noted hopefully that the face of each elf brightened as Arien rode past.

Still, Del wondered how that could make a difference against the overwhelming odds they faced. He took his place alongside Arien and Ryell in the middle of the Illuman line and kept quiet his doom saying.

But, distinctly, he heard Ryell mutter, "Twenty to one."

Arien, intent on his personal preparations for what was to come, did not reply.

Then a fanfare of trumpets sounded from the Calvan lines, and Ungden, Overlord of Pallendara, Commander of the Calvan Empire, made his grand entrance onto the field, bedecked in golden-hued plated armor. His mount, a fine white gelding, was outfitted likewise and prancing gracefully in white-furred boots. A great gem-covered helm with feathered plumes adorned the Usurper's head.

A score of the Warders of the White Walls surrounded Ungden protectively with their own white chargers, well muscled, finely bred stallions specially trained for the elite guard of the Overlord. The Warders wore their traditional white uniforms and sky-blue cloaks, with white-plumed helms and shields adorned with a gauntleted fist clutching a sword above four bridges and four pearls, the original standard of Pallendara.

Some traditions even the arrogant Ungden did not dare to challenge.

Del grimaced in anger when he recognized the two

riders within Ungden's protective circle. Mitchell, his chest puffed out in gloating pride, rode at the Usurper's right. Reinheiser followed, continually looking from side to side as though he was searching for someone.

On the ledge overlooking the field, Sylvia notched an arrow to her bow as Ungden's entourage moved to the center of the field in front of the first rank of Calvan soldiers. The Usurper was within her range, though his fine armor would probably deflect an arrow at this long distance. Her shot would have to be perfect to penetrate. And if she missed her mark, the plans for an ambush would be ruined.

"Stay your hand," came a voice behind her. "Ungden is too well protected for any such attempts."

Startled, Sylvia spun around and, seeing the speaker, obediently lowered her bow and ducked back to the safety of the cliff wall.

Ungden absently waved a gloved hand and a standard bearer rode out from the Calvan ranks toward the elven line. He crossed the narrow field at a gallop and, spotting Arien's arrayments, pulled his horse up a few yards in front of the Eldar. His wide-eyed amazement in confronting the legendary night dancers belied the deadly serious business of the day.

The Calvan studied the elven forces for a moment, noting their number, and addressed Arien with arrogant confidence. "Do you speak as leader of your people?"

Grim-faced, Arien did not reply.

Undaunted by the imposing stare, the soldier continued. "Night dancers, heed my words!" he called to all the elves. "While it would be but a small task for the army of Pallendara to defeat you by the sword—clearly, you cannot hope to win—it is not the wish of the Overlord to see you destroyed. Lay down your weapons. Accept Ungden as the true and sole king of Ynis Aielle and your lives will be spared. You cannot resist!"

Not an elf stirred or softened the set of his visage. There was no room for compromise in their determination. They were a free people, and they were more than ready to die in defense of that freedom. Ungden and his cocky charges apparently didn't appreciate their resolve.

They would teach the Calvans better, though their deaths would surely be part of the scenario.

"What say you?" demanded the messenger. "Will you yield to the will of the true king?"

Ryell, next to Arien, spat on the ground in front of the Calvan. For the first time in a long while, he and Arien were in complete agreement.

Arien stepped his horse out from the elven line and the Calvan, despite his outward arrogance, backed off an equal distance in cautious respect.

"Why are you here, serpent?" Arien asked. "You have no quarrel with us, nor do you have any claim over us. We are free, our land is our own, and we recognize no self-proclaimed ruler! Now be off, else you shall be the first to feel the cold edge of my blade!" In a flash, he had Fahwayn drawn and readied, its blade shining with the inner glow of its magic.

The messenger had his answer. Terrified by the calm confidence with which the elf-king promised his death, he wheeled his horse around and fled back across the field to report to his Overlord.

Ungden laughed when he was informed of the elves' defiance. With a wave of his hand, he sent the messenger back to his place in the ranks and set his war machine into motion.

A horn blew. On cue, the sergeant of the elite guard drew his sword and raised it high above him. Man and elf alike tensed.

A second horn blew. The commanders of the Calvan forces walked their groups into position in front and at the sides of Ungden's entourage. Del was sweating now, and finding it difficult to breathe.

A third horn blew. Ungden let a few more tantalizing seconds pass, then motioned to his sergeant. The blade fell and the thunder of 20,000 pounding hooves shook Mountaingate to its core. Screaming battle cries and clashing their weapons against their shields, the Calvan army fueled its frenzy with every charging stride.

Under the leadership of Sylvia, the archers waited patiently for the best possible moment to spring their ambush. As the Calvans passed the midpoint of the field, reaching their closest point to the ledge, the elves sprang from their concealment and loosed a shower of arrows, concentrating their fire on the front riders. Horse and rider tumbled to the earth and those directly behind trampled them or were tripped up. The Calvan line wavered and nearly broke down altogether in confusion, their battle formations shattered by the deadly surprise attack. Arien recognized the opportunity to release his warriors, but for some reason, almost as if some other will imposed itself upon him, he couldn't speak his command to charge.

The Calvan commanders quickly realized the impact of the trap on their troops. With professional efficiency they swung the army in a loop and short retreat to reform the battle groups and regain their composure. Many Calvans had gone down under the flurry of arrows, though not nearly enough to give the Illumans any hope of victory.

"We should have attacked!" Ryell insisted.

Arien could not rebuke the scolding. He still did not understand what had held back his command. He couldn't believe that he had frozen under the pressure.

"Their ranks seem not at all thinned," moaned Ryell. "If we ever had even a slight chance, it is gone now."

The Calvans prepared to resume their attack. Now knowing the danger from the cliff, they moved to the western side of the field and covered their flank with their shields. The arrows wouldn't hinder them this time.

Yet even as they kicked their horses into motion, a bearded old man in a light blue robe and a pointed cap walked out among the archers. Sylvia and the others lowered their bows.

"Ardaz!" Del cried when he noticed the wizard. "On the ledge, Arien!"

It was true, the Silver Mage of Lochsilinilume had come. He held his arms outstretched, one hand clutching his oaken staff and the other reaching for the power of the heavens, and chanted in an arcane tongue, the invocation of fire. The Calvans began their second assault, unaware of the doom that was about to befall them.

"Now we get our fight!" Ryell yelled to his comrades.

"Hold, my friend," commanded Arien with a knowing smile, understanding now the will that had stayed his charge. "Ardaz is come. He will have a trick or two for Ungden."

"Again you act the part of a fool, Arien," retorted Ryell. "The antics of that buffoon will not stop the Calvans. We must meet their charge!"

The Calvan force closed in quickly, but Arien put his full trust in the wizard and held his troops at bay.

Ardaz's invocation reached a feverish pitch. A red flame sprang from the top of his staff, flickering, yet not consuming the wood. He pointed the staff across the field and spoke the final rune. Instantly a wall of flames, stretching the breadth of the field, ignited in front of the charging riders. Those that could not stay their mounts plunged headlong in, bursting into white flame, and fell as charred corpses.

This time the training and expertise of the Calvan commanders could not prevent a panic. Horrified by the bared power of the wizard, the surviving Calvans swung back wildly in full retreat. But Ardaz wasn't finished.

"This business must be ended here and now," he explained to Sylvia, almost in apology for his next action. He raised his arms again and called out in a voice godlike in power, "Ungden, Usurper! Too long have you imprisoned the peoples of this land with your unlawful rule! By the fires of the sun above, I purge Aielle this day of your evil stain!" He aimed his deadly staff again and a second flame barrier sprang up, directly behind Ungden and his guard, boxing in the entire Calvan host.

On command from Ardaz, a tear of sorrow in his eye, the killing walls began to converge.

Trapped Calvan riders spun wildly and banged into one another, some falling from their mounts only to be trampled into the dust. Crazed horses, blind to the urgings of their masters, rushed for the western ledge, the only escape route, and plummeted hundreds of feet to Blackemara.

Relentless, merciless, the fire walls closed in.

Though horrified, Sylvia and the other archers watched the grisly spectacle. They felt it their responsibility to bear witness to the momentous tragedy of this day, and they realized that Ardaz, nearly broken by the slaughter he had invoked, needed their support.

In the rank of elven horsemen, outside the fire wall, Del and the others could not see what was happening to the Calvans. But the screams and wails of their dying foes told them all they needed to know.

"The antics of a buffoon," Del echoed somberly to Ryell.

"I apologize," replied Ryell, his words reflecting both awe for the mage and pity for the tortured Calvans within the fires. "There is perhaps more to Ardaz than I have believed."

"Call him not Ardaz," Arien said. "Call him by his true name." He extended his hand toward the bent figure, now leaning heavily on his staff. "Behold Glendower! Woe be to those who invoke the wrath of the Silver Mage!"

Calvans died by the score in the panic, some caught by the wizard fires, others trampled, and still more leaping to the swamp. Then there came a barely audible buzzing sound, and as suddenly as it had started, the riot ended. Barren of all emotion it seemed, almost zombielike, the remainder of the Calvan army moved back into battle groups.

Still the walls converged.

But not a man screamed.

And not a horse reared or snorted in terror.

Only the crackling of the rolling fires consuming grass and flesh disturbed the eerie stillness.

Ardaz understood and was afraid.

A swirling cloud of red smoke floated out from the Calvan line, growing more tangible as it moved. Soon it resembled a rider and horse and then it was; a red-cloaked man, cowl pulled low to hide his face, atop a gaunt, yellow-eyed black stallion that snorted smoky flames through its flared nostrils and pawed the ground as though it hated the living grass below it.

"Istaahl?" Sylvia asked Ardaz, but the distracted wizard did not reply.

The red-cloaked rider reached his bony arm toward the west, clenching and unclenching his fist as though he was gathering up the air from the distant expanses. Then he swung his arm at the cliff, as if throwing something, and a great gust of wind smote Ardaz, extinguishing the flame atop his oaken staff.

And the fire walls were gone.

"The wizard of Caer Tuatha?" cried Ryell when he saw the red-cloaked mage.

"It cannot be," replied Arien, surprised. "Istaahl gathers his power from the sea. This mage is too far inland."

"The master is come," hissed an evil voice from under the red cowl. Ardaz's face went bloodless. The red-robed wizard pulled back his hood, revealing his pallid, hairless head, and the many-faceted black sapphire that was his mark. Ardaz groaned audibly, though he had already guessed that Thalasi had come.

"May the Colonnae be with us!" gasped Arien, for he, too, recognized the mark of the Black Warlock. "Angfagdul, the utter blackness, is come again!"

Chapter 24

Jericho

Tucked away into a small corner of his subconscious, in a place reserved for childish, supposedly irrational, fears, Del retained an image resembling Morgan Thalasi, a demon embodied in human form. Thalasi's withered body appeared broken and sickly beyond anything which could be alive. Yet the life force within the Black Warlock exuded an aura frighteningly, paralyzingly evil, and a strength sufficient to hold two armies at bay.

On the ledge, Ardaz spun about and waved his arms wildly, summoning all of his strength in a desperate effort to battle Thalasi. The air about him crackled as his power mounted; Sylvia's hair tingled and was drawn outward toward the wizard by the growing charge. When he knew that he had reached his limits and could contain no more of the energy, Ardaz uttered a rune of evocation and stamped his staff on the rock, releasing a blue bolt of lightning. Its flash blinded all who witnessed it for several seconds; the corresponding rumble of thunder rolled throughout the mountains for miles around.

But Thalasi had anticipated such attempts and had prepared himself accordingly. A protective globe of defensive energy encircling him dispersed the bolt into a shower of many-colored, harmless sparks before it ever reached its mark.

Thalasi curled a thin lip over his rotted teeth in a smile that seemed more a grimace, and drew out a thin, iron-shod rod. Pointing it at the ledge, he demonstrated his mastery, controlling elemental powers that Ardaz could only ask for assistance. Uttering only two simple runes, he returned Ardaz's attack tenfold with a mighty white bolt.

The Silver Mage had worked frantically to construct his own defensive barrier when he saw Thalasi draw the rod, but he was overmatched. The violence of the white bolt shook the whole mountain, sending cracks deep into the stone from the ledge all the way down to the field, and the archers were thrown from their feet. The brunt of its malice focused on Ardaz, ripping through his defenses, charring and splintering his fine oaken staff and hurling him into the rock face at the rear of the ledge. He lay crumpled against the stone, patches of his clothing blackened and still smoking, his newly grown hair singed, and the fingers on the hand that had been holding his staff burned and blistered.

Sylvia regained her footing and rushed to his side. Blood streamed from the wizard's lips as he mouthed the name of the Black Warlock. And then he fell silent.

Half in anger, half in desperate fear, the archers began firing at Thalasi. He laughed at them and turned aside, ignoring them, for their attempt was pitifully inept against his shielding; the arrows were reduced to windblown ashes when they hit the defensive globe.

Knowing his doom was upon him, Arien determined that his demise would be unyielding to terror. He called for his troops to gather their courage with him and charge.

But this, too, proved futile.

Grinning broadly, Thalasi faced the elven line and began twirling the wand like a baton. Compelled by his dominating will, the Illuman horses responded in kind, turning circles of their own, oblivious to the commands of their riders. Ungden, and then his troops following his lead, broke out into taunting laughter at the sight of the helpless elves struggling vainly to control their mounts. And all of the horses were dancing.

All except one.

The white mare snorted in fury and steeled her eyes against the onslaught of Thalasi's wicked attack. Summoning every strength of will within her, she cleansed her mind of Thalasi's insinuation and began to slowly walk toward the bringer of perversion, bearing on her a confused and terrified DelGiudice.

Onward she marched, now crossing the grass blackened by Ardaz's fire, her stride growing bolder as she became more assured that she could resist the Black Warlock. Del was caught in the middle of a struggle between two powers far beyond him. A helpless pawn in their battle, he held tightly to the mare's mane with both hands and prayed that Arien or anybody would come to his aid.

Thalasi was deceived. Assuming the mare to be guided by the great will of her rider, he directed his next attack at Del. Extending one bony hand, he spoke a curse, and violently closed his fingers into a tight fist.

Del shrieked in agony as he felt an icy hand grasp and squeeze his heart. Horrified, he released his grip on the mare and clutched his chest.

He felt a lump in his shirt pocket.

Acting solely on his instinct to survive, Del tore open his shirt and pulled out the little derringer. His eyes bulged from the inner pressure, his breath would not come, and consciousness was slipping away, but he somehow managed to fumble the silver bullet into the chamber and point the pistol at Thalasi. The sight of the weapon amazed Thalasi, and in his surprise, the Black Warlock released for a moment his deadly grip. Del's lungs expanded immediately, taking in a deep breath of revitalizing oxygen, but he wasted no time enjoying the sensation. Closing his eyes in anticipation of the explosion and kick, he put his finger on the trigger.

He couldn't do it.

The Calvans were no longer laughing. They stared curiously at Del, who had resisted their wizard and who held this strangely shaped piece of metal. Mitchell grunted in anger when he saw the gun, revolted by the possibility of his most hated enemy destroying his plans for conquest. Yet, certain that he would be Del's primary target if he exposed himself, the captain made no move to rush to Thalasi's aid.

Reinheiser, though, recognizing the danger to his master, reacted quickly and without regard for his personal safety. He broke through the line of Warders and galloped his horse flat out across the field.

Del stared at the derringer helplessly, feeling deceived by his own conscience, disgusted at his failure in this time of need, and in the paralyzing resurgence of pain as Thalasi, now understanding the full potential of Del's threat, renewed his assault even more furiously. Del would have dropped the weapon altogether had not one voice rung clear with reason in his ears. "Do it!" Billy Shank cried out to him.

But Del could not bring himself to move. He looked down at his hand, trying to fight against his own revulsion and Thalasi's insidious assaults. He was dismayed by the sight of his arm; veins engorged with blood from the tremendous pressure, and bruises on his forearm where smaller veins had already begun to rupture. He realized that he was beaten, no match for the power before him, and knew with the utmost revulsion and horror that soon he would virtually explode.

Reinheiser pulled up alongside Thalasi and saw with relief that the master was again in complete control.

Sylvia saw it, too. The black cloud that was Morgan Thalasi would soon consume Del, and then the doom would fall upon the rest of her people. Desperately, she grasped at the one faint hope she could see and ran to the side of the fallen wizard. "Please, Ardaz," she pleaded, cradling his head. "You must help us! Angfagdul will destroy us all!"

Ardaz opened one eye. "Nasty shot, you know," he gasped. "Really quite beyond me." He started to drift off again, but Sylvia shook him. "Of course, of course," he groaned in reply. "We must do something. Perhaps . . ." He silently mouthed some words, trying to remember a spell.

"Bring me an arrow," he instructed. Quickly Sylvia handed him the finest arrow she had remaining in her quiver. Ardaz stroked its wooden shaft and chanted a spell of seeking. The effort cost him the last of his strength and he fell silent, his eyes closed once more.

Sylvia slipped the arrow from the wizard's loose grip and fitted it to her bow as she ran back to the ledge. She prayed that the enchantment had been completed, and that it would be enough to get the arrow through to Thalasi. With a deep breath to steady her trembling arms, she took a bead on the Black Warlock and fired.

Del would have been dead by then, except that Thalasi was taking his time, savoring the torment of this man who dared oppose him.

Sparks flew as the arrow's stone tip struck the magic barrier. It deflected slightly, but was not destroyed, and though it did not hit its mark, it came close enough to surprise and distract Thalasi. For the second time, Del was free.

Furious at the attempt on his life and even more at the intrusion into his play, Thalasi spun at the ledge and loosed a second white bolt of destruction. Instead of waiting to see if her arrow found its mark, though, Sylvia was already moving. She dove back to the safety of the mountain wall just as the blast splintered the lip of the ledge into chunks of rubble.

Reinheiser, seated next to his master, hadn't been so quick to react. The bolt crossed directly before his face and the intensity of the flash stunned and blinded him.

"Sylvia!" Del screamed in rage, and he thrust the pistol toward the Black Warlock, who countered by holding his staff horizontally in front of him with both hands and clenching down on its iron tips. Like the edged blade of a sword, waves of energy sliced viciously at Del. His shirt ripped and a line of blood oozed from his chest. But he would not be stopped this time. He thought of Ardaz and Sylvia, both of whom he believed killed by Thalasi's thunderous attacks; he remembered again the image of Captain Mitchell on the beach, proclaiming himself a god. In his rage, Del found the strength to ignore the pain and resist the will of his foe.

As his sight returned, Reinheiser saw the look of undeniable determination on Del's face and knew that his master was in mortal danger. "No!" he yelled, and he leaped at Thalasi.

Too late. Del fired, and the bullet of the fourth magic, technology, sundered Thalasi's black staff at its midpoint with a flash of brilliant green and tore into the Black Warlock with a fury heretofore unknown in Ynis Aielle. Reinheiser dove across the back of the hell-spawned stallion and fell headlong into the ground. In his hands, he held an empty cloak. There was no sign of Thalasi, no sign that the warlock had ever been there, save a broken staff and a red cloak with a bullet hole in it.

Reinheiser pondered this turn of events for just a moment, until he felt warm blood trickling between his eyebrows and over the bridge of his nose. "Must have landed on a rock," he mumbled as he slipped out of consciousness.

The white mare started in surprise at the gunshot, and Del, in his weakened state, tumbled to the ground. The pain in his chest was gone, but his life's blood flowed from numerous cuts and gashes. Del didn't notice, he was too busy staring at the little pistol.

And the blood on his hands.

Reinheiser's horse flattened its ears and backed away as the white mare and Thalasi's gaunt stallion squared off. Bent on destruction, the black horse reared and snorted its fire. Then, as if it suddenly realized the true nature and power of the being it faced, it dropped its head in submission, dissipated into vapors, and was gone.

In the northern end of the field, the elves' horses stopped dancing. On the ledge, the archers reached for their remaining arrows.

The battle of magics was ended.

The battle of swords was about to begin.

Suddenly, a lone rider burst through the Calvan ranks, pushing all aside in his blind fury. Mitchell charged across the field, his great shield held high to protect against attacks from the ledge and his spear level, leading him unmistakably toward his prey. Arrows cracked into his shield and whistled all about him, but he was not deterred. His eyes saw nothing other than his quarry; his rage and frustration led him down a narrow tunnel toward this man who had disrupted all of his plans.

By the time Arien realized the identity and intent of the rider, he knew it was too late to save Del. Angered at his failure to react, he spurred his stallion into motion and the elven charge was begun.

Rallied only by the threats of Ungden and their commanders, the Calvan army, hesitant and unsure, answered the elven assault.

Mitchell reared up alongside his helpless enemy, dipping the tip of his spear just above Del's head. "Now you die!" he snarled, a victory smile stamped upon his face. He raised his weapon for the death plunge.

Del's eyes fixed upon the wicked tip of the spearhead, its image ringing unnaturally clear in the field of his blurred vision like the balancing point of his consciousness. Dazed and slipping from reality, he could not truly appreciate that he was about to die.

Still, somewhere in the back of his mind, Del understood a sensation of relief when he saw, even as he fainted away, the blur that was the white mare's hind leg smash into Mitchell's side.

Sylvia viewed the whole scene from the ledge. Not understanding the true nature of the white mare, she could hardly believe that this beast had come to the rescue.

Then the battle was joined and her joy left her, for even with all that had transpired, the Calvans badly outnumbered the elves. The sorceries had been played out; this clash was now solely sword against sword. And in that context, with no more tricks to spring, the elven cause seemed hopeless.

"Pick your shots carefully," Sylvia told her companions. "We haven't an arrow to waste."

One of the other archers, a young maiden with eyes too pure to be witnessing such carnage, walked over to her. "Lady Sylvia," she said. "Arien declared me message bearer to those that departed the city. I await your word on how I should proceed."

Sylvia turned back to the field. Already the sheer number of Calvans had created a distinct advantage. A portion of Ungden's army had swung around the elven line and Arien's warriors were flanked on three sides and being driven back toward the drop to Blackemara.

"Go then, now," Sylvia instructed the maiden. "Find our brothers and sisters in the mountains and tell them not to forget us or the noble cause we undertook that they might live freely."

The maiden began to weep.

"Be at ease," Sylvia assured her. "Take comfort in the knowledge that all who died here this morn accepted their fate willingly.

"Any who wish to leave may go now," she said to all the others on the ledge. "Those of us who remain behind shall pass no judgment upon you, and of you all we shall ask is that you do not forget us."

But the elves truly believed in their cause and the maiden Arien had appointed as messenger departed alone.

Backed into a corner, the elves fought with unbelievable fury and many Calvans were cut down. Fahwayn rang again and again and soon the Calvan troops backed away whenever Arien, Deathbringer they called him, moved toward them.

Amidst all the confusion, the white mare reared up on her hind legs over Del's body and shrieked an unearthly howl that scraped the marrow of even the sturdiest warriors, and from that moment neither man nor elf dared approach her or the man she protected.

Still more Calvan warriors fell, but fatigue and sheer numbers were playing more and more against the elves as the minutes of unrelenting battle passed. Fresh Calvans pressed in on their weary foes and elven blood mixed with the blood of the humans on the scarred grass of Mountaingate, and elven screams of pain and death rivaled those of the Calvans.

The archers on the ledge had little to offer their brothers on the field now, and Arien knew that the battle was nearing an abrupt end. The Calvans continued to avoid him wherever they could, allowing him virtually free movement on the field, and that maneuverability offered him one desperate flicker of hope. Back toward the far end of the field sat Ungden, surrounded by two seemingly impregnable rings of guardsmen. With Thalasi gone, and Mitchell and Reinheiser out of the battle, only the fear of the Overlord's wrath kept many of the Calvan soldiers committed to the fight.

Nearly blind with rage, Arien bolted at the Usurper and was promptly intercepted by two of Ungden's outer defensive line. And behind them, two others from the inner ring stood at the ready should Arien, against all odds, force his way through. The remaining elite guardsmen held their posts, alert for any further attempts.

Fury drove all the weariness from Arien's muscles and his sword work was nothing short of magnificent. Yet these were the Warders of the White Walls that he faced, the finest warriors that Calva had to offer, and though none of them could have withstood his assault alone, two were more than his equal. Every time he launched Fahwayn into a deadly thrust at one of his opponents, he was forced to withdraw and parry a well-aimed counter by the other. As the Warders grew accustomed to the feints and dodges of the Eldar, they were able to keep him almost exclusively on the defensive.

Before long the frustration of his ineffectiveness tempered the rage that had given Arien strength. He was tiring now, and making mistakes that he knew would eventually cost him his life.

He lunged desperately, but the flashing speed wasn't

there, and his intended target deflected Fahwayn aside while the other Warder drove his sword at the opening in Arien's defenses. The Eldar felt the cold tip begin to bite at his chest and recoiled instinctively, though he knew it was too late.

Yet he still lived.

Blood trickled from a wound just below his breast, but the puncture was not deep. Something had stayed the Warder's hand. Fahwayn now on guard before him, Arien studied his opponents. In their eyes he saw respect rather than bloodlust. "You could have finished me," he said to the Warder.

"Nay, you were the quicker," was the reply.

"You had me dead!" Arien insisted. "Yet you held. You have no heart for this fight!"

In rebuttal, the Warder swung mightily, Arien easily deflecting the blow. "I'll have the Usurper's worthless head!" he proclaimed.

"That we cannot allow," said the Warder, but his voice was unconvincing and Arien knew that his perceptions of contempt for Ungden among the Warders were correct.

Then a horn blew, and so clear and strong was its note that for a moment the fighting stopped and all heads turned toward Avalon. There, at the edge of the field by the magical wood, hovered Calamus, winged Lord of horses, and atop him, dressed in shining mail, set Belexus, an ivory horn pressed to his lips and a huge sword raised triumphantly. Below him, emerging from the wood, straight-backed and proud on mighty steeds, came the rangers of Avalon, swords bared and faces grim.

Barely two-score strong, yet preceded by a whispered reputation of ferocity that was the meat of valorous tales throughout the taverns of all Aielle, they struck a chord of fear in the hearts of Calvan and Illuman alike.

For neither side understood the purpose that brought the rangers to the field of battle this morn, or could guess whose cause this legendary order would champion.

The question was soon answered. "What crimes huv ye done by the Children o the Moon?" cried Belexus. "Ware me sword, Ungden. Throne-stealin murderer, now ye get yer due!" And on came the rangers.

Calamus, soaring on mighty wings, quickly outdistanced the other horses, and from his high vantage point, Belexus spotted Arien and understood at once the elf-king's desperate attempt.

They shared much, these two warriors who had never met. Akin and unrivaled in their battle prowess, adhering to a common code of morality and justice that would not tolerate one such as Ungden the Usurper, elf-king and ranger prince realized immediately an empathetic bond.

Even as he noticed several of the Warders closest to Ungden pull long glaives off of their mounts to protect against an assault from the air, Arien knew without doubt what action the mighty ranger would take.

Timing was the key.

Bearing down on the Overlord of Pallendara, Belexus shared Arien's fire, blood coursing hot with rage through his veins.

Arien moved sluggishly now, intentionally tempering the pace of his fight to dull the edge of his foes' wariness. He had no margin for error; there would be no second chance.

A fleeting shadow passed as Calamus swooped, and as Arien had hoped, it caused a slight distraction in the eyes of his opponents.

The flashing speed returned to the Eldar's sword arm. Fahwayn razored across the chest of one Warder, and with a subtle twist of his wrist, Arien continued the same motion of the blade and drove its point under the breastplate of the other. He finished neither move, having not the time or the will to kill either of his worthy adversaries. But his attack was successful. Both Warders, falling back to avoid Fahwayn's fell cut, stumbled aside and Arien saw the path to Ungden cleared before him.

For Belexus now executed his role in the assault. He had started, predictably, toward Ungden, bringing up a wall of pole arms. But then he swerved Calamus aside and as Arien cracked through the first line, drawing the attention of the two Warders of the second ring, Belexus was upon them.

A battering ram of flesh and muscle, the ranger and his winged steed smashed into the first rider and drove him and his mount into the second and beyond. Belexus had played his part perfectly and the demon in his blood was placated when he felt the rush of air as Arien charged through the gap behind him.

Desperately, the Warders closest to the Usurper tried to swing their cumbersome weapons about. To their dismay, Arien was already beyond them, and for that moment it seemed to the Eldar and to the Usurper that they were the only two people on the field. All other sights were reduced to meaningless blurs by singular, all-consuming emotions: the anger in Arien, and the terror in Ungden.

Pitifully, Ungden drew his ornate sword, hardly able to hold the heavy blade steady in his feeble arms. Fahwayn twirled above Arien's head once, then smashed into Ungden's sword, driving it from his grasp. There was no mercy staying Arien's rage. He didn't even realize that his wimpering opponent was now unarmed as he brought Fahwayn above his head again in a twirl. Without the slightest hesitation, he unleashed all of his anger into one mighty swing and lopped off the Usurper's head.

Ungden's body held its position for a moment, as if frozen in disbelief, then slumped onto the back of its horse. Arien watched with grim satisfaction as the head rolled about in the dirt. He expected the Warders to rush in and kill him now, but the only rider approaching was Belexus, bending low over the side of Calamus to scoop up the head.

Soon the ranger was soaring over the field displaying the gruesome trophy and blowing wildly on his horn.

To Arien's amazement, the Warders of the White Walls saluted him for his victory and, heads down, started back across the field. The Eldar looked upon them with pity now, honorable men broken by the bindings of an oath that had forced them into servitude to a tyrant. Only by defeating them in battle had Arien and Belexus freed them of their responsibilities.

With the sight of their own champions leaving, and the great ranger (with two-score of his brutal allies charging down upon them) holding their Overlord's severed head, the Calvans' heart for this fight was shattered. Some fought on, more in fear than in anger, but most rode wildly back across Mountaingate and fled into the cover of Avalon. Many merely dropped their weapons and pleaded for mercy.

The Battle of Mountaingate was ended.

Chapter 25

To the Victor . . .

"Dance with me!" she teased, and twirled across the moonlit field, the short cape tossing about her naked form as she ran, heightening his hunger. He could not resist her, was defenseless against her innocent smile, her bewitching eyes, amd her simple purity. She could break him with a word.

And yet he knew only security in her presence.

The cape rode up high as she spun with a careless laugh, her thighs catching the quiet rays of moonlight in a soft, enticing glow that held his longing gaze.

A long moment passed and still the light commanded his full attention. Subtly the light transformed, intensified, an entity unto itself now.

It should have been gone . . . the cape would fall back down . . . surely she must have moved again.

But it remained.

And she was gone, and the field. He tried to recapture the moment, the feeling, but they were no more. Only the light remained.

The light.

He became aware of something chill and wet against his cheek. Gradually he realized that he was lying facedown.

Doggedly, Del willed one of his eyes open. The brightness soon came into focus as bedewed grass, holding a crystalline sparkle that could only be the light of morning. Beyond were the arching silver telvensils that formed the gateway to the paths up the mountains.

He was on Mountaingate, and the name triggered other recollections. Slowly he rolled over and propped himself up on his elbows to survey the field. A harsh reality awaited him.

Mountaingate, once proud and fitting entrance to the great Crystal Mountains, lay in ruin. Beneath the maddened charge of armies, its waving grasses had been trampled and churned into broken sod, now slick with the blood and gore of the fallen. Crumpled and broken forms, elven and human alike, littered the field, and riderless horses wandered mournfully about in aimless confusion. Wisps of gray smoke still rose from the areas charred and blackened by wizard's fire, dulling the vision with a dreamlike quality.

But Del understood the reality. A bitter mixture of revulsion and anger welled in his throat as he gazed upon the carnage. He thought of the beauty and magic of this land, given to Man as a gift from the Gods, and one word alone escaped from the bile in his mouth, "Sacrilege."

He turned away, unable to face Billy and Sylvia as they approached.

To the western side of Mountaingate by the drop to Blackemara, the Calvan prisoners sat huddled and miserable under a brutal guard of unsympathetic elves. The wretched humans were not allowed to move or speak, and punishment for any disobedience came swift and harsh, the butt end of a spear or a well-aimed kick.

"Their hate runs deep," Billy said, noticing that Del had taken an interest in the scene.

Helplessly, Del shook his head. He wished he could block out all of the grisly scenes before him. "Ardaz?" he asked suddenly, remembering Thalasi's assault on the ledge.

"He is well," Sylvia replied. "Angfagdul's attack wounded him." She mimicked Ardaz's voice lightheartedly, "But we wizards are a sturdy lot, you know, tougher than the stones in a mountain, though a bit more cracked, I do daresay!" But even Sylvia couldn't hold her smile. "He is at council now, with Ryell and Arien and the other Eldars," she said.

"And Erinel?"

Billy and Sylvia looked to each other for support.

"Gone, Del," Billy answered grimly. He looked forlornly over the blasted field. "Like so many others."

"Did the council go well, Father?" Sylvia dared to ask when Arien found them later that morning.

"Hatred," Arien replied sadly. "It is my belief that the destruction of Ungden and Morgan Thalasi ended this war. Caer Tuatha will not attack us again."

"Why would they want to?" Billy reasoned.

"Such was my argument," said Arien. "But the death of kin and friend breeds vengeance."

"Oh, damn," Del groaned. He looked again at the miserable Calvan prisoners and the unchanging grimace of the elven guards. "And what of them?" he asked somberly, fearing the answer.

Arien hesitated and shrugged. "The Calvan dead shall be left on the field for the carrion birds, and the prisoners tried before the council for crimes against Illuma. Some may be set free to give the appearance of justice, but most, I fear, are doomed."

Del trembled on the edge of control. "And those that fled?"

"Hunted down and punished."

"You have to stop this!"

"I am helpless!" Arien shouted back at him. The Eldar calmed at once and true sorrow was in his eyes. "Never have I felt so alone among my people. None but Ardaz stood beside me at council."

As if on cue, Ardaz walked by at that moment, though he paid no notice to his friends. "Terrible," he muttered to himself, wandering off toward the cliff wall. "Just terrible."

The wizard pulled the black cat off of his shoulder and blew gently into her face to awaken her. "Des," he said, "I need you now, my sweet. Get to Avalon, bring us some help!" And at his bidding, Desdemona became a raven and flew off into the afternoon sky.

The searchers Arien had dispatched arrived on the field later that day with the group of elves that had fled to the mountains. All were overjoyed at the unexpected return to their homeland, yet there was grim business still to be done and the celebration of the victory would have to wait.

Using responsibility and respect to their dead as a shield against grief, the elves worked tirelessly long after sunset to complete the huge pyre. And when the many-tiered wooden tower, beautifully crafted and worked to be a fitting monument to the heroic dead, was completed, all of Illuma looked on solemnly as nearly four-score Children of the Moon, friends who should have lived for centuries to come, were gently laid upon its benches.

Then the midnight hour was upon them, and the orange flames roared into the night, consuming the mortal bodies of the fallen and lifting their spirits on hot winds to the heavens above.

And carried, too, on the winds were the wails and cries of the living. Death was not a common visitor to the land of the ageless elves, and grief of such magnitude had never before been known.

Throughout the ordeal of the funeral loomed Ryell, a specter of singular purpose. With boundless energy, he seemed to be everywhere at once, consoling mourners and sharing in their grief for the fallen. Yet, though his grief was genuine, his actions were calculated, subtly nurturing in his people the same seeds of vengeance that drove him. He spoke of the dead always in terms of glory and honor, and ended each encounter with a reminder that the Calvans had brought this upon them.

Fearing for their safety as angry eyes turned upon them with increasing frequency, the Calvan prisoners huddled close together.

"They'll rally behind him," Del remarked to Arien.

Arien understood the awful truth of the words. One elf even pulled a small stick from the pyre and threw it at the prisoners. It fell harmlessly short of its mark, but drew a cheer from several other of Arien's people.

Relentlessly, Ryell stepped up his prodding, rushing to and fro about the fire, sweeping up excited and angry followers in his wake. Soon the whole group was gathered around him and he raised his arms for silence.

"This is not good at all, no, no," mumbled Ardaz. "Arien, stop him now! Who will wash the blood from our hands?"

Arien shrugged helplessly and dropped his eyes.

"It seems that the trial has begun," said Del. Sylvia glared at him, not appreciating the bite his sarcasm put on her father.

"Friends! Kin!" Ryell called loudly. "This is a night of sorrow, to bid farewell to our brave brothers. But do not linger in grief for them, for they died with the knowledge that their sacrifice would help to free us from the bonds of our imprisonment. I only hope that my own death will be glorious and purpose-filled!

"How many injustices have we suffered at the hands of the humans? Are their any among us who have not lost kin at this very battle? And have you not, as I, felt the belittlement when you looked out over the southern fields and knew that you could not travel them, even if you so desired, because you were not born of the proper heritage?

"That degradation is ended! The army of Caer Tuatha is smashed and all Calva is open to us!"

Arien flinched and sank even deeper at the chorus of wild shouts that arose in support of Ryell.

His daughter squared off in front of him, forcing him to look her in the eye. "When the army of Ungden threatened, you fought, though you had no hopes of winning," Sylvia said sharply. "You drew your strength from the righteousness of your cause, and from the injustice of your enemy. Look at Ryell. Hate drives him. Is he any better than Ungden?"

"With our victory in the Battle of Mountaingate, we began the age of Illuma!" Ryell proclaimed above the hysterical cheers. "Let us tonight begin the lessons we shall teach to all of Calva!'' He pointed his menacing sword at the helpless prisoners while elves all about him scooped up sticks or drew their own swords.

''They brought this pain upon us,'' Ryell cried. ''Let them feel the sting of their folly!'' He started the mob toward the prisoners.

Arien's jaw clenched as a spasm of renewed anger burned through him, and he rushed to intercept Ryell.

''Move aside,'' Ryell snarled, and his sword point came up threateningly.

Arien grasped Fahwayn's hilt and held his ground. ''This is wrong,'' he declared flatly. ''This is not the way of our people.''

''Your day is passed, Arien Silverleaf,'' Ryell asserted, though he dropped the sword point and backed away a step. ''The people will not listen to you.''

''They are maddened by the same demon that possesses you,'' Arien retorted. ''Hear me!'' he cried, but the mob, beyond reason, shouted him down.

''Move aside, Arien,'' Ryell said again. ''You cannot win.''

Suddenly there came a great flash behind the Eldar, and from the ensuing smoke emerged, coughing, the wizard Ardaz, the raven, Desdemona, returned to his shoulder. ''Wait!'' he cried. ''A rider is coming! From the south, from the south!''

The crowd fell silent and as one peered southward.

''I see no rider!'' snapped Ryell.

''Hush!'' Ardaz scolded. ''Have a care, Ryell, your impatience tries my patience!''

Ryell glared at him but, having witnessed Ardaz's power, did not challenge him further.

It would have been pointless anyway, for the sound of a galloping horse was soon heard approaching. The tall silhouette of a ranger crossed through the light of the fire. He paused to observe the gathering for a moment, then walked his mount over to Arien.

''Lord Silverleaf,'' he said respectfully as he dismounted, stooping right down into a low bow.

Arien nodded.

"I am Andovar, courier from Avalon. Bellerian, Lord of Rangers, sends his greetins."

"And ours to him," Arien responded. "Your names are welcome in Illuma. Our debt to your people is great."

Andovar surveyed the mob and the huddled prisoners. "Vengeance?" he asked Arien.

"Justice," Ryell spat back at him.

"As ye wish," the ranger conceded calmly. "It seems, then, that I huv come just in time, for Bellerian bids ye to take no action before the morn."

"For what reason?" demanded Ryell.

"Tis no for me to say. Accept that the dawnslight will bring new tidins."

Ryell moved to argue, but Arien cut him off and ended the grumblings of the crowd. "Silence!" he commanded. "Is there no limit to your rancor? Were it not for the rangers of Avalon, your corpse and mine would be numbered among the dead. Surely we owe them the respect to trust in their request without question."

Having no rebuttal, Ryell shook his head and walked away. The crowd, too, settled back into uneasy appeasement and both Arien and Andovar breathed easier.

"I should like to speak to the prisoners," Andovar asked.

Most of the Calvans stood up as the ranger approached and some even saluted. Andovar's eyes, though, met with those of one who neither stood nor saluted. In the distance, Billy and Del saw him, too.

"Mitchell!" cried Del.

"And that's Reinheiser behind him," Billy added.

The captain and the ranger stared each other down.

"I warned ye," Andovar growled.

Mitchell spat up at him.

"Lord Arien," called Andovar, "for meself, I am beggin a favor o ye. Will ye grant it?"

"If I may," Arien replied cautiously.

"A sword for this man. I've a debt for settlin."

Mitchell squared himself before the ranger. "A

weapon of your world, not mine,'' he growled. ''You made the challenge; I choose the weapons.''

Without hesitation, Andovar handed his own sword to an elf beside him.

''Fists''—Mitchell chuckled wickedly—''and nothing else. I want to kill you with my bare hands.''

''Suren ye'll die slower,'' Andovar replied with the same evenness. ''But suren ye'll be just as dead.''

''Wait!'' Del called, rushing over to them.

''Ye look better than when I left ye yesterday,'' the ranger greeted him. But Del was in no frame of mind for courtesies.

''It's my fight, Andovar,'' he said as he and the captain locked in unblinking stares. ''It's been my fight for a long, long time.''

Andovar surveyed the two men. He feared for his friend, believing Mitchell to be the stronger, but realized that he had no right to take this battle away from Del. Reluctantly, he stepped aside.

Del knew what he had to do. ''Violence is not the answer,'' he reminded himself softly. He took a deep breath to steady his nerves.

He felt that he had himself settled then, but he wasn't prepared for the viciousness of Mitchell's initial attack. The captain charged like an angry bull, knocking Del backward, and began his onslaught, raining blow after blow on his stunned opponent.

Unnoticed in the background, Martin Reinheiser held a single blade of grass in his hand, softly stroking it and whispering unfamiliar words.

Del somehow managed to stagger away from Mitchell and regroup. Dazed, the sickly-sweet taste of blood rich in his mouth, he had almost gone down under the brutal beating. ''I'm not going to fight you, Mitchell,'' he said. ''I won't lower myself.''

Mitchell didn't understand Del's motives, but he roared in again. And Del had to wonder if he was proving any point, or simply showing himself to be a fool.

Then, slipping in from somewhere in his subconscious, came the words of Belexus, advice the great warrior had given him several weeks before. "The greatest advantage o a true warrior is not strength or quickness, but courage," Belexus had told him.

Del gritted away the pain and stood tall against the punishment. He was right; this had to work!

Reinheiser marveled at how easily the transformation spell had been completed. In disbelief of his own handiwork, he gingerly fingered the razor edges of the small knife he now held in his hand.

Mitchell's hands found Del's throat. Grinning with murderous glee, the captain drove Del to his knees. But Andovar had seen enough. He rushed over and grabbed Mitchell, pulling him free of Del. Then, with strength that horrified the helpless captain, the ranger tossed him back, sending him sprawling into the Calvan prisoners.

The elves stood silent, confused and shocked, as if Del had held a dark mirror up to them.

Reinheiser moved over to Mitchell and roughly pulled him to his feet. "Kill DelGiudice," he instructed as he slipped Mitchell the dagger. "On your life, kill him!"

Mitchell shuddered at the sudden coldness in the physicist's eyes and stumbled back out from the crowd.

Andovar stepped defensively to block the captain, but Del regained his footing and pushed him aside. Andovar looked at him in disbelief.

"I must," Del told him. "They have to learn."

"You are indeed brave, Jeffrey DelGiudice," said Andovar. He clasped Del's shoulder and stepped aside.

"It's over," Del told Mitchell.

Mitchell shook his head and lashed out, the tip of the concealed dagger sticking out from between his fingers. Del deflected the blow aside, then felt a burning pain. Amazed, he looked down at the bleeding gash in his hand.

Mitchell smiled wickedly and struck out again, but

Del, realizing the danger, was quick to dodge back from the blow.

He recited Belexus's advice again to keep from panic as he backed from the stalking captain.

"You're running out of room," Mitchell taunted as they neared the ledge overlooking Blackemara.

Del's heels slipped out over the ledge. He hoped his death would make his point.

Mitchell bared the dagger now, caring for nothing but his lust for Del's blood. He raised his arm to strike.

But an arrow found his wrist.

Stunned, both he and Del looked to the side—where Ryell stood, grim-faced, bow in hand.

The knife dropped and Mitchell toppled in agony.

Instinctively, Del retrieved the blade and straddled Mitchell's chest, putting its point to the captain's throat. Caught up in the frenzied celebration that suddenly erupted all around him, he almost struck. A wave of nausea swept over Del when he realized what he was about to do and when he looked at the elves crowding in close and shouting in wild glee for Mitchell's death.

"Stop it!" Del screamed at them as he jumped away. He flung the dagger over the cliff, far into the night, and charged through the confused crowd, wanting only to get away from the infectious madness.

Billy and Sylvia ran over to calm him. But they had no answer for Del when he looked them squarely in the eye and said, "Are you so sure the right side won?" Then he darted across the field and through the silver archway, seeking out the sanctuary of the mountain trails.

With the attention of the elves diverted, Reinheiser calmly strolled over to Mitchell. "Do not worry," he said. "Our escape is at hand." He pointed over the ledge.

Mitchell, clutching his wounded wrist, peered into the gloom, trying to understand what Reinheiser was talking about.

He felt an icy cold, incredibly strong hand pushing on his back and he was falling.

Some of the elves noticed then, just as Mitchell went over. Reinheiser answered their dumbfounded stares with a shrug of his shoulders, then laughed evilly and leaped off the cliff.

Andovar rushed over, but the two men had disappeared into the dark night. "It is good they are dead," the ranger said. "Suren they'd've bringed harm t'our Aielle."

The calm that followed ignited Ryell. He ran to the brighter area beside the pyre. "Let us not forget our great victory!" he shouted, fearing that the crowd's confusion would steal his momentum. "This is a night of celebration!" Welcoming emotions that buried the disturbing accusations Del had raised, most of the elves responded with renewed and heightened enthusiasm.

A helpless shake of his head was the only apology Arien could offer to Andovar.

Reinheiser wasn't dead.

He cast a simple spell as he fell, manipulating the air currents to slow his descent and cushion his landing. He stepped down gently into Blackemara just a few feet from the crumpled and twisted body of Captain Mitchell.

Amazingly, the captain managed to half open one eye.

"You will be dead soon," Reinheiser assured him.

Mitchell knew the truth of the physicist's words, for his lungs had collapsed and he could not draw any breath.

"Before, you were merely an inconvenience," Reinheiser explained. "But now, with your knowledge of weapons and your obsession with power, you have become a danger to me." In a hissing voice that was not his own, he added, "Ever you would remain a simple Faustus!"

Mitchell's eyes widened in terror at the evil aura that suddenly engulfed him. He felt his gaze drawn up the trail of dried blood on Reinheiser's face to the physicist's forehead, where the cut tip of a shining black sapphire was just beginning to show through the skin.

"Your soul is mine!" Reinheiser proclaimed.

Blood and bile rose in Mitchell's throat as he realized his eternal doom.

He died without hope.

Del ran on along the dark and twisting paths, desperate to outdistance the sounds of the renewed party on the field below. Finally exhausted, he slumped back against a boulder. Great patches of dark clouds raced furiously across the sky above him, driven by a violent wind that had come slicing through the mountain gaps from the northern peaks.

He could still see the field. The fire had been refueled, its wild flames leaping high into the night, clearly outlining the silhouettes of the elves as they danced in orgiastic frenzy.

Del could not hold back the tears as he watched his utopian fantasies dispelled. He had dared to believe that he could make a difference in the future of Aielle, had allowed himself the naive optimism that the course of civilization could be different here than in his own war-ravaged time.

He sat tormented by the cruel visions for a long while, until sleep mercifully overtook him.

On Mountaingate, the vicious party raged.

Chapter 26

The Challenge

Del thought it was the sun that stole his troubled dreams, but it was not. Calae stood before him, bright and glorious as the dawn itself.

"You expect much of us," Del said to the Colonnae Prince.

"We expect nothing and ask nothing," replied Calae.

"And give nothing," Del quipped sharply. He wanted to retract the insult as soon as he heard it spoken. Certainly the Colonnae, who had given salvation to his race in its darkest hour, did not deserve such words.

He felt even more ridiculous when Calae laughed softly, accepting the sarcasm with good-natured understanding of the frustration behind it.

"Can't you help me?" Del pleaded. "Can't you stop them, show them what they're doing?"

"What would be the gain?" Calae replied. "The destiny of Mankind lies in the hands of Man. If it were otherwise, there would be no meaning. Your race is free, DelGiudice, you would have it no other way. Man must bear his own burdens and accept the responsibilities of self-reliance."

Del's eyes dropped as the weight of salvation fell with heavy finality onto his shoulders.

"You may find that you have the strength to win your fight," Calae comforted. "There are stirrings in Avalon that offer hope." His words trailed away.

Del looked back at him, but had to shield his eyes as the light intensified, blurring the image of the Colonnae Prince. The first rays of the new dawn had found their way over the Crystals, and by the time Del was able to sort through the glare, Calae was gone.

Del considered the words and looked to the field far below. Shadowed by the high cliff along its eastern border, Mountaingate had not yet seen the dawnslight. The fires burned low and most of the elves slept, their celebration interrupted by physical and emotional exhaustion.

Del rushed down the mountain paths, spurred by the undeniable truth of Calae's observations and determined to face his responsibilities bravely, to bear the weight of his duties with his back stubbornly straight.

"You have become a pitiful sight, Arien Silverleaf," Ryell taunted a short while later, the mob behind him, nearly all of Illuma, agreeing with his every word. "Sworn to the service of your people, yet you stand against them. What form of consistency is this?"

"We gave our promise to the ranger that we would wait for word from Bellerian," Arien reminded his adversary.

"We agreed to wait until morning," Ryell retorted. "The dawn is come; I have heard no messages from the cursed wood."

"I hold for the just course," Arien stated.

"You are alone in your folly."

"Not true. I stand alone before you because the others who are able to perceive the evil that has befallen our people fear to oppose you. You feed upon the sorrow of many, Ryell. They follow you that they might shield their grief in anger and hatred, black thoughts easily sated by vengeance. Is it not the same for you and your loss of Erinel?"

"You should have stayed away longer," Billy said grimly when he saw Del approach from beneath the shadows of the telvensils. "Ryell has just announced the decision of the council."

"Innocence will not defend the prisoners from his unmerciful blade," stuttered Sylvia, and she turned away, ashamed, at that moment, to be numbered among the people of Lochsilinilume. "He is going to kill them all."

"The hell he is," Del growled as he started foward. Billy grabbed him by the arm.

"You can't," he said.

"Let go," Del ordered, his eyes unyielding as he stared down at his friend. "A few days ago you convinced me that we were brought here to help the right side win. That battle isn't over."

"Get out of our way, Arien," Ryell threatened, regaining his composure against Arien's stinging reference to Erinel. "Or we shall cut you down as a traitor."

Appalled that the demon possessing his onetime friend had gained such control, Arien's hand went for his swordhilt. But Del stepped in front of him, face-to-face with Ryell.

"This is none of your affair, human," Ryell spat at him.

"Oh, it is," Del retorted. "I won't stand by and let you murder innocent people."

"Innocent?" Ryell balked. "They marched against our homes! Had they won, would they have shown mercy?"

"I don't know," Del answered sincerely. "But that doesn't give you the right to do this. Can't you see that these men came here honestly believing in their cause? They were misinformed by evil, and we can only guess what magical persuasions Thalasi exerted over them.

"The Black Warlock is dead, Ryell. Ungden is gone and can harm your people no more. Do you really believe that these men here remain a threat to you? Or do you just want revenge?"

Ryell spoke now to the crowd as much as to Del. "I want to teach a lesson to Calva that the humans will not forget!

"All you'll breed is hatred!" Del shouted back at him. "You cannot know the horrors of the world before Aielle." He stepped out to the side, that all the crowd might see him. "Hear me well," he cried. "For my purpose in returning from that past age is upon me now." He looked Ryell straight in the eye. "Wars breed war; killing breeds killing. Once you begin that cycle, there can be only one end.

"When my world burned, Ryell, five billion people died with it. Five billion.

"Five billion hopes, five billion hearts." He hated to speak his next words, but shock was his only weapon. "Five billion Erinels.

"There will be no reprieve from the horror you begin this day."

Flames simmered in Ryell's eyes. His sword came from its sheath. "Move, human," he snarled. "Or my blade shall find your head."

Del's smile bore the serenity of truth. He held his arms outstretched. "Then do it," he said impassively. "My faith in your people is undaunted. When your venom has played itself out, they will look upon their bloodstained hands with horror. They will remember this moment, Ryell. What will become of you when they realize the truth of the path you led them down?"

Ryell's sword tip dipped. He thought of Del's fight with Mitchell the previous night. How could this man so willingly accept death?

Suddenly, a frantic cry of alarm rang out. "Look to the south!" yelled one of the elves, and the others soon understood his panic.

Streaming out of Avalon and northward across Mountaingate, spear tips and helms glistening in the early sun, came the regrouped remnants of the Calvan army, even now more than a thousand strong. The elves realized at once that they had been caught unawares, never imagining that the scattered and leaderless army could be turned back on them so quickly.

"Deceiver!" cried Ryell in hopeless rage, and he spun back and cut a deadly arc at Del's throat.

Ardaz was quicker, though, throwing a spell with a wave of his hand that stayed the blade and held Ryell motionless in midswing.

"Hold calm!" Arien commanded his people as the

Calvans, still walking their mounts and showing no signs of breaking into a charge, passed the midpoint of the field. "The Rangers of Avalon are among their ranks!"

The army stopped a short distance from the stunned elves and three men rode out from their ranks. A fair-haired young man atop a great roan stallion, dressed like a king in a flowing white robe with golden trimmings, rode in the middle, flanked on his right by the warrior Belexus, upon Calamus the Pegasi, and on his left by the ranger Lord Bellerian. In his arm, Bellerian cradled a coral crown, pinkish white and inlaid with dozens of lustrous pearls.

Following closely came a line of eleven, ten Warders of the White Walls centered by Andovar, who bore a furled standard.

Arien grew more at ease when he noted the sincerity of the fair-haired young man's keen, dark eyes. There was noble blood in the lad; he was not diminished by the mighty rangers flanking him. He eyed Arien for a long moment, then raised his clenched fist above his head.

The Calvans had come too close if they meant to charge, but still Arien started defensively when the lad dropped his arm in a quick movement.

And to the utter amazement of the elves, the entire Calvan army, and the rangers riding with them, threw their weapons to the ground and remained at silent attention. At the same time, Andovar unfurled the standard—four white bridges and four pearls set against a blue field.

The banner of Pallendara before the reign of Ungden.

"I am Benador," announced the young man in a strong, clear voice befitting his station. "Heir to the line of Ben-rin and rightful Lord of Pallendara. I was but an infant when Ben-galen, my father, and Darwinia, my mother, were murdered by Ungden the Usurper, and I owe my life to venerable Bellerian and the wizard you call Ardaz."

Ardaz blushed and lowered his eyes from the many glances that came his way.

"For they hid me away from Ungden's fell knife," Benador continued. "And for lo these thirty years I have lived as a farmer's son.

"Several months ago I came north to the fair wood of Avalon that Bellerian might prepare me for the day when I would claim the throne that is rightfully mine.

"That day is come," he proclaimed sternly, his arms outstretched and his eyes raised skyward. "Be it known here and now, and let the word go out throughout all Aielle, that the line of Ben-rin is restored to the throne of Pallendara!"

When he looked back at Arien, his friendly and unpretentious smile had returned. "And in the true spirit of Ben-rin," he said softly to the Eldar, "it is my first act to surrender my army to the night dancers." The astounded elves didn't even know how to react.

"My people have committed many sins against you and yours, Lord Eldar Arien Silverleaf, the worst being the battle that was fought yestermorn. I cannot undo those wrongs, but I desire that the feud between Calva and Illuma end now." He dropped his arms and his gaze. "We trust in your mercy."

At once, all eyes focused on Ryell.

"Let him go, Ardaz," Del insisted. Released from the wizard's spell, the confused Ryell hesitated.

"Here is the chance of your world," said Del. "Peace is yours if you only reach out and grab it!"

He put his hand on Ryell's shoulder. "Erinel is dead; the price has been high—too high. But if this doesn't end now, then Erinel's death means nothing. Then all of this will happen all over again."

Ryell looked to Benador and the Calvan army, waiting patiently for his decision.

Unarmed.

"No tricks," Del assured him. "I promise."

"What say you, Ryell?" asked Arien. "I know my answer to the rightful Lord of Pallendara. It is an answer that I give willingly, with all of my heart. Yet many of our people have come to value your words above mine and it is important that our stand in this matter be undivided. So what say you?''

''The whole future of Aielle rests with your decision,'' added Del. ''Will your world start down the same bloody path that led my world to its destruction? Or are you going to rise above this stupid violence?''

Ryell dropped his gaze, trying to sort through the sudden confusion this day had brought. How could he be expected to accept peace with the hated Calvans with an Illuman victory at hand?

His eye strayed to the funeral pyres of his dead comrades, the pyre of Erinel, joy of his life.

He glanced at the bodies of the fallen Calvans, some black with carrion birds, lying scattered about the field, and thought of the children back in Calva, standing in their doorways and crying for their fathers who would never return.

Such were the horrors of war.

Humbled and embarrassed, Ryell faced Arien, tears flowing freely down his cheeks. ''Too much blood has been spilled already,'' he said softly.

He threw his sword to the ground.

Chapter 27

Changing of the Seasons

"We do not accept your surrender, Lord of Caer Tuatha," Arien said to Benador. "Only your friendship."

Benador dismounted and extended his hand to the Eldar, and as Arien moved to accept it, he undid the clasp holding his scabbard and let Fahwayn fall to the earth beside the sword Benador had cast down. It was at that moment of friendship between the Eldar of Lochsilinilume and the Overlord of Pallendara that many elves and men alike came to know and share Del's hopes for the future of Ynis Aielle.

"You're free now," Del said softly to Ryell. "Free of the hate that's darkened your life for so long."

Ryell could not manage a smile from his tear-streaked face.

But he offered a handshake to Del.

The funeral fires brightened the evening sky once again on Mountaingate. But this night, the grief of the survivors was not masked under cries of hatred or false glory. Both human and elf accepted their losses as a tragic lesson and vowed never to repeat the grievous error they had made.

In an act of the highest faith and trust, Arien, without opposition from any of his people, laid open the once-secret paths and led his human guests to the Silver City. There a great feast was prepared and many bonds were made and oaths were spoken. The solemn celebration lasted a full week, its high point an invitation by Benador to the elves and rangers to share in the ceremony of his coronation in Pallendara in the spring of the next year.

On the morning the Calvans were to depart, Del went early to Billy's room to rouse his friend.

"We did it." Del laughed, his enthusiasm born of pride. "We were brought here to straighten things out, and damn it, we really did!"

"I wouldn't go that far," Billy replied as he rolled out of bed and stretched. "You've forgotten your own world. Hundreds of years of prejudice and hatred don't disappear overnight."

Looking at his black friend, Del could only agree. He moved to the window and threw the curtains aside.

And then he fell entranced as he looked out over the magical valley at the sight of elves and humans bidding fond farewells and trading sincere handshakes and hugs. Serenity flooded over Del; every care and worry seemed to fly from him at that moment, for somehow he knew these to be honest glimpses of Aielle's future.

"It'll take time," he said through a hopeful smile, turning to face Billy. "But they're on the right path."

Billy cocked his head curiously at his friend's sudden, and overwhelming, visage of calm.

Yet another summer passed into autumn, but he could not know that. He had forsaken all hope; it could bring only torment in a timeless dilemma that knew no cure.

Salvation lay only in meditation and thus he had grasped at the one spell available and turned inward, suspending all but his thoughts in time. How many years had passed? How many yet would?

He knew not, and cared not. As physical suspension eliminated his needs and preserved his body, contemplation of deeper universal truths preserved his mind.

But what had disrupted his spell? What physical change had occurred in the constant to disturb his enchanted sleep?

The latch clanked again and the tiny cell door swung in. Most of the light from the corridor was blocked by the silhouette of a figure stooping to enter, though it still seemed painfully bright to this man who had known only the darkness of dungeons for three decades.

"The blessings of the Colonnae forever upon the head of Ardaz!" cried Benador when he viewed the prisoner. "True was his guess, and Istaahl the White is returned to the side of Pallendara's throne!"

A quiet blanket of snow lay deep all about Illuma Vale, though winter neared its end.

Del knew there would be no sleep for him again this night. He rolled out of his bed and moved to the window. Soon the trails would be open again, back to Avalon.

Avalon.

How many months had it been? After the battle, Del had tried vainly to get back into the enchanted forest, even traveling around the Southern Crystal Mountains to find a different route.

But Brielle had shut him out.

He had sought out the rangers. But, alas, they had no answers for him.

Summer had turned to autumn, autumn to winter. And the snows had forced him from Mountaingate, back to Illuma, and shut the trails behind him.

Still Del should have enjoyed these times. The scars of the battle were fading and the elves had returned to their dance and merriment. The harsh winter could not daunt their eternal play, and now, with the season turning again, and the coronation of Benador fast approaching, their joy seemed tenfold.

But an awkward perception, the feeling that he was trapped in a land where he did not belong, had grown within Del like a cancer. He could not escape the fact that he was from a different world, one of ambition and responsibility, and though he had always rebelled against those aspects of his society, the tendencies of his former life were painted indelibly on his mind. The trivial frolics of the elves did not satisfy his needs.

And his restlessness, he feared, might bring his dangerous knowledge crashing down on this innocent world.

His depression had only deepened with the wintry season. A beard now adorned his face; he wouldn't be bothered with shaving, and he rarely left his room, for interaction with the elves only reminded him that he was not of this place called Aielle.

He dressed and moved to Billy's room and could not help but smile at the contented snores of his friend. Billy had grown to be at home here. His friendship with Sylvia had blossomed into something more, something wonderful.

Del thought of the crowning of kindly Benador, and of the bond that would strengthen between the races, and he smiled again. "Bear witness for me," he whispered into Billy's ear, and he left the grand house.

Bordering on desperation, he made his careful way up the invisible stair to Brisen-ballas, seeking Ardaz, the one man who might understand his troubles.

But the wizard was nowhere to be found.

So Del wandered under the crisp, star-bright skies of winter's last night. He could not deny the truth of his fears and his feelings, yet he could not escape who he was.

The sounds of the dance of Tivriasis wakened him to his surroundings. He had wandered to Shaithdun-o-Illume, the shelf of crystalline reflections. The haunting beauty of the place captured him at once and he suddenly understood Arien's protectiveness of this realm and just how much was at stake.

Del glanced back at the tunnel he had just come through. His personal needs seemed insignificant and selfish at that moment. He was free of their hold over him and his eyes held a renewed gleam as he watched the growing glow of the moon on the mica walls.

When the moon has passed beyond the western horizon and the stars sparkle brighter against a darker sky, when the last notes of the evening's voices have faded from thought and the first hints of the music of dawn have yet to sound, a man might then truly explore the murmurs of his soul. So it was for Del that night on Shaithdun-o-Illume. He found a time of the present, where his inner contemplations could run free of the world's noise.

He took no notice, sometime later, of the unnatural mist that drifted up from the pool to hover a short distance from the ledge, nor did he see the specter that appeared within its cloudy vapors.

"DelGiudice," spoke the figure, and the angelic tones filled Del with a sense of joy.

"Calae!" he replied.

"You are troubled, my friend."

"A woman," Del explained. "And a world. Loves that I cannot have."

Down from the mountains, in the quiet magic of Avalon, the woman leaned heavily against a tree.

"Oh, Rudy," she cried. "I huv breaked me covenant!"

"That is quite obvious, dear sister." Ardaz chuckled. "Yes, yes, quite obvious!" He became more serious when he realized that Brielle was truly distressed.

"No need to worry!" he said. "The Colonnae rejoice! They themselves sent me to you!"

"Help me," she begged, taking comfort in his words. "Please ye must. Ne'er huv I known such fright."

"I'm afraid, too, Calae," continued Del. "Afraid of myself and the things I might do."

"Have you cause?" asked Calae.

"This is the world I always dreamed of," Del began. "The world of all my fantasies, and I can't stay because of the things I learned in the world I despised. My knowledge, my ways, could bring ruin to Aielle. I couldn't bear to do that."

"Could you not keep this dangerous knowledge to yourself?"

"Maybe," replied Del. "But I can't take the chance. I'm not like Billy. He can accept it all with a shrug and a smile, but I'll always be trying to improve things. Aielle doesn't need that." He looked deeply into the blue flames of Calae's omniscient eyes. "They survived their Jericho; their battle is won. I am the only danger now."

"Your fears are valid, my friend. It was necessary that you come to this realization on your own. I see your pain and wish that I could tell you otherwise."

"It's not fair," Del said quietly. "To have found my heaven only to have it pulled out from under me."

"I am truly sorry."

Del fought back his tears. "What then?" he asked through a stoic front. "Will you send me back to my own time, where I might live out my life."

"That I cannot do," Calae replied. "The rivers of time flow at different speeds, but, alas, their waters move ever in the same direction. The moment of your existence in the earth you knew has passed. Even if this were not so, the experience of your world would pale beside the beauty of Ynis Aielle. You would not be happy there."

The Colonnae Prince extended his arm toward Del. "Come with me, Jeffrey DelGiudice," he said. "Come, that we may travel the stars together."

Del eyed the entrance of the tunnel to the elven city, then felt his gaze drawn southward, through the crack in the mountain wall to the impenetrable black veil shrouding Avalon. "How can I let it go? Or her?" He looked back at Calae, the wetness on his cheeks twinkling in starshine. "It's all over?" he mumbled.

Calae remained unchanging, his arm extended and his visage beckoning.

Del shook his head and smiled, accepting his fate at the hands of the trusted Calae. He cast a final, dreamy glance at the enchanted forest.

Then stepped off the ledge.

Perhaps it was merely the winds within the stillness of the night, but more likely it was the magic of Calae, or of Ardaz or Brielle, carrying a final comfort to the man of yesterday who had so touched their lives, as the last sounds of Ynis Aielle carried to Del's ears were the birth cries of a baby. A child was born unto Brielle, a beautiful girl. Rhiannon, she would be called, the name of a woman who had graced that long-lost world with wisps of mystery and enchantment.

Also at that moment, snow began to fall across Aielle. Driven by the sea wind, it whipped with blizzard fury against the black walls of Talas-dun, where Reinheiser, the new Black Warlock, sat on his dark throne, awaiting the day when he would rise once again. It fell indifferently on Pallendara, barely visible against the whiteness of the newly polished walls. It shrouded sleeping Illuma, and descended gently on Avalon, where a new mother suckled her child.

That was to be the winter's last snow, for the dawnslight came bright and clear, the first day of spring.

Epilogue

To the elves, she was Caer Tuatha, the City of Man, and Billy found comfort in that description. For if the human spirit could be moved to such heights of creative achievement as this wondrous city of twisting spires and many-tiered fountains, there was indeed hope for the race.

Much of the decay wrought by Ungden had already disappeared by the time the elves and rangers reached the city, for the heaviest toll imposed by the unlawful rule of Ungden was a decline of the spirit. Now, with the return of the rightful Overlord, the pall had been lifted off the city and the music of minstrels once again issued from the open gates, a heartening sound of gaiety and promised comfort to all who would enter.

And the white walls shone with renewed luster at the return of the heir of Ben-rin. Twas rumored in the city, and perhaps it was true, that Pallendara's walls held within their sculpted buttresses and murals the contented souls of the long-dead artists who had dedicated their lives to crafting them.

Then, a time of tingling excitement and hope, when dreamers spout visions of fairy-tale kingdoms and even the staunchest of pessimists grant themselves a peek through a rose-tinted window, the coronation of Benador was carried off with enthusiasm and regal splendor that exceeded the highest expectations of anyone in attendance. People thronged into Pallendara from all the wide reaches of Calva to witness Aielle's new dawn. Ungden was no more, and delivered unto them in his stead was a man of the stock to put things aright. Thousands as one, their hearts lifted in cheers, song, and dance as Benador accepted the pearly crown from Istaahl, the White Mage. And many a tear was shed when the new Overlord recommissioned the Warders of the White Walls as the palace guard and accepted their oath of loyalty.

The celebration lasted for a score of days and beyond, and gaining momentum through it all was the rebeautification of Pallendara. Billy's heart jumped as he viewed ballistae and catapults broken down and packed away, and gardens planted or statues erected in the niches the weapons had occupied.

He knew that Del had won.

A Note on Language

English is the language common to all the races of Aielle, even spoken, though in a broken form, by the wild talons of the eastern wastes. This is merely a carryover from the times before the holocaust, English being the predominant language of the children on the ships the Colonnae guided to Aielle's shores.

The Gaelic flavor of the rangers' speech is due to the influence of Jennifer Glendower (Brielle). Alone in her domain for many centuries, the witch often wove spells of cell memory, seeking her ancestors through her genetic heritage. And from those encounters she acquired the more colorful phrasings and rhythms of the speech of her Scottish highlander forefathers. These she passed along to Bellerian when he came north to live under the boughs of her wood, and he in turn imparted them to the children who would become the rangers of Avalon.

Enchantish is the tongue of wizards, its rolling multisyllabic words an integral component of spellcasting. In Aielle it is most prevalent among the elves, who incorporated it into their everyday speech through their close association with the wizard Ardaz. Ironically, *enchantish* also has Gaelic overtones, for the language of the ancient Celtic peoples reflected their symbiosis with the land and the natural forces around them, the same forces from which wizards draw their power.

Glossary

Aielle—the land of rebirth
Ancient Ones—the survivors of the *Unicorn,* delivered unto the future land of Aielle to teach the new race of man the lessons of the past
Andovar—a ranger, friend to Belexus
Angfagdul—(*enchantish*) "the utter darkness," referring to Morgan Thalasi
Ardaz—the Silver Mage of Illuma, one of the four wizards trained by the Colonnae at the dawn of Aielle
Arien Silverleaf—Eldar to the elves of Illuma, the first elf born of elven parents
Avalon—a magical forest located southwest of the Crystal Mountains and bordering the field of Mountaingate
Backavar—(enchantish) "iron-arm," referring to Belexus
Belexus—a ranger, son of Bellerian, and reputedly the mightiest warrior in all Aielle
Bellerian—the Lord of the Rangers of Avalon
Benador—heir to the line of Ben-rin and rightful Overlord of Pallendara
Ben-galen—father of Benador, killed by Ungden the Usurper
Ben-rin—beloved Overlord of Pallendara at the time of the second mutation of man
Billy Shank—navigator of the *Unicorn*
Blackemara—(*enchantish*) "black mere," a festering swamp in a box canyon just north of Avalon
Brielle—mistress of the First Magic, the Emerald Witch of Avalon and one of the Four

Brisen-Ballas—the tower home of Ardaz on the cliff overlooking Illuma Vale

Brogg—the Brown Wastes, a land desolated by Thalasi to discourage intruders from finding his stronghold

Caer Tuatha—(*enchantish*) "the city of man," referring to Pallendara

Calae—angelic Prince of the Colonnae

Calamus—a pegasus rescued from a dragon's lair by Belexus and serving as his mount in return

Calva—the grasslands of south-central Aielle, under the rule of the Overlord of Pallendara

Castel Angfagdt—(*enchantish*) "the castle of darkness," referring to Talas-dun

Clas Braiyelle—(enchantish) "home of Brielle," referring to Avalon

Colonnae—angelic beings who served as guardians to the second race of Man immediately following the holocaust

Crystal Mountains—two great, mica-strewn ranges forming the northern border of the Calvan plains

Darwinia—wife of Ben-galen, murdered by Ungden the Usurper

Desdemona—Ardaz's shape-changing familiar, usually in the form of a black cat

Doc Brady—ship's doctor on the *Unicorn*

e-Belvin Fehte—(*enchantish*) "the killing fires," referring to the holocaust that destroyed the original race of Man

Elves—the second mutation of Man, driven into exile by the Calvans

Erinel—an elf, nephew of Ryell

Fahwayn—Arien Silverleaf's magical sword

Four—the four adults saved from the holocaust by the Colonnae and trained as wizards

Four Bridges—structures spanning the River Ne'er Ending in southern Aielle; site of a legendary battle between the talons and the Calvans

Hollis Mitchell—Captain of the *Unicorn*

Illuma—the secret mountain refuge harboring the fugitive elves

Illuma Vale—the magical valley wherein lies Illuma

Istaahl—the White Mage of Pallendara, one of the Four

Jeffrey DelGiudice—Del, Junior Officer on the *Unicorn*

Jennifer Glendower—Brielle's name before the holocaust

Justice Stone—site of Ardaz's deception of Umpleby, where the wizard pretended to slay the elves while in reality shuffling them off to Illuma

Kored-Dul—(*enchantish*) ''mountains of shadow,'' located in northwestern Aielle and harboring Talas-Dun

Loch-sh'Illume—(*enchantish*) ''the moon pool,'' the mountain pond located at the base of Shaithdun-o-Illume

Lochsilinilume—(*enchantish*) ''land of the enchanted moonlight,'' referring to Illuma

Luminas Ey-n'Abraieken—(*enchantish*) ''dance of the brightest moons,'' a celebration started by Arien Silverleaf to honor the beauty of the light of the full moon upon Shaithdun-o-illume

Martin Reinheiser—a civilian scientist aboard the *Unicorn*

Michael Thompson—an engineer on the *Unicorn*

Morgan Thalasi—the Black Warlock, one of the Four and evil practitioner of the Third Magic—domination

Nuset—''National Undersea Exploration Team,'' sister organization of NASA

Pallendara—Aielle's greatest city, located on the southern coast

Perrault—Istaahl's name before the holocaust

Rangers of Avalon—the children of the nobles of the court of Ben-galen when Ungden usurped the throne, stolen away to safety and trained as warriors by Belerian

Ray Corbin—First Officer of the *Unicorn*

Rudy Glendower—Ardaz's name before the holocaust

Ryell—an elf, friend of Arien Silverleaf

Shaithdun-o-Illume—(*enchantish*) ''mountain shelf of

moonlight,'' the special place of celebration for the elves of Illuma

Silver City—the city of the elves, Illuma

Sylvia—an elf, daughter of Arien Silverleaf

Talas-Dun—Morgan Thalasi's black fortress

Talons—the first mutation of Man, a wicked race serving as evil pawns in Morgan Thalasi's designs for power

Telvensil—a silvery, white-leafed tree common to the southern slopes of the Great Crystal Mountains

Thomas Morgan—Morgan Thalasi's name before the holocaust

Tivriasis—the singing stream of Shaithdun-o-Illume, named by Arien Silverleaf in memory of his late wife

Umpleby—ancestor of Ungden, a ruthless land baron opposing Ben-rin, then Overlord of Pallendara

Ungden—''the Usurper,'' self-proclaimed Overlord of Pallendara who gained power by means of a bloody coup in which he killed Ben-galen and Darwinia

Unicorn—the deep-diving submarine that took the ancient ones to the depths of the Atlantic, and ultimately, to the waters of the new world

Warders of the White Walls—an order of knights bound by absolute oath to the Overlord of Pallendara

Witching Prophetics—a series of prophecies by Brielle foretelling the coming of the ancient ones

Ynis Aielle—(*enchantish*) ''isle of rebirth''

About the Author

Since bursting upon the fantasy scene in 1988 with THE CRYSTAL SHARD, Bob Salvatore has published four other novels, reached *The New York Times* bestseller list, and made his mark as a leader in the genre.

Born in Massachusetts in 1959, Bob, who holds a B.S. in Communications/Media and has worked as a mailman and an English teacher, is now a service representative for a high-tech company. When not writing, chances are he's playing street hockey or softball. He, his wife, Diane, and their three children make their home in Leominster, Massachusetts.

SIGNET FANTASY (0451)

WORLDS OF WONDER

☐ **BARROW A Fantasy Novel by John Deakins.** In a town hidden on the planes of Elsewhen, where mortals are either reborn or driven mad, no one wants to be a pawn of the Gods. (450043—$3.95)

☐ **CAT HOUSE by Michael Peak.** The felines were protected by their humans, but ancient enemies still stalked their trails to destroy them in a warring animal underworld, where fierce battles crossed the species border. (163036—$3.95)

☐ **THE GOD BOX by Barry B. Longyear.** From the moment Korvas accepted the gift of the god box and the obligation to fulfill its previous owner's final mission, he'd been plunged into more peril than a poor dishonest rug merchant deserved. Now it looks like Korvas will either lead the world to its destruction—or its salvation. . . . (159241—$3.50)

☐ **MERMAID'S SONG A Fantasy Novel by Alida Van Gores.** In the world under the sea, the Balance hangs in jeopardy. Only Elan, a beautiful, young mermaid can save it. But first she must overcome the evil Ghrismod's and be chosen as the new Between, tender of the great seadragons. If not, the Balance will be destroyed—and darkness will triumph for all eternity. (161131—$4.50)

☐ **ANCIENT LIGHT—A Fantasy Novel by Mary Gentle.** Lynne de Lisle Christie is back on Orthe, caught in a battle to obtain high-technology artifacts from a bygone civilization, while struggling to protect the people of Orthe from its destructive powers. But who will protect *her* from the perils of discovering alien secrets no human was ever meant to have? (450132—$5.95)

Prices slightly higher in Canada.

Buy them at your local bookstore or use this convenient coupon for ordering.

NEW AMERICAN LIBRARY
P.O. Box 999, Bergenfield, New Jersey 07621

Please send me the books I have checked above. I am enclosing $________ (please add $1.00 to this order to cover postage and handling). Send check or money order—no cash or C.O.D.'s. Prices and numbers are subject to change without notice.

Name________________________________

Address______________________________

City ____________ State ____________ Zip Code ____________

Allow 4-6 weeks for delivery.
This offer, prices and numbers are subject to change without notice.